Do Opposites Attract?

Do Opposites Attract?

Kathryn Freeman

Published 2014 by Choc Lit Limited
Penrose House, Crawley Drive, Camberley, Surrey GU15 2AB, UK
www.choc-lit.com

A CIP catalogue record for this book is available
from the British Library

ISBN 978-1-78189-101-8

Printed and bound by CPI Group (UK) Ltd, Croydon, CR0 4YY

To my men. My sons, who put up with their mother's weird desire to write about romance. And my husband, who didn't laugh too loudly when I said I wanted to give up work and write. He told me to go for it.

This book is your fault!

Acknowledgements

My mum insists she always knew I'd become a writer one day. Her belief in me, based on the tenuous evidence of scribbled letters rather than any great literary prose, says a lot about a mother's blinkered love. Thank you Mum (and Dad because I know you watch over me).

Of course writing is one thing. Writing a story that others might want to read is something else. There were many dark days when I thought this would never happen, so a huge thanks to the rest of my family for keeping me going – David and Jayne, my other Mum and Dad, my lovely Northern relies from Fleetwood. You all rock! And I will never forget the support from friends (Charlotte, Priti, Jane, Lisa, Fiona, Sonia, Gill, Anissa, Bee, Janet, Michele, Sheyline, Laura, Tara) and from work colleagues (Stockley Park, Bagshot, Zurich and North America). You all rock, too.

Do Opposites Attract? would not have been the book it is today without the insightful advice from the Romantic Novelists' Association New Writers' Scheme or the guidance of my wonderful editor. Thank you to them, and to writers everywhere who have been kind enough to welcome me into this exciting world.

Finally, a huge, heartfelt thank you to my publisher, Choc Lit, for being brave and kind enough to take a risk on an unknown author. This book is your fault, too!

Chapter One

The ballroom was dazzling. The jazz band played, diamonds glittered. Waiters strutted round with silver platters filled with canapés and the finest champagne. Wealthy men in their handmade tuxedos danced with glamorous ladies in eye-wateringly expensive silk dresses. It resembled a scene from the nineteenth century, when girls in their finery would set out to snare a rich husband. Two centuries later it looked like very little had changed – bar a reduction in simpering and an escalation in blatant flirtation.

Brianna was so bored, she wanted to scream. She didn't want to spend yet another Saturday night in the company of these pampered, idle rich. Not with men who seemed increasingly dull, or with women who cared about nothing but spending money and looking good. Her greatest fear was that she was fast becoming one of them.

Across the sea of black tuxedos and vibrant designer dresses, Brianna caught sight of Melanie. She smiled as their eyes locked. Melanie had been her best friend from school; was her best friend now. She too had more money than she knew what to do with. With an understanding borne of years of friendship, they simultaneously moved towards the exit.

'When are you going to dance with me, Brianna?'

Her escape temporarily halted, Brianna turned to find Henry Doherty following her. He was attractive, if you liked men with bland, even features. Brianna didn't.

'Maybe later,' she replied, giving him a cool smile. 'And maybe never,' she muttered under her breath, gliding quickly through the hotel and into the welcome fresh air of the London evening.

'I see you're much in demand again.' Melanie had followed her out and was looking furtively up and down the street to check nobody was watching them. With a nod of satisfaction she delved into her satin evening bag and proceeded to light two cigarettes.

Brianna didn't smoke. Neither did Melanie. At least not when they were sober. In fact, Brianna hated it with a passion and refused to go out with any man who smoked. But every now and again, when she'd had too much to drink, or was feeling low, a cigarette was just what she needed. Tonight it was a combination of both.

Taking a deep drag she rested against the cool wall of the hotel. 'I didn't see you standing around like a wallflower either,' she remarked as the nicotine slowly seeped into her veins, relaxing her.

'One of the privileges of being your friend is that I seem to acquire the men you reject.' Melanie grinned and rested against the wall next to her. 'Of course the downside of that is they always know they're getting second best.'

Brianna emitted a very unladylike snort. 'What a load of bull. Look at you with your shiny blonde hair and baby blue eyes. You could never be second best.'

Melanie shook her head, though she was still smiling. 'And look at you, Brianna Worthington. I might be the cool blonde, but it's the sexy brunette the men are desperate to meet.'

Brianna took another drag from her cigarette. 'Bollocks. It's my trust fund they're chasing, not me.' As the sole, fourth generation heir to the Worthington family business, being fabulously wealthy was something she'd grown up with. 'Still, who cares? Far easier to be the one being chased than the one doing the chasing.'

'Speaking of your trust fund, how is life in the family emporium? Found a job you actually enjoy yet?'

Brianna snorted again, a sound totally at odds with her appearance. 'Sure. Running a chain of shops is exactly how I see my life unfolding.'

'Good heavens, only you could call the illustrious Worthington department stores a chain of shops. If your father heard you, he'd disown you.'

'Sometimes I think that might be a good thing,' Brianna admitted quietly.

Melanie shot her a look of disbelief. 'You're kidding me. Then you'd really have to work for a living.'

'So? You don't think I've got the stamina to do a nine to five, five day week?'

'Stamina, yes, boredom threshold, no. You'd be tearing your hair out after a fortnight.'

'Only if I chose the wrong job.'

'And what, pray, would be the right job?'

The conversation was becoming way too serious for a Saturday night. 'Okay, you win. I can't imagine anything I'd want to do seven hours a day, five days a week.' She shuddered. Taking a final puff of her cigarette, she crushed the stub under her five inch silver Jimmy Choo's. 'Come on, my friend. Let's go back and party.'

Grabbing Melanie by the arm, the pair of them strode confidently back into the hotel, oblivious to the envious glances of other women and the frankly lustful gazes of the men. They both lived in a world where they were used to being pursued and adored.

On entering the glittering ballroom once more, Brianna paused. There was Henry again, his eyes scanning the room. With a sinking feeling in her stomach, she guessed he was looking for her. Bugger. She liked him well enough, and had certainly *known* him long enough because their mothers were great friends, but it didn't mean she wanted to spend the rest of the evening with him. Especially as he seemed to be angling to move their relationship on from friendship to something more. It simply wasn't going to happen. He might be good-looking, but romantically, Henry left her cold. What was it about rich men that made them dull? Maybe they didn't feel the need to try. Or maybe their lives were so empty it left them with nothing interesting to say.

'Henry's on the prowl for you,' Melanie whispered, nodding her head in the man's direction.

'Which is why I'm about to make a run for it.'

Her friend chuckled. 'Coward.'

'I prefer to think I'm being kind.'

'Abandoning me is kind?'

'Not giving Henry grounds for false hope is kind. Abandoning you is a necessary step, but one I know a best friend will forgive.'

Not allowing Melanie a chance to reply, Brianna darted out of Henry's line of vision, offering her friend a silent apology when his gaze fell in her direction. Feeling every inch the coward she'd been accused of being, Brianna sneaked round the outside of the room and headed for her mother's table.

Dull and rich. The words haunted her as she walked. They applied just as easily to women, too, and were exactly what she feared was happening to her. It was all very well being rich and pretty, but really, what did she actually *do*? What was her purpose? If she wasn't careful, she was going to end up being a bland, rich lady. One of those who lunched, played tennis and waited for their equally boring partners to come home.

It was a sobering thought, sobering enough to dim the champagne high she'd been slowly cultivating all evening. Time to head to the refuge of her mother.

Approaching her table, she found her deep in conversation with Henry's mother, Abigail.

'I'm sure it won't be long before Henry and Brianna get together,' she overheard her mother saying. 'They make such a lovely couple. And I wouldn't have to worry about my in-laws coming for tea.' The two ladies chuckled.

Anger fizzed up Brianna's spine and her first instinct was to pull the two women apart and announce that hell would need to freeze over before she'd ever contemplate marrying Henry. But mid-stride, she halted. She was twenty-six years old. Old enough to have learnt to curb her temper. Well, almost. So instead of rushing in with both feet, Brianna hung back, accepted a drink from a passing waiter and let her anger cool.

All her life she'd done as her parents had asked, sometimes going against her own wishes. She'd trooped off to ballet lessons when she'd rather have been learning to salsa. She'd struggled with the classical piano, although she'd wanted to rock the electric guitar. She'd even spent endless hours perfecting her topspin forehand, whilst enviously watching the girls from the local school play football. But marrying Henry was a step far too far. How could her mother think that someone like him was right for her? For marriage, she needed love. And for love she needed someone far more exciting than Henry.

Abigail started to make a move and Brianna took her opportunity and sidled onto the now vacant chair next to her mother. 'Mum,' she greeted her, landing a kiss on both her cheeks. 'What have you and Abigail been plotting?'

Her mother had the grace to blush. 'Plotting? Don't be ridiculous. We were just having a chat.'

Brianna narrowed her eyes. 'You were discussing me, Mum. Apparently I'm going to marry Henry. Which, I have to confess, is news to me.'

She'd expected embarrassment, but a broad smile lit up her mother's face. 'Well, what do you think? Wouldn't he make an ideal husband?'

'Ideal how, exactly?' She was trying to curb her tongue, she really was.

'Isn't that rather obvious, darling?'

'Not to me.'

A faint crease lined her mother's brow, her one and only sign of annoyance. She didn't do big scenes. Didn't shout or rant, which drove Brianna mad, as she did both, frequently. 'Your father and I both think Henry would make the perfect husband for you. We've known his family for years, he's independently wealthy, and has charming manners.'

'And that's all it takes? Money, a pedigree and a few basic manners? Mum, we're talking about my life here, my future,' Brianna snapped, exasperated. So much for curbing her tongue. 'There's no way I'm going to let you and Dad determine who I'm going to marry. God knows you've chosen everything else in my life, but not this. Never this.' She pushed her chair back and stood up. 'What about love, Mum? Am I not allowed to marry for love?'

'Of course you are, my darling.' Instantly her mother was by her side, an arm draped around her shoulders, hugging her tight. 'Love is the most important thing. But you can learn to love the right person,' she added quietly, 'rather than someone who might be unsuitable. Who might want you for your money.'

'Don't you trust me enough to find that person by myself?' Brianna replied sadly.

'Oh shush, of course we do. I was just trying to help, that's all. Give you a push in what I thought was the right direction.' Gently she pulled Brianna back down onto the chair. 'What is it, my love? Your father and I are worried about you. You don't look happy any more; you haven't done for a while. That's why we started talking about Henry. We thought maybe you were ready to settle down, but not sure who to settle down with.'

Brianna sighed and leant back against the chair. 'Oh, Mum, I'm far from ready to settle down, and especially not with Henry.' She toyed with the stem of her wine glass. 'I feel restless. I'm halfway through my twenties and I still don't know what I'm doing with my life. I don't just want to get married and have babies. In time, yes, but not now. I want to do something useful, something worthwhile. Not become yet another spoilt rich kid.'

'I thought you were going to work with your father?' her mother prompted cautiously. 'Make use of that business degree you worked so hard for.'

Brianna let out a deep chuckle, releasing the last of the tension between them. 'Very tactful, but you know as well as I do that I haven't exactly excelled in that direction so far.'

'I know that buying and finance weren't your forte,' her mother replied generously. 'But I thought you enjoyed the marketing section?'

Brianna thought back to her time in the Worthington family business, affectionately known as the big W due to its single letter logo. Yes she'd enjoyed looking at ways to improve the branding and promotion of the company, but it hadn't lit any fires in her. Running a chain of shops – sorry high end department stores – simply wasn't what she wanted to spend the best part of her life doing. 'It was fun,' she replied slowly, 'but I'd soon grow bored of it.'

Her mother squeezed her arm. 'Brianna, you're beautiful, smart and determined. You'll find your path in life, my dear.' She considered her daughter for a moment. 'You know I think you should talk to Margaret. She's here this evening. You've met her before, I think?'

Brianna nodded, recalling being introduced to a feisty, grey-haired lady at the last charity ball her mother had coerced her into attending. 'Yes, she runs the charity tonight is in aid of, doesn't she? She's one scary lady.'

Her mother laughed. 'She's not so scary, at least not when you get to know her. Mind you, she has to have a certain amount of pluck to be able to do her job. I was wondering if maybe spending some time working with a charity, a cause you feel is worthwhile, might help you determine your direction. Margaret heads up Medic SOS, a charity I'm rather proud to be the patron of.'

Brianna looked guiltily at her mother. 'I haven't really paid much attention to your charity work, have I? I should have done. What do they do?'

'Well, Margaret can tell you more, but in a nutshell they provide immediate medical help to any place in the world struck by a natural disaster of some sort. I came to know about them when they saved the life of my friend, Tilly. Do you remember how she was caught up in the tsunami disaster in Thailand? The local medical services were hopelessly overburdened, but she was lucky enough to be taken to a Medic SOS tent when she started to have trouble breathing. It turned out that she'd fractured a rib, which then punctured her lung cavity. The team operated on her there and then, and literally saved her life.' At that moment, her mother glanced up and waved. 'Look, here comes the lady herself. I'll ask her to have a chat with you.'

Over the next ten minutes Brianna listened attentively while Margaret described the work of Medic SOS. The more she listened to the older lady's rather gruff tone, the more Brianna started to feel a spark of interest. Maybe her mother was right. Perhaps it was time she considered a new direction, something far removed from traditional business. Goodness knows it hadn't exactly captivated her so far.

'We've got a team out in South America at the moment,' Margaret was saying. 'They've been there for two days now, dealing with the aftermath of a destructive tornado. If you're interested you could fly out and see for yourself the work they do.'

'Really?' Nobody was more surprised than Brianna when the word shot out of her mouth.

Or when Margaret actually cracked an answering smile. 'Yes, really. Just contact the office on Monday and we'll sort everything out for you. Mitch McBride is the lead doctor down there. He's our most experienced medic. You couldn't ask for a better person to demonstrate the practical side of what we do. I'm sure he'll be happy to show you around.'

When Brianna drifted away from the ball later that evening, her head wasn't full of dancing or champagne. Instead she was trying to imagine what a poor area in South America might look like after a tornado, and whether she could possibly be of any help in putting things straight. For the first time in a long while she felt a zip of excitement.

Chapter Two

If Mitch had overheard Margaret telling the young socialite how happy he'd be to show her around, he'd have possibly burst into uncontrollable laughter. But that would have been after he'd thumped his fist against something hard and uttered several filthy swear words. Showing a visitor around the crude camp that so many were now calling home was the bloody last thing he had time for. He was far too busy trying to administer medical help under a leaking tent and without half of his much needed supplies. They were apparently still making their way across the flood stricken muddy tracks that passed for roads. And still it rained.

'Mitch, they're bringing in another crowd.'

Midway through examining the arm of a five year old boy for fractures, Mitch glanced up to see Tessa, his senior nurse, point towards a bedraggled group of varying ages shuffling into what was laughingly called the waiting room. In reality it was a smaller tent adjoined to the larger treatment tent.

'Thanks, Tessa.' Mitch smiled briefly at the head nurse before focussing all his attention back on the child. 'It looks like you've broken your arm, buddy.' He spoke softly in Spanish to the little boy with the large brown eyes. 'But we'll put a cast on it and soon have you as good as new.' He ruffled the boy's hair. 'Have you got any family here with you?' The boy simply shook his head, the fat tears that trailed down his cheeks telling the story far more eloquently than any words. 'Did you get separated?' Mitch continued gently, holding the boy's hand.

The boy nodded and Mitch sighed. Sometimes he hated his job. 'Don't worry. You stay here with us. We'll look after you until we can find your family. Okay?'

He walked the boy over to Tessa. 'Can you sort this brave lad out with a cast and a sling?'

Tessa smiled. 'I'm sure that can be arranged.' She glanced in the direction of an adjoining tent. 'Have you checked on the main ward recently? We're filling up fast.'

Mitch ducked his head through the entrance and went to see for himself. The main ward was a preposterously grand name for what was simply yet another tent, this time filled with rows of temporary beds, most, as Tessa had implied, already occupied. With a heavy heart he ducked back to the treatment tent.

'Poor sods,' he muttered to Tessa. 'And to think they're the lucky ones.' At least they'd managed to escape from what was left of the remote villages that had once been their homes. All too many hadn't.

'We do what we can. If we weren't here, even they wouldn't be lucky.'

She was right. In fact *we do what we can* was a mantra he'd repeated to the team often enough. But not for the first time he wondered how much longer he could continue to work amongst such obvious suffering.

The trouble was, having done a seven-year stint as an army doctor, he'd found it hard to settle into mainstream hospital work. Partly because treating patients who were there through their own fault – too much alcohol, too much food, too little exercise – had bugged the hell out of him, but mostly because he'd missed the thrill of life on the edge. Of never quite knowing what was going to happen next. It was while he'd been slowly going out of his mind with boredom that he'd attended a lunchtime lecture on Medic SOS. The rest, as they say, was history. Three years on and he was now the Chief Medical Officer in charge of an established core of doctors and nurses he could call on as the circumstances dictated.

But much as he loved it, the job was beginning to take its toll. He couldn't remember the last time he'd let his hair down. Done something frivolous, just for the hell of it. Being surrounded by human tragedy on a regular basis was turning him into a tougher, more serious-minded man than he'd ever intended to be. At some point he needed to have a break, take some time to relax and just enjoy life again.

With a deep sigh he walked back to the treatment room. There he was greeted with rows of traumatised faces, all waiting to be helped. These poor sods had lost their homes, probably somebody they loved, and damn near their own lives. His own life was positively privileged in comparison. *Stop moaning, Mitch. Your holiday can wait.*

It was late by the time the queue of waiting survivors had all been attended to. Some had been bandaged up and sent to the temporary camp to search for missing loved ones and find a place to sleep. Others were settled into the ward, too injured to be moved.

Having completed his final round and checked that each patient under their care was stable, he turned to Tessa. 'Time for a quick team meeting, I think. Can you rally the troops?'

While Tessa disappeared off, Mitch pushed together a few chairs at the back of the treatment tent and waited for his small unit to arrive. To the outside world they probably appeared an odd bunch, but they were united in their desire to provide help to those who needed it most, usually with little concern for their own personal comfort or safety. When discussing their jobs with friends in the bar back home, the life of a medical charity worker probably sounded exciting. Reality was a much bleaker picture. A tough hide was needed to withstand the unrelenting misery of the situations they were thrown into, and the crude conditions they were expected to work and live in. Many who joined in a haze of enthusiasm and desire to do good didn't last more than one trip. The team on this tour though were a seasoned group, part of his core team. He felt a rare surge of emotion, even affection, towards them as they slowly straggled in towards him.

'Come on you ugly bunch. I've got places to go, people to see.' His statement was met with the chorus of derisory sniggers he'd expected.

'Even if you said that back at the office, we'd laugh in disbelief. The only places you go are work and bed.'

'Thanks, Tessa,' he remarked dryly as his head nurse took the seat next to him. He knew, because he'd seen her CV, she was in her early forties, but she had a face and body that could have passed for a decade younger. She'd joined Medic SOS following a divorce, determined to start her new single life in a very different environment than her married one.

'She should know. She's tried to entice you out often enough.' That was from Toby, another nurse who came as a pair with his wife, Jane. They'd joined after finding out they weren't able to have children.

Mitch grunted at Toby's remark, uncomfortably aware of the truth behind it. When he turned to see Tessa blushing next to him, red enough he could almost feel her heat, his discomfort increased a hundred fold. She was his right hand woman. Someone he trusted, admired and enjoyed working next to. Period. He prayed that was all she felt, too. Not only did he not think of her like that, but women and work didn't mix. Frankly women and him didn't mix that well, either. He'd had his fair share of affairs – probably more than his share – but for reasons he couldn't fathom, women often tried to shift things from casual and easy to permanent and complicated. Something he had no interest in.

'Thanks, but my personal life isn't on today's agenda,' he told the group gruffly just as Stuart and Roger joined them. Stuart was the other doctor in the team, not long out of medical school. Young and single, what he lacked in experience he made up for in enthusiasm. Roger was a huge, burly, no-nonsense individual who made a surprisingly gentle and caring nurse. He was married, but his wife seemed to tolerate his frequent stints abroad. Some speculated that was what made their marriage work.

'So will it be on a future agenda then, boss?' Dan, the last one in the team, grinned as he plonked himself on the remaining chair. Single and in his mid-twenties, he was handsome and he knew it; a total ladies' man. Officially he was in charge of logistics. Unofficially he was also the unit's entertainment co-ordinator, which usually meant locating the nearest available bar. A place they could unwind and, for a few hours at least, block out the misery they'd witnessed during the day.

'My personal life will never be an agenda item. Not as long as I'm still breathing,' Mitch muttered darkly, and they all laughed.

'Sure thing, boss. You're our man of mystery. You're single, like to run and swim and enjoy an occasional beer. It's all we need to know.' Dan grinned again, flashing a set of even white teeth. 'Speaking of which, I've located the nearest watering hole. Any chance of you joining us tonight?'

Mitch shook his head, surprising nobody. They always asked, but he rarely came. Thrust together under circumstances that made for real, lifelong friendships, Mitch remained a man alone. It wasn't that he was unfriendly. Just that he didn't allow anyone to get close to him.

'Right, down to the real agenda,' Mitch announced abruptly, determinedly steering the topic of conversation back to work. 'Dan has managed to track down the rest of our supplies and they should be with us tomorrow evening. In the meantime, the stuff we have has been borrowed from the hospital in the next town. Use it wisely.'

His grim expression said all it needed to. They weren't to waste it on patients who weren't going to make it.

'On a lighter note, we have a visitor, Brianna Worthington, joining us tomorrow for a week. As she's the patron's daughter, I guess that means we'll have to be on our best behaviour.' His wry grin caused his eyes to crinkle and the hearts of the women to flutter. 'Without the money, we don't exist.'

'Better put me in charge of looking after her then,' Dan interrupted cockily.

Mitch chuckled and his harsh features temporarily relaxed. 'I can't think of a man more suited for the job. I was going to say she'll be in safe hands, but frankly with you, I'm not so sure.'

'She might prefer the quieter, more sensitive type,' Stuart interjected, a determined glint in his eye. 'I think I should be responsible for showing her around.'

Mitch shook his head. 'Come on, guys. The woman hasn't even arrived yet and already she's causing trouble. She might be fat and ugly for all you know.'

'Yeah, but she's going to be loaded,' Dan replied sheepishly. 'That would sure make up for any disappointment in the looks department.'

Rolling his eyes heavenwards, Mitch sighed. 'Well someone has to pick her up from the airport tomorrow. Maybe you boys should flip a coin. Meanwhile go and make merry, but for God's sake behave yourselves. Roger and I will hold the fort.'

Mitch watched them bustle out of the tent, their minds already on a well-deserved night off. Sometimes he wished he could be like that. It must be great to drink, relax and share experiences, but he hadn't been made that way. He couldn't do small talk. He couldn't share confidences. Heck, he couldn't even relax properly in the company of others, even those he knew well. All of which meant there were very few people in his life he had ever been close to. He had a couple of friends from the army but they were now married and he felt like such a spare part when they all hooked up, it seemed easier not to bother. Besides, he was happy with his own company. Frankly he preferred it to the effort of making conversation with others.

'Sleep or ward duty?' he asked Roger, who shrugged his massive shoulders. 'Okay, toss you for it.'

'Heads.'

Mitch flipped the coin, took a quick look and then thrust it back into his pocket. 'Unlucky. You're on duty.'

'Hey, wait a minute. I didn't see that.'

'Calling me a liar?'

Roger chuckled – a sound quite incongruous with his big, brawny looks. 'Sly and sneaky, yeah, but a liar? Nah. Heads it is. Enjoy your kip.'

While Roger went to take his turn on ward duty, Mitch made his weary way back to his tent. Luxurious it wasn't. A camp bed, an oil lantern and a table and chair that doubled up as a desk when he needed to catch up with his paperwork. Something he'd fully intended to do when he'd called tails on a coin that had turned up heads. But the moment he spied the bed, exhaustion crept up on him and instead of sitting at the makeshift desk, he lay down. In this job he'd learnt to sleep whenever he got the opportunity.

Chapter Three

Brianna breathed a huge sigh of relief when the small plane finally touched down onto the tiny airstrip. Relief, because she'd finally reached her destination after twenty-four hours of travelling and relief that the churning motion of the little propeller driven plane had finally come to an end. That being said, she climbed down the steep steps with a great degree of trepidation. She'd seen from the air the devastation the recent tornado and subsequent flooding had caused. The affected area was vast and she wasn't particularly looking forward to seeing the results close up. Hers had been a privileged existence so far. In all her twenty-six years the only hardship she'd witnessed had been on the television. This next week was going to be one heck of a giant step into the unknown, that was for sure.

The heat and the barrenness of the landscape hit her as she reached the cracked tarmac, a sharp warning of the discomfort that lay ahead. Part of her, the part that delighted in luxury, was already starting to regret her rash decision to come here. At this very moment she could be flashing her credit card round the Knightsbridge shops – a world away from where she was now. But that was the whole point, wasn't it?

Looking up she caught sight of a tall, rangy man walking towards the plane. The long stride, loose-limbed gait and straight back bore the hallmarks of a man who was confident in his own skin. A man who knew where he was heading. Her eyes skimmed over his muddy desert boots, creased khaki shorts and plain white T-shirt. Was that the hint of a black tattoo on his bicep, creeping beneath the shirtsleeve? After acknowledging the pilot with a wave of his tanned arm, the man turned and strode towards her.

Dark blond hair, in need of a good cut, surrounded a sun-bronzed, rugged face. It was a face too harsh, too strong to be called handsome. But it made her look, nonetheless.

'Brianna, I presume?' He looked directly at her, his eyes cool and assessing, his voice deep and curt. It was a voice used to issuing commands, used to being in control.

Control was something Brianna was also familiar with. As was the fact that men usually came on to her when they were first introduced. That sounded vain, and it wasn't something she encouraged, just something she lived with. Men seemed to want to flirt with her, whatever their age. Clearly this one was an exception. The fact that he couldn't even muster a smile for her was intriguing. It didn't upset her. Just made her determined to make him take notice. 'You presume correctly,' she replied, smiling broadly and holding out her hand. 'Pleased to meet you.'

The man glanced at the offered hand, but ignored it. 'Have you any bags in the hold?'

She muffled the gasp, but couldn't prevent a sharp intake of breath. Her world might be very different to his, but surely simple courtesy had a place wherever you were? She couldn't work out if he was simply as coarse as he appeared, or if he was deliberately trying to rile her. If it was the latter, he was succeeding. Clutching at manners ingrained in her from an early age, Brianna bit her tongue and continued to smile. 'Thank you, yes. There's my holdall and two boxes.'

Without a word the man swung round and marched over to the plane where he opened the cargo door and pulled out the items. As she watched, the biceps on his arms bunched and the tattoo became clearer; a black panther. An involuntary tremor ran down her spine and for the first time since she'd embarked on the trip, Brianna thought about her own safety. Here she was, in a foreign country thousands of miles from home and dependent on this man to take her to where she needed to go. A man who wore a bold tattoo and an air of ... well, frankly menace. At the very least, he was pretty intimidating. A view that wasn't altered when he thrust one of the boxes into her hands and strode towards the jeep without a backward glance.

Brianna had no choice but to follow. The alternative was to remain alone in an empty airfield in the middle of nowhere. Wordlessly he dumped the luggage into the back of the truck and went to sit in the driver's seat. She stared in open-mouthed astonishment, the box she was left carrying nearly slipping from her hands. Whoever the heck this man was, he was certainly no gentleman. With a hiss of irritation she hoisted the darn package into the back and stalked to the passenger side. As she struggled to open the stiff, heavy door and climb up into the battered seat, she realised she'd taken for granted the charm and effortless good manners of the men she usually mixed with. Apparently opening the car door for a lady didn't come instinctively to every man. Clearly not to the one who sat beside her, his eyes fixed forwards.

Perversely, the ruder he was, the more determined she became to show him the social skills he clearly lacked. 'It's kind of you to come and pick me up. How are things at the camp? Are they on top of the situation yet?'

Briefly the man paused in the action of starting the engine to give her a cold look. 'Villages have been flattened, electricity and water cut off, families torn apart. We're still pulling people out of destroyed buildings and flooded rivers. No, I don't think you could say we're on top of things.'

Bastard, Brianna thought angrily. How dare he talk down to her like that? She hadn't meant anything by her simple question – just some small talk to ease the journey. 'Thank you for your assessment,' she replied frostily, deciding not to pursue any further conversation. She could only thank God she wouldn't have much to do with this man when they arrived at the camp. He was clearly the driver. Hopefully the medical team would be friendlier.

Mitch watched the temper flare briefly in Brianna's eyes at his reply and smiled to himself. He had no doubt she wasn't used to being spoken to like that. She probably had a group of sycophantic friends who followed her around, hung on her every word, told her what they thought she wanted to hear. He guessed that was what it was like in the rich world she lived in. Of course he didn't know. When he thought of the contrast between his own upbringing and hers ... he shook his head in disgust. Even he could see the massive chip that sat firmly on his shoulder. The fact that it was still there and that it only took someone like Brianna to reveal it, annoyed the hell out of him. He'd done well for himself, achieved respectability. Where he'd come from shouldn't matter. But it did, particularly when he met people like her. Which was why, instead of being polite and civil, things he knew he was quite capable of, the devil inside him made him act just the opposite. He became the rough, ill-mannered man synonymous with his upbringing. He hadn't missed the look of shock on her face when he'd thrust the parcel at her. Nor had he missed her look of disdain when faced with having to open her own door. Well, this was his turf. While she was here she would have to learn to play by his rules. Which meant not being waited on hand and foot and not being mollycoddled. It also meant doing as she was told.

He smiled grimly to himself. It was going to be interesting to see how she'd cope with all that. He'd promised Margaret he'd show the patron's daughter round and give her an insight into the work they did and he would. Just not cap in hand. If he had to babysit the woman for a week, she'd have to take him as she found him.

As the jeep bounced over the ruts in the road, he idly

glanced over in her direction. One thing was for certain, she was trouble with a capital T. Dan and Steve had already argued so much about who was going to pick her up that in the end Mitch had snatched the keys and driven off himself. And that was before they knew she wasn't a fat, ugly heiress. Jeez, when they found out she was actually a flaming beautiful one, they were going to be unbearable. With flashing green eyes, shiny brown hair and a curvaceous figure no man could ignore, and believe it, he was trying, she was one sexy lady. Not the type he wanted hanging round an overworked, increasingly stressed camp. Added to which, the flirtatious smile she'd first directed at him told him she was a lady used to enjoying the company of men. Used to wrapping them around her little finger.

It was going to be a very long week.

Their journey to the camp was conducted in an uneasy silence, Mitch very aware of Brianna quietly fuming next to him. He smiled grimly to himself. She could choose to sulk, or choose to listen. It made no odds to him.

'Mitch!' As he pulled up by the Medic SOS tents, Jane came hurrying out to meet him.

Brianna turned her head sharply towards him, astonishment written across her perfect features. '*You're* Mitch McBride? Well, it would have been nice if you'd bothered to introduce yourself.'

Before he could reply, Jane interrupted. 'There's an emergency, Mitch. You're needed on the ward.'

As Jane hurried away, Mitch jumped down from the jeep. 'Sorry, honey. I've got more important things to do than smooth your ruffled feathers.' Midway to the tent, his mind already focused on the emergency, he paused and shot Brianna a brief look over his shoulder. 'Stay in the jeep. I'll get someone to come and sort you out.'

Brianna let out a snarl of sheer frustration. How bloody

rude. Irritated, she deliberately climbed out. The sight that met her was awful enough to push her petty annoyance into the background. My God, the place looked stark. Row upon row of battered, makeshift tents in a huge muddy field. She shuddered, unable to stop the totally selfish thought that she wasn't going to be getting a nice hot shower to ease away the discomfort of a day and night travelling. And, to top it all, the man she'd been assured would be happy to help her understand the work of the charity, seemed to be anything but happy. The words surly, rude and arrogant came to the top of her mind.

'Brianna?' A handsome young man approached her, a wide grin on his face. 'Wow, we really hit the jackpot with you. First time we get a visitor and she's drop dead gorgeous. Well, welcome to hell. I'm Dan and I'm here to look after you. Anything you need, just ask me.'

For the first time since she'd set out on this adventure, Brianna felt her shoulders start to relax. Here at last was an admiring man with a friendly face. 'Great to meet you, Dan. I suppose a hot shower is out of the question?' The words blurted embarrassingly from her lips but Dan simply laughed.

'Well, it's pretty basic and there might be a problem with hot water, but we can manage something resembling a shower. Come with me.'

'Really, a shower?' Right now she didn't care what it looked like or if the water was freezing. Anything that removed dust and grime was okay with her.

'Really.'

He plucked her holdall and both boxes out of the truck with an ease that reinforced her earlier impression; Mitch had been out to make a point when he'd made her carry one. Either that or he was a weakling. A clear image of taut, muscular biceps flooded her mind and she stumbled on the uneven ground.

'Watch your step. Don't want you banged up with a twisted ankle on day one.'

Dragging in a lungful of air, she focused on the man she was with. 'What's your role in the team then, Dan?' she asked as they skirted the larger marquee-like tents that she guessed substituted for a hospital and made their way towards a cluster of much smaller ones.

'Logistics,' he replied, another quick-fire grin lighting up his face. 'Which basically means I do everything that isn't connected with the medical care. I sort out supplies, put up the medical tents and equipment, work with the other charities to make sure we get food and shelter for ourselves. Plus I look after any visitors,' he added with a wink.

Brianna bet Dan knew all about looking after visitors, female ones in particular. He had a natural, easy charm and, together with his obvious good looks, it made him very attractive. But much as she was enjoying his attention, Brianna knew she wasn't going to be one of his conquests. She preferred the slightly less obvious, the less easy. In truth, although she hated to admit it, Mitch was the one who'd grabbed her interest. Overbearing and ill-mannered he might be, but his surprising deep brown eyes drew a woman in, and his forceful personality made her sit up and take notice. Even though she might not want to.

Dan had moved ahead of her and was now unzipping the entrance to a tatty looking white tent she guessed she'd be calling home.

'Here you go. It might not be much, but after a day around here, trust me, you'll be glad to get back to it,' he remarked as he placed her luggage on the floor. 'There is a temporary shower just around the corner. The water's cold, but it will definitely freshen you up. Alternatively, some of us go and bathe in the lake. It's okay, as long as you watch out for crocodiles.'

Brianna shivered. 'I think I'll go for the shower.'

'Probably a wise choice,' Dan agreed with a grin. 'I'll leave you to sort yourself out. When you feel like some company, come to the main medical tent. There are sure to be a few of us around.'

Left on her own, Brianna sank down on the camp bed. Okay, she didn't sink. That would imply a degree of give in the brick-like mat that was trying to pass for a mattress. Oh heck, she so wanted to cry, but that would be weak and she was determined not to act like the spoilt brat some probably believed her to be. Mitch for one. Then again, why should his opinion of her matter? He was just a jumped up doctor. If she wanted, she thought with a flash of anger, she could get him fired.

As quickly as it had arrived, the anger vanished and she was left feeling stupid and a tiny bit scared. That was exactly the type of attitude she hated. Sure Mitch had been less than welcoming, but at the end of the day her only real gripes were that he'd given her a box to carry and not opened the truck door for her. Considering what he had on his plate at the moment, they were hardly crimes of the century.

Half an hour and a cold shower later, Brianna was feeling a little more human again.

'Have you managed to find everything you need?'

In the act of folding her towel over the end of the bed, Brianna looked up with a start, shocked to find Mitch walking unannounced into her tent. 'Do you always come into a woman's room uninvited?'

Mitch raised an eyebrow. 'It depends on the woman.'

'Well this woman wants you to wait until you're invited.' She didn't want to act like a brat, but she wasn't going to let him trample all over her, either.

'But then I might be waiting a long time,' he replied calmly, nonchalantly leaning against a tent pole.

Something she couldn't deny. 'What did you want?' she asked somewhat churlishly.

Mitch sighed. 'Look, I came to check you were all right, that's all. I apologise for not knocking first, but it's damn hard to do that on a tent.'

Against her will, Brianna's lips twitched slightly. 'Point taken. And yes, thank you, I'm fine. I feel a lot better after a shower and change of clothes.'

'I'm sorry we couldn't arrange an en suite for you.' Mitch regarded her with steady brown eyes and she didn't know if it was a joke, or a dig. Probably the latter, though this time she wasn't going to rise to the bait. 'What's in those?'

Brianna followed the direction of his gaze, over to the two large brown boxes. At the time, her idea had seemed like a good one. Now, under Mitch's tough scrutiny and having seen the grimness of the situation first hand, she wasn't so sure. 'Just something I brought from home I thought might be ... useful.' She tried to distract him. 'Have you got time to show me the medical tent now?'

Mitch nodded. 'Yeah. But not until you've shown me the boxes. I take it you checked with Margaret what to bring? We're really struggling for some medical supplies.'

Oh wow, he really knew how to make her feel small. Then again, she couldn't blame him for this blunder. It was entirely down to her own ignorance. 'Umm, no, I didn't think to ask. I only checked what I should bring in terms of clothes. For me.'

The disbelieving look he gave her said it all. 'What on earth is in them then?'

She stared at her feet, way beyond embarrassed. 'I guess you'd better see for yourself.'

When she dared to look back up Mitch was crouched down on his haunches, tearing open the first box with a penknife. After peering inside, he burst out laughing.

By rights, she should have been highly offended at his reaction, and some of her was. She may not have had the foresight to find out what they needed, but at least she hadn't come empty-handed. But she found herself unable to muster any anger because she was too busy goggling at the sight of the attractive man crouched over the box. Gone was the harshness, the brooding. In its place was a youthful, almost boyish expression. God, he was positively gorgeous. A smile lit up his face, warmed his chocolate-brown eyes, and even created a set of cute dimples on either side of his mouth. She would never have put cute and Dr Mitch McBride together in the same sentence. But here he was, looking so damned sexy she almost couldn't breathe.

'Teddy bears?' Mitch asked when he'd finally finished laughing. 'Well, I'll give you ten out of ten for originality, if only one out of ten for practicality. But then I don't suppose someone like you knows much about practicality.'

The sting of his words brought Brianna crashing back down to earth and she immediately reversed her opinion of him. Not cute at all. For a moment she'd glimpsed someone else; a relaxed, attractive, fun-loving man. Now the harsh face was back and with it the sarcastic tone. 'They aren't for you,' she replied stiffly. 'They're for your patients. I did bring some things for you and the team, but if that's going to be your attitude, I think I'd prefer to take them home with me.' Inside she cringed at the knowledge of what was in the other box. If he'd laughed at the teddy bears …

Mitch took in Brianna's flushed cheeks and fiery green eyes. She really was a beauty and her temper only added to her sensuality. But for crying out loud, when he thought of all the things she could have brought, and he was left staring at a box of ruddy useless stuffed bears. No, he was damned if he was going to apologise for laughing at her. He could, however, extend an olive branch. 'I'm sure the kids will love the bears.'

She raised her chin and looked him in the eye. 'But medicines would have been more useful and might have saved a few lives.'

He met honesty with honesty. 'Yes.'

With a sigh she nodded over to the other box. 'I suppose you might as well see what I got you.'

Intrigued, despite himself, he took out his penknife again and sliced open the second box, pulling out a couple of bags. 'Shower gel and body lotion?'

She bit her lip. 'No, that's for the women. Jane and Tessa, right?'

He nodded and dived back into the box. 'Whisky?' He could see she was still embarrassed because her eyes weren't quite meeting his now.

'Yes,' she replied diffidently. 'A bottle for each of the men. Even you.'

Laughing grimly, he tucked the bottle under his arm. That just about summed up the difference between them. She'd packed luxury items. He'd have given his eye teeth for some essentials. Disposable razors maybe, because he was running out. Batteries for his torch. Toothpaste, though maybe he could gargle with the whisky instead. 'Thanks.'

She acknowledged his pretty lame gratitude with a cursory nod. 'Now, if you've finished poking fun at me, I'd like to see where you attend the patients.'

Mitch stared back at her, at the proud way she carried herself. At the steel he glimpsed behind the beauty. Thank God rich pampered girls weren't his type. Women like her lived privileged lives in ignorant bubbles. He preferred his women savvy, experienced and down to earth.

As she sauntered out of the tent ahead of him, head held high, her slim curvy figure clear underneath the tight canvas trousers and black T-shirt, he thought he'd do well to keep reminding himself of that during the week ahead.

Chapter Four

It didn't take long for Brianna to begin to understand the importance of the work of the Medic SOS team. Within minutes of being shown round the medical tents she could see for herself how many patients were being looked after and how many were still waiting to be seen. She finally understood what people meant by the term heart-wrenching.

'Do you want a drink of anything?' Mitch asked, moving towards a vast chrome container of what was presumably hot water.

Struggling to take in the fact that he was actually being polite, Brianna said the first thing that came to her mind. 'Yes please. Have you got any herbal tea?'

Mitch just looked at her. He didn't need to say anything. His disgust was written all over his face. Blimey, of course they didn't have any herbal teas. Where the heck did she think she was, the Ritz? Squirming with embarrassment, Brianna tried to smile. 'I can't believe I just said that,' she admitted, shaking her head. 'Anything hot and wet will be fine.'

She hung back as he filled two plastic cups with hot water and goodness only knew what else. Whatever it tasted like, Brianna knew she was going to have to drink it. All of it. As he handed her the cup, he was interrupted by a blonde nurse.

'Mitch, they're bringing in a child. He's thought to be about five or six years old. Found by the banks of the river in a hypothermic state.' Mitch nodded at the nurse and turned to Brianna.

'Brianna, this is Tessa, our head nurse. She's the one who really runs this place. Without her, we'd be lost.'

Brianna turned to shake Tessa's hand, watching with interest as the nurse flushed a vivid shade of scarlet. As Mitch and Tessa went off to prepare for the arrival of the child, Brianna studied the body language between doctor and nurse. She guessed Tessa was older than Mitch, though it was hard to be sure. The nurse wore her age well, whereas Mitch had a face that looked like it had lived through hard times. Tessa was certainly attractive, with short blonde hair and big blue eyes. What was also evident, from the way she hung on Mitch's every word, was that Tessa was head over heels in love with the doctor. For his part, Mitch was professional, but Brianna couldn't see anything to indicate he returned the feeling. In fact she wondered if he had any idea of the crush his head nurse had on him. She doubted it. He didn't look like a man who cared overly much what others thought of him.

The child was brought in on a stretcher. Brianna stood to one side, out of the way but close enough so she could observe as nurse and doctor worked together on him. They seemed to have a routine that required little verbal communication. Occasionally Mitch would utter a few words, such as 'oxygen' or 'warm IV fluids', but most of the time they worked in silence.

'You must be Brianna.' She turned to find herself greeted by a tall, lanky young man. He had a pleasant face and a shy smile. 'I'm Stuart, one of the doctors. Good to have you with us.'

'Hello, Stuart, and thank you. It's good to be here. I think,' she added with a half-smile, looking back to where Mitch was still hovering over the new patient.

Stuart nodded. 'Doesn't look like much fun, does it? But trust me, it is possible to enjoy yourself here, at least when you're not on duty.' His eyes rested on Mitch. 'Well, it is possible for most of us, that is.'

Despite the circumstances, Brianna giggled. Laughter for her was a much needed release. 'He's not a bundle of joy, is he, your boss. I've gained that impression already.'

'He certainly isn't. Oh, don't get me wrong, he's not a tyrant or anything. But he does take it all very seriously.'

Brianna took in the rows of traumatised patients, the makeshift beds, the lady with the mop fruitlessly trying to clean up mud from the floor. 'I guess it's a serious business.'

'It is,' Stuart agreed. 'But everyone needs some down time, away from the sharp end. Otherwise you just get dragged down with it.'

'So what do you do on your time off?' Brianna was intrigued as to what they could do in such a godforsaken place.

Stuart shrugged. 'Well, Dan usually finds out the nearest bar in a town that's still open. This time around it's about forty minutes in the jeep, but well worth the effort to mix with normality for a while. In fact last night we rented a room in the local inn and had a hot shower. It was bliss.'

Brianna laughed. 'Don't tell me the highlight of your social life is having a hot shower. I really am going to go mad.'

'Hey, don't knock it. When you've been here a few more days, you'll be begging to come with us.'

'Stuart, there are people waiting to be seen.' Mitch's curt order cut into their conversation.

Stuart flushed. 'Definitely not a bundle of joy,' he muttered to her under his breath before scuttling off with his tail between his legs.

Brianna's sympathy went out to him. 'Was that really necessary?' she asked coolly as Mitch came to join her, the young boy he'd been working on now hooked up to monitors.

'You think it's acceptable to be flirting when there are

people in pain waiting to be helped?' Mitch glared at her and Brianna had a feeling he was looking down at her from more than just his physical height.

'He wasn't flirting, he was being polite,' she returned, aware that her upper-class accent had risen a notch in her anger. 'A gentle word would have been just as effective and far less embarrassing.'

'Anything else you'd like to tell me I'm doing wrong?' His eyes flashed dangerously.

'Don't you also have patients to see?' she shot back, determined not to let him have the upper hand.

'I had rostered Stuart on this afternoon so I could talk you through the way we work. However, if you're not interested ...' He let his sentence trail off and began to walk away.

She fumed. She had never met anyone as annoying as Mitch McBride that was for certain. But she was here to learn what the charity did and like it or not, as the doctor in charge, Mitch was key to that. She had to find a way to get on with him, or she'd have a difficult and probably fruitless week. With a determined effort she swallowed her pride. 'I am interested,' she spoke to his retreating back. 'Please, I'd like to hear about your work. That's what I came here for.'

At last, Mitch thought, a touch of humility. He turned round, pathetically glad he'd finally made Brianna say please. When she'd berated him about his treatment of Stuart, it had felt like the lady of the manor remonstrating with one of her servants. A guaranteed way to put his back up. Why did the rich think they could order people around just because they had money?

'Okay then, princess, why don't I start with the tour I was planning on giving you, until we were interrupted.'

'My name is Brianna,' she replied with icy politeness. 'Please use it.'

He watched as temper flashed once more in her vivid green eyes, and grudgingly found himself admiring her. She was certainly no pushover. Probably too accustomed to getting her own way. He wondered how much of her almost regal attitude would still be there when it was time for her to go home. 'Well then, Brianna,' he said with emphasis, 'you've already met our other doctor, Stuart. We're a small team here this time. Generally we call on a few more doctors to help us, but on this particular trip other organisations have brought quite a lot of medical staff, so we've come with just the minimum.'

'I don't quite understand how you fit in with the other aid agencies. I mean, why do you need Medic SOS when you've got organisations like the Red Cross?'

Mitch nodded. It was a common question. 'The Red Cross is only so big. It hasn't got the capacity to help out in every crisis that comes along. The same goes for other medical charities. Sure, they always attend the big ones, the tsunamis or earthquakes that hit the headlines. But they're stretched very thin, especially with their support in the war zones. Medic SOS help make up the numbers, usually attending the smaller crises that might otherwise get overlooked. Plus, being small, we're nimbler and can get out to a place within only hours of it being brought to our attention. We're usually the first team on site. Once the other teams arrive and things are under control, we withdraw and wait for the next crisis.'

'How often are you called out, on average?'

He could see he had her attention now. It was quite a heady experience, being pinned down by those intelligent green eyes. 'How long is a piece of string?' he answered simply. 'In our world, there is no average. We could go weeks, on occasion months, without a call and then find ourselves called out every week. It really is hard to say.'

'I can't imagine a life like that,' she admitted. 'Waiting for the next phone call. Not knowing what you might have to face when it comes. What do you do with yourselves in between trips?'

'Sleep usually,' he replied dryly.

Brianna studied him seriously. 'You're not kidding, are you?'

'No way. I never joke about sleep.'

He was rewarded with a small smile. 'And after you've slept?'

He shrugged. 'Paperwork, there's always a lot of that. We assess our supplies and determine what we need to replenish. Then there's skills training, attending courses to make sure we're up to date with the latest techniques and equipment.'

'And waiting for the phone to ring,' Brianna finished for him.

'Yep. It's not the job I'd recommend for a family man, or someone who likes routine. But it suits me.' No chance of anyone missing him when he was called up. Which was exactly how he liked it.

For the next hour, Mitch gave her his undivided attention. He answered her questions as politely as he could, which was easy because they were surprisingly astute. He showed her the equipment they used and how it differed to that in a regular hospital. He explained the typical injuries they came across and how they worked with the other agencies. If she was bored at any point, she didn't show it, though by the end her barrage of questions did start to dry up.

'Why don't you get some rest,' he told her, taking in her very pale face.

'I'm fine. I don't want to miss anything.' She ruined the statement by yawning widely.

'Grab a couple of hours and come back for the medical review meeting at six.'

'The what?'

Yeah, he had made it sound fancier than it was. 'It's just our daily catch up meeting. A chance to check on the progress of the patients and discuss any issues.'

She gave him a tired smile. 'Thanks. I'd like that.'

He watched her walk away with a puzzled frown on his face. A pampered princess, but with brains and a desire to learn. Interesting.

Brianna was woken by her alarm and for a moment she had trouble remembering where she was. As she sat up in the cramped bed and listened to the sound of rain against the canvas, the reality came back all too quickly. She'd gone to catch up on a few hours' sleep, but set the alarm so she didn't miss Mitch's meeting. He'd been considerate enough to invite her, the least she could do was accept. And turn up on time.

They seemed to have come to a sort of truce. Certainly on her part she'd started to develop a grudging respect for the man. He might be gruff, arrogant and lacking in manners, but he was extremely knowledgeable and seemed to genuinely care about the work he did.

With an effort she dragged herself out of bed and splashed cold water on her face from the jug left in her tent. With a quick flick of the hairbrush, she was ready to face the world again. It was a far cry from the hours she usually took to get ready at home. Here there wasn't even a mirror to check her appearance, so she had to assume she looked okay. Even if she didn't, there was no time to fix it. She didn't need much of an imagination to picture Mitch's face if she turned up late.

By the time she'd navigated her way to the Medic SOS tent – not as easy as she'd thought as one tent looked pretty much the same as the next – the team had already sat down. Thankfully they all seemed far too engrossed in what they were saying to notice her sneak in. Moving quietly to the vacant chair, she settled back to listen.

Much of what was said went over her head. They talked about patients she hadn't met and medicines she'd never heard of. She was almost falling asleep on her chair when Mitch started to discuss the little boy who'd been brought in with hypothermia.

'I've rung the hospital in the capital and they do have capacity to admit him,' Dan was saying. 'I think you were after a dialysis unit?' he checked with Mitch. 'Well, they do have one.'

'What would that be for?' Brianna asked. It was the first time she'd spoken since the meeting had begun.

'In some severe cases, it can be possible to take the blood out, warm it up, and put it back,' Mitch explained. 'You can do that using a dialysis unit.'

'Shall I sort out an air ambulance for him?' Dan asked, looking at Mitch.

Mitch shook his head. 'No,' he replied shortly. 'It's not worth it.'

Brianna stared at him, aghast. Had he really said that? 'What? You're telling us this child's life isn't worth it?' she exclaimed, horrified. 'Do you mean not worth the expense, or not worth the hassle? Because if it's the expense, I'll flipping well pay for it myself.'

A hush came over the group. 'Not every problem can be solved by throwing money at it,' Mitch replied quietly.

The condescending sod. Brianna leapt to her feet. 'Good God, I can't believe I'm hearing this. I thought medicine was a caring profession. That you were in it to save lives. And yet here you are, casually dismissing the chance of saving the life of this young boy. You heartless bastard.'

'Brianna, stop this. You're getting over-emotional,' Mitch told her roughly.

'We're talking about a child's life here,' she interrupted angrily. 'Of course I'm emotional. You should be, too. Remind me never to get sick when you're around. You might think I'm not worth the bother, too.' Tiredness from the journey, coupled with the emotion of the situation seemed to strip away all her control. As the harsh words flew from her mouth, she stalked towards the exit. 'Excuse me,' she spoke into the now deadly silence. 'Suddenly I have other things I need to do.'

A few moments later she was back on her bed, tears she'd been trying so hard to contain now gushing out, like water from a leaking dam. She cried for herself, because she felt tired and lonely, and she cried for the little boy whose life was slowly ebbing away.

When there were no tears left, she got back up and went to the ward. At least she could show the boy somebody cared.

Chapter Five

Mitch had watched Brianna stalk out of his meeting with an air of resignation. Why were people outside the profession unable to grasp that it was impossible to save everybody? And she'd twisted his words. He hadn't said *the boy* wasn't worth it. Just that the exercise of calling for an air ambulance wasn't worth it. Sadly they'd found the kid too late and Mitch knew no amount of effort was going to save him now. All moving him would do was make the poor soul less comfortable and hasten his departure.

'I don't think our visitor has been around death before,' Tessa observed, speaking into the silence that had greeted Brianna's departure. 'Perhaps, in a few more days, she'll come to understand that not everyone makes it.'

'Perhaps.' But Mitch had his doubts. He had a sense that if Brianna set her mind to it, she would never give up, never let go, whether that was on a project or a person. She was a determined woman, a quality he would usually respect. At the moment though, she seemed to have set her stubborn mind on going up against him. Perhaps because he didn't tug his forelock every time he spoke to her.

They finished the meeting without any further histrionics. Gathering together his notes, Mitch wandered back out to the ward, his mind on Brianna. He had to admit her reaction had been a bit of a shock. He hadn't expected to find her so concerned with the welfare of a child she didn't know.

When he entered the ward and caught sight of her sitting at the boy's bedside, he immediately thought his mind was playing tricks on him. He'd been thinking about her so much, now he was starting to see her. Then he heard her murmuring to the boy and watched as she settled one of her ridiculous teddy bears next to his face. The very real sight touched something deep inside him, a place that hadn't been warmed in a very long time. Out of her comfort zone and exhausted from the travel, she hadn't taken off to her tent as he'd thought she would, as she actually had a right to do. Instead she'd decided to offer comfort to a boy she'd never met. He liked to think he was a pretty good judge of character, but as he watched Brianna stroking the young boy's hair, Mitch wondered if perhaps he'd misjudged her. Beneath the posh, glossy exterior there was clearly a compassionate heart. It was almost as surprising a find as the sharp brain he'd witnessed earlier.

Slowly he walked up to her. 'Brianna.'

She looked up with a start, her dislike of him very much in evidence when her beautiful face turned from soft to haughty in the blink of an eye. 'I know you believe he's not worth any of your precious time,' she told him in a voice so cold icicles seemed to hang off each word. 'But you can't stop me from being here.'

Frustrated, Mitch jammed a hand roughly through his hair. Then, acting on impulse, he reached out, grabbed her arm and dragged her off the chair and outside the tent. Although she protested, his grip was so tight she was unable to do anything but follow him.

'Damn you, Brianna,' he uttered under his breath. 'You're putting words into my mouth.' He paused, fighting to control his temper. 'I didn't say he wasn't worthy of our compassion, just that there was nothing else we could do to save him.'

Brianna looked down at the hand that gripped her arm. Mitch wondered what she saw. The strength? Or the fact that it was rough and calloused.

'Let go, you're hurting me.'

If she'd slapped him, he couldn't have let go any quicker.

'Sorry, I didn't mean to.' Angry red bruises marked the delicate creamy skin where his hand had been and he winced at his roughness. 'I just wanted to make sure you followed me out,' he tried to explain. 'Although the boy isn't conscious, nobody knows whether he can hear or not. I didn't want to subject him to this conversation.'

Brianna nodded briefly, then turned away from him and disappeared back inside the tent. Mitch was left standing outside like a fool, annoyed and frustrated. It seemed nothing he did was going to please the lady. It shouldn't matter to him, but it did. And damned if that realisation didn't escalate his annoyance and frustration.

Brianna spent another hour with the boy and then gave in to the tiredness she'd felt since she'd arrived. Travelling, coupled with the trauma of the day, had left her so exhausted that even the little camp bed seemed like the height of luxury. As soon as her head touched the pillow, she fell asleep.

When she woke, the clock by her bed said it was only four in the morning, but her mind told her it was time to get up. That was the trouble with jet lag. Frustrated, Brianna climbed out of bed and got dressed. With nothing to do in her little tent to while away the hours – no TV to watch, no music to listen to – she decided to check up on the little boy. See if he was still hanging in there.

Easing quietly through the entrance to the medical ward, she was heading towards the boy's bed when she came to an abrupt halt. Good God, was that Mitch at the boy's bedside? From across the dimly lit tent she could just about make out his broad-shouldered figure, smoothing what she guessed was a damp cloth gently across the boy's parched lips. Not wanting to disturb them, she backed out and bumped straight into Tessa.

'Sorry,' she said hastily. 'I was awake, so I thought I'd see how the boy was doing. But I see he already has company.'

Tessa nodded. 'I'm afraid he's nearing the end now, that's why Mitch is with him. Nobody under his care ever dies alone, not if he can help it. It's something he's done ever since I've known him.' They both gazed at the poignant sight of doctor and patient, man and boy. 'Often in our work the patients don't have their friends and families with them. They get split up in the chaos. It's hard enough to keep tabs on who is alive and who's dead, never mind where they might be. So in cases where there's no family around, Mitch makes sure whoever is on duty calls him if the patient is slipping away. No matter what time it is he comes to hold their hand.'

Tessa moved past her and into the ward but Brianna hung back, her mind choked with emotion. Though it might go against the grain, she realised she owed the man a pretty big apology. She'd taken his abrasive, tough attitude as a sign of somebody who didn't care, when in fact that couldn't be the case. Why would anybody do this job, living and working in the crudest of conditions, witnessing human suffering on an agonisingly large scale, if they didn't care? No doubt they had to grow a tough hide, but she'd been wrong to assume that meant they were unaffected by it.

Quietly Brianna entered the ward again and walked over to the bed where the boy was taking his final breaths. As she stood alongside them, Mitch glanced up. From the look of his haggard face, he hadn't had any sleep.

'I'll take over now, if you like,' Brianna said softly.

He shook his head but nodded in the direction of another chair. 'Come and join us.'

Twenty-four hours ago, Brianna would have been annoyed that Mitch hadn't got up to fetch the chair for her. Already she felt like a different person. This Brianna could accept that manners weren't actually that important. They could be learned, but they didn't define you. Other attributes, such as strength and compassion, did. Mitch had them both, in spades. So she silently forgave his lack of manners and went to get the chair. Together they sat with the boy while his life slipped away.

Finally Mitch stood up and gently drew the sheet over the boy's head. 'He's gone now,' he whispered. 'Come on. I don't know about you, but I could use a drink.'

Surprised by his invitation and desperately in need of one herself, Brianna followed Mitch to his tent. It was similar to hers, though larger as it had room for a table, currently playing host to several piles of haphazardly thrown together files. Mitch delved into the canvas bag beside his bed and brought out the bottle of whisky she'd given him. Following a quick swig, he wiped the top and handed it to her. 'Just what was needed, after all,' he remarked dryly.

Not wanting to turn down his gesture of friendship, Brianna took hold of the bottle, brought it to her lips and took a sip. Used to drinking whisky out of a crystal tumbler, she found it hard to judge how much of a mouthful she was taking and ended up spluttering. Calmly Mitch took the bottle back from her. Though his face was expressionless, she felt sure his brown eyes were laughing at her.

He gestured for her to sit on the chair while he went to lie on the bed, rubbing at his face and eyes as if to wake himself up.

'Rough night?' Brianna asked.

'You could say that.'

Seeing his shattered face she felt a sharp pang of guilt. 'Mitch, I'm sorry for what I said in the meeting. I'm sure you did all you could to save him.'

Mitch glanced at her, his dark eyes holding hers. 'Yes, we did. But maybe you were right. Situations like this occur far too frequently and we start to treat them as normal, using phrases we shouldn't. I never meant the child's life wasn't worth it.'

'I know,' Brianna admitted quietly. And she did. He might not be crying, shouting, or wearing his emotions on his sleeve, but the man in front of her was suffering because he'd lost a patient. 'It must be hard, watching a patient die like that. It's the first time I've done it and I don't think I could bear to do it again.'

'Watching them die isn't the hardest part. It's feeling so damned useless that tears at you.' He shrugged awkwardly then, as if embarrassed to have let slip that little morsel about himself.

'How long have you being doing this job?' she asked, partly because she was interested and partly to get them talking about something less harrowing.

'With Medic SOS? Three years.'

She thought of what she had already seen in the short time she'd been here. 'How do you stand it?'

'What, the primitive sleeping conditions? The cold river water shower?'

She glared at him, not sure whether he was joking with her, or mocking her. His face was so flipping hard to read. 'I meant how can you stand seeing suffering on such a scale?'

Mitch drew himself further onto the bed and lay back against the pillow, putting his arms behind his head. 'I guess, like most things in life, you get used to it after a while. It doesn't make it easy to live with, but you aren't shocked any more. Before working with Medic SOS I was in the army, so I'd already seen some pretty grim stuff.' Abruptly he stopped, turning the tables on her. 'What about you, Brianna? Why is someone like you spending a week here?'

At his use of the words *like you*, she bristled. 'Look, I know you've got me pegged as a spoilt rich bitch and maybe you're right,' she conceded crossly. 'But I don't want to be like that. I don't want to spend my life falling out of clubs drunk on champagne.'

'Doesn't sound too bad to me,' he drawled. Then he smiled. Just as the laugh had earlier, the smile transformed his features, warming his dark brown eyes, smoothing the harsh planes of his face. If she was poetic she'd have said it was like a glimpse of sun on a cloudy day. It made her very much aware of him as a man, and not just an irritating person she was forced to temporarily put up with.

Of its own volition, her body responded to him, her blood feeling warmer, her stomach all fluttery. Please no. She didn't want to be attracted to this man. Hastily she turned away, pretending an interest in the floor. Anything to stop looking at him. 'Well, I want to do something more with my life,' she finally stated.

When there was no reply, she stole a look at the bed. He was fast asleep. She watched the rhythmic rise and fall of his chest with a strange sort of relief. At least she could now escape his scrutiny. Hopefully, by the time she saw him again, she would have this crazy desire back under control. They'd just watched a patient die together. Clearly her emotions were all over the place.

She rose from the chair, but couldn't resist a final look at his sleeping form. Now, instead of an uncouth man, she could only see one who was strong, tough and downright sexy. With a despairing shake of her head, she fled his tent and returned to the safety of her own. It was still only half five in the morning so she chose to lie back on her bed and try and get some more sleep. She must be over-tired if she was starting to find the rough, gruff Dr McBride attractive.

Chapter Six

Brianna knew for certain how far this trip had already changed her when she cleaned up the last mouthfuls of a bowl of glutinous porridge in the catering tent. Last week she would have rejected the food without a second thought. This morning she was simply grateful for something to fill her stomach. If Melanie could see her now, she'd laugh her dainty little socks off. Thinking of her, Brianna was hit with a sharp pang of loneliness. She missed a friend, someone to talk to, to laugh with. How long had it been since she'd laughed? Not since she'd arrived here, that was for certain. The team were friendly, but they treated her with the politeness of strangers. She wanted to talk to someone who knew her, who would tell her how it was. Glancing at her watch, and quickly calculating time differences, she reckoned it was lunchtime in the UK. Melanie might just have woken up.

'Brianna?' She sounded distinctly groggy.

'Don't tell me I've woken you up?'

'Of course you bloody have,' came the grumpy reply. 'It's only five in the morning.'

Brianna started to giggle. 'Oops, I must have got the time differences wrong. Sorry.'

Suddenly her friend woke up. 'Bugger, sorry, tell me everything,' she screeched. 'And you'll have to shout because this is a really lousy signal.'

'Of course it is. I'm using a satellite phone because I'm in the middle of flipping nowhere.'

'Well, apart from being in the middle of nowhere, how the heck are you?'

'I can't believe I'm about to say this, but I miss your ugly face, my friend,' Brianna replied with a smile, gratefully easing into their usual banter.

'Boy, things must be really bad.'

Brianna chuckled. 'No, they aren't, not really. In fact everyone has been really good to me. It's just not the same as being with your friends. They tend to treat me with kid gloves here.' Her mind wandered back to Mitch. 'Well, most of them do. They're probably scared I'll go telling tales to Mum.'

'Any hunky men?'

'Melanie,' Brianna exclaimed in mock disgust. 'I'm here to understand how the group rescue and care for injured people whose lives have been ripped apart by a tornado. I'm not here to pick up men.'

'Well, generally speaking, they try to pick you up,' her friend replied dryly. 'I'm sure even the most devoted rescue worker isn't blind to a beautiful woman.'

Brianna sighed. 'Maybe, but I have to say, it is all pretty depressing. It certainly puts my own life into perspective. I can't help but think how flipping lucky I am.' There was a moment's silence, and Brianna wondered if Melanie was still there. 'Melanie?'

'Hey, I'm still here buddy. I hear what you're saying, but don't get too serious on me. Sure, do what you can to help, but you still have your own life to lead. And anyway, you didn't answer my question. What about the men?'

Brianna thought of Mitch. How would Melanie react if she admitted she thought she was falling in lust with the head doctor? A rough looking man with an abrasive personality. She couldn't even explain the attraction to herself, never mind her best friend. 'Nobody you'd be interested in,' she replied truthfully.

Quickly she caught up on the last few days of trivial but amusing gossip from back home, ending the call with a promise to phone again if anything interesting happened.

‘I thought I might find you here,’ Dan announced as he walked towards her. ‘If you’ve finished your breakfast, would you like a tour of the main camp? I’ve got to pick up some supplies and thought you might fancy a ride.’

‘What, a chance to get away from here for a while?’ She smiled at him. ‘What are we waiting for?’

Brianna knew a trip around the camp wasn’t going to be scenic, but at least it was away from the depressing sight of patients in hospital beds. It also took her away from the close proximity of Mitch, which was definitely a good idea. She was still alarmed by her sudden attraction to him in the early hours of the morning. With a bit of luck, time away would bring her equilibrium back to an even keel.

First Dan drove to the small airstrip where he hauled several large crates marked Medic SOS into the back of the truck. He refused her offer of help, for which she was grateful. If she’d gone with Mitch, no doubt she’d have been the one left lugging the boxes while he watched. And told her to put more effort into it.

Driving back, Dan stopped to introduce her to a twinkling-eyed older man called Sam, who was in charge of the whole set-up, and then detoured so she could see the full extent of the refugee camp.

‘I wonder how they manage to live, eat and sleep all under one small canvas roof?’ she wondered out loud, staring at the huddled rows of tents the poor villagers now called home.

‘It’s probably easier when your original home wasn’t much bigger.’

She nodded, uncomfortably aware that even before the tornado these people had lived in homes probably no larger than the garage her father parked his car in. As she scanned the faces in front of her she didn’t see any of the emotions she’d expected. There was no weeping, no angry tantrums. If this had happened to her, she’d be doing both.

Instead there was a quiet acceptance of what had happened. Most people seemed simply grateful to be alive and holding someone they loved.

'I can't imagine how it feels to suddenly lose everything. Your home, possessions, maybe members of your family.' She felt sick at the thought.

'I doubt it's much fun, but then again it depends on what you had to lose in the first place.'

'I guess.' The sheer extent of her privileged existence hadn't been clear to her, until now. Would any of the crowd she partied with really understand the hell other people were living through? Even Melanie had changed the subject when Brianna had tried to explain what she had seen. Whatever she did with the rest of her life, Brianna promised she'd never forget the hardship she'd witnessed on this short trip. Or the grace with which the villagers handled the cruel blow fate had thrown them.

'So, are you enjoying your stay with us so far?' Dan's voice interrupted her thoughts.

'I'm not sure enjoying is the right word. It's certainly been an eye-opener. You read about this sort of thing in the newspapers, but until you've actually seen it for yourself, well, it just doesn't seem real, does it?'

Dan glanced over at her. 'I guess you're right. I've been doing this job for a couple of years now, but I can still remember my first camp.' The jeep shuddered as it went over a few craters in the road. 'Still, we can't have you going back remembering just the tough stuff. You have to have some fun. It's how we manage to cope with the rest. Me, Jane and Toby are going out to the town for a drink tonight. Will you join us? We're a lot more entertaining when we're not on duty.' He grinned, his eyes lighting up in invitation. The message in them was clear.

'Perhaps,' Brianna replied cautiously. She longed for a

few drinks and a bit of light relief, but she didn't want to give Dan any wrong ideas. 'I'll see how I feel later. What about the others? Aren't they coming?'

'Roger doesn't fancy it and Tessa and Stuart are on duty.' He veered sharply to the right to avoid a giant pothole. 'Mitch rarely comes out, but maybe if you invited him, he would.'

Brianna laughed at that. 'After our little altercation yesterday, I sincerely doubt that.' Thank goodness only she knew how her pulse had rocketed at the suggestion. She gave what she hoped was a nonchalant shrug. 'But I'm happy to give it a try.'

They were on their way back to the medical tent when Dan's phone went off. 'Yes, no problem, we're nearly there.'

After finishing the call he turned to Brianna. 'We've got to get a move on. They need the truck to get out to a child who's been found in the rubble of one of the houses. Apparently a metal pole has speared straight through his chest.'

Brianna shuddered violently. 'Oh God.' The images that flashed through her mind were enough to make her feel faint.

'The family had evacuated to the camp a couple of days ago but this morning the mother noticed her son was missing. It seems he'd wandered back to his old home for some reason. When they found him he was trapped by the pole, still alive but unable to move.'

Dan continued to talk but Brianna heard very little of the rest. It took all her concentration to stay conscious. And not heave all over the dashboard.

They screeched to a stop outside the medical tent and Dan dashed inside. Brianna waited in the truck, desperately trying to be strong. It wouldn't be pleasant but she wanted to go with them. This was the type of situation they must regularly come face to face with. She wanted to see for herself how they dealt with it.

'Brianna.' Mitch opened the truck door. His hair was dishevelled, his eyes tired and his chin wore a couple of days' worth of stubble. It didn't stop her heart doing cartwheels in her ribcage as he glared at her. For all his roughness, perhaps because of his roughness, he was the sexiest man she'd ever met. 'We need to take the truck. You'll have to get out.' No please, just a command.

She stayed seated. 'I'm coming along.'

Mitch started to grab her and pull her out of the truck. Then he looked down at his hand gripping her arm and dropped it faster than the proverbial hot potato. 'For God's sake woman, why won't you do as you're told?' he thundered, clearly exasperated.

'I'm here to see what you do, so I'm staying. I'll sit in the back if you like, but I won't remain behind.'

'This isn't a flaming outing to the park,' he replied tightly. 'There's a boy impaled with a pole. It won't be a pretty sight.'

She raised her chin. 'I'm not stupid. I know that. But what's the point in me coming all the way out here if you won't let me see what you actually do?'

Mitch could see there was no point arguing with Brianna. Other than manhandling her out of the truck – and she probably still had the bruises from the last time he'd put his grubby hands on her soft flesh – he had no choice but to let her stay. He was damned if he'd ever met a woman more stubborn, or more arrogant. 'Fine,' he snarled. 'But there's only one person we'll be focusing on. You feel faint, or sick, you're on your own.'

He slammed the door shut and went to check the equipment Dan was putting in the back of the jeep.

'Will you need to operate on site?' Dan asked, heaving a medical bag over his shoulder.

'I hope not.' The preference was always to get a patient into hospital with injuries like this. The reality was that the hospital was hundreds of miles away. With no smooth roads and no ambulance with soft suspension, it was highly likely such a long trip would cause more damage. He'd have to assess it when he was there. The most realistic scenario was he'd have to bring the boy back to the medical tent and operate on him there. It was primitive, but he'd done it before. He just hoped Brianna didn't stick her pretty little nose in too far. He knew how traumatic the sight would be when they got there. He'd seen it many times before, both with Medic SOS and on the battlefield. She hadn't. He didn't have the time or energy for more than one patient.

'What's she doing in the truck?' Tessa looked pointedly at Brianna, who was staring defiantly out of the window.

'Apparently she's coming with us,' Mitch replied absently, his mind already thinking ahead to what he might find, what he would need.

'You've got to be kidding. She'll just get in the way.'

Clearly incensed at being discussed as if she wasn't there, Brianna yanked open the door. 'I can hear, you know,' she told them. 'And I won't get in your precious way. I'm just here to observe.' With that she slammed the door shut again.

Tessa raised her eyebrows at him, but Mitch merely shrugged. He wasn't going to get embroiled in a female spat. Taking the coward's way out, he helped Dan load up the rest of the equipment.

The atmosphere in the truck was tense as he drove to where the boy had been found. Next to him Brianna folded and unfolded her arms, wrapped her hair into a ponytail, and finally stared out of the window. Behind him, on the back seat of the truck, Dan closed his eyes and a stony-faced Tessa glared at the back of Brianna's head.

Once again, Brianna shifted in her seat. 'Having second thoughts about tagging along now?' he asked.

'No.'

He almost smiled. As if she'd admit to being wrong. 'Ever seen a bad injury?'

'My mother once cut her hand on a kitchen knife.'

He couldn't help himself. He snorted. 'Don't tell me. She needed one, no maybe two plasters?'

'She needed stitches,' Brianna muttered, refusing to look at him.

Casting his eyes down to her hands, he saw how tightly she clutched them together and felt a twinge of sympathy. 'You want my advice? When we get there, don't look.'

He brought the truck to a halt outside the ruined remains of a small house and flung open his door. Leaving it up to the rest to bring the equipment, he headed straight towards the cluster of people. A woman, presumably the mother, lay on the ground, weeping loudly and cradling the boy's head in her arms. They all looked up as he approached.

'Doctor, doctor,' the mother cried in Spanish, tears streaming down her face.

Mitch nodded at her and hunkered down next to the boy. He might have seen several such injuries, but it didn't take away the immediate feeling of repulsion. Poor little mite. Gently he began to examine him, trying to find out if the pole had skewered any vital organs. Thankfully the boy was unconscious, though the family confirmed he'd been awake when they'd got there.

'It looks like it's just missed his heart,' he reassured the mother in his serviceable Spanish.

While Mitch and the others raced to the child, Brianna hung back. From what she judged to be a safe distance, she allowed her eyes fleeting glances of the scene, keeping them at head height so she wouldn't accidentally glimpse the poor boy on the ground. She felt really, really shaky. Mitch and Tessa had been right. She had no place here.

Suddenly the crowd around the boy moved away, and Brianna's eyes unthinkingly shifted downwards, towards the child. Instantly she knew she had to look away, but found she couldn't. It was as if someone had hit the pause button and she was left staring at the grotesque sight of a long rusty pole sticking out from the top half of a child's body. *Oh my God.*

A tidal wave of nausea hit her, clawing at her stomach, and the air she sucked in came out in short, rasping breaths. She felt cold and clammy and rubbed absently at her arms, trying to warm herself, all the while her eyes fixed on the distressing sight in front of her.

'Brianna!'

Through a fog of horror, Brianna heard Mitch's harsh voice yelling at her. She blinked and slowly moved her head, as if coming out of trance. Dimly aware of him motioning for her to move away, she turned and took a few steps towards the truck. That was when her knees gave way. Quickly she crouched onto the ground and put her head between her legs, letting the blood rush back to her brain. Bugger, bugger, bugger, she'd been about to faint. Would have done if Mitch hadn't called out. Just as he'd predicted she'd nearly added to his problems.

'You okay, Missy?' One of the men who'd been standing by the boy came up to her, speaking in halting English.

Weakly she smiled up at him. 'Yes, thank you, sorry.' Her eyes involuntarily flickered towards the scene, but this time Mitch's large body obscured her view. Hastily she looked away. 'Is he your son?'

The man shook his head. 'My nephew. He in bad way.'

Brianna reached out and squeezed the man's arm. 'Yes, but he has good people looking after him. They will do everything they can.'

Together they sat and waited. Brianna found she was

unable to resist looking over again, but this time she kept her eyes on Mitch. Whether it was because the initial shock had worn off, or because she was now focused on Mitch instead of the boy, she wasn't sure but she no longer felt she might black out. Or heave.

'He must have nerves of steel,' she whispered out loud. The boy's uncle clearly didn't understand, but smiled as if he did.

The more she watched Mitch work, the more her admiration for him grew. There was nothing hesitant or unsure about his actions. Rather they were decisive, confident. If she'd been the mother she would have felt immensely reassured that this man was looking after her child. He had the air of a man who wouldn't let anything beat him. It was wildly inappropriate, but she felt a stir of desire. There was something incredibly sexy about the sight of the calm, self-assured doctor at work.

Disgusted with the way her thoughts had turned, she forced her mind back to the reason they were there. 'Do you know why your nephew came back here?' she asked the man at her side, trying to take both their minds off what was happening.

'I think he miss his things,' he replied sadly. 'He look for them.'

Brianna waited until they were putting the boy onto the stretcher before walking up to the ruins. She wondered if there was something in particular the boy had been searching for. Something important enough to him that he'd walked all the way from the camp to find it. There, under a sheet of corrugated iron, she caught sight of the furry ear of a toy rabbit. Lifting up the iron sheet, she tugged out the soft toy. It was dirty, but nothing a wash couldn't solve.

Back at the medical tent Mitch and the team operated on the child while Brianna waited anxiously with his mother and father. It had been two hours now and they'd still not received any news. Restlessly she stood and started to pace. Putting her hands in her pockets, she felt the soft fur.

'Here.' She handed the cuddly toy to the mother. 'I found this in the rubble. Maybe it was what your son was looking for?'

With trembling hands the mother reached for the rabbit, tears running softly down her face as she cuddled it to her. 'Gracias, gracias.'

Brianna reached over to give her a hug. She had nothing else to offer.

Suddenly the tent door swished open and Mitch walked in. Dressed in green overalls, sweat beaded across his forehead and locks of sandy hair plastered to his face. He looked shattered. 'He's stable.' He spoke the words softly in Spanish to the parents, but Brianna got the gist of what he was saying from the look of relief on his face, and delight on theirs.

The couple hugged each other tightly and then went to shake Mitch's hand. 'Doctor, you save his life, you are miracle worker,' the father told him.

Mitch shook his head. 'I'm afraid not. He still has a long way to go, but you can see him now.'

He took them off to see his young patient and Brianna collapsed back on one of the chairs. She felt exhausted too, though all she'd managed to do was get in the way. Leaning forward, she put her head in her hands and closed her eyes.

As Mitch left the parents with their son, he noticed the mother tuck a toy rabbit into the boy's arms. It was the same rabbit he'd seen in Brianna's hands as they'd left what had remained of the family's home. For some inexplicable reason, it made him smile. Damned if she didn't have a real thing about stuffed animals. He went in search of her and found her sitting where he'd left her, though now she was hunched over, head in her hands. Glorious chestnut hair straggled out of the confines of its band and escaped in ribbons over her face.

'Tough afternoon.'

Brianna looked up with a start. Her face was so pale. Far too pale. 'For you and his family, definitely,' she replied softly.

Mitch looked at her through narrowed eyes. 'For you too, I think.'

'A bit.' Squeezing her fingers together, she sat back in the chair, her face suddenly alive with a mixture of anger and disgust. 'You were right, damn it. I shouldn't have gone. You nearly had two casualties on your hands.'

Mitch went to sit next to her. 'Don't be so hard on yourself,' he told her quietly. 'Seeing a person so badly injured is incredibly traumatic. Even more so when that person is a child. It would knock anyone sideways.'

'Which was why you didn't want me to go.'

'Yes,' he agreed. 'But you're not used to doing as you're told, are you?'

Her eyes flickered with a hint of amusement. 'No, I guess not.'

He held her gaze. It was the first time he'd really looked into her eyes, at least when they weren't spitting anger at him. They were beautiful. Clear and as green as a forest on a sunny day. He felt drawn to them and to her. Alarmed at the thought, he abruptly rose to his feet. 'Go and get some rest,' he told her roughly. 'And this time, do as I damn well say.'

Brianna smiled, producing pretty grooves on either side of her mouth. Grooves he wanted to run his tongue over. She was one hot lady, but that was a big part of the problem. He was anything but a gentleman. 'Yes, sir,' she replied mockingly.

'That's more like it.' He looked at her a moment too long and felt a kick of desire. Sharply he turned and retreated to the safety of his tent.

Chapter Seven

Mitch was catching up on his paperwork when Brianna strolled, unannounced, into his tent. Although he'd done the same to her the previous day, her cockiness rankled with him. This was his turf and he didn't take kindly to people walking in and out as if they owned the place. Even people who looked as gorgeous as she did.

'Dan asked me to invite you to come out with us tonight.' She stood confidently in the middle of his tent, hands on hips, a disarming smile on her face.

He dragged his eyes away from her and back onto his notes. 'Thank Dan for the invitation, but no, not tonight.' A night out with Brianna was the last thing he needed. She irritated the hell out of him, but maddeningly at the same time he wanted her. It was an urge he had no intention of following up on.

'God, are you always this boring?' she asked in exasperation, green eyes mocking him.

He darted another glance at her. 'Are you always this rude?' he countered evenly.

She shrugged nonchalantly and his eyes were drawn to her slender shoulders and the glossy hair cascading over them. He imagined running his hands through that hair. Placing his hands on those shoulders and pulling her tightly against him. Shit. What in God's name was he thinking? Clearly he'd been without a woman for too long.

'You know the saying,' she continued, thankfully oblivious to his train of thought. 'All work and no play.'

Mitch turned away again and sighed. She was right of course. Hadn't he told himself a few days ago he was getting too dull? When was the last time he'd been out for a drink with his colleagues? After the day he'd had, a night out would do him the world of good. As long as he kept away from Brianna. 'Okay, okay, point taken. Give me five minutes and I'll be there.'

With a nod of her head and a confident sway of her hips, she was gone. Mitch sat back in his chair and let his mind play out their conversation. Had he just been smoothly railroaded into going out tonight? Reluctantly he laughed, admiring her style. In fact, the more time he spent with her, the more he found to admire. She still had the arrogance of the fabulously wealthy, but even he had to acknowledge part of his resentment towards that came from knowing his own roots were very different. Wealth was only part of the picture. He'd never had the luxury of a proud heritage, something the Worthington name gave her. Even he, a fashion philistine, had heard of it. But he respected that she'd been prepared to rough it out here for a week and take an interest in the charity. On a baser level, he also admired the way her smooth rounded buttocks pulled on her canvas trousers. And the way her breasts jiggled invitingly under her T-shirt.

Desire washed through him once again and he growled in frustration. It was time to get his libido in check. He valued his job far too much to want to risk a quick tumble in the sheets with the patron's daughter. No matter how sexy she might look.

Five minutes later Brianna found herself wedged in the back of the jeep between Mitch and the door. Jane was on the other side of him, with Dan and Toby up front. As they bounced over the rough terrain, Brianna was constantly thrown against a brick wall. At least that's what Mitch's body felt like. His expression was about as forgiving, too.

'You know, for a man on his night off, sandwiched in

the middle of two women, you're not looking particularly happy.'

He grunted. 'This is my happy face.'

'Crikey. Don't let your patients see your miserable one then. It will put their recovery back a week.'

She shot a quick grin at him, but there was no answering smile. No warmth in his eyes. Did anything make him happy? From what she'd seen so far, he rarely laughed, seldom even looked pleased. She'd have dismissed him as boring had there not been that edge to him, the sexy sense of danger.

'You know most men on a night out with a couple of women would try and charm them. At the very least entertain them.'

She heard Jane snigger on his other side.

'I'm not most men.'

She exhaled in exasperation at his curtness but couldn't disagree with his statement. Certainly he was very different from the men she usually went out with. They liked to talk, normally about themselves. They also didn't feel quite so ... solid when she brushed against them. The jeep shuddered and once again she was jolted against his side. There was nothing soft about him there. Nothing soft about him anywhere, to her knowledge. Tough, hard and uncompromising were better adjectives. Which made it really hard to understand why her fingers itched to run through his shaggy hair and trace the lines of that strong jaw.

She sucked in a deep breath and looked away. God she wanted him, and the knowledge stunned her. Not only was the target of her desires so unlike anyone she'd ever dated before, but her thoughts were also totally inappropriate, given the circumstances. She was here to understand how the medical charity saved lives. Not get tangled up with the head doctor. On every level she could think of, that was just plain wrong. But it didn't stop her wanting.

'What are you drinking?' Toby asked as they parked outside a little bar that stood on the corner of a muddy road.

'Beer will be great, thanks,' she replied, remembering her earlier faux pas over the herbal tea. Hopefully beer was a safe choice.

Walking behind her, Mitch raised his eyebrows. 'What, no champagne?'

'Only when I'm wearing my diamonds,' she replied tartly, her eyes sweeping round the nearly deserted bar. It was a far cry from her usual drinking establishments: walls screamed out for a coat of fresh paint and worn chairs and rickety bar stools clustered around scratched wooden tables. She settled her gaze back on Mitch. 'How much longer are you going to keep up the rich girl jibes?'

He visibly flinched. 'Fair point,' he conceded quietly. 'I'll try and rein them in from now on.'

'Good. In that case why don't we find somewhere to sit? I have a thought I want to throw by you.'

They found a table big enough for them all to sit at, but Brianna sat close to Mitch because she wanted to pick his brains. Watching the muscles of his arm bunch as he pulled out his chair, she had to admit his brains weren't the only part of his body she wanted to grapple with, but they'd have to be enough. At least for now.

'Okay, shoot.'

Mitch took a deep gulp of his beer and focused his steady brown eyes on her. As usual, they were cool and guarded. For a brief moment she wondered if they ever burned with desire, or warmed with joy. 'Is it my imagination, or do Medic SOS receive more than their fair share of the difficult cases?'

Briefly he smiled and reached again for his beer. 'It does seem to be that way these days. It wasn't when we first started but now, when we're supporting other medical agencies, they tend to ask us to handle the acute traumas.' He shrugged. 'I'm not complaining. It keeps life interesting.'

'Why do you think that is?'

'I guess because we're good at it.'

'Same question. Why?'

Mitch sighed. 'I thought I was meant to be coming out tonight to play? This sounds like work to me.'

'Humour me, just for a little while. Then you can play with me all you like.' She grinned, fully aware of the suggestive nature of her comment. She was hoping for a teasing reply, something to suggest her attraction wasn't all one sided.

He gave her a sharp look through lidded eyes. 'Most of my medical experience is from serving in the army,' he stated matter-of-factly, totally ignoring her attempt to flirt with him. 'I'm used to operating under harsh conditions. When I came out of the army and went back into civilian medicine, I specialised in A & E, doing further acute trauma training. That was where I met Tessa. When the opportunity to work at Medic SOS came along, we both volunteered. I guess over the years we've shared that experience within our group and built up a solid skills base. Gradually the larger agencies have started to see what we're capable of.'

Brianna rested back against her chair and gave voice to the idea that had been niggling at her. 'I think Medic SOS should make more of that niche. From a marketing point of view, that is.'

Mitch raised an eyebrow, his interest snared. 'What do you mean?'

'Look, I don't know anything about medicine, as you've already gathered, but I know a lot about money and a fair bit about marketing. If Medic SOS was branded as specialists in acute trauma, I believe it would secure a lot more funding than it does currently. People would be able to see how it offered something different from other medical agencies. I know it sounds harsh, but it would give the charity an edge. There are so many organisations competing for people's money. It's important to stand out from the rest.'

Mitch considered Brianna's words. He had no concept of business, but it didn't take a genius to see the merit in what she was saying. Besides, it was only mirroring what they were already doing in the field. Why shouldn't they make more of that specialism when they promoted the charity to sponsors? Especially if it brought in more funding. 'Sounds like you're talking yourself into a job.'

She blinked and for a split second she looked speechless. Then her face lit up in a delighted smile. 'Hey, maybe I am.' Shaking her head, she reached for her drink. 'I could do this, you know, I could really do it.'

He'd meant his comment as a joke. After all, why would a woman like her need a job? But she looked so impossibly chuffed he started to wonder if she was seriously considering it. 'I have no doubt you could do it. You're pushy and stubborn as hell. Just the right attributes for squeezing money out of big business.'

He'd been half afraid he'd gone too far, but she burst out laughing.

'That was rude,' she replied, playfully digging him in the ribs.

He felt a jolt of pleasure at her touch and had to focus on the wall ahead to steady himself. 'So, when do you start?'

Again, he meant to provoke, but she didn't hesitate. 'As soon as I get back to London and persuade Margaret I'd be excellent in the role.'

'I don't expect you'll find that too difficult,' he replied wryly.

'You mean because I'm the patron's daughter?'

The amusement in her face faded and the cool haughty look came back in force. He definitely preferred the former. 'No, I didn't mean that,' he countered with a touch of frustration. 'I meant I'm sure you can be very persuasive when you want to be. You got me out tonight, didn't you?'

She slipped him a sly look. 'Umm, yes I did, didn't I? So tell me, Dr Mitch McBride, what do you usually do on a night off?'

He shifted uneasily on his chair at the change in topic. This was exactly why he didn't usually socialise. He was crap at talking about himself. Didn't like it, didn't want to do it. 'On camp? Or at home?' he asked, throwing the question back as if it were a ticking bomb.

Her lips twitched. 'Let's start with on camp.'

'I catch up on my paperwork, go for a run, read a book.' So what if he sounded boring? He wasn't interested in appearing attractive to her. What else was there to do on a ruddy refugee camp, anyway?

'And when you're home?'

He regarded her suspiciously. Couldn't she see he didn't like this sort of small talk? Her eyes stared back with their all too innocent expression. Of course she knew. It was exactly why she was subjecting him to this torture. 'At home I ...' What did he do when he was home? Other than the same lame things he'd already stated. He stood up. 'Who's for another drink?' Buying a round had to be better than being interrogated by Brianna.

Brianna watched Mitch stride up to the bar, his movements fluid and confident. Looking at him, he could have been a cowboy, or a stuntman. Any job based outdoors involving an element of risk. He didn't look anything like a doctor, certainly none she'd ever met. Somehow she couldn't picture him in a sterile hospital ward, or a GP surgery. She guessed it was why the job he did now suited him so well. But if that part of him was obvious, a lot wasn't. He kept so much hidden and she had a feeling it would take far more time than she had left to uncover it.

Mitch brought the drinks to the table and turned to discuss football with Toby, cleverly evading any further questioning from her.

'Have the last few days given you an insight into what we do then, Brianna?' Jane asked, clearly equally as bored with the discussion on the merits of the new Manchester United striker.

'It's been incredible,' Brianna said with true feeling. 'I was telling Mitch, it's inspired me to get involved with fund-raising when I get back.'

'Fantastic, we can always use more money. Sometimes I look at the equipment we have to work with and wonder how we save any lives at all. But raising money is tough and there are a lot of charities competing out there. All of them are doing worthwhile things and many of them much closer to home.'

'I know, but I've got a bit of experience in marketing so maybe I can help.' She looked across at Mitch, his face now much more animated. Had his reluctance to talk to her been due to her questions, or because she was a woman? 'I was thinking Mitch would make a great front man for the charity. You know, the real face of Medic SOS.'

Jane giggled, making Brianna warm to her even more. Sparky and fun, she seemed to have no side to her. 'You're so right. He could do that sexy, brooding, male model pose so well. I'm not sure you'd be able to persuade him into it though.'

'Persuade who into what?' Dan asked, having overheard the last part of their conversation.

Jane rolled her eyes and looked helplessly at Brianna. She obviously wasn't keen to embarrass her boss. Brianna, on the other hand, had no such compunction. 'Persuade Mitch into posing for the Medic SOS advertising materials.'

Mitch, who had just taken a swig of his beer, nearly choked on it. 'What?'

'How better to promote the charity than with the image of its head doctor?' she explained. 'Plus you have the advantage of being good eye candy.'

He stared at her in total shock. She'd never seen anyone so wrong-footed. 'You're joking, right?'

She shook her head. 'Not at all. Far better to use a real person, especially if he's sexy, rather than a boring model.'

Now he resembled a startled deer. 'You're trying to tell me my picture on an advert would entice people into donating their money? What bloody rubbish.' Slowly he got up. 'I'll leave you to play your games. I'm going to get some fresh air.'

Brianna sighed as she watched him stalk out. Bugger, she'd embarrassed him. Who would have thought the tough doctor was capable of being embarrassed? 'I'd better go and apologise.'

Jane looked at her sympathetically. 'You shouldn't have to. Calling him sexy was hardly an insult.'

No, Brianna thought, it wasn't. She found him outside, leaning back against the wall and staring into space. 'I meant it, you know,' she said as she walked up to him. 'You would look great on a billboard.' He ignored her, staring stonily into the distance. 'Haven't you been called sexy before?' Brianna was intrigued.

'No.' The word had to be prized out of his clenched jaw.

'Well it's about time you were.'

Finally he turned to look at her. 'What is it you want from me, Brianna?' he asked softly.

The sexual chemistry that had bubbled dangerously between them right from the start flared into life and suddenly the air felt hot and heavy. 'I call a man sexy and all of a sudden he assumes I want something from him.' She tried to smile, but the joke fell flat.

What would he say if she told him the truth? That what she wanted was for him to take her to bed. She opened her mouth to tell him exactly that, but faltered at the harsh expression on his face. Even she, confident in her ability to attract the opposite sex, couldn't be that bold with him. 'Look, I didn't mean to upset you. I happen to think you would do a great job at selling the charity. But you clearly don't want to get involved with that, which is fine.' She shrugged. 'I might not be able to put any of my plans into action, anyway.' Turning away from him, she started walking back into the bar. 'Come and finish your drink.'

The rest of the evening passed uneventfully, though the atmosphere between her and Mitch remained. She desperately wanted to know if he found her attractive, too. If he wanted to sleep with her as much as she wanted to sleep with him. So far, she'd shown her hand, but he'd kept his well hidden.

Chapter Eight

The following morning the team huddled together in Mitch's tent to go over the plans for the day.

'The final item to discuss is the temporary school,' Mitch was saying, his eyes skimming through his notes. 'They're looking for English speaking volunteers to do a stint with the children.' He glanced fleetingly at Brianna. 'I thought it was something you could help with.'

'Because I'm useless here?'

His expression changed from bland to irritated. 'No. Because nobody here talks the Queen's English better than you do.'

It was another dig at her background, but Brianna held back a retort. After last night, she needed to find a way back into his good books. 'Okay, no problem. I'd love to help. I can give them the rest of the bears I brought.'

He looked like he was going to add a comment about that, but thankfully he didn't get a chance because Dan spoke. 'I'll go with you. Can't have them all talking like posh people.'

Mitch narrowed his eyes and glared at the logistics man before seeming to pull himself together and nodding. 'Okay.'

When the meeting was over, Mitch pulled her to one side. 'Make sure you take some water bottles with you. I presume you read all the bumph about never drinking water that isn't out of a sealed bottle?'

Really, did she look stupid? 'Of course.'

Dan appeared at her side. 'Hey, don't worry about her, boss. I'll make sure she's okay.'

Mitch thinned his lips. 'I'm sure you will.'

When he was out of earshot, Dan whistled. 'What's got into him this morning? He's even grumpier than usual.'

Brianna had a horrible feeling it was down to her meddling last night. She'd told the guy he was sexy enough to be billboard material and now he hated her. Go figure.

Shrugging off Mitch's irritation, she went to gather the box of remaining bears from her tent and followed Dan to the jeep. As he drove she thought about the day ahead. Talking with the school children would be fun. As would being in the company of Dan. What a flipping shame that next to Mitch, Dan was like a young boy, still wet behind the ears. It wasn't just the difference in ages, though there was probably ten years between them. Dan was all on the surface. What you saw was what you got. Mitch was deep, complex. He intrigued her. Where did he get his mental strength from? Why was he so unwilling to let down his guard? Why did he find it so hard to smile?

'Here we go.' Dan jumped down from the jeep and went round to open the door for her.

Thanking him, she scrambled down and surveyed the school tent. 'I'm amazed they're bothering with schooling at a time like this.'

'It helps the kids to have some sort of normal routine in their lives.' He grinned. 'And gives the parents a bit of a break.'

Quietly they crept into the back of the tent, but in no time at all they were spotted and drawn into the conversation. Brianna had worried whether she'd even be able to talk to the children, but she found between her limited grasp of Spanish and their surprisingly good English, they managed fine. And the teddy bears went down a storm. So there, Mitch.

In between the smiles and laughter there were some touching moments, most particularly when the children haltingly described when the tornado had hit. Brianna wasn't the only one with tears in her eyes. Thankfully the teacher called a temporary break after that and Brianna escaped outside for some much needed air.

'You want drink?'

A smiling girl with dark curly hair and big brown eyes offered her up a cup. 'I, umm.' She could feel the bottle of water weighing heavily in her trouser pocket, but how could she refuse the girl? It seemed far too rude. 'Thank you. That's very kind.' She took the cup and took a tiny sip. She'd throw the rest away when the girl wasn't looking.

'Your pleasure.' The girl gave her a wide, toothy grin.

Brianna laughed and gently touched her cheek. 'You say *my* pleasure.'

'My pleasure.' She stayed where she was, still smiling, still watching.

Brianna took another sip. 'Lovely.'

The girl nodded and skipped away.

It wasn't long afterwards that Brianna started to experience the most intense, griping stomach cramps. She excused herself from the class and flew outside. A few moments later Dan came to find her. He took one look at her white face and clammy skin and bundled her straight into the jeep.

'Don't tell me you drank the water.'

'Only a sip,' she protested, then moaned as another cramp made her double up in pain.

'That's all it takes,' he told her, but Brianna wasn't listening. She was too busy retching out of the window.

Mitch watched as Brianna staggered out of the truck and swore. 'You fool.'

She grimaced. 'Thanks for your concern, but you don't have to worry about me. I'll be fine.' He took hold of her hand to steady her as she tried to walk towards the medical tent, but she snatched it away. 'No, I'm okay.' Then she projectile vomited all over his shirt. 'Oh my God.'

Before she had a chance to say anything else, her legs gave way. Mitch caught her in his arms and carried her inside. Crikey, she was a lightweight.

She wriggled. 'No, I don't want to go here.' Her pale, anguished face pleaded with him. 'Please. Take me to my tent. I just need to rest.'

He knew she was mortified at being sick in front of them and guessed being shoved onto a hospital bed would only compound her embarrassment. He turned to Dan. 'I'll carry her to my tent. I've got paperwork to do anyway, so I'll keep an eye on her at the same time. Make sure Stuart is about. Oh and grab me a drip and stand. Thanks.'

She was obviously feeling lousy because she allowed him to put her on his bed and fix up the drip with no protest. Following a few more, blessedly dry, heaves she fell fast asleep. In between literally and figuratively mopping her brow, he took the opportunity to change out of his vomit-patterned shirt, take a quick shower and tackle more of his blasted paperwork.

A couple of hours later he heard a groan from his bed and turned to find her trying to sit up. Her hair was a mess and her face washed out, yet her very vulnerability tugged at him. 'Welcome back,' he told her gruffly.

She held out the arm with the drip in it. 'What's this doing here? I'm not ill.'

'It's replacing the fluids you splattered over my shirt.'

Instantly she clasped her other hand to her mouth in horror. 'Shit, now I remember. I'm so sorry.' She hung her head. 'I can't believe I puked up all over you. God, and it would have to be you, wouldn't it?'

'What do you mean by that?'

'I mean, you're ... well ... you're you.' She bit her lip. 'You already think I'm a total moron. Now I've thrown up all over you, you'll hate me even more.'

What the blazes was she going on about? 'Number one, I don't hate you, don't be so ridiculous. Number two, do I look like the type of man who's bothered by a bit of sick?'

It stopped her in her tracks. At least long enough to study him. He tried not to squirm. 'No, I guess not. But I expect you are bothered by the fact that I forgot to do as you told me.' She shook her head. 'No, that's not true. I didn't forget. It's just the girl who offered me the drink looked so adorable, and I didn't want to disappoint her.' He was about to say something, but she wasn't finished. 'Instead I disappointed you.'

'Jesus, Brianna, I'm not disappointed in you.'

'Then why are you so cross with me?'

'Cross?'

'Yes. When I got out of the jeep, you called me a fool. And just now, when I woke up, you looked almost angry.'

He was angry, but not with her. With himself, for being so bloody attracted to her. Hell, when Dan had offered to go with her today, he'd been hard pressed not to punch the guy. 'I'm not cross,' he told her shortly. 'I was worried. Do you have any idea how many diseases you can pick up from contaminated water?'

She shook her head, and he sighed and went to feel her forehead. It felt normal. If soft, silk-like skin could be called normal. 'I think you'll be fine. Dan went back to the school and the water they used was originally from a bottle, though it wasn't fresh. I think whatever upset you has probably been flushed out by now.'

'All over your shirt.'

She sounded so flat, as if she'd had the stuffing knocked out of her, that he almost smiled. He should enjoy this subdued version of Brianna while he could. She was a lot easier to handle. 'I'll take the drip out and you can go and rest a while in your own bed.'

He quickly removed the line and helped her to her feet. She looked a little shaky. Like a newborn foal, all large eyes and cute. Yeah, definitely cute. Hastily he dropped his hand to his side. 'Are you okay to make your own way back?'

She eased her feet into her boots, holding onto his bed to steady herself. 'Yes, thanks. I've caused you enough trouble.'

Okay, now this almost chastened version was beginning to frustrate him. 'It's no trouble. Looking after sick people is what I do.'

He received a small smile for that. 'I know. And you're pretty good at it.' Her smile grew wider. 'Though your bedside manner could do with softening up a bit.'

With that she was gone. He stared after her as the doorway flapped back down. He should have walked with her, made sure she was okay. It was just he wasn't sure, if he tucked her back into her own bed, whether he'd be strong enough to leave.

She unsettled him, he admitted it as he sat back at his desk, and he didn't like the feeling. Not one little bit. She was flirting with him, damn her, but it wasn't clear why. Even less clear was what on earth he was going to do about it.

Letting out a deep sigh, he flung open a file.

Chapter Nine

Back in her tent, Brianna dozed for a bit but soon realised she wasn't going to get any more sleep. That was when she pulled out her notepad and began to scribble a list of thoughts, questions, musings around her ideas for the charity. She worked until her stomach started to rumble, a sure sign she was feeling better. Automatically she threw back the sheets, ready to get up, but then she halted. If she moved from here, she might bump into Mitch. Could she face him, having humiliated herself in front of him yet again? Nearly blacking out at the sight of the boy skewered by a pole had been bad enough, though perhaps understandable. But chucking up over him, after he'd expressly warned her to drink only her own water?

Groaning, she curled back into bed. Wow, she really knew how to impress a guy. The stupid thing was, she *did* know how to dazzle a man. Just not this one. With Mitch she seemed to press all the buttons he hated being touched. She let out a long, deep breath then slipped her feet back onto the floor. She had to face him sooner or later. Might as well get it over and done with.

After finding a few slices of bread to line her stomach, she wandered into the ward where she found Mitch checking on the boy whose life he'd saved yesterday. Quietly she moved to his side. 'He looks a lot better than the last time I last saw him,' she whispered. The boy was sound asleep, a good colour in his cheeks, a peaceful expression on his face. More importantly, there was no pole sticking out of his chest.

'I could say the same about you.' He held her eyes for a pulse-humming moment before looking down at his patient.

'He's well on the road to recovery. I had to remove a rib and he'll always have a scar, but other than that I expect him to be back to normal in a few weeks.' Mitch nodded at the toy bunny. 'Was that your doing?'

Brianna felt a hot flush creep up her neck. 'Umm, yes, I found it where he was trapped. Figured it might have been what he went home for.'

Mitch nodded. 'That was pretty astute of you. The rest of us were so focused on the trauma, we didn't take in the detail. Details can be important.'

Now her cheeks were flushing furiously. As they moved away from the boy's bed and towards the waiting area she was pathetically grateful that Mitch was one step ahead of her. 'Have I turned you into a fan of cuddly toys then?' she asked, once her cheeks had cooled.

He flashed a rare grin. 'Fat chance.'

Wow. When it actually surfaced, his smile was to die for. Almost of its own volition her body swayed towards him and her hand moved to touch his arm. 'Mitch.'

He jerked away, as if she was too hot to touch. 'What?'

She didn't know what she'd been about to say, but whatever it was, it died on her lips at his reaction. Men usually wanted to pull her towards them, not push her away. Feeling incredibly foolish, she took a step back and cleared her throat. 'I wondered if I could catch up with you later. I want to find out your wish list of provisions for Medic SOS, if money was no object.' That was better. Cool and professional. 'If the charity want to ask people for more money, it's good to have a real handle on what you plan to do with it.'

'Fine. I'm on call tonight, but I'll be in my tent if I'm not needed on the ward.'

It was a date then. Of sorts.

* * *

Brianna showered in the cold river water, something she was becoming surprisingly used to, and changed into clean jeans and a fresh shirt. As she towel dried her hair, she wished once again for her hairdryer. Not necessarily to dry her hair – the temperature was so hot that wasn't a problem – but to tame the stupid curls that seemed to spring out of nowhere. Checking her face in the little compact mirror she'd found in her handbag, she added some blusher and a hint of lipstick. Yes, it was vanity, but she wanted to look as good as she could. In a few moments she was going to Mitch's tent. Sure ostensibly it was to discuss the charity, but that wasn't all she had planned. Frankly she'd done with tiptoeing around and attempting light flirtation. It had got her nowhere. Tonight she was going to seduce the man. At the very least, she was going to try.

Her stomach churned, and this time it wasn't because it was empty. She knew what she was about to do wasn't sensible. Heck, even the thought of it made her cringe. But the days were flying by and she needed to find out if he wanted her as much as she wanted him. If he didn't, fine. She'd plaster a cool look on her face, grit her teeth and get through the rest of the week. Then she'd climb on board a plane and never have to see him again.

If he did want her ... a flush of longing swept through her body and she had to sit on the bed for a few moments to steady herself.

When she'd gathered her wits sufficiently, she slipped out of her tent and went to stand outside his, letting out a small cough. 'Can I come in?'

'Yes.'

The single word was neither warm nor inviting, but she squared her shoulders and walked in. Surprise, surprise. He was at his desk, poring over papers. 'Don't you ever stop working?'

He turned his chair so he could see her. 'I think we've already established I'm fairly boring.'

Brianna bit back a smile. Boring was absolutely the last word that came to mind when she thought of him. With no other seating available, she opted to lie on his bed. It might help her seduction; now he wouldn't have to imagine her there. 'I don't remember saying you were boring,' she replied softly.

Immediately he tensed. 'So, what did you want?' he asked abruptly.

It wasn't a promising start but it was a cue she couldn't ignore. Slowly she rose from the bed and sauntered over to where he sat, swaying her hips just slightly more than usual. She could only hope she was getting this right, and not coming across as a desperate call girl. She'd never tried to seduce a man before. Hadn't had to, hadn't *wanted* to, until now. Carefully she perched on the corner of the table, knowing full well his head was now level with her chest. 'I want you to tell me what you wish for.'

She heard him suck in a breath. 'Why have you really come here tonight?' he asked roughly.

Brianna couldn't resist a smile at his obvious discomfort. Since she'd met him he'd been the one in control. The confident, domineering one. But right now, in this tent, the reins had been passed to her. 'I would have thought that was pretty obvious.'

Mitch shoved back his chair with such force it nearly toppled over. 'Stop playing games, Brianna.'

'Who said it was a game? I'm deadly serious.' To prove it, she reached out her hand and deliberately rubbed it down his fly.

Instantly he hardened under her caress, but before she had a chance to savour the victory his fingers had clamped over her wrist, removing her hand. 'We're surrounded by people whose lives have been devastated, and all you're interested in is a quick romp in the sack?' he asked coldly.

He might not have physically slapped her, but his cutting words were just as effective. And like a bucket of cold water, they extinguished her desire, leaving her utterly humiliated. The worst part was he was absolutely right in his condemnation. She'd been acting like the spoilt rich girl she so desperately didn't want to be. 'Sorry,' she whispered, utterly ashamed. 'I can see you're not interested.' She jumped off the table, anxious to flee as quickly as possible. As she landed, she accidentally bumped into him, bringing her body hard against his.

The spark of lust Mitch had been trying to ignore suddenly ignited. Roughly he grabbed Brianna's shoulders and pulled her towards him. 'I didn't say that,' he growled before crushing her to him, bending his neck so he could savage her mouth.

The kiss was so hot he wouldn't have been surprised to find their mouths on fire. But as the passion raged, suddenly a kiss wasn't enough. Pushing the paperwork aside with one sweep of his hand, he roughly pushed her onto the table. With his lips still firmly pressed onto hers, he pulled at her shirt, popping the buttons in his haste to get at the full breasts beneath. The red mist descended on him. He was out of control.

'Is this what you wanted?' he declared harshly, his fingers unclasping her bra and releasing her delicious breasts into his hands. 'To make love to a bit of rough from the wrong side of the tracks?'

Through the fog of sexual desire, he was aware of Brianna stilling. Of her grasping the hand that had been playing with her nipple and slapping it away. 'How dare you,' she spat at him, shoving him off and clutching at her shirt to preserve her modesty. 'Do you really think that's what this is all about?' She shook her head and stood up. 'How little you must think of me. And yourself,' she finished coldly.

Mitch tried to settle back to his paperwork but his mind just wouldn't focus. His eyes kept straying to the pillow where she'd laid her head for the second time today. When he went to sleep, if he ever did, he was going to smell sultry flowers, or whatever the hell it was she washed her hair with.

With a groan he shut his eyes. Bad idea. Now all he could see was the straight, proud lines of her body as she'd walked away from him. How many other women would have left with such arrogance after what he'd done? The throbbing heat between his legs was still there, a painful reminder of how much he'd wanted her. Still wanted her, damn it. She might have led him on, but he was the one who'd lost control. He was the one who'd shoved her down on the table, mauling her like she was a common slut. His mind flooded with self-disgust. He bet none of the pompous, toffee-nosed men she dated had ever treated her like that.

With a cry of frustration he forced himself to his feet. He was an effing genius. He'd managed to humiliate not just himself, but her, too. And they still had another four days left in each other's company.

There was nothing else for it. He had to go and apologise.

Feeling like a man on the way to the gallows, he went to find her tent. The entrance flap was down. 'Brianna,' he spoke through the canvas.

His word was greeted with silence, and for a moment he wondered if she was actually in there. Then came a muffled reply. 'What?'

'Can I come in for a moment?'

'Why?'

'I'd rather have this conversation in private, if it's all the same to you.' He half expected her to tell him to bugger off, but instead she told him to come in.

He found her lying on the bed, clutching a pillow to her chest. Her hair was loose and her cheeks were wet. She looked young, wary and impossibly vulnerable.

'Sorry,' he said quickly, anxious to get this over and done with. He hated eating humble pie. 'I acted like a jerk.'

'Yes, you did.' She held his gaze unflinchingly, though her usually sparkling eyes were rimmed with red.

'Damn,' he muttered into the silence. 'You're not going to make this easy for me, are you? What else can I say? I apologise. I'm not used to female company on these projects. I guess I just flipped.'

Brianna stared at him for several long, tense moments. Then she dropped her gaze to the floor. 'Yes, well, I probably provoked you.'

He raised an eyebrow. 'Probably,' he replied dryly. 'I was rough. I'm sorry if I hurt you.'

'Hurt me?' she exclaimed, eyes glittering. 'You think I'm angry with you because you were rough? Of all the ridiculous ...' She shook her head. 'It's not what you did, Dr McBride. It's what you said.'

Mitch looked baffled. 'What I said?'

'You really think I wanted to kiss you just so I could see what it was like to kiss a man who has less money than I do? You think I'm that shallow?'

He took a moment to study the woman on the bed. Nobody had made her come here. She didn't need a job, like he did. She was here of her own free will, because she wanted to make a difference. 'No, I don't think you're shallow,' he replied quietly. He held her gaze and something moved between them, something that stirred him, frightened him. He was beginning to like her, as well as fancy her. Never mind shallow, he was in danger of being dragged out of his depth.

He broke the gaze and shoved his hands in his pockets before he was tempted to do anything with them. Like run them down those amazing curves of hers, for starters. 'Look Brianna. I need to focus on what I'm doing here, without any distractions, tempting though they might be. You're only here for a few more days, so I suggest we forget about what happened. To avoid any further complications, let's stay out of each other's way.'

Brianna watched as Mitch ducked back out of her tent. Possibly he was right. Probably he was right. Certainly staying away from him was exactly what she'd planned after she'd left his tent. Never had a man made her feel so cheap. But now her anger had vanished. Call her foolish, but despite his sometimes cruel words, she saw something in him she hadn't seen in any of the other men she'd dated. It wasn't just lust, though his kiss had been far beyond anything she'd ever experienced. Never had she been handled with such wild ferocity, such white-hot passion. He thought he'd been rough? She'd never felt more aroused.

But he was more than a sexy doctor with rugged good looks and an athletic build. Beneath all that there was toughness, layers. She couldn't fully put a handle on it. Mitch wasn't a man a woman could ignore. Love him or hate him, he made a mark. He certainly had on her. Yes she wanted his body, but she was also desperate to understand his mind.

She wasn't sure she was ready to give up on him quite so readily.

Chapter Ten

When she woke the following morning, Brianna could still feel the heat of Mitch's lips on her mouth and the hardness of his body against the softness of her own. With a groan of pure exasperation, she threw off the sheets and climbed out of bed. Why oh why did she have to fall in lust with the one man who had no intention of following up on the spark between them? She hated this tense, aching feeling that she could only guess was sexual frustration. It was totally alien to her. She was used to turning down what was being offered, not being turned down.

As she sat having breakfast with a few of the team, she realised it wasn't only her body that had become sensitised to Mitch. It was also her mind. Whenever his name was mentioned, she felt the quickening of her pulse and her eyes automatically scanned for his tall, lean frame. She was acting like a schoolgirl with her first crush, which was frankly ridiculous because she hadn't indulged in such childishness even when she *had* been a schoolgirl. She'd had no time for crushes. She'd been too busy deciding which males to date and which to ditch.

In her determination not to brood any further on her fixation with Mitch, Brianna went back to the medical tent and offered her help to Stuart and Jane. With no medical training, she was pretty useless, but at least she could wash floors, serve out drinks and give an encouraging smile or two. The gratitude of the patients was humbling.

It was when she returned from refilling the water jug that Jane tapped her on the shoulder. 'Just to let you know, there's been a mudslide a few villages down. It caught everyone unawares and I think a lot of the villagers were still in their homes when it hit.'

Brianna's heart sank into her boots. These poor people, hadn't they suffered enough already? 'Oh my God,' she muttered. 'Are you going to help?' When Jane nodded and turned to go, Brianna held her arm. 'Can I come? I know I'm not much use but—'

'An extra pair of hands is always useful,' Jane interrupted. 'Come on.'

She had never seen so much mud. It was horrific, like something out of a disaster movie. Everywhere she looked was brown and wet. Rescue workers were knee deep in the stuff, only their bright orange vests telling them apart from their surroundings. They dug and dug, some with spades, some with mechanical diggers, some with just their bare hands. Those who'd been lucky enough to be rescued were huddled together in a group. Dirty, shivering, eyes wide with terror. She spotted Mitch at the bottom of the mudslide, hunched over a prostrate body. Grimly she watched as he shook his head at the rescue worker standing next to him. A sheet was pulled over the dead body, and it was stretchered away.

In a daze, Brianna strode up to him. 'What can I do?' she asked softly, numbed by the catastrophic scene in front of her.

He turned towards her, eyes like dark, sunken pools. 'Keep out of the way,' he replied bluntly.

Brianna flinched. Eyes burning with tears, she stumbled away.

'Brianna, wait a minute.' Jane chased behind her. 'Ignore him. He might work like a machine, but he's a human being underneath it all. He's knackered. I think he meant to say, keep away for your own safety.'

'Maybe.' She wasn't so sure. Mitch saw her as a useless upper-class bimbo who was more likely to cause trouble than to help. And with her current track record, she guessed she couldn't blame him. 'Jane, I feel so useless. Is there anything I *can* do?'

Jane smiled and gave her a reassuring hug. 'Come on, lovely, I've got just the job for you. See those terrified children standing over there?' She pointed to a grubby, forlorn-looking group. 'Alice, one of the WHO team, has gone to get some fresh clothes and towels for them. Why don't you help her clean them up?'

At the sight of their huge sad brown eyes, Brianna's heart melted. Plastering a smile on her face, she went to help.

For the next few hours she worked with Alice, helping to clean up the uninjured. She tried to offer comfort and a distraction from the fresh disaster that had befallen the area. No sooner had they ferried one group over to the camp, a fresh huddle would form. It was both heartbreaking and uplifting. The more villagers they tended to, the more had been rescued. She tried not to look at the mounting pile of body bags on the other side of the mudslide. She focused on the living, the well. That was traumatic enough.

Mitch had experienced many bad days in his line of work, but today had to rank with one of the worst. They'd rescued more than were killed, but only just. The saving grace had been that the village buried under the mudslide had been small. Those who'd made it out alive were able to tell them how many people should have been there. He'd worked on much larger mudslides, when they had no hope of knowing how many people had remained buried. That made rescue work really hard, not knowing when to give up. Thankfully, this time, all the villagers had been accounted for, one way or another, by nightfall.

Having showered off most of the grime of the day, Mitch made his way back to his tent. He was used to feeling tired, it was something that never left him when he was on site. Today though, the exhaustion was physical as well as mental. Pulling victims out of the mud had been a thankless task, one that had strained at every muscle and sinew. He stopped for a moment, rolling his shoulders to release some of the tension. That was when he caught sight of a slender female figure with her back against a tree. Her face was lit up by the amber glow of a cigarette. It was a face of great beauty, but tonight it held a hint of fragility. Of course the sensible course of action was to walk by and go straight to his tent.

Right now he didn't feel like being sensible.

'They can kill you.'

Brianna's head shot up. 'So I hear,' she replied in her cultured voice.

He wanted to dislike it, as he wanted to dislike her, but there was something about the posh husky tones that sent a shiver up his spine. 'I didn't have you down as a smoker.'

She smiled slightly. 'I'm not. At least not unless I'm very drunk, or emotionally overwrought.'

He leant back against the tree next to her. Close, but not touching. 'Well, unless you've snuck into my tent and pilfered my whisky supply, I guess it's the latter that's led you to nicotine tonight?'

'Umm, but I wouldn't mind indulging in some of the former right now.' She took a long, deep drag. 'I don't know how you do it.'

'Watching you smoke?' he asked, deliberately misunderstanding her. 'It's hard, especially as I used to smoke and had a devil of a job giving it up.'

She smiled, as he'd hoped she would. 'I won't offer you one then.' She watched as the smoke trailed up from the end of the cigarette. 'But that isn't what I meant, as I think you know.'

'It's part of life,' he replied simply.

'But doesn't it make you sad, or angry, seeing so much death?'

'I used to get angry, on the battlefield. When I saw the body bags build because of a pointless war, it really got to me. This is just nature doing her thing. It's tough on those caught up in it, but then life is tough.' He gave her a sideways glance.

'At least it is for most people. That's what you're thinking, isn't it?' Temper rippled through her, mixing with the sadness and anger he saw in her eyes.

'Yes,' he agreed, keeping his voice deliberately calm. He sensed she wanted to fight, but tonight he didn't fancy being her punchbag. 'Most people do have a tougher life than yours.'

'You don't know anything about my life. How can you stand there in judgement?' He raised an eyebrow, daring her to continue. The temper fled as quickly as it had arrived and she sighed. 'Okay, you're right, I have had it easy.'

'I didn't say your life was easy,' he qualified. 'But I don't think it has been tough.'

'My first car was a Porsche,' she admitted.

Mitch felt his lips curve upwards. 'Impressive. How long did it last?'

'Two days. I crashed it into a ditch going round a corner too fast. I was grounded for a week.' She caught his grin and smiled. 'What was your first car?'

Mitch settled further back against the tree. 'Owned or borrowed?' he countered.

'Let's go for borrowed.'

'A Ford Capri, when I was twelve.'

'I take it the owners didn't realise you'd borrowed it?' He

just grinned, a flash of white teeth in the moonlight. 'Did you give it back?'

Mitch thought back to the Capri that had landed in the ditch, mangled by a tree. He and his two mates had been lucky to get out of it alive. 'I crashed it. I don't think the owners would have thanked me for returning it.'

'At last, we've found something in common. We're both bad drivers.'

The laugh whooshed out of him. It had been so long since he'd had a really proper laugh, he was surprised his body still remembered how to do it. 'In my defence, lady, I was only twelve and couldn't reach the damn brake pedal.'

She conceded his point. 'Hey, this is fun.'

'What is?'

'You and me actually having a conversation.' Her grin was infectious and he found his muscles starting to relax. 'My first birthday party was held in the Savoy,' she continued. 'For my eighth we took ten of my friends to Disneyland Paris.' She cocked a look at him. 'What about you?'

'Birthday parties were for sissies.'

'Aw, come on, you must have had at least one.'

Instantly his muscles tensed again. This was not a topic he wanted to discuss tonight. Or any night. 'Let's just say my mother wasn't one for making too much fuss.' He pushed his body off the tree and moved to stand in front of her. 'You did well today,' he told her, quickly changing the subject.

'You mean I kept out of your way?'

He saw the teasing light in her eyes and smiled. 'I guess I was a bit curt.'

'A bit, but then again, nothing I haven't seen before.'

An involuntary smile spread across his face and he watched as it was mirrored across her own. His body stirred. God, he was losing himself in those dancing green eyes. They were dazzling him, sucking him in. Instinctively he placed his hands on her shoulders. But as he bent his head towards hers, he suddenly stopped. *You're playing with fire, McBride.*

Swiftly he pulled back, thrusting his hands deeply into his pockets. 'Goodnight, Brianna.'

Watching Mitch's retreating back, Brianna played out the scene again in her mind. She knew the predatory look that entered a man's eyes when they were about to pounce. She'd seen it in Mitch's eyes, just before he'd broken away. Why was he so determined not to get close to her?

Feeling restless, her head full of questions, Brianna wandered back to her tent. If ever there was a time she needed a chat with her best friend, this was it. Pulling the clunky satellite phone from her bag, she dialled Melanie's number.

'Brie? Wow, hey there.'

Instantly a smile tugged at her lips. 'Hey yourself. What are you doing? It must be, what, afternoon with you?'

'Pardon? Blimey, you sound like you're in a toilet. Speak up girl.'

'I said what are you up to?' The signal was pretty scratchy but the tenuous contact with home was worth the frustration of trying to hear.

'I'm shopping. What do you expect me to be doing? More to the point, what are *you* doing?'

Brianna gave her friend a quick rundown of the last two days, and though she tried to keep her voice neutral when she spoke of Mitch, Melanie's gossip radar was far too sensitive. Even thousands of miles away. And with a poor signal.

'So this Mitch you keep mentioning. Do I take it he's a bit of a hunk?'

'My God, how can you tell that?'

'Because your voice goes all husky when you mention his name. So, dish the dirt. Have you kissed?'

'Sort of.'

'What did you say? *Sort of*?'

'Yes, okay, we've definitely kissed. It was ... amazing, magical.'

'And?'

'And he doesn't want it to go any further. He doesn't want anything to distract him from his job, apparently.'

'Do you believe him?'

Wasn't that the million dollar question. 'No, I don't think I do. He seems pretty good at closing off all his emotions and focusing on the issue at hand. I think it's to do with my money.' Men fell into two main camps when it came to her wealth. The confident charmers were attracted to it. The shier, hesitant men were overawed by it. Mitch didn't fit into either camp, but the very fact he'd mentioned it several times, proved it was an issue.

'Well, the days are ticking by, sweetie. What are you going to do? Leave it, or go after him?'

Brianna took a nanosecond to make up her mind. 'Go after him,' she replied decisively. 'I guess it will come down to who's the more determined to get their way.'

Melanie let out a long, lusty laugh. 'Well, watch out Mitch McBride, whoever you are. You don't know what's about to hit you.'

Chapter Eleven

Following a good night's sleep, Brianna woke the next morning fresh and alert. Something she hadn't thought possible when she'd gone out for a smoke the previous night, all keyed up by the grimness of the day. The unexpected banter with Mitch had obviously succeeded in unwinding her, as she'd drifted off to sleep with absolutely no trouble.

Peeking her head cautiously out of the tent, she was pleased to find the sun was shining for once. With a bit of luck the weather was breaking, which would allow the area to start the difficult job of getting back on its feet again. It was just the morning to try out a swim in the lake.

Quickly she slipped on a T-shirt and trousers and after grabbing a towel, she headed off towards the clearing. The birds chattered and the sun shone through the trees. It was hard to believe that only yesterday they'd been rescuing people from a horrific mudslide. The calm water of the lake glistened, positively inviting her to take a dip. Carefully she scrutinised the surface. No crocodiles, at least none she could see. And no people either. After stripping off her clothes she ran stark naked into the cool water, letting out a gasp as she went under. Invigorating was certainly a word that came to mind. So did flipping freezing. She swam quickly at first, warming up her muscles. Then she floated on her back, drinking in the rays from the sun.

As Mitch drew up to the lake, he couldn't believe his eyes. He'd swum here every morning with nothing to disturb him apart from the wildlife. Today it appeared the lake was already taken. As he zeroed in on the body floating serenely on its back, he drew in a sharp breath. Brianna. And what a sight she was. She looked like a mermaid, the water gently cascading over her sun-kissed body.

His body responded instantly, pulsing into life, and he groaned. He should go. God knows, there was enough sexual tension between them without her catching him gawping at her like a randy teenager. With a sigh of frustration he turned to walk away.

'Don't go on my account.'

Abruptly he halted. A twig snapped underfoot as he slowly turned round, the sound echoing across the still lake. Still except for the few gentle ripples that surrounded Brianna who was now treading water, a teasing smile on her face. Hell, she looked like a siren, set to seduce the hapless sailor. Or in his case, swimmer.

'Come and join me.'

'Thanks, I'll wait,' he replied tersely.

Feeling foolish, he sat on the ground. To leave now would give the impression he was embarrassed, or worse, scared. No way was he was going to give her the satisfaction of mocking him about running away. Determinedly he drew up his legs, rested his chin on his knees and watched as she finished her swim. He knew she was naked. Even from a distance he could make out the full curve of her breasts. He wasn't going to look away when she came out, he decided. She should be the one embarrassed, not him.

At last she emerged from the water, and he stared straight at her. It was an image that would stay in his mind for a very long time. Her body was magnificent. With a confidence that only the truly beautiful exuded, she walked easily onto the shore, her body glistening in the sun. Arousal shot through his system, so sharp, it was painful.

'Would you mind passing me my towel?' She stood in front of him, a wet, dripping picture of perfection.

'God, Brianna.' He grabbed at the towel near his feet

and shoved it at her. 'Damn you.' With a strangled oath he stood and dragged her to him, his mouth coming down roughly on hers.

Brianna let out a low moan as Mitch plundered her mouth and for the second time in as many days, he lost his control. Never a man who made love with finesse or gentleness, his hands wandered roughly up and down her body, moulding her closer and closer to him. One minute they were standing, the next he'd manoeuvred her to the ground and was lying on top of her. God she felt so bloody good, so soft, so smooth where he was hard and rough.

The contrast set off alarm bells in him and he leapt off her, rolling to his side, his chest heaving in time with his ragged breaths.

'What the hell am I doing?' he asked out loud, disgusted at himself. He had to be out of his mind. She was making him go out of his mind.

'Pretty well, I thought,' Brianna replied on a laugh.

He didn't know whether to be angry or amused. She was playing with him, damn her, much like a sleek aristocratic cat toys with a poor dumb mouse. But the knowledge didn't make his body ache any less. He was so sorely tempted to give in and let her play, despite the complications it would bring. But people like him and Brianna were never meant to mix, not on any intimate level. She wasn't from his world. He didn't even know which rules she played by.

He sat up, thrusting a hand through his hair, his movements jerky. 'This is wrong, on so many levels,' he muttered darkly.

'Why?'

'You really need me to tell you? We're out in the open where anyone could see us. There are people suffering agonies of injury and death all around us. Your mother is patron of the charity I work for. Saints alive, do I really need to go on?' Of course there were also the things she didn't know about him. The things that would make someone like her run like blazes if she ever found out. He sighed and got to his feet, reaching for the abandoned towel. 'Here, dry yourself off, get dressed and get the hell out of here.'

Brianna couldn't argue with Mitch's first two objections, but she wanted to clear up the third. 'You don't really think my mother cares who I sleep with, do you? I'm a grown woman. As long as I'm happy, she's happy. I mean, it's not as if you're going to lure me down the aisle, is it?'

His head shot round. 'Damn right.'

The words were said with such feeling she had to laugh. 'Well, at least we've got that clear.' She tugged on her T-shirt and the trusty canvas trousers she'd been living in these last few days. They would be going in the bin as soon as she got home. 'I'm just saying, another time, another place.' She twitched her shoulders in a careless shrug, though inside she felt anything but casual. The intensity of their kiss had shaken her to the core. She enjoyed sex, but what she'd just experienced with Mitch had staggered her. If she'd had her way, they would still be making love to each other now.

But it seemed Mitch was calling the shots. And he'd turned his back on her and was pulling off his shirt as he marched towards the lake. She had a brief, stunning view of his broad, tanned back before he dived into the water.

Brianna found the day long and hard. Where had all these injured people come from? They lined the walls of the tents, waiting patiently to be seen. The nurses were run off their feet, triaging the injured, making sure those who were worst off were seen first by Mitch or Stuart.

Occasionally she caught glimpses of Mitch, stethoscope round his neck, a calm, authoritative air firmly on his shoulders. He was called out several times, only to return with a casualty on a stretcher, who was then rushed straight into the area where they operated. Breaks were few and far between. How did the team cope with such full-on days? How did doctors like Mitch cope with such a never-ending stream of critical, life or death decisions to be made? She thought how she would have spent the day had she been at home. Flitting round the shops, lunching with friends. A glance at her watch told her it was nearly nine o'clock at night. Heck, no wonder she felt exhausted. She'd never spent so long on her feet. Nor had she ever spent so much time helping others, she thought with a rush of shame. Not that she'd been much help here.

'Miss.' An elderly man in one of the beds called over to her.

Pleased at last that somebody needed something from her, she hurried to his bedside. 'How can I help?'

He looked uncomfortable. Eyes darting everywhere but at her, he spoke in halting English. 'Need toilet? Help me?'

She watched as he struggled to pull back the sheets. Nodding, she stood with her arm around his shoulders, acting as a lever as he swung his legs out of the bed.

'No!' Tessa rushed up and, none too gently, pushed Brianna out of the way.

'He needs to go to the toilet,' Brianna explained with more patience than she was feeling. 'I was just helping him.'

Tessa gave a stern shake of her head and eased the man back into bed. 'He mustn't try and walk.' Reaching down, she handed the patient a urine bottle from under the bed, speaking to him in fluent Spanish.

When the patient had understood, Tessa took Brianna's arm in a firm grip and led her away. 'Didn't you see the notice on his bed?' the nurse fumed at her, gesturing to the clipboard. 'For God's sake, stop interfering in things you've no training in.'

'What's going on here?'

Brianna glanced up to see Mitch staring down at them. Just what she needed. It wasn't enough that she'd been humiliated by the nurse, now she faced a tongue lashing from him, too.

'I caught Brianna helping a patient out of bed who shouldn't be walking. It's time you reminded her she's only here to observe.'

Several of the team and quite a few patients were now watching with undisguised interest. Beyond embarrassment, Brianna avoided Mitch and glared straight back at the nurse. 'Thank you, Tessa. I think even someone of my limited capabilities has received that message now.'

She turned and walked out of the ward with as much dignity as she could muster. When she was sure she was out of sight, she ran the rest of the way to her tent and collapsed, crying, onto the bed. Damn the woman for making her feel totally inadequate.

Mitch stood at the entrance of Brianna's tent, listening to the muffled sobs. 'Can I come in?' he asked through the canvas wall.

'Help yourself,' came the voice from the other side, followed by a loud sniff. 'But I'm warning you, there's no way you can make me feel any more useless than I do already. So if you've come to yell at me too, you're wasting your time.'

Cautiously he walked into her tent. He took one look at the slender figure sitting on the bed and his heart went out to her. It had been one hell of a long day, for all of them. Of course he and the team were used to it. Brianna wasn't. Tears rolled down her cheeks and her glorious eyes looked utterly miserable. 'I'm not here to shout,' he replied gently. 'I'm here to check you're okay.'

'Thank you, I'm fine.'

She looked anything but. With a sigh he sat down next

to her on the bed. 'Tessa didn't mean to embarrass you like that. She was just concerned for the patient.'

Brianna glared at him. 'Yes, she was concerned for the patient. But she sure as heck enjoyed humiliating me, too.'

Mitch shook his head. 'No, Tessa's not like that.'

'Are you really so clueless? Tessa fancies you.'

An uncomfortable flush crept up his neck.

'Yes she does,' Brianna insisted. 'Consequently she doesn't like me. She sees me as a threat.'

Embarrassed, Mitch leapt up off the bed. 'That's ridiculous. Tessa doesn't think of me in that way and I certainly don't think of her that way.'

'What about me, Mitch?' she asked softly. 'Do you think of me that way?'

Hell's teeth. This was no longer embarrassing, it was excruciating. He thrust his hands into his pockets. 'You know I do.'

Instantly the atmosphere in the tent changed. Tension, dark and heavy, mixed with the spark and crackle of sexual chemistry.

'Then what are you waiting for?' she whispered.

Mitch tried to take his eyes away from hers, he really did. Somehow they wouldn't budge. He couldn't seem to force them to look at the floor, at her chin. God, anywhere but at those dazzling green emeralds that were telling him, quite clearly, what she wanted. 'We've been here before,' he told her thickly.

'I believe we've solved two of your issues. Nobody can see us here and my mother has nothing to do with you and me.' Slowly she stood and walked towards him. 'Of course we are still in the middle of a disaster-stricken area ...' she left the sentence hanging.

Mitch swallowed. Then swallowed again. This stunning beauty was practically offering herself to him on a plate. What the blazes was he meant to do now?

Chapter Twelve

Brianna's eyes were still on his, her body close enough he could inhale her wild flower scent. Her lips so damn close, Mitch could almost taste her. Call him selfish, but right now he wasn't thinking about the patients lying in the ward. He wasn't thinking about the bleep in his pocket either, destined to go off at any time. All he could think about was the woman who stood in front of him. He only had to stretch out his hand and he could touch her. She was his for the taking.

'Mitch?' His name was a whisper from trembling lips. He heard her inhale an unsteady breath and then she bit into her lower lip. This time the gesture wasn't coy, or deliberate. It was uncertain, scared almost. It was a heady moment, knowing he could unnerve her. She'd done it to him often enough.

His hands twitched in his pockets, but just as he started to pull them out, to drag her to him and take what he wanted, she spun abruptly away from him. 'I'm sorry, you obviously don't want this.' Her voice caught as she stood with her back to him. 'I think you should go.'

Mitch stared at her in stunned disbelief. Had she really taken his hesitation as a sign of indifference? Was this gorgeous creature really that unsure of herself? Heck, if she'd been any other woman, he would have thought a lot less and moved a lot quicker. The fact that he hadn't, told him he knew this had the potential to be far more than a quick romp between the sheets. It bothered him enough to hesitate. But not enough to stop.

He reached out and snatched at her arm, pulling her back towards him. 'Not so fast.'

At the sound of Mitch's rough, husky voice, Brianna's legs, already shaking, nearly gave way. Had it not been for his arm supporting her, she'd be a crumpled heap by his feet. Jeez, she was crap at seduction.

But then she turned to look at him, and her stomach almost fell to the floor.

Dark eyes, almost black, gazed heatedly back at her, filled with desire and a hint of the danger she found so exciting about him. Her pulse scrambled and someone – was that really her? – let out a breath that was half moan, half gasp.

He tugged on her hand. 'My tent,' he snapped, his voice hoarse. 'It's got a larger bed.'

With her heart hammering against her ribcage, she followed him. When they were both inside he zipped the door firmly shut. Then his mouth came crashing down on hers.

There was nothing tender about the way Mitch set about making love. He was fever and fire. His kisses left a burning path in their wake. His hands ... Oh God, his hands were everywhere. There wasn't a part of her left untouched by his heat.

'There's something you need to know about me,' he muttered between hot kisses. 'I don't think much of long foreplay.' With that he unceremoniously yanked off her clothes and threw them across the tent.

It was fierce, wild and utterly thrilling. Caught up in the fervour, she tried to get to his flesh. She wanted to touch his naked body, to see how the muscles she'd glimpsed beneath his T-shirt played out across his chest. To feel their strength. Pushing up his shirt she snaked her hand up his back.

He batted it away 'We'll get to that.'

He was like a tornado, whipping over her body, intent on getting his fill of what he wanted. And that seemed to be to devour every part of her. From her breasts, to the liquid centre between her legs, he explored, leaving a scorching trail in his wake.

'Please, Mitch ...' she implored him, suddenly not confident enough to ask for what she wanted. What she needed.

He seemed to understand, for he lifted her into his arms and lowered her onto the bed before finally tearing off his own clothes. Brianna watched, fascinated, as he stretched to pull off his T-shirt, giving her a blissful glimpse of hard, well defined muscles, a dramatic black tattoo and a sprinkling of dark blond hair.

After pulling a condom from his holdall he quickly sheathed himself and launched on top of her. With a single fluid movement he pushed her legs apart and drove himself inside. He didn't ask, he just took. As he thrust his powerful body into hers, she thought she'd die with the pleasure. He felt ... incredible. She cried out, only to have his hand brought down firmly onto her mouth.

'Canvas walls,' he muttered.

She was too far gone to care. All she wanted was for his body to keep pounding into hers, again and again, harder and faster. Finally she bit down on his hand as an intense orgasm ripped through her system. It seemed to go on and on, leaving her totally shattered. As she lay in a post-climactic haze, she was dimly aware of him stiffening inside her, taking his own release.

For several pulsating minutes he lay, fully stretched out, on top of her. When he finally eased onto his elbows and looked down at her, his hair was mussed and his eyes like deep pools of liquid chocolate. 'I think we've successfully established this is what I wanted,' he announced roughly.

He was still inside her. Even as she smiled and wrapped her arms around his neck, she was aware of him hardening again. 'Umm, I can see that.' She arched her hips to encourage him. His brown eyes darkened further and his mouth descended onto hers once more.

Lying on her side, totally spent, Brianna cuddled up close to Mitch and rested her head on his chest. His bed might be larger than hers, but it was still narrow, forcing them together. She took the opportunity to study the body pressed up against her. It wasn't the prettiest male body she'd ever lain next to, but it was the toughest. The panther tattoo crept intimidatingly across the top half of his arm, adding to his wild boy aura. His tanned chest wasn't the sort artfully created by hours in a gym. It was one that matched his face, rugged and strong. Several scars ran haphazardly across it. Gently she ran a finger across the ridge of the most ragged scar. 'A war wound?'

Mitch looked down at the dainty fingers brushing across his skin, sliding over the scar he'd received from a knife fight when he was thirteen. He swore softly to himself. Those soft, well-manicured hands didn't belong on him. What the hell was he doing with her? But even as he wondered, his body responded to her touch. How could he want her again? He'd harboured a faint hope that taking her to bed would get her out of his system, but his body was emphatically telling him something entirely different. 'Unless you're up for another round, I suggest you put that finger away.'

She looked up at him through a tangle of glossy chestnut hair. 'I wouldn't say no, but I'm going to need a rest first. You've worn me out.' She bent to kiss the scar.

Uncomfortable with her scrutiny, Mitch pulled up the sheet. 'You can't play with the goods if you're not prepared to handle the consequences.'

A giggle burst from her but she obediently lay her hands over the sheet, snuggling in further to his side. 'Tell me a bit about Mitch McBride.'

He stilled. 'What do you want to know?'

She cocked her head up from its resting place on his chest. 'Well, start from the beginning. Your parents.'

'What about them?' He clasped his hands behind his head and tried to relax.

'Are you close to them?'

'No.'

Brianna sighed. 'This is worse than getting blood out of a stone. Are they still alive?'

Mitch glanced down at her. Hadn't she got the message yet? She was clearly one of those women who wanted cosy conversation after making love. Well she'd chosen the wrong guy for that. And most definitely the wrong topic of conversation. 'No,' he replied shortly.

'Any brothers or sisters?'

'No.'

'Come on, Mitch, can't you say anything but no?'

'I don't recall saying no tonight.'

Brianna sat up in frustration, the sheet dropping off and leaving her breasts exposed. 'Come on, these are simple questions. Why all the secrecy?'

He let out a long, exasperated breath. Women. She sat there, taunting him with her bare breasts, and expected him to have a conversation about his family? Something he didn't talk about. Ever. Even if bare breasts were nowhere in sight. 'Why all the questions?' he countered.

Brianna glared at him. 'I want to know a little bit about the man I'm sleeping with, that's all. You know all about me.'

He dragged his eyes from her delicious breasts and focused on her face for a moment. 'Brianna, this is just sex. We're not about to start a relationship. We don't need to waste time on conversation when we could be putting that time to much better use.'

Before she had a chance to protest, he captured one of her breasts in his mouth and pushed her back down onto the bed.

'Where are you going?' Through the haze of sexual satisfaction, Brianna became aware of Mitch pushing her aside so he could get out of the bed.

'I've been bleeped.' He was shoving his long legs into his trousers and grabbing at the nearest T-shirt. 'I don't know how long I'll be.'

There was a pointed silence. Though she waited for the words telling her to go back to sleep, he'd join her when he was finished, they weren't forthcoming. 'Right. I'll go back to my tent then.'

Mitch simply nodded at her and vanished. Slowly Brianna eased back against the pillow. She felt hurt, slighted, though why she'd expected anything different, she didn't know. He hadn't exactly been tripping over himself to charm her into bed. No, it was she who'd done the chasing. He might be up for sex, but clearly that was all. Spending the night cuddling up in his bed had never been on the cards, whether he'd been bleeped or not. She should have known that, readied herself for it.

Annoyed with herself, she moved out of the bed and hunted around for her clothes – clothes that had been discarded earlier with ruthless abandon. Well, it might not have had the ending she'd hoped for, she acknowledged as she zipped up her trousers, but it had certainly been a night she would never forget.

When Mitch made it back to his thankfully empty tent an hour later, he had the first opportunity to mull over what the hell had happened. God, he'd never been more pleased to be bleeped in the middle of the night in the whole of his life. When he'd first opened his eyes, he'd been horrified to find he'd fallen asleep with his arms around Brianna, her body nuzzled against his. They'd looked like a real couple, rather than two people who were together just for sex. He'd been so damn shocked he'd pushed her away with more roughness than he'd intended, subconsciously knowing he'd wanted to wake her up. Had wanted to make sure she wasn't in his bed when he'd got back.

It was a mystery to him why women thought having sex with a man automatically gave them the right to wake up next to him. He preferred to wake up alone, something that had led to him being called cold and heartless on many occasions. Probably he was, but he was a loner. He liked his space, his freedom, his independence. It was how it had always been. He'd stopped relying on other people a long time ago. Since he'd done that, accepted that he was on his own, that there was nobody to look out for him but himself, life had been a lot simpler. It was how he intended it to stay.

Chapter Thirteen

The time had finally come. Her last day at the camp. When she'd first set foot in this part of South America and seen for herself the grim reality of life here, the week had stretched ahead of her like an eternity. Now, incredibly, it was nearly over, leaving her with decidedly mixed feelings. She was desperate to get back to civilisation. A hot bath and television. A comfortable bed and wardrobe full of clean clothes. Those were the basics. Then there were the simple pleasures. A meal in a restaurant. A drink with her friends. Things she'd taken for granted, but now couldn't wait to enjoy again. In fact, when she looked at it hard, there was actually only one reason why she didn't want to go home. And that reason was currently sitting down in the camp dining room, eating breakfast.

'Did you manage some sleep?' she asked as she deliberately went to sit opposite him. He wore his intimidating look – unshaven and unsmiling – but it was water off a duck's back to her now.

'Some.' He glanced up at her briefly, eyes hooded, then carried on eating his porridge.

'Is there anything you need me to do today? Anything I can help with?'

He shrugged. 'I'm not sure. You'll need to check with Tessa and Stuart. I won't be around much.'

Brianna felt a flare of intense disappointment. This man had feasted on her body last night. He had been more intimate with her than any man she'd ever known. And now he was spending her final day somewhere else. It hurt, as did the fact he couldn't even be bothered to look her in the eye when he told her. 'I see. You are aware this is my last day here. I go home tomorrow.'

Finally his eyes rested on hers, but they were anything but friendly. 'We're trying to save lives here. It doesn't all stop just because you're going home.'

Ouch. He knew how to hurt. 'Yes, you're right, I'm sorry.' Ashamed she lowered her head and pretended an interest in her breakfast. She was being totally selfish, thinking only of what she wanted. His skill-set was rare and much in demand. If this week had taught her nothing else, it had taught her that.

Mitch cleared his throat. 'Sorry, too. I do the jerk thing quite well.'

Her heart melted and she smiled. 'Yes, you do.'

'There's been further chaos downstream and I've been asked to go and help, but before that I'm going to check on a suspected case of cholera in the camp. You can come with me, if you like. But I'm warning you now, it won't be pretty. The main symptom is diarrhoea.'

'With an invitation as appealing as that, how can a woman possibly refuse?'

His lips twitched, but he also shook his head, as if caught in two minds whether to laugh or cuss at her for being so flippant.

A short while later she was sitting in the truck next to him, bumping over the hard ground towards the back of the camp.

'Do I have any instructions?'

'Smile, stay out of the way and, for the love of God, don't eat or drink anything offered.'

She huffed. 'That's it? You really do think I'm a waste of space, don't you?'

He pulled the truck to a stop. 'No. I think you're bright, strong and determined, but your talents lie in a different direction than nursing.'

Slightly mollified, she climbed down from the truck. 'You only said all that so I'd do as I was told.'

He tried to look offended, but the bugger was clearly having a hard time suppressing a smile. Funny, for most of her stay she'd wanted to make him smile. Now he was, she wanted him to take her seriously.

Mitch hauled his medical bag out of the back of the jeep and together they walked up to the large tatty tent. Even from a distance she heard the cries of a baby.

'Here.' He thrust some disposable gloves at her. 'In case you ignore the *stay out of the way* instruction.'

Giving him a hard glare, she snapped on the gloves.

Mitch bit back a smile. Brianna looked so cute when she was in a huff. He'd fully intended not to see her at all today, figuring it would save them both the embarrassment. But she'd looked so hurt this morning when he'd ungraciously barked at her that somehow he'd ended up inviting her along.

And now here he was, feeling an almost overwhelming need to smile.

'Médico.'

Abruptly he looked up to see the worried face of a woman beckoning to him from inside the tent. Time to get his head screwed back onto his job.

The smell was the first thing that hit him when he lifted up the tent flap. He was used to bad smells, but the stench of diarrhoea wasn't one you wanted to hang around long in. He turned to the woman, clearly the mother, and started asking all his usual questions; who had diarrhoea, when had it come on, how many bowel movements, when he heard a muffled squawk from behind him.

Brianna appeared momentarily in the doorway. Her face went sheet-white, she gasped, croaked out 'Oh … sorry,' then threw a hand to her mouth and disappeared.

He found himself having to stifle another smile. 'She's not quite used to life in a refugee camp yet,' he explained to the mother.

Not that she'd ever be used to it, he reminded himself as he started to examine the children. She was going home tomorrow. Back to her highly privileged, highly sanitised life. A fact he'd do well to remember.

There were four kids affected in all, and he quizzed the older child.

'Where were you drinking from?'

He looked sheepish. 'The lake.'

Mitch shook his head. It didn't seem to matter how many times these kids were told not to drink from lakes and rivers, they did it anyway. 'You know you only drink treated water.' He grabbed another few packs of purifying tablets out of his bag and tossed them over to him.

'Yes, Médico.'

It was exactly the same voice Mitch had used when he'd been that age and teachers had told him not to get into any more fights, not to get into trouble.

He delved into his bag and gave the mother some rehydration sachets. 'You need to mix these in the water I'm leaving you and get the kids to drink lots of it.' Then he explained, yet again, the importance of good hygiene. Washing their hands with soap after going to the toilet and before cooking or eating. Treating the water before drinking it. Finally he nodded over to the youngest. 'Someone will come and collect him and take him to the hospital tent. He needs to be put on a drip for a while.'

'Thank you.'

After saying his goodbyes, he went in search of Brianna. He found her sitting near a small clump of bushes, hugging her legs.

He nodded over to the bush. 'Is that where your breakfast ended up?'

She stared resolutely past his shoulder. 'Yes.'

Hunching down next to her, he smoothed back her hair.

'Sorry. Bringing you here wasn't one of my best ideas. I didn't think.'

'It's not your fault I seem to have this propensity for throwing up at the drop of a hat.' She nodded to his shirt. 'At least you weren't in striking distance this time.'

'I guess I should thank the bush for taking the hit.'

Suddenly she let out a sob and thrust her face into her hands. 'God, why am I so flaming useless?'

He felt a strange fluttering sensation in his chest and had to fight not to fling his arms round her. She was leaving tomorrow. He might have let his guard slip last night, but he had to shove it firmly up again now. 'I told you, you're not useless. Just not cut out for life in a refugee camp.'

'I guess not.' She glanced sideways at him. 'Did you fix them?'

'I'm not sure that's the right terminology, but yes. They'll be okay. If you catch it early enough, cholera is easily treated by rehydration.'

'That's it? No hour long operation? No fancy drug cocktail? Just drink some fluids?'

He chuckled. 'A lot of what we do here is very simple.'

For a few moments they sat side by side, gazing out over the camp. Mitch was very much aware of her next to him, but not only as a woman. In every way they were diametrically opposite and yet ... and yet he could sit here, next to her, and feel not just comfortable, but strangely content.

But that was dangerous. Because he didn't want to feel any closeness towards her, Mitch suddenly jumped to his feet. 'Right. I need to head on downstream. I'll give you a lift back.'

Once more Brianna sat next to Mitch in the truck. It had been a strange morning. She'd humiliated herself again.

Okay, nothing odd in that. At least not on this trip. But what had been odd had been Mitch's attitude towards her when he'd sat with her by the bush. For a few wonderful moments he'd been warm, relaxed. Of course he'd quickly smashed whatever had started to grow between them, almost as if he'd been afraid of letting her get close.

'Got any plans for your last night?' They were the first words he'd spoken to her since they'd set off back to base.

'No, I hadn't thought of it.' Liar. Images of Mitch making love to her all evening danced through her mind. She bit the inside of her cheek and went for broke. 'Will you be around?'

'I'm not sure. Maybe if I get back in time, we can drag a few of the others out and go for a farewell drink?'

Not exactly the images in her mind, but she was pathetically grateful for the offer nonetheless. 'Sounds good, but if you go out twice in a week they'll think you've had a knock on the head.'

At last he smiled at her. 'When in truth, I've been corrupted by the patron's daughter.'

'I think it was you who did the corrupting last night.'

Mitch eyed her speculatively. 'You didn't look like you were complaining.'

She returned his gaze steadily. 'I wasn't. I'm not.'

The electricity crackled between them once more. They were poles apart when it came to background and personality, but when it came to physical attraction they were dynamite together. As his eyes darkened with desire, she knew at least on that front, they were in agreement.

Chapter Fourteen

Brianna spent the rest of the day helping Dan out with the medical supplies. She was a liability everywhere else in the camp, but at least with Dan she felt useful. And welcome. He flattered and charmed her, a welcome change from Mitch, who seemed determined to do neither.

When her muscles finally screamed at her to stop, she sat wearily on one of the many medical supply boxes they'd collected from the airport.

'I certainly won't miss all the back-breaking unloading,' she complained, rubbing at the small of her back.

'Will you miss any of it?' Dan asked, plonking himself down on another box.

'Umm, let me think. Showering with cold water, no. Sleeping in a tent, no. Eating what seems to be porridge three times a day, no,' she replied, counting them off on her fingers. Then she grinned. 'The people, yes. Are you up for a night in town again, a farewell drink? Mitch said he would try to get back for it.'

Dan's eyebrows shot up. 'Mitch did?'

'Don't sound so shocked. I'm sure there's a human being in there somewhere. It just needs a bit of coaxing to come out.'

'Or maybe it needs a beautiful woman.'

Brianna flushed. Not from the compliment, she was used to those, but from the implication. Had Dan guessed she'd shared Mitch's bed last night? Had he heard them? 'I doubt Mitch would bow to the bidding of any woman, whatever she looked like.'

Dan laughed. 'Yes, you're right there. We've had a few foxy chicks drift in and out over the years, but he hasn't seemed too bothered.'

'No?' She told herself it was just idle curiosity. It wasn't as if she was that interested in Mitch's love life, not really.

'I don't think Mitch is aware of the effect he has on the opposite sex. He's great with his patients, but that seems to be where his people skills end. Anyway, you know me by now. I'm definitely up for a night out. I'll gather the troops and we'll head off around seven?'

Seven o'clock came. Everyone gathered by the jeep, ready to go out. Everyone except for Stuart and Roger, who were on call. And except Mitch, who was nowhere to be seen. Brianna ignored the spike of disappointment and hustled everyone into the jeep. It didn't matter that Mitch wasn't there. Dan, Jane, Toby and Tessa were. They would go and have a good night out.

And they did. Without Mitch around, Tessa became a lot friendlier and after several rounds of beer, all five of them were laughing and joking.

'So, confess up.' Jane's attention turned to Brianna. 'Was it you in Mitch's tent last night?'

Suddenly four pairs of eyes rounded on her. Three held amused interest, one a flash of cold dislike. Brianna paused and took refuge in her drink. 'Why do you ask?'

'Because,' Jane said with a giggle, 'Toby and I share the tent next to his. We definitely heard a female scream, though it was quickly muffled.'

She stifled the groan, but only just. Oops. What on earth was she meant to do now? Would Mitch be livid if she admitted to his team that she'd slept with him? Probably. She certainly knew one person who'd be more than cross at hearing the truth. In fact, if looks could kill, Tessa would have shot her right between the eyes by now. 'It surely can't be the first time you've heard a woman in his tent,' she prevaricated, trying not to look directly at anyone.

Toby laughed. 'I can't imagine he's a monk, but he doesn't usually entertain women when he's on camp. So, was it you?'

Brianna wondered if she could get away with ignoring the question and asking if anybody wanted another drink. But looking at the very interested eyes resting on her, she doubted it. 'It might have been.'

'Well, knock me down with a feather,' Toby exclaimed, clearly enjoying the gossip.

'And I thought you were saving yourself for me,' Dan piped up, though he had an easy smile on his face, indicating he wasn't seriously bothered.

Tessa, on the other hand, was clearly extremely bothered. 'I'm just going to the ladies,' she stammered as she lurched up from her chair, the blood fast disappearing from her face.

Brianna watched her go with a rush of genuine sympathy. It must be hard, carrying a torch for someone who didn't return your feelings.

Jane placed a reassuring hand on Brianna's arm. 'Don't worry about Tessa,' she whispered as Dan and Toby stood up to get another round. 'It might do her good. She's pined away for Mitch for far too long. At least now she knows there's no hope for her in that direction.'

Brianna resisted the impulse to burst into uncontrollable laughter. 'Hold up there. You're putting two and two together and making a lot more than four. Mitch and I just had a little fling. I'm not sure we'll even repeat the experience.'

Jane gaped at her. 'Hey, you're not about to shatter my dreams and tell me Mitch is a disappointing lover, are you?'

Now it was Brianna's turn to look shocked. 'It's okay, Jane, your fantasies are still very much intact. But he would die if he knew we were having this conversation.'

'Very probably. But this is just between you and me. I love Toby, of course.' Her eyes hastily scanned the bar, checking her husband was out of earshot. 'But Mitch? Well, he's most women's fantasy man, isn't he? Sexy, moody, but underneath a heart full of compassion. He just needs the right woman to crack him. Maybe he's found her.'

'Oh no, slow down there. Mitch and I shared one night of, albeit amazing, sex. I don't want you reading anything more into it.' She bit her lip and found herself sighing. 'He certainly isn't.'

'And you?'

Brianna flushed. 'Just between you and me, I'm smitten,' she admitted softly. 'Which is quite possibly the most stupid thing I've ever done.'

'Or perhaps, the best.' Jane gently squeezed her arm. 'Give it time and see where it leads.'

Back at her tent, Brianna packed up the few items she wanted to take home with her. Everything else she was leaving for the poor villagers, partly in a bid to help where she could, partly because she never wanted to see them again. Then she climbed into the hard, narrow bed for the last time. As she lay back against the lumpy pillow, she thought guiltily of how much she was looking forward to her goose feather one back home.

Then she thought of what she'd be leaving behind, or rather who.

She'd missed Mitch tonight, more than she'd wanted to, far more than was healthy, and she couldn't understand why. Heck, she'd met and turned down men who were more handsome than him, far richer than him. Men with charm and sophistication. Men who knew how to flirt with her and how to make her laugh. So why was she fast becoming obsessed with this man? Was it simply the emotion of the setting? Far from home, she was living in circumstances that would play havoc with any woman's heart.

'Brianna, are you still awake?'

Her heart lurched at the sound of the rough, deep voice on the other side of the canvas. Quickly she scooted up in the bed. 'Yes, come in.'

Mitch had spent the day with casualties of a further mudslide that had resulted from last night's torrential, but thankfully localised, rain. Rain he hadn't even been aware of while he'd had Brianna wrapped around him. As he lifted up the flap and ducked into her tent, the sight of her sitting up in bed in a skimpy vest top was enough to gladden even his exhausted soul.

'Sorry I couldn't get back any earlier.'

She gave him a warm smile. 'No problem. How was it?'

The sympathy in her eyes made him suddenly long to put his arms around her and bury his face in her glorious hair. But he wasn't a man who needed comfort, so he remained where he was. 'Pretty grim.' His eyes fell on her case. 'Have you packed?'

'If you can call throwing a few items into a bag packing, then yes, I have. Early start tomorrow. Dan said he'd take me to the airport.'

He nodded. 'Right then, I'll say goodnight and leave you to get some sleep.'

Brianna gave him a lopsided smile and then slid out of bed. 'Don't I get a goodbye kiss?' she asked, her eyes glinting dangerously.

Mitch watched, entranced, as she walked the few paces towards him. The vest top did little to hide the fullness of her breasts. The skimpy shorts revealed slender, shapely legs. How much could he stand before he gave in to the urge to push her onto the bed and take her one last time?

'You know as well as I do that if we kiss, it won't just end there,' he replied, his voice sounding like sandpaper, his arms already settling on her hips, pulling her against him.

'I was hoping not,' she admitted huskily.

Maybe it was the grimness of the day, which contrasted starkly with the pleasures she was offering. Maybe it was just Brianna. Either way, he could no longer remember why taking this beautiful woman to bed was a bad idea.

With a groan he lifted off her vest top, enjoying the sight of her breasts as they bounced free. They were incredible; round, pert, a perfect handful. He bent his head to suckle.

'You have too many clothes on,' she gasped, her hands rushing to grab his shirt and pull it over his head.

God, the feel of flesh on flesh. The horrors of the day fast slipped away as she rained kisses over his chest and unfastened the buttons of his trousers, beginning to work them down his legs.

Quickly they divested the rest of their clothes. Then she took his hand and led him to the bed, laying down and pulling him on top of her. As his hard edges came into contact with her softness, he groaned with pure pleasure.

'These beds are too damn small,' he muttered a short while later. In a flash he was on his feet and lifting her up. As she anchored her legs around his hips and her arms around his neck, he used his free hand to grab the blanket from the end of the bed and throw it onto the floor. Then he lay her down on top of it and spread his rangy body alongside hers. 'Now we've got room to move, to explore.'

She turned to give him a sexy smile, her eyes sparkling with desire and promise, and he decided to show her exactly what he meant by exploring. With his lips, his tongue, his hands, he ravished every inch of her. When he was satisfied he'd left no part untouched, he entered her in one fierce, life-affirming lunge. Whatever he gave, she gave back and together they proceeded to make full use of the floor space available. First he pushed her onto her back, then her side, finally she climbed on top of him, never missing a beat.

When at last her muffled scream brought about his own shattering climax, he knew he wouldn't remember today for all the death he'd seen. He'd remember it for this moment.

They lay together, each catching their breath. Feeling deliciously relaxed, Brianna trailed her fingers across Mitch's bare chest, which was rising and falling in time with his slowly recovering breaths. Had a man's body ever excited her as much as this man's did? She didn't think so. It was scarred, not perfect. Rough, not smooth. Strong, not beautiful. But she couldn't keep her hands off it.

'I thought you had an early start?' he asked as he snared her fingers.

'Plenty of time for sleep when I get home.'

They lost themselves in each other once more.

Chapter Fifteen

When her alarm went off at 5.00 a.m., Brianna was forced awake from a deep and dreamless sleep. With her mind still foggy, she sat up in the camp bed and looked around the place she'd called home for the last week. Her discarded shorts and vest top were the only clue as to how she'd spent most of the night. She could remember, vividly and with the utmost pleasure, rolling around on the floor with Mitch. But she couldn't remember when Mitch had left her, or how she'd got into bed. Sadly, memories were all she'd have from now on. It was time to go home.

She dressed quickly and walked out to wait for Dan.

'Are you off then?' At the sound of the cool female voice, Brianna turned to find Tessa behind her.

'Yes.' She smiled warmly at the head nurse. They hadn't spoken to each other since that episode in the bar, Brianna figuring it best to stay out of Tessa's way. Though she'd never experienced unrequited love, she'd seen how hurt Tessa was and had felt for her. 'I hope there are no hard feelings,' Brianna began, but Tessa's stony glare stopped her in her tracks.

'It won't last.'

Brianna gave a casual shrug. 'Who says I want it to last?'

'You're not right for him.'

'And you are?' The sympathy she'd been feeling was fast receding.

'You think just because you've got money, you can get anything, or anyone, you want.' The words were laced with bitterness. 'Well, don't think Mitch will be that easily bought. He'll always be his own man, not some sort of lapdog to a pampered princess.'

God how she hated that term, but she was too busy laughing at the picture of Mitch as her lapdog to take offence. 'I know that. And as his own man he can choose who he wants to sleep with. He chose me.' Oh, what was she doing, getting involved in a demeaning war of words over a man? It was ridiculous. 'Look, let's not argue over this. As you say, it's not as if Mitch and I will ever be an item. To be honest, I don't even know if we'll even see each other again.' Hearing Dan coming towards them in the truck, she stared directly into Tessa's eyes. 'It was good to meet you, Tessa. You do a great job here, you really do.'

Gratefully Brianna climbed into the passenger seat. All of a sudden she was desperate to get home. Away from injured children, traumatised villages, and a tall, fair-haired man with intense dark brown eyes and a rough, tough attitude.

Many weary, bone-shaking hours later, Brianna reclined in the first class cabin of a 747 that would whisk her back to London. As the bubbles of champagne fizzed delicately over her tongue, she reflected on her trip. Already she felt a different person from the one who'd flown out, only seven days ago. Now she had a focus, a purpose. She knew what she wanted to do and even had a plan of how to get there. All that remained was to convince Margaret her ideas were sound and that she was capable of carrying them out.

Leaning back against the soft pillow, she took another sip of the liquid nectar and decided to be honest with herself. The change in her wasn't all to do with her desire to work for the charity. Some of the increased spring, the giddiness, euphoria almost, was to do with a very different desire. She'd finally found a man who really interested her. Not just sexually, though he did that in spades, but emotionally. Mitch McBride had captivated her. She wanted to spend more time with him, to get beneath the tough outer layer he showed to the world. Even as she was flying away from him, she knew she'd have to see him again.

She'd just have to.

While Brianna was sleeping in the luxury of the first class cabin, Mitch was in the middle of his ward round with Tessa. Was it his imagination or was she being frosty with him? He respected Tessa hugely, but couldn't say he understood her. Most of the time she was friendly, but there were times he had the distinct impression she was angry with him. Like now.

'Is everything all right, Tessa?' he asked when they'd finished checking on all the patients.

'Yes, why wouldn't it be?' She busied herself with filing away the patient's notes. 'I saw Brianna go off this morning.' Suddenly she looked up and scrutinised his face, obviously waiting to observe his reaction.

Mitch knew they were all aware he and Brianna had slept together. Toby had taken much delight in watching his boss squirm when he'd let slip that little nugget. But it was his business, his alone. He wasn't about to discuss it with anyone.

He turned to leave, but Tessa hadn't finished. 'I'm surprised at you, Mitch, sleeping with her.'

Still with his back to her, he struggled to rein in his temper. His private life was just that. But he'd been reckless enough to conduct a physical relationship whilst on camp, something he'd vowed never to do, and now he was paying the price. Biting his tongue, he replied in what he considered to be a pretty measured tone. 'Not that it is any concern of yours, but why do you say that?'

'I didn't think spoilt little rich girls were your type.'

Instinctively he opened his mouth to defend Brianna. She was rich, yes, spoilt no. But then he closed it again. Did he really know what she was like? At the camp she'd been out of her usual environment. Back on her own turf, with all the trappings of her wealth around her, she was probably a very different person.

'They're not my type,' he replied shortly. On that they could agree. However much he might have been attracted to Brianna, she most definitely wasn't the right type for someone like him.

Thankfully his bleep went off before Tessa could get in any further digs. He'd stick to concentrating on his work from now on. It was the one blasted thing he was good at.

It had taken the best part of a day and a night, but Brianna was finally home. Home was the house she still shared with her parents. Not that they were on top of each other. With four floors, umpteen bedrooms and acres of square footage, it wasn't what most people were lucky enough to call a home. Brianna had an apartment on the first floor of the impressive London mansion house. Her place had its own entrance and stretched all the way from the front of the house to the rear. Four bedrooms and bathrooms, three reception areas, a study and her own kitchen. She had all she needed for her own independence, with the comfort of knowing her parents were just down the hallway. Sometimes she could go days without seeing them, though usually at some point she'd open the interconnecting door and wander down the corridor for a chat. She was incredibly lucky, and not just in material terms. More important than any amount of wealth, she was loved and cherished. The apple of her parents' eye. Sometimes it was hard being the only child, the sole focus of all that devotion. But mainly it was heart-warming, comforting. Whatever happened in her life, her parents were always there to pick up the pieces. To console her and then encourage her into the next venture.

Brianna found her mother in the family kitchen, discussing recipes with the cook. She stood and watched for a moment, appreciating her mother's grace, the way she spoke to the cook in a way that made her an equal, not a member of staff. When she finally caught sight of her daughter, a huge smile swept across her face. Brianna dropped her bag and rushed to hug her. Now *this* was what she called home. Not the bricks and mortar, but her mother's arms.

'You look happy, Brianna,' she announced when she'd checked her over from head to toe. 'The trip has obviously done you good.'

'Oh, Mum, I can't begin to tell you some of the things I've seen. It was heartbreaking and inspiring. Depressing but strangely uplifting.'

'Wow, it certainly seems to have made a big impression.' She squeezed her daughter's hand. 'Come with me. Let's sit down with a cup of tea and you can tell me all about it.'

Her mother made the drinks and they carried them through to the sitting room, where Brianna took her mother through all she'd experienced. She made her laugh with tales of the primitive accommodation and the cold shower. She made her cry with tales of the mudslide and the mounting body bags. Finally she conveyed her real admiration for the medical team out there, how hard they worked, how many lives they saved. Brianna was careful not to mention any names specifically. Her mother had an uncanny ability to sniff out the merest hint of any gossip and Brianna wasn't sure she was ready to share Mitch with her yet.

'So you see, I really think getting Medic SOS to specialise in the serious trauma cases is the way forward. Not only would it give them a clearly defined role, but it would make fund-raising easier, helping them to stand out from the other charities.'

Her mother sat back on the sofa. 'Look at you, my darling, your eyes all bright with excitement. You've no idea how pleased I am you've taken this to heart and I'm sure Margaret will be delighted to hear your ideas.' She held her daughter's hand and studied her face. 'Now tell me what else has you so buoyed up.'

Brianna blinked. Surely her mother's romance radar wasn't that good? 'What do you mean?'

'My darling child, I know you. It isn't just the idea of working with the charity that's put a smile on your beautiful face. What else has happened?' She smiled as her daughter's cheeks began to turn pink. 'Ah, it must be a man.'

'How do you do it, Mum?' Brianna shook her head and laughed. 'I'm never going to be able to keep a secret from you, am I?'

'No, and don't you forget it. Now tell me who is responsible for putting a sparkle in my daughter's eyes.'

'Mitch.'

'Mitch McBride? The chief medic?' She waited for Brianna's nod of affirmation. 'I remember him. Serious, somewhat distant, but with an edge to him that was rather attractive.'

This time Brianna's laugh was rich and explosive. 'That's just him, to a tee. He's all those things, and more. Oh, Mum, he's not just sexy, he's dedicated. You should have seen him out there, cool, calm, in control, saving lives.'

'Can this really be the same daughter who is usually so dismissive of men? Who delights in telling me all men are weak and pathetic, apart from her father?'

'Up to now, that's been true. But Mitch is neither weak nor pathetic. In fact I've never met someone so mentally strong, so sure of himself.'

Her mother studied her carefully. 'Watch out, Brianna. You mustn't let your admiration for his skill build up into anything more than that. I know it's exciting, meeting someone a bit different to your usual type, but don't go doing anything foolish. He moves in very different circles to ours.'

'Now you're being a snob.' Brianna dismissed her mother's concern. 'Just because he doesn't have rich parents. Not many men do.'

'That's not what I meant,' her mother replied seriously, her pale blue eyes showing nothing but love and concern. 'I remember when Margaret first talked about giving him a permanent job with the charity. She ran it by me, as her checks had revealed he'd been in trouble with the police when he was younger.'

'I'm sure it was just childhood rebellion,' Brianna replied dismissively, recalling her conversation with Mitch about cars.

Her mother rested a hand on her arm. 'I'm sure you're right,' she agreed softly. 'That's why we decided to recruit him anyway. From what I hear he's doing a sterling job and Margaret has never regretted it. He's a good man, I have no doubt. But I don't want you to get hurt, my darling.' Tenderly she tucked a loose curl back behind Brianna's ear. 'Your father and I have a really happy marriage. I think that fact alone gives me some right to advise you. The reason we get on so well is because we're two similar people, from similar backgrounds, wanting the same things out of life. As exciting as Mitch may seem, he is very different to you. He doesn't look the type who'd ever want to settle down. From what I recall, he pretty much went from the army into this job. He's never put down roots. Remember that.'

'Come on, Mum, it's not like I'm thinking of marrying him.' Brianna forced herself to smile, though the truth of her mother's words stung.

'Good, because I'm not sure he would be right for you.

You want someone more like your father. A man who understands you and where you come from. Who can mix with your friends. A man who loves you for you and not the money you come with.'

Though it hurt, Brianna knew what her mother was saying made sense. 'Well, you don't have to fret. Mitch and I haven't even arranged to see each other again. It was probably just a thing of the moment. A build-up of the emotion and tension that was part of being at the camp.'

They exchanged another long hug and Brianna disappeared thoughtfully back to her apartment. Why did it feel like she was deceiving her mother and herself with her words of reassurance? If it was just a casual fling, why did her heart lurch whenever she thought of him? Why, when she closed her eyes, could she still picture him so vividly? His stern, rugged face and deep brown eyes.

Brianna went to the bathroom and turned on the taps to the bath. She was tired from the journey and wasn't thinking straight. What she needed was a long, hot soak and a good night's sleep. Please God, when she woke up in the morning let her silly schoolgirl crush be a thing of the past.

Chapter Sixteen

Brianna felt slightly foolish as she walked towards Margaret's sparse, functional office at Medic SOS. All morning she'd told herself this *wasn't* a job interview. It was just a chat with one of her mother's friends about some ideas she had for the charity. But somehow her mind had got carried away and here she was, dressed in a smart suit, her heart thumping, her clasped hands trembling, feeling very much as though she was going into the most important interview of her life.

Just outside the open office door, Brianna paused and took a deep breath. She was offering to help, to provide her services to the charity for free. She had absolutely nothing to be nervous about. Other than making a total tit of herself, of course. Oh heck, maybe she could just sneak out without anyone noticing?

'Ah, Brianna. Please, come in.'

So much for disappearing. Plastering a smile on her face, she lifted her chin and walked into the office to shake Margaret's outstretched hand. The smile the other woman gave her was friendly enough, but Brianna knew Margaret. She wouldn't hold back if she disagreed with what she had to say.

'Thanks for seeing me.' Brianna returned the hearty handshake and sat down gratefully on the offered chair. At least now nobody could see her knees knocking.

'No problem. I was intrigued by your phone call.' Margaret sat opposite her, pushing her chair back a bit so she could lean comfortably against it. 'But before we get round to what you wanted to discuss, how did you find the trip?'

Brianna considered her words. 'A real eye-opener,' she confessed. 'You might hear about these disasters on the television, but nothing can prepare you for the reality of seeing tragedy up close. I have utter admiration for all the people working there.' Did she sound too gushing? Brianna paused and took another deep breath. 'Have you heard from them recently? How are things now?'

'They're getting there. Mitch thinks they should be back in a week. The rest of the agencies will be there for a few more months, helping to rebuild, but our work should be done. What were your impressions of the team?'

Brianna swallowed hard. Discussing the team was fine, but how could she do that without talking about Mitch? And how could she talk about him, without giving away her silly crush? At the mere mention of his name, her heart had jumped. 'They're professional, hard-working, capable, compassionate,' she replied quickly. 'I just don't know how they keep going back for more. I felt emotionally and physically drained when I left. I couldn't go back again.'

Margaret smiled. 'You say that now, but in a few weeks you might think differently. We always try to make sure that the staff have some time off before sending them out again. You're right though, it is exhausting work, on both the mind and the body.'

'Margaret,' Brianna began before the older lady could ask her any further questions, 'while I was there I had some thoughts about Medic SOS and how it could re-position itself amongst the relief agencies. I think it would make them more attractive to donors.'

'Well, don't hold back. Go for it. I'm always receptive to new ideas, especially if they help bring in the funding.'

With her heart in her mouth, Brianna handed over the report she'd compiled. 'I've outlined everything in here, so perhaps I can take you through it?'

Brianna spent the next hour discussing her plans and the details she'd worked up. Margaret listened attentively, asked searching questions, but gave away little of what she was thinking. So little that Brianna started to feel she was wasting her time. Maybe she was being ridiculous. After all, Medic SOS had survived very nicely for many years now. Moreover, it had grown from being a list of on-call doctors to a dedicated team. Who was she to think that, after one brief week, she could change the direction of the charity? She didn't even know anything about medicine.

But you know something about marketing, her mind kept telling her. You just have to make Margaret understand that.

'So you see,' she continued, trying desperately to make an impression, 'I think Medic SOS really has the potential to attract more funding by making it clearly different from the other aid agencies. In Mitch you already have a Chief Medical Officer who is known as an expert on severe trauma care, and who's built a team with similar capabilities. I've seen it for myself. Medic SOS get the tricky cases because they have the experience to deal with them. If the charity capitalise on this expertise in their marketing, it would make it easier to promote and thus bring in more revenue. With the increased funding you could expand, recruiting and training more personnel and buying further specialist equipment.'

Brianna didn't realise her eyes shone with enthusiasm, or that her voice betrayed her excitement. She only knew that she'd pitched her ideas with all her heart. If they fell on stony ground, then so be it. She had tried.

'You've obviously given this a great deal of thought,' Margaret replied, her face pleasant, but nothing more. 'However, I have to ask myself, what does this young lady know about medicine, or the work of medical staff in times of disaster? One week doesn't make you an expert.'

Brianna's heart sank. She had always known the charity head would be a tough nut to crack. 'I understand your reservations, believe me. If someone had told me a couple of weeks ago I'd be pitching an idea to market and expand a medical relief charity, I would have laughed in their face. I don't have experience of working in disaster areas, you're right, but I do have experience in marketing. It's what I did much of my degree in, and what I've focused on in the family business. I've also spoken to Mitch about my ideas and he thinks they have value.' Brianna felt she'd just played her last card. If the old bird didn't respect the thoughts of her Chief Medic, then she was a fool. Brianna didn't think she was.

At last, Margaret's face relaxed into a smile. 'I'm sure he did think that. Who wouldn't? You've put together an excellent proposal, Brianna. One I endorse wholeheartedly. Sometimes a fresh pair of eyes can see things that should have been blindingly obvious to those who work here day in, day out. The only question I have is would you be willing to see your ideas through? To work for the charity?'

Brianna thought her grin must be a mile wide. 'Yes, yes please!'

'I'm afraid we can't pay you much.'

'Good heavens, I don't want paying. Just the chance to make a difference.' Crikey that sounded corny, but Brianna's throat felt unusually tight and she had the uncomfortable feeling she was only a short step away from crying. She had to be crazy, getting emotional over taking an unpaid job. Or maybe, just maybe, the tears were because she'd found a direction for her life.

'Well, you'll certainly get a chance to make a difference.' Either Margaret hadn't seen her wobble, or she was discreetly ignoring it. 'One final thing, Brianna. I will expect you to work normal office hours. That means being in the office for nine o'clock each morning. I'm afraid I can't have you wandering in late and leaving early. It isn't fair on the rest of the team.'

For a moment Brianna hesitated. She thought of her life, of the parties, of the long, luxurious mornings lying in bed. She'd have to give up both in order to do this. Was it what she really wanted? Then she thought of the traumatised faces of the people she'd met in South America, and of the hard work the team put in to save lives. Really, working in a centrally heated office and going back to her elegant home each night wasn't so difficult. 'No problem.'

Margaret stood and shook Brianna's hand. 'Then welcome on board, Brianna.' The hand that clasped hers squeezed tightly, leaving Brianna to wonder if Margaret really was the battleaxe she pretended to be.

'Come and meet the office crew and find yourself a desk,' her new boss was saying. 'If you're going to work with us, there's no time like the present.'

With a laugh Brianna picked up her bag and followed Margaret out into the main office. It wasn't large, just a few simple workstations, a small kitchenette, two printers, and a couple of potted plants. When she'd worked for her father she'd been given a plush office, a leather chair, her own secretary. Here she was one of a small team in a basic environment.

She'd never felt more proud, or more delighted to be anywhere.

Several hours later, Brianna was finding it hard to remember why she'd been so excited about working for a living. Her eyes ached from looking at a computer screen and her brain ached from trying to understand how the charity worked, and who was responsible for what. She must be mad, she thought, as she drank her third cup of coffee that afternoon.

She could be sitting in a spa, or shopping. She sipped from the chipped cup. Or having freshly roasted coffee with her friends. What was she doing in a shabby little office, drinking instant coffee and trying to get her head around the workings of a medical relief agency?

'How are things, Mitch?'

Brianna's head shot up at the sound of his name. Sally, the office manager, was smiling into the phone. All of a sudden the middle-aged mother of three was acting like a coy schoolgirl. 'Well, just you take care of yourself, you hear me? You've been out there for nearly three weeks now. Time to come home.'

On impulse, Brianna scribbled a note to Sally asking to be put through to Mitch when she'd finished. Then she waited, heart hammering in her chest, for her phone to ring.

'Mitch, how are you?'

There was a pause. 'Brianna?'

Why did the sound of his deep voice cause her to tremble? If she'd thought a few days away from him would cure her of her infatuation, she was wrong. If anything, it was getting worse. 'Yes, it's me.' Not a cool, measured reply. More a breathy squeak.

'You convinced Margaret then?'

'Sure looks that way.' She hesitated, picking up a pen, then putting it down again. 'So I guess you and I will be seeing each other again from time to time.' Immediately she cringed.

'I guess we will,' he drawled with a casualness she'd tried, but totally failed, to convey.

'How is everybody?' she asked, wanting to keep him on the line.

'Well, Tessa's not talking to me. Apparently spoilt rich girls aren't my type.'

Brianna let out a chuckle. 'I got that impression from

her, too.' There was a pause during which she wanted to ask him if Tessa was right, but she swallowed the words. Too keen. There were lots of other things she was bursting to ask. How was he, really? Had there been any more mudslides? When exactly was he coming home? When he swam in the lake, or lay down in bed, did he think of her? The questions died on her lips. Always so confident around men, now she felt tongue-tied and awkward. 'Well then, I'll see you around.' Slowly she put down the phone.

'I hear you've met our Mitch.' Sally pushed back her chair and went to collect her coat.

'Yes, I was out there with them all last week.'

'My sources tell me he showed you more than just the camp.'

Brianna looked up sharply, but was pleased to find Sally was grinning. 'What can I say? He's a sexy man.'

Sally laughed out loud. 'You won't have any of us arguing with that. Well, good luck to you, love. Many have tried to crack him, but none have succeeded so far.'

'Oh, it's not serious,' Brianna replied quickly, anxious to get this part straight. 'We had a bit of fun, that's all.'

Back at the camp, Mitch turned the phone off thoughtfully. He had to admit to a fair degree of surprise that Brianna had actually gone and joined the charity. His money had been on her going back home and not giving the place a second thought. But no, the enthusiasm she'd shown at the camp, the desire to help, seemed to be genuine. Whilst that was great for the charity, it was going to be bloody awkward for him. Not least because, when he bumped into her in the office, he knew damn well he was going to find it very hard to keep his hands off her. Even now, just imagining her, he could feel the heat pulsing through his body. But continuing to sleep with a woman who was now a work colleague, as well as the patron's daughter, wasn't going to work. Relationships ended, at least his always did, and with the end came bitterness and bad feeling. He couldn't afford to taint his career with that, not when working for the charity meant so much to him. Not when it was all he had.

'Can I come in?'

Mitch turned from his desk to find Sam, the man in charge of the whole refugee camp and an old friend.

'Sam,' Mitch greeted him with a warm handshake. 'I wondered when I was going to see you.'

'Well, you could have come and found me, you know,' he replied, walking into the tent. 'Dan did. He also introduced me to your newest recruit.'

Mitch frowned. 'Pardon?'

'That gorgeous, classy bird with the shiny brown hair and flashing green eyes.' Sam grinned and wriggled his eyebrows expressively in appreciation.

'Umm, let me think, it's still hard to pin down.'

Sam laughed and slapped Mitch on the back. 'You old devil. How do you do it? Every time I look round you've added another woman to your harem. What with Jane—'

'Who's married,' Mitch interjected.

'And Tessa, who's not,' Sam replied with a sly smile. 'I thought you had enough on your plate. Now you add Brianna.'

'I haven't added anyone. Brianna is the daughter of our patron, and came to see what we were up to. If you've spoken to her, I'm sure you'll know all that already.'

'Well, if you had any sense you'd be grabbing that one with both hands. It's not often someone like you will get to meet such a classy lady. And smart too, from what I could gather.'

Mitch knew Sam meant no slight, but the truth of his words stung. 'She's not my type, Sam,' he told the older man. 'High maintenance and way out of my league. Now what was it you wanted to talk about, or did you just come here to wind me up?'

They sat down and went about discussing the business of transferring any outstanding casualties to the outlying hospitals. Medic SOS had been on site for nearly three weeks. It was time to begin the process of packing up and going home.

Chapter Seventeen

Though she was ashamed to admit it, this morning Brianna had taken extra care over getting dressed. The skirt she wore had been deliberately chosen to show off her legs, ending as it did several inches above her knees. She'd topped it with a deep green blouse, knowing it clung to her curves and accentuated the colour of her eyes. Finally she slipped on kitten-heeled sandals. They helped to dress down the outfit, but still added that touch of sexiness she was looking for. The mirror told her that her hair was smooth and casually styled, that her make-up was subtle but emphasised the shape of her eyes and the high cut of her cheekbones.

Today Mitch was back from South America. The word in the office was he'd be coming in, as he always did, to sort out the paperwork before heading home. It had been a week since she'd last seen him, but the time apart hadn't dimmed her desire one iota. If anything it had heightened it. So today she wanted to look irresistible. He'd seen Brianna on camp. Now she wanted him to see Brianna in her own environment; glamorous clothes, sophisticated make-up, sleek blow-dried hair. She wanted to knock him dead.

It was well into the afternoon by the time she managed to catch up with him. Having been holed up with Margaret for over an hour, he was making his way towards the open plan office as she was coming out of the ladies.

'Brianna.'

'Mitch.' Pretending casualness, she nodded in his direction, taking the opportunity to appraise him carefully. The last week hadn't dulled his sex appeal, but it had added to his dishevelled and frankly shattered appearance. The deep brown eyes were bloodshot, the lines on his face deeper and harsher than before. 'When was the last time you had a decent night's sleep?' she asked sympathetically, feeling a deep and alarming rush of tenderness towards him.

He half smiled. 'I can't remember.'

'You're on your way home, to bed, I hope.' Inside she cringed. She sounded like his damn mother.

His lips tightened, but he nodded his head, 'Yes, ma'am.'

'Well, I hope you're not planning on driving. Not in your condition.' Oh heck, now she'd gone from mother to matriarch. 'Sorry, that didn't come out like I'd planned.'

If anything his jaw clenched further. 'I'll be the judge of whether I'm capable of driving or not.'

'Well, when you're making that judgement, just remember that if you fall asleep at the wheel, it won't only be your life that's put in danger.' Oh, why was she firing off at him like a pompous twit when all she really wanted to do was fling her arms around him and tell him she'd missed him?

'I'm quite aware it wasn't my welfare you were concerned about,' he replied in a clipped voice. 'But the point is mute. My car's at home. I'm going back by train.'

'Oh.' Brianna sighed. This wasn't at all how she'd hoped their reunion would go. Far from being blown away by her looks, her stupid remarks, which she could only blame on nerves, had made him cross and irritated. 'Can I give you a lift to the station?'

It was on the tip of Mitch's tongue to say no, he was perfectly capable of getting to the damned station by himself, but he stopped himself. He was justified in being pissed with Brianna for treating him like her son – as if there were any similarities, any at all, between her and his mother – but to refuse a lift would be churlish. He was her work colleague now. He needed to get his act together and start behaving like one. Not stand here wishing she'd run up to him and thrown her arms around his neck. 'A lift would be good. Thank you.'

God but she was a sight for sore eyes, he thought as he followed her out. And his exhausted eyes were definitely that. He'd forgotten how bloody stunning she was. He could see the curves of her pert bottom ahead of him and his hands itched to touch. Heck, he was so damn punch-drunk with tiredness, he might just do it. Might just forget all the reasons why he shouldn't. Swiftly he shoved his hands into his pockets.

As they entered the small car park round the back, it didn't take much intuition to work out which was Brianna's car.

'Don't tell me, yours is the Jag.' It was the only one expensive, stylish and new enough to have possibly been hers. And it wasn't just any Jaguar. No, Brianna had to have the top of the range sporty XKR model, all power and understated luxury.

She pressed her key fob, and the Jag's indicators blinked in reply. 'Any complaints?'

He shrugged. 'I guess it beats a cab.'

'You silver-tongued devil.' Shaking her head, as if she couldn't believe his boorishness, she nodded to the passenger door. 'Don't expect me to open it for you.'

He grunted and let himself in. Nestling into the warm, leather interior, he was too tired to worry about his grouchy behaviour. Or to fret about comparisons between her sleek sports car and his own basic four-wheel drive.

Within moments, his eyes grew heavy and he was asleep.

Knowing Mitch wasn't one for conversation, Brianna didn't realise he'd fallen asleep until she arrived at the station. He looked so peaceful she hesitated to wake him up. What was the alternative? Should she take him home? She glanced in his direction once more. He was breathing slowly and deeply, the harsh lines on his face blissfully relaxed. Waking him up wasn't an option. It was too cruel. She reached into her handbag for her mobile phone.

'Sally? It's Brianna. I was taking Mitch to the station, but he's fallen asleep in the car. I thought I might as well take him home instead. Can you give me his address, please?'

She noted it down with interest. So, he lived by the sea did he? The man was full of surprises. She would have had him down for a city apartment. She put the address into her navigation system and saw it would take about an hour and half to drive him home. Well, that wasn't such a big deal. It wasn't as if she had any plans for the evening. At least none more important than taking Mitch home.

'Either a lot has changed in the last three weeks, or this isn't the way to the station.'

Brianna jumped at his voice and quickly turned the radio down. 'You fell asleep. I thought I might as well take you home.' She knew she sounded defensive, but she was worried he'd be cross with her.

Instead of the sharp retort she'd expected, his body relaxed. 'Do you know where you're going?'

'Address from Sally, instructions from the satnav.'

'Well, you seem to have everything under control.' And with that he fell back to sleep.

An hour and a bit later, Brianna turned the car onto the seafront and smiled to herself. There was something about the sea and the pounding of the waves that lifted the soul. Instantly she could see why he lived out here. Doing the job he did, how better to unwind, to get away from it all, than to come to the sea? Though it was May, today the clouds were grey and the sea reflected the dull shade. Not put off, she stopped the car, let down the sunroof and sucked in a deep breath. The smell of the salt spray, the sound of the waves as they crashed onto the shingle beach. She glanced sideways. The sexy man in her passenger seat, making her feel so very alive. It was glorious.

'I take it we're nearly there.' Mitch sat up in the car and fixed his sleepy brown eyes on her.

God, she ached to kiss him so much it was driving her mad. 'I thought the sea breeze would help wake you up,' she replied with a grin.

'Well, gee, thanks.'

Ignoring him, she carried on down the road and pulled up outside the address she had on her satnav. 'Oh, what a charming house.'

Delighted, she bounded out of the car, impatient to take a closer look. When Mitch made no move to get out, she turned her back on him and walked down the front path. Did he seriously expect her to just drop him off, turn round and go back? She'd driven him all the way here, the least he could do was let her see where he lived.

Slowly Mitch eased out of the car, stretching out his legs. Wasn't charming another word for small? He looked at his house and tried to see it through Brianna's eyes. A Victorian building, backing on to the sea. He kept it in good order, even doing a spot of gardening when he'd run out of other chores to do, but he had no doubt his *charming* house could fit into hers several times over.

Pulling his holdall out of the back, he tried to shrug off the chip weighing heavily on his shoulder. 'Thanks for the lift,' he said belatedly, catching up with her on the step. 'I'd offer you a drink, but I'm not sure whether Edna has stocked up the supplies or not.'

'Edna?'

'My elderly neighbour. She insists on knowing when I'm coming home so she can turn on my heating and fill up the fridge.'

'Well, why don't we go in and see? And if she hasn't I'm sure we can think of something else to do.' She trailed off, giving him a coy, flirty grin.

Despite his tiredness and his wariness around her, Mitch couldn't help but laugh. 'I think we'd better hope she's been in. I doubt I'm capable of much more than boiling the kettle.'

He opened the door and before he could say mind the step, she'd darted in. He was close behind, noting the post neatly stacked on the sideboard, a strong indication Edna had, indeed, already been in. The relaxing warmth from the radiators confirmed his suspicion.

'Well, it looks like we're in luck. Coffee, tea?' he asked.

'Tea would be great, thank you. I won't expect herbal.' After giving him a teasing smile she slipped off her shoes and wandered into the front room.

He filled the kettle but as he waited for it to boil he couldn't resist craning his neck round the corner, observing her as she had a poke around. Did she notice the large patio doors opening onto the wooden sun deck? The original open fire. The state of the art flat screen television. Or did she see a worn rug and battered leather sofa. Books and magazines scattered untidily across a stained coffee table. A wetsuit thrown carelessly over the back of an old armchair.

He huffed and turned his attention back to the tea. It didn't matter what she thought, he told himself. It was his house, his choices.

When he went to join her she was curled up on his sofa, looking for all the world like a regular visitor. He felt a dart of annoyance, but couldn't explain why. Was it because he felt safer pigeonholing her as a stuck up rich bird, than seeing her looking so at home on his sofa?

He thrust the steaming mug of tea under her nose. 'Sorry I couldn't find the Royal Doulton.'

It was an ungracious comment. He knew it. So, by the look she gave him, did she. Irritated that he felt so damn awkward in his own house, he went to sit on the armchair, pushing the wetsuit onto the floor. It landed with a plonk, the sound bouncing round the otherwise silent room.

'Do you surf?' she asked, just as the quiet was becoming uncomfortable.

'Occasionally.' He was about to leave it at that, but he'd already made a big enough prat of himself. Time to show her he could be decent. When pushed he could even make polite conversation. 'But the waves aren't really big enough on this coast. Mostly I go windsurfing.' He swigged at his tea, then forced a smile. 'Look, thanks for driving me home, Brianna. If you hadn't I'd still be on the train, probably fast asleep and having missed my change.'

'It was my pleasure. That's what work colleagues are for.'

None of his previous colleagues had ever sat on his sofa. Or looked so damn sexy doing it. He cleared his throat. 'I guess this is where I should say welcome to Medic SOS. If I'm honest, I didn't really think you'd follow through on your ideas.'

'Oh?' She pinned him with those green eyes. 'Of course, you still have me down as the flighty rich girl who hasn't done a day's work in her life.'

He shrugged to hide his discomfort. Her words were very close to the truth. 'You don't exactly have to work for a living.'

'No, I don't, but that doesn't mean I'm not prepared to try.'

Her chin was angled, her head held high, daring him to disagree with her. This time his smile was spontaneous. 'I can see that, and I admire you for it.'

He was amused, and surprised, to see her blush at his small compliment. It made him wonder if she was ever complimented on anything other than her looks. 'I take it Margaret liked your ideas?'

Her face lit up with pride. 'Yes, she did. She's agreed we should look at making Medic SOS a specialist trauma group. It's there already, really. We'd just be formalising it and then capitalising on it.'

His interest piqued, he sat forward on the chair. 'We'd need more equipment and training. Definitely more staff, as we'd need specialists rather than the on-call generalists we tend to rely on. That all requires money.'

'I can get that.'

He raised his eyebrows and couldn't resist a short laugh. 'I bet you can.'

They discussed the charity for a bit longer and it was dark outside when Brianna finally stood up. 'I guess it's time I hit the road. You look done in.'

As she eased off the sofa and bent to pick up her shoes, Mitch's breath caught in his throat. It was right that she was going, he reminded himself as his body made a mockery of his tiredness by becoming instantly alert at the sight of her rounded backside in that tight skirt. Those endless legs. They couldn't continue to sleep together. Not now she worked for the charity.

'You don't have to go.' Christ, where on earth had those words come from? He'd just broken every one of his promises to himself. He was weak, so flaming weak – but he wanted her. In fact at that moment it went beyond a simple want. He needed to have her.

She straightened up, her face looking as shocked as he felt. 'I thought you said you weren't capable of doing anything more than boiling a kettle?'

Slowly he raised himself off the armchair and stood in front of her. Mouth aligned with her inviting lips, chest aligned with the curve of those tantalising breasts. 'A man would have to be comatose not to be able to respond to you,' he replied hoarsely.

A grin split her face and she raised her arms to encircle his neck. 'So you do give out compliments.'

He shook his head. 'It wasn't a compliment. I just tell it the way I see it.'

'Well then, I'd be delighted to stay.' She moved in and lightly kissed his lips. With a groan he yanked her harder towards him and deepened the kiss.

As her body moulded to his, Brianna was very aware of Mitch's lean shape and strong muscles. Also of his very obvious desire for her. This was what she'd dreamt about for the last week, she acknowledged as she melted in his arms. But as the kiss grew hotter and his hands snaked underneath her clothing, he abruptly pulled away, resting his forehead against hers.

'For both our sakes, I need a shower first.'

Brianna leant in and took a deep smell of musky, travel-worn man. 'You don't have to on my behalf.'

Groaning he grabbed hold of her hand and started up the stairs. 'Come and have a shower with me.'

Clothes flew around the room and it wasn't long before they were standing under the hot, steamy spray of the shower.

'I hope you're not expecting foreplay,' he said roughly as he pushed her against the shower wall.

Intoxicated by him, she laughed. 'Nope. You've already told me you're not a fan of that.'

His eyes fell to her breasts and he dipped his head. 'Maybe with you I'll make an exception.'

As his tongue played with her nipples, her breath came out in a lusty moan. 'Umm, I'll look forward to that. But not this time.' Reaching her arms around his neck, she pulled herself up so her legs were round his hips. 'Take me now, Mitch. I'm all yours.'

As he thrust hungrily into her, Brianna had just enough time to wonder about the truth of the words she'd spoken. Then she lost the ability for any conscious thought.

Chapter Eighteen

The following morning Brianna was carefully watching a pan of spitting bacon when she heard a knock on the door. She looked up at the stairs, but there was no sound from the bedroom where she'd left Mitch half an hour ago, still sound asleep. Should she answer it? Or was that too personal a thing to do for a man she didn't really know?

There was another knock.

'Hello, Mitch. Are you there? It's Edna.'

Hearing the old lady's voice through the letter box, Brianna turned the gas down low and went to open the door.

'Oh, hello dear. Sorry, I didn't realise Mitch had a lady friend over.'

Brianna smiled down at the visitor. She was short, only reaching her shoulders and her hair was neatly scraped into a grey bun at the back of her head. Edna's face carried the wrinkles of old age, but the blue eyes currently scrutinising every inch of Brianna were far from dull. They were lively and, at that moment, very interested.

'I'm afraid Mitch is asleep,' Brianna explained cautiously, well aware the old lady was putting two and two together and making more than a casual night spent in Mitch's bed actually justified. 'I'm Brianna. You must be the helpful neighbour he talks about. Pleased to meet you.' Brianna went to shake the wizened old hand.

'Well, it's good to see he's finally found somebody to look after him. I keep telling him, it's not right for a man of his age to live alone. Especially with all the travelling he does. He needs someone to come home to.' Edna didn't wait to be invited in. She breezed past Brianna and into the kitchen where she settled herself down on one of the chairs.

'Oh, it's not like that. Mitch and I, we're just ...' Brianna trailed off, feeling silly. What exactly were they? Lovers? Maybe, but could she really call them lovers after a few rounds of passion? And anyway, she couldn't say that to Edna. Friends? She wasn't even sure she could call them that. 'We're just work colleagues,' she finished.

'Really? Work colleagues never made bacon and eggs for each other in my day.' Edna twinkled back at her. 'I'll leave you to it, my dear. If you want some advice from me, I would snap that young man up. If I were thirty years younger, I would do it myself. Sometimes I wonder where all the time went.' She patted Brianna on her arm. 'He can be a bit surly at times, but deep down he's a good man. You look after him.'

Mitch had slept like the dead, but woke with a raging hunger. He thought back to the last twenty-four hours and realised it was hardly surprising, as he hadn't eaten. He'd meant to eat before he went to bed, but he'd been distracted by Brianna. He smiled as he remembered last night. Definitely worth missing a meal for. Lazily he stretched and, grabbing a pair of jeans, padded down the stairs to find something to eat.

Two things struck him as he walked towards the kitchen. First was the smell of bacon, which had his digestive juices churning in his stomach. Second was the sound of female voices. The first delighted him, the second didn't.

'There you are, Mitch. I was just saying to your young lady, she needs to look after you.'

Much as he liked Edna, at that particular moment he could happily have throttled her. He didn't bloody well need looking after. Not by any woman, and certainly not by Brianna. He was perfectly happy with his life as it was, thank you very much.

He must have telegraphed his annoyance because Brianna

glanced warily over at him. 'Edna just came round to check you were okay,' she told him in a tone a zookeeper might use to calm a mean-looking lion.

Mitch nodded and battled to get his temper under control. Edna had his best interests at heart. He might not always want or need her help, but that didn't mean he couldn't show some gratitude for what she insisted on doing. When his temper was back on its leash, he walked over to the older woman and planted a quick kiss on her lined cheek. 'Thanks for filling the fridge, Edna. And for coming over. As you can see, I'm still in one piece.'

Edna looked him up and down. 'Only just. You look tired and too thin.'

He laughed briefly. 'I'm going to sleep and eat for the next week. I promise.'

'Well then, I'll leave you to it. It looks like you're in good hands.' She smiled over at Brianna.

Mitch caught the glance and sighed. God save him from meddling women. Needing some space before he spoke to Brianna, he walked Edna to the door.

Having seen out the first of the two women, Mitch turned back and wondered what he was going to do about the second. Much as he'd enjoyed Brianna last night, he wasn't comfortable with having her in his home this morning, cooking in his kitchen. It smacked of an intimacy he had no desire for. Women didn't sleep in his bed. They didn't stay over. Those were his rules. Rules he seemed to have totally forgotten last night during the grip of lust.

'You don't want me here, do you?' Brianna noted as she leant back against the cooker.

Wearing yesterday's clothes, her hair gloriously tangled and her face without make-up, she shouldn't look more desirable than she had the day before. And he shouldn't still want her.

'I didn't say that,' he replied stiffly.

'You didn't have to. It was clear when you came down the stairs. It was there in your eyes, in your body language.' She turned round to turn off the gas. 'Well, you don't have to worry. I'm on my way out.'

Mitch cast his eyes over to the work surface where she'd found a tray and put on it two pieces of buttered bread, a glass of orange juice and a mug. She'd obviously been intending to bring him breakfast in bed. Brianna, who had probably never cooked a meal in her rich little life. He glanced from the tray to her. The way she chewed at her bottom lip and stared at him with large, mutinous eyes. Moments ago he'd felt irritated at the sight of her in his kitchen, now he was inexplicably touched.

As she turned to leave, he caught her by her shoulders. 'Stop, please. I'm not used to having women make me breakfast, that's all.'

'It's not much of a breakfast,' she muttered, tears hovering in her eyes. 'I'm no good at cooking. The bacon is burnt, and the coffee looks so strong I think the teaspoon is standing up in it.'

Mitch laughed, long and deep. 'Well, I appreciate the gesture, honestly.' God, how could any man be safe around her? She was so damned gorgeous he ached. He bent to kiss those lovely full lips. A few minutes ago he'd wanted her gone. Now he couldn't get enough of her.

Trying to claw back his control, he slowly drew back. 'Much as I'd love to continue this, my stomach is screaming with hunger.'

He poked at the bacon in the pan and scooped some up to put between the bread. 'Aren't you having any?'

She shook her head. 'I've had some toast.' She watched as he took a swig of the coffee she'd made. 'I'm impressed. You're not pulling a face.'

'I am inside.' She gave him a sharp dig, enough to make him grunt.

'So, what are you doing this weekend?'

Warily, he shrugged. 'No real plans. Probably some windsurfing at some point.'

'Good. You can teach me.'

'Now wait a minute ...' He swallowed down another mouthful and stared at her. 'That depends,' he countered.

She raised an eyebrow. 'On what?'

'On whether we both know where we stand. We work together. I don't want this getting messy. No strings, just a bit of fun.'

She smirked slightly and fished around in the pan for some bacon. 'Umm, fun. I didn't think you knew the meaning of the word.'

'Maybe it's about time I learnt.' He abandoned his plate and reached for her. 'Starting from now.'

With a laugh Brianna wriggled away from his grasp. 'Much as I would love to stay, I've got a job to go to.' She gave a self-deprecating chuckle. 'Now those are words I didn't think I'd ever utter. I'll be here at eleven o'clock on Saturday.'

Before he had a chance to disagree she closed her lips firmly over his, giving him one final toe-curling kiss. When he was totally churned up, to the point of getting ready to drag her upstairs again, she spun out of his grasp and let herself out.

As the door closed behind her, he lifted his eyes to the ceiling and exhaled slowly. He must be going soft in the head. He didn't do relationships. So why had he just allowed Brianna to make plans to see him at the weekend?

It could only be because he wanted to see her sexy little curves in a wetsuit.

With a resigned smile he went to clear up the mess she'd

left behind her. The girl wasn't kidding when she said she couldn't cook. Debris from her attempt was littered all round his kitchen. Scraping the charred remains of the bacon into the bin, he reflected he was due some fun, and Brianna was certainly that. She was also so plainly out of his league, there wasn't going to be any of the usual pressure for anything heavy.

She wanted to experience life outside her usual social circle for a change. He needed to relax and enjoy himself more. Both of them knew the score.

Chapter Nineteen

If anyone had said to him a month ago that he would be sitting on his balcony on a Saturday morning waiting for a classy lady to turn up in her Jaguar, he would have told them where to get off. But here he was. Even more surprising, he was looking forward to seeing her. Whether he would still be saying that by the end of the day was another matter.

Right on time, she knocked on his door. Today she was dressed in casual jeans and a leather jacket. She still exuded enough sophistication and glamour to knock him sideways.

'Are you going to stand there all morning, or are you going to let me in?' With a swish of her silky hair she glided past him and into the house. When she'd reached the sitting room, she turned and smiled back at him. 'So, what are the plans?'

His mind filled with the sight of her, it took him a moment to realise she'd asked him a question. 'Plans? I thought we were going windsurfing?'

'Yes, we are,' she agreed happily. 'But we're not going to do that all day, are we?'

Like wading through a bog, he slowly came to grips with the conversation. What on earth was she expecting? Was he supposed to have prepared an itinerary, laid on a few surprises? Is that what men did in her world? 'Brianna, are you playing games here? What else do you expect?'

Some of the happiness left her face. 'Well, nothing, I guess. Windsurfing is fine.'

'But you were hoping for ... what?'

She shook her head. 'Look, it doesn't matter. I'm happy doing whatever you want. As long as it's with you, I don't care.'

'Even if it means windsurfing all day?'

Dropping her bag on the floor, she slowly walked up to him, placed her hands on his shoulders and moved in for a kiss. 'Yes,' she murmured softly.

As if she'd flicked on a switch, his body was instantly on fire. Within moments his hands were under her shirt, undoing her bra, teasing her breasts.

'Bedroom?' she asked on a breathy whisper.

He shook his head. 'No time.' He pushed her back on the sofa and systematically removed her clothes with barely controlled aggression. Then base instincts took over and within moments he was inside her, taking her with a ferocity that blew his mind.

Carefully he levered himself up from the sofa and thrust an unsteady hand through his now dishevelled hair. What was it about Brianna that made him unable to keep his hands off her? She'd barely been in his house a few minutes before he'd torn off her clothes. He glanced at the discarded items littering the floor. He hadn't even let her go upstairs to the bedroom, for God's sake. He'd acted like an animal on heat. Remembering their time in the camp, when he'd accused her of wanting to find out what it was like to make love with a bit of rough, he felt ashamed. Now she knew.

'Sorry,' he apologised grimly, hauling himself off the sofa.

Brianna lifted her head and raised her eyebrows. 'Err, what for exactly?'

Simmering with embarrassment and a fair amount of self-disgust, he found his boxers and yanked them on. 'I could at least have offered you a drink first.'

'You could,' she agreed slowly. 'But I much preferred your alternative welcome.'

'What, being jumped on before you'd even taken your jacket off?' He'd like to bet her usual dates didn't greet her like that.

Brianna stood up from the sofa and, clearly comfortable in her nakedness, slid her arms around his waist. 'Absolutely. Do I look like a woman who hasn't been totally and utterly pleasured?'

Mitch studied her face. Her eyes danced, her lips curved. She sure didn't have the appearance of someone who'd been forced to endure something they didn't want to do. In fact she looked happy, satisfied and downright gorgeous. 'No, you don't.' He shook his head. 'If your parents could see you now.' With that he moved away from the circle of her arms and went to retrieve his discarded jeans.

Thoughtfully Brianna began to pull on her underwear. He was right. If her parents could see her now they probably wouldn't be best pleased. Her mother had already warned her off Mitch and Brianna was prepared to admit she might have a point. There was a lot about the man she didn't know. She cast him a surreptitious glance as he pulled on his shirt, the muscles of his chest rippling, the panther tattoo flashing menacingly before being hidden by the sleeve. But it was that very hint of bad boy about him that made him so irresistible.

'Did you bring your wetsuit?' Mitch asked as he did up the buttons on his fly.

Brianna nodded, looking around for her jeans. She spotted them thrown over the back of the leather armchair. 'It's in the car.'

Mitch crooked a smile, staring at her matching midnight-blue bra and pants. 'If you go out dressed like that, Edna will have a heart attack. I'd better get it. Where are your keys?'

Several minutes and some hysterical laughter later, at least from Brianna, they headed out of Mitch's patio doors and down to the beach. Brianna had never worn a wetsuit. She'd only bought it the day before and couldn't believe how tightly they fitted, or how they emphasised every bump.

'I feel positively indecent going out like this,' she complained as they walked across the pebbles.

He gave her a dark look. 'I can't say it leaves much to the imagination. But it will give me something to look at while you're falling off the board.'

She punched him heartily on the arm. 'No way. I'm going to be good at this. Just you watch and see.'

An hour later, Brianna was eating her words, along with most of the English Channel. 'It's impossible,' she spluttered, glaring at the board as she fell off yet again. 'You windsurfers must have special shoes or something that stick you to the board.'

He flashed one of his rare smiles. 'Staring down the board, daring it to throw you off, isn't going to work you know.'

She tried in vain a few more times until finally he took pity on her. 'Here, why don't you have a rest and watch me for a bit.'

'Nothing like showing off,' she muttered, but gratefully plonked herself down on the beach. She wasn't going to let him know it, but she was dying to see how good he was. If he was anything like as good to watch in the water as he was to watch out of it, she would enjoy the next hour a lot more than she had the last.

She arranged herself comfortably on the beach, propping her head up against her bag and prepared to ogle. A woman was entitled to ogle, especially if she was sleeping with the man she was ogling. Stretching out, she let out a sigh of pure female admiration. He looked heavenly in his gear, the wetsuit emphasising the breadth of his shoulders, the lean lines of his body. His trim, athletic backside. Several times this morning she'd had to ask him to repeat himself as she'd been distracted by the sexy grin, the humour-filled brown eyes. This relaxed, dryly amused Mitch McBride was very different to the austere, distant persona she'd seen at the camp. She found she liked him. A lot.

They stopped for lunch at a little kiosk on the seafront where he ordered them both hot tea and sandwiches. The day had turned out different to her expectations, which she was ashamed to admit had included only a short stint in the water followed by a very long lunch in a fancy restaurant, but as she sat next to Mitch on the beach, she couldn't remember ever appreciating the seaside more.

'This is nice,' she sighed, leaning back against the stones, enjoying the warmth of the sun on her face.

'What? A kiosk sandwich and a cup of stewed tea?'

She glowered at him. 'Being by the sea, in the sun.' She wanted to add *being with you*, but wasn't sure how well it would be received. 'On dry land.'

His answering laugh was a deep rumble that made her toes curl. 'I hate to say this, princess.' He merely grinned when she frowned at the use of the nickname. 'But you asked me to teach you how to windsurf. I'm not stopping until I've done just that. Time to get up, and back onto that board.'

He stretched out a hand and pulled her up sharply, causing her to bounce into him. Instantly his mouth swooped on hers and they shared a long, deep kiss. 'Now you're just trying to distract me,' he murmured as he drew back.

'We could ditch the windsurfing and go back to yours,' she suggested coquettishly, fluttering her eyelashes at him.

'Don't tempt me.' He took her firmly by the arm and led her back to the board.

By the end of the afternoon she finally had the hang of

it. She wasn't stylish, but she was actually standing upright, turning the sail and manoeuvring the board in vaguely the right direction. Her sense of accomplishment was huge and so, she thought ruefully, would be the bruises.

After arriving back at his house exhausted but content, she went up to get a hot shower. The perfect cure for a day in the cold sea. As the spray pummelled her body, she studied the bathroom for telltale signs of Mitch. His shower gel smelt of the fresh sea air and brought back memories of the first time she'd slept with him and inhaled that same smell from his skin. On the sink was a single toothbrush, reassuring her he was a man who lived by himself and didn't often have female visitors. He must wet shave, as his shaver and foam were on the shelf by the sink. It was fascinating, these little glimpses into his life.

'Feeling warmer?' Mitch asked as she made her way back down the stairs.

'Much better, now I'm not being plunged into ice cold water.' She eyed the glowing flames from the fire he'd just made and sighed. 'All I need now is to snuggle down in front of that fire.'

Mitch watched as she did just that, tucking her feet up under her and lying back against the soft cushions. She was certainly making herself at home and he wasn't quite sure what to make of it. On the one hand it was his space, his sofa by the fire. On the other, she looked so beautiful and seemed to fit the place naturally.

Brianna caught him staring at her. 'What's wrong?'

Aware he'd been stuck in some sort of trance, Mitch mentally shook himself. He was too obsessed with his own independence. She was only staying the night. At least he guessed that was what she was planning and, considering the lateness of the hour, the long drive back to hers and the fact that she'd stayed over the last time, it wasn't an unreasonable intention. Still. It left him feeling slightly on edge. A smidgen unnerved. His *no stopping over* rule tossed straight out of the window again, twice in a week. 'Nothing's wrong,' he muttered, moving to the door. 'I'm going to have a shower. Grab yourself a drink.'

When he came back downstairs he found her exactly where he'd left her, only this time with a glass of wine in her hand.

'Fish and chips okay for you?' he asked, belatedly realising he hadn't thought this day through at all. What guy has an elegant lady staying in his house and offers her fish and chips? A total loser, that's who. 'Then again, maybe you don't eat food that comes wrapped in paper?'

She flinched. 'Of course I do.'

'Sorry.' He put up his hand in a gesture of peace. 'That came out without me thinking.' Or more accurately, it came out because he was pissed off with his own lack of sophistication.

'Mitch, I'm a normal human being, you know.' Her sharp glare revealed both hurt and anger. 'Just because my parents are wealthy it doesn't make me any different from the next person.'

'Perhaps, in some respects,' he agreed. 'But your experiences are very different to mine. That can have a profound effect on your outlook, on how you think and feel.'

'Well, right now I'm feeling like you're having a dig at me. I can't help being rich.'

'No.' He couldn't help where he'd come from, either. But it didn't make the two of them right together. Sighing, he picked up his car keys and turned towards the door.

They ate their fish and chips off their laps. Mitch had come back in a better mood than he'd gone out in and, between the glow from the fire, the food in their stomachs and the alcohol, the atmosphere was cosy and relaxed. It still rankled with Brianna that he couldn't seem to see her simply as a woman, rather than a rich woman, but she had to let that go. In time he would grow to see her differently. If he'd let them have that time.

'Mitch, why did you join Medic SOS?' Brianna asked as she put down her empty plate. 'You said you worked in the army, and then A & E in a civilian hospital. So why change?'

He took a drink of his beer and settled back into the fireside chair. 'I was bored. It might sound stupid but I missed the challenge of working in difficult conditions. Medic SOS gave me back that challenge, plus the knowledge I was helping real suffering, in areas that badly needed that help.'

Brianna nodded. She could see what he meant, but it still seemed like a tough career choice. 'Joining the army is an unusual move for a graduate doctor, isn't it? Why that rather than a traditional hospital?'

'Why not?'

Exasperated, Brianna poured herself some more wine. 'Come on, that's no answer. I'm interested, that's all. Why is asking you any questions about your private life like pulling teeth? You know it's because you're so evasive that I think you're hiding exciting secrets. If you were more open I wouldn't probe so much.'

'Is that a promise?'

She eyed him through her lashes. 'Yes, so spill the details, doctor.'

He put his hands up in mock surrender. 'Okay, okay. I joined the army because it sounded exciting and because I didn't have any family or a base that tied me to any particular place.'

Now she was getting somewhere. 'So your parents had died by this time?'

'I never knew my father, but yes, my mother had died.'

'When?'

'Several years before, when I was fourteen.'

'Oh, Mitch, you poor thing. I am sorry.'

'I wasn't.'

His blunt statement shocked her. As did the way his face suddenly turned as harsh as his voice. 'What did she die of?'

For a fraction of a second his hand clenched on his glass. Then he carefully schooled his features back into a blank mask. 'It's not important.'

His reaction said otherwise, but she'd learnt enough about the man to know he wasn't going to be pushed anywhere he didn't want to go, so she changed tactics. 'Who looked after you when your mother died? Did you have a stepfather?'

'I didn't have a stepfather, no.'

Brianna fought to keep the impatience from her voice. 'So who took care of you? Relatives? Foster parents?' When he simply gave a slight shake of his head, Brianna's heart crumpled. 'Oh, Mitch, you didn't go into care, did you?'

'No.' He paused, his expression so guarded she thought that was all he was going to say on the matter. It was a surprise when he spoke again into the silence. 'I was lucky to find a woman prepared to take me in. She looked after me for a while. Put me on the straight and narrow. She even paid for me to go to university.'

Briefly his eyes flickered, giving her a sense that this person was important to him. 'She sounds like one special lady. Are you still in touch with her?'

Instantly the shutter came down again. 'No, I'm not. She broke the contact.'

He stared broodingly into the fire, his face set back into

hard lines and Brianna kicked herself. Why had she spoilt the mood by insisting on finding out more about him? She wanted the relaxed man back, the one she'd been with all day. Slowly she uncurled from the sofa and went to sit on his lap. 'I think that's enough questions for now, don't you?' she asked, smoothing his hair from his brow.

With a groan, he settled his arms around her and sought out her mouth. 'Come to bed.'

She laughed. 'I thought you'd never ask.'

Chapter Twenty

It seemed natural they spend Sunday together. At least it did to Brianna, who'd shown no signs of heading home after breakfast. Mitch was surprised to find he had no desire to push her out. It was the first time he'd spent a weekend with a woman yet so far he'd had no urge to reclaim his space. He hadn't felt irritated when she'd perched where he usually sat on the sofa, and had even enjoyed her commentary on the newspaper she'd been reading. As they strolled back from a relaxing pub lunch, he wondered what it was about her that made her such good, easy company.

'Come on, show me your stone skimming skills. I'll wager ten pounds I can do more skips than you.' Brianna bounded down to the sea, her hair flowing in the wind, cheeks flushed and face alive with laughter.

There was his answer. She was such good company because she was fun. He'd never met anyone so full of life. She made him feel young. He bent down to snatch up a flat stone. 'You're on.'

The contest was hard fought and Mitch was more than a little surprised she was so good at skimming stones. 'Where did you hone your skills then?' he asked after one particularly good throw had bounced off the sea six times.

'My parents have a house by a lake in Italy. We used to go there a lot when I was a child, usually with a group of friends who also had children. I was the only girl, so I was determined to beat the boys.' She eyed up his stone. 'Go on then, see if you're man enough to beat a girl.'

Mitch grinned, put his arm back and produced a beauty. They watched it skip ten times before it sunk into the sea. 'Ten pounds I believe?'

'Damn you. I bet you wouldn't have done that if I hadn't riled you.' Just then her mobile phone rang. 'Hello? Hi Melanie ... I'm with Mitch.' She cast a furtive look at him. 'Umm, yes, very well. Details later.' She giggled, blushing slightly, and he had no doubt what was being discussed. Before he had a chance to be put out, she was laughing. 'Very funny. As it happens we're not in bed, but it would take us too long to get there so we'll have to pass. Thanks for asking though. Bye.'

Mitch quirked an eyebrow at her.

'My friend, Melanie. A crowd of them are going to watch a polo game this afternoon. She was asking if I wanted to go along.' She grinned. 'Providing we'd made it out of bed.'

He chose to ignore the fact that these two women were discussing his sex life. 'Polo?' he asked instead. 'Is that really what you do on a Sunday?'

Brianna sighed. *Here we go again*. Mitch was wearing that look. The one that said she was rich, and he wasn't. Would he ever forget about her damn money? 'No, of course it isn't,' she retorted sharply.

'Never?'

She squirmed slightly. 'Okay, yes we go to polo sometimes. Satisfied?'

'What do you do when you're not at polo?'

Relieved they were back onto more neutral ground, Brianna threaded her arm through his. 'There's a crowd of us that tend to go round together. Sometimes we go to each other's houses, sometimes to a party or club.' When he asked, she named a high profile club in London. 'What about you?'

'Very similar,' he replied dryly.

She elbowed him sharply in the ribs. 'Come on. This is called conversation. I tell you a bit about me, you tell me a bit about you. You'll get the hang of it in time.'

He shook his head, laughing softly. 'I'm not sure I will, but okay. I run along the beach, windsurf, read the newspapers, relax.'

'That sounds a bit lonely,' she remarked quietly.

He raised his eyebrows in surprise. 'I'm not lonely. I enjoy my own company. When I'm working, I'm surrounded by people all of the time. When I come home, it's nice to chill.'

But even when you're on camp you don't socialise, Brianna wanted to retort, but she thought better of it.

It was a lazy Sunday and Brianna was amazed to find it after six o'clock when she finally looked at the time. They were snoozing together on the sofa, having spent most of the afternoon making love. When it came to sex, Mitch had both stamina and a voracious appetite, a very welcome combination in her book.

'I guess it's time I hit the road.' She sat up slowly, uncaring that she was naked. He loved her body. She knew by the way his eyes darkened when he looked at her. It felt incredible to know she had that power over him, physically at least.

'Have I tired you out?' He stretched his tall frame across the sofa, arms folded behind his head, his hair flopping messily over his forehead.

God he was beautiful. Not conventionally of course. His face was too rugged for that. But there was so much coiled strength, both in his mind and his body. She hadn't realised what an aphrodisiac that was. Cocking him a grin, she reached over to run her fingers over the hard planes of his chest. As his taut abdominal muscles quivered, she felt another stirring of desire.

'Brianna, you need to stop that now, or you won't be going anywhere.'

Pouting provocatively, she bent to pick up her clothes. Suddenly she was grabbed from behind.

'Damn you woman, why can't I get enough of you?' His voice was harsh, almost angry.

Brianna turned to say something, but her mouth was captured by his and once more she was lost.

'I really have to go now,' she said a little while later as she finally moved off the sofa and started to get dressed.

For a moment his eyes rested heatedly on her chest. 'I'll be sorry to see those breasts tucked away, but it's probably for the best. If we carry on like this I'll end up hospitalised with clinical exhaustion.'

She was thrilled she had that effect on him but much as she loved the sex, she wanted more. Would he let her in? 'When was the last time you went to the cinema?' she asked, shrugging on her shirt.

'Cinema?' He'd hauled himself off the sofa and was tugging on his jeans, concentrating on the buttons of the fly. 'I can't remember. Probably to see *The Guns of Navarone.*'

Brianna widened her eyes in shock, then threw a sock at him. 'Very funny, though knowing you it won't be too wide off the mark. Why don't you come up during the week and I can show you what normal people do on a night out?'

Her invitation was met with a wall of silence. She couldn't read his expression, his head was bent, but she saw his fingers falter on the buttons. Damn, she'd pushed him too far.

Wordlessly they finished dressing. Then he walked over to the patio doors and looked out at the rolling waves. 'Brianna, I just want to get one thing clear. I don't do relationships. If you want cosy dates, followed by hearts and flowers, you need to go and find somebody else.'

Her heart plummeted and her hands shook slightly as she wrestled the remaining boot onto her foot. 'Well, you're certainly honest.' When she'd finished she stared up at his profile, so aloof, so distant again. What was he so bloody afraid of?

'I believe in total honesty,' he replied, turning slightly so she could see his full face. Not that it helped, he was so flaming unreadable. 'That way nobody gets hurt.'

It's too late for that. 'So, if I don't get hearts and flowers and protestations of love, what do I get?'

'Heat, passion. You and me, in bed.'

He wasn't wrong there, but she was starting to wonder if that was enough. Her feelings were running beyond simple lust and into something ... more. He wasn't immune to her, she could see that, but he had this big wall around him he didn't seem to let anyone through. Would he let her in, given time?

'Mitch, have you ever had a proper relationship with a woman?'

He looked slightly taken aback. 'Define proper.'

'You know, a commitment between two people that you're not going to see anybody else. A relationship where you make plans to see each other again, go on dates, enjoy weekends away.'

He looked back at her through narrowed eyes. 'No, not in those terms.'

'Why not? What are you scared of?' she asked softly, walking up to him and putting her arms around his rigidly set shoulders.

Impatiently he shrugged her off. 'I'm not scared of anything. I learnt long ago not to rely on anybody else. It's a philosophy that's stood me in good stead and I'm not about to start changing it now.'

Hurt that he wouldn't let her close, Brianna had half a mind to tell him to bugger off. But then she caught a glimpse of pain in his eyes and her heart melted. There was a reason for his aloof nature, his determination not to let anybody into his life. 'Who hurt you, Mitch?'

He gave her a long, cool stare. 'Why do you assume somebody has?'

'Because the man I've seen hold a child's hand as he died, the man who gives up most of his life to care for others, the man I've just spent the weekend with, he's different to the man who's standing in front of me now. When you're not consciously thinking about blocking people out, you're a wonderful, warm person. So something happened in your past that's made you wary of letting anybody get close to you.'

His eyes were flat, unmoved by her speech. 'Or maybe I'm just a selfish person who prefers his own company and has no desire to ever share his life with anybody else.'

Exasperated, angry with him for being so cold and herself for caring too much, she bent to pick up her overnight bag. 'Message received, loud and clear. I'll let myself out.'

Mitch watched as Brianna opened the door and slammed it firmly behind her. The sound of finality echoed around him. What was wrong with him that he was pushing this beautiful, vivacious woman out of his house? She'd wanted to go to the cinema with him. Was that such a major crime? Hadn't he just had one of the most relaxing, most enjoyable weekends he could remember? And hadn't that been mostly down to her? Before he could think about what he was doing, Mitch thrust open the door and ran down to where Brianna was starting the engine.

'Brianna, wait.' As he reached her, the Jaguar purred into life. Cocooned inside, she couldn't hear him, so he tapped on the driver's window.

Her head twisted towards him and he received an icy stare.

Undaunted, he tapped again.

Glowering at him, she finally lowered the window. 'Did

I forget something? I'd hate you to be left with a reminder of the weekend you were forced to share your precious company with another person.'

He winced. 'I guess I deserved that. Look, I'm sorry. I enjoyed this weekend. More than I thought,' he added wryly. 'I'm not used to spending time with a woman and still wanting to see her again. You're a first.'

Brianna rested her hands on the wheel and stared straight ahead.

He ducked down so he could look her in the eye – if she ever bothered to face him. 'I'm not sure I'm capable of a relationship,' he told her gruffly. 'But I can't stand the thought of not seeing you again.'

Time seemed to stand still as he waited for her reply. He was aware of the tension in his shoulders, the way his hands fisted at his side. Of how much her answer mattered to him.

Magically, she tilted her face towards him and curved her lips into a smile. To his astonishment, she then reached up and placed a hand on either side of his face and gave him a long, drugging kiss, which had the tension washing straight out of him.

'Okay, Mitch, we'll take it slow. Wednesday night. Meet me after work. We'll go to the cinema and share a bag of popcorn. Not too scary for you?'

He grinned a touch sheepishly. 'I guess it's a date.'

'I guess it is.'

Chapter Twenty-One

As he sat on the back row of the cinema with Brianna, Mitch felt like a teenager again. Then again, he'd rarely gone to the cinema as a boy. And never made out with a girl as classy as Brianna.

'Why don't you follow me in your car,' she suggested as they walked out into the night.

'Follow you where?'

She looked at him as if he was stupid. 'Back to mine.'

Slowly he shook his head. 'I don't think so.'

'But why ever not? I thought from the way you were kissing me in the cinema ...' She flushed slightly. 'Well, I guess I just assumed one thing would lead to another.'

He sighed and ran a hand through his hair. 'You share your place with your parents, Brianna.'

She stopped walking. 'So? I live in a floor of my parents' house, one that has its own entrance so you won't come across them. Anyway, even if you did, why would it matter?'

He felt the heavy weight of that damn chip on his shoulder again. 'I'm hardly their idea of good boyfriend material,' he muttered tightly, angry he cared what they'd think of him. He was a decent man, earning a decent living. He should be damn proud of himself. Usually he was. So why, when he was with Brianna, did his past keep creeping back?

'Is that what you are, then? My boyfriend?'

And now she was teasing him. 'I don't know what the hell I am.'

'You're my lover, Mitch.' She kissed him lightly on the lips. 'So, are you following me home, or not?'

The moonlight made her green eyes shine. Her smile was

provocative, promising a night of passion. He was a man. There was no choice. 'I'll follow you.'

He tried not to gawk too much when he parked his car. Tried not to let the magnificence of the town house, set in an exclusive residential area of London, bother him. It was only bricks and mortar, after all. But even as he undressed her in the bedroom, he couldn't help but notice the sheer opulence. Where his house boasted comfort, hers was bespoke designer.

It shouldn't matter that her apartment alone was worth many times more than his house by the sea. But it did.

Then Brianna's hand reached for his belt, undoing it with deft, perfectly manicured fingers and he couldn't think any more.

'Mitch?'

'Umm?' He raised a sleepy eyelid, realising that once again he'd stayed the night at Brianna's. Since their date at the cinema a few weeks ago, it had started to become a habit.

'There's a couple of things I need to talk to you about before I shoot off to the office. One involves work, and the other pleasure. Which do you want to start with?'

'Pleasure is always a good place to end.'

She smiled. 'We'll start with work then. We're holding a fund-raising ball next month and I'd like you to speak at it.'

He opened both eyes. 'You want me to do what?'

'You don't really need me to repeat it, do you?' He must still have looked stunned because she gave him a *crikey I thought you were brighter than this* roll of her eyes before explaining more fully. 'The people who come to these charity balls have only two thoughts in their mind; having a great time and getting drunk. I know, because I've been one of them. And that's fine, in a way, because as long as they buy the tickets and enjoy themselves, we've made money for Medic SOS. But I think we're missing a trick. We could be showing them exactly what the money they've donated goes towards. Make them see how important, how vital the charity is. I can't think of anybody who'd be better at getting that message across than you.'

Mitch sat up further in the bed and crossed his arms over his bare chest. 'I'm not a public speaker, Brianna, I'm a doctor.'

'Yes, and one who believes passionately in what he does. I watched you when you were explaining your role to me. This will be just the same, only a few more people will be listening.' She smiled and kissed his furrowed brow.

'I might not even be in the country when the event takes place.'

'I know, but if you are, will you do it. Please?'

'Why do I feel like I've been manoeuvred into this by a master in the art of persuasion?' He eyed her suspiciously, his voice resigned. He didn't like the idea much, but if she thought it could help the charity he didn't see how he could reasonably refuse.

She gave him a smug grin. 'Because you have.'

'I think we should focus on pleasure, now.' He started to move his fingers lightly over her breasts, smiling when she lay back against him and moaned softly.

'I've been invited to a party this weekend,' she murmured, her eyes glazing over. 'It's at a friend's house in the country. We've all been asked to stay over. Would you come with me?'

His fingers stilled. 'I thought we were taking this slow, Brianna.'

'We are, but this will be fun.' She turned and rained feathery kisses on his chest, obviously designed to soften him up, to placate him. 'They're a good crowd, you'll like them. Please?'

Mitch lay back against the headboard, his body for once not distracted by Brianna's touch. This was not his idea of one step at a time. He had deep reservations about meeting her friends. Fathoms deep. It was hard enough being with Brianna, but to mix with a crowd of wealthy Hooray Henries? For a man who didn't do small talk, and was very much aware of the shortcomings in his own background, fun definitely wasn't the word he would use to describe it. 'We'll see.'

He'd gone all quiet on her again. Taking one look at the stiff set of Mitch's jaw, Brianna figured now was the time to take a shower. Maybe when she'd finished, he'd have loosened up again.

However, when she came back out he was putting away his phone and looking very serious.

'What's up?' she asked, drying her hair with the towel.

'There's been a monsoon in the Philippines. We've been called in. I've got to go.' He started to put on his jeans.

'Oh,' was all she could manage. Crestfallen that he'd be going away she said the first thing that came into her head. 'Do you have to go today?'

He stared at her pointedly. 'What do you think?'

'Well you're not the only doctor who works for the charity. Maybe you could catch up with them later. After the weekend.'

It was the wrong thing to say. She knew as soon as she saw him yank on his shirt with barely controlled fury. 'People are dying, for God's sake. I think it's a little bit more important than going to a party, don't you?'

Ouch. He was so good at making her sound like a selfish bitch. 'Thank you, Mitch. I don't need to be reminded of that. But would it kill you to show a hint of regret? I was looking forward to spending the weekend with you.'

'This is who I am, Brianna,' he replied brusquely. 'This is what I do. If you don't like it, tough. I won't change.'

Her temper, always quick to flare, boiled over. 'How dare you twist my words. I'm not asking you to change. Just show a bit of disappointment that you can't be with me this weekend.'

'Honestly?' He looked directly into her eyes. 'I'm not sure I am disappointed. If I'd gone, it would have been for your sake, not my own. Maybe it's better this way. You'll have more fun without me.'

'I won't.' She slumped onto the bed, aware she was pouting, being melodramatic, but unable to stop herself. 'How can I? I love being with you. Besides, you won't just miss the weekend. You'll be gone for weeks.' A sob caught in her throat.

'I know.' Finally he stopped dressing and sat next to her on the bed. 'Brianna,' he began more gently. 'When I said I didn't think I could do relationships, I wasn't joking. God knows, as a person I'm difficult enough to get on with.' His lips crooked into a small smile. 'But it's not just me, it's also my job. Perhaps this is a good opportunity to say goodbye. It was fun while it lasted.'

An agonised sound exploded from her throat but he ignored it, tucking a hand under her chin so her eyes were forced to meet his. 'I don't want to hurt you,' he continued in a tone she imagined he'd use with a confused patient, 'but if we carry on like this, I will. I live for my job. Mentally I'm already packing my bags. I don't have the time or energy for any of the emotional baggage having a woman in my life will inevitably cause. I'm sorry.'

Brianna ignored her breaking heart and buried all of her pride. 'No, Mitch. You're not ending this. I won't let you.'

His dark eyes looked almost kind. 'Think on it while I'm gone. Go to your party. Mix with your friends. In a few weeks you'll feel differently.'

He kissed her on the lips; a quick, rough kiss. Then he left.

When the weekend arrived and Brianna met up with Melanie at the country mansion in the Cotswolds, she'd managed to shift her crushing disappointment into a more healthy anger. How dare Mitch talk about ending their relationship? Men didn't finish with her. She was the one who did the finishing, when she grew bored. And she wasn't bored yet.

Unwillingly her mind flashed back over her past relationships. The men she'd turned down. She liked to think she'd let them down gently, but had their hearts bruised as badly as hers was doing right now? God, she hoped not, because this really hurt.

Sadly she trailed her fingers over the slinky red party dress she was about to change into. She'd bought it with Mitch in mind, looking forward to seeing the expression on his face when she sidled up to him in it. She'd had visions of him ripping it off her and dragging her to bed. No chance of that happening now.

'Brie, are you all right? You look a bit down.' Melanie, getting changed in the same room as her, had just struggled into a tight midnight-blue number.

'Hey, never mind me, you look fabulous. How did you manage to wriggle into it? With a shoehorn?'

Melanie huffed. 'Please don't make me laugh. I'll bust the seams. And don't change the subject. What's up?'

'Nothing really. I'm just a bit upset Mitch can't be here.' She left it at that, not prepared to admit to herself, never mind her best friend, that what she'd shared with him was over.

'I guess that's the trouble with men who work for a living.' Melanie grinned impishly. 'You know, it might not be a bad thing, Mitch not being here.'

'Oh?'

'I happen to know that Frederick, the son of the Earl of Lincolnshire, has been invited tonight. Trust me, Brianna, he's just your type. Tall, dark, handsome and richer than you are.'

Determinedly Brianna thrust aside the image of a tall, fair, rugged doctor. It was time she went back to her own world. And her more usual type. Glancing down at her dress, she slipped her friend a wry smile. 'Well, it seems the dress might not be wasted, after all.'

An hour, and a few glasses of champagne later, Brianna started to feel a bit happier. Her old friend Henry had been attentive, complimenting her on her dress, begging for the first dance. Last time they'd met, she'd escaped him at the ball. This time she allowed him to lead her onto the floor. It did a woman good to be fawned over once in a while, she reminded herself. Mitch had hardly bothered to pay her any attention in that respect.

As a passing waiter refilled her glass for the third time, Melanie came into view, a startlingly handsome man in tow. 'Brianna, let me introduce you to Frederick.'

Frederick took her hand and raised it to his lips. 'Wow. When Melanie told me she wanted to introduce me to the most beautiful girl in the room, she wasn't joking.'

Light-headed from champagne, her heart and ego bruised, Brianna beamed at his compliment. Maybe Melanie was right. Frederick was just the tonic she needed. 'Pleased to meet you, too.'

They talked, they danced, they flirted. It turned out that Frederick lived in London too, and was currently contemplating dabbling in politics. He knew many of the people she knew, so many it was a wonder they hadn't met before. They compared favourite haunts, agreeing that Mahiki was the best place for a champagne cocktail. They discussed countries they'd holidayed in, the finest mountains to ski down, and the most perfect beaches. It was the easy conversation of two people from similar backgrounds. When the band played a slow waltz, it seemed natural that they walked back onto the dance floor, gliding across it like two seasoned professionals.

Brianna kept telling herself this was much more like it. Even if he could, which she doubted, Mitch would never have waltzed with her. He'd have hung at the back of the room, brooding. She hadn't discussed ski slopes or night clubs with him, but she knew he wouldn't have an opinion on either. Perhaps her mother was right. Mitch had been something different. A passing fancy, but nothing lasting.

'Will you come out onto the veranda and look at the stars with me, Brianna?' Frederick whispered into her ear.

How charming, how romantic. *And how unlike anything Mitch would ever say to her.* Brianna smiled brightly and allowed herself to be led outside. Once there, in a slick move, Frederick twirled her gracefully into his arms.

'That dress has been driving me crazy all night. You have been driving me crazy all night. Do you mind if I kiss you?'

Brianna looked into the deep blue eyes of the handsome Frederick. Before she'd visited the Medic SOS camp, before she'd met Mitch, this was exactly the type of evening she would have craved, and Frederick exactly the type of man.

But not now. Something had changed inside her. Even as his lips descended onto hers, she knew she wouldn't feel the jolt of desire she should, that she wanted to. Her mind was with another man. One who kissed without asking, who was rough, not gentle. Passionate, not sensitive. Strong and proud, but not rich. She wanted to forget him, to lose her mind in the moment, but she couldn't.

Damn Mitch McBride. Even when he wasn't with her, he

was invading her senses. He'd not only ruined her weekend, it seemed he'd ruined her taste for other men.

Angry with herself, Brianna drew away. 'I'm sorry, Frederick. It's been a wonderful evening and you have been a charming escort, but I'm afraid I can't do this.' Placing a kiss on Frederick's cheek, she started to move away.

He stopped her with a gentle hand on her elbow, giving her an ironic smile. 'Just my luck. I meet a beautiful woman, but she doesn't share the attraction.'

'No, it isn't that,' Brianna replied sadly. 'Believe me, you're every woman's dream man. Handsome, charming and a true gentleman. It's just that ... there is someone else. He couldn't be here tonight, but it hasn't stopped him being in my thoughts. I'm sorry.'

She left him standing on the veranda and went to find her bedroom. The party was over for her. It seemed nothing in her life would ever be quite the same again.

Chapter Twenty-Two

The first few days in the Philippines had been sheer hell, but then Mitch had expected that. They always were, with any new disaster. The chaos, the numbers of casualties, the basic equipment and supplies they had to work with until they could get their hands on more. His small team were groaning under the workload, made especially difficult as the airport runway had been damaged just after their arrival, delaying the other aid agencies. They had put in monster days and regularly interrupted nights. Now, thankfully, the airport had re-opened and things were easing. For the first time in over seventy-two hours, Mitch returned to his tent anticipating a solid night's sleep.

That was when he saw a package on his desk. At first he didn't think much of it. Sometimes he would receive samples, or specialist medicines that way. But he did a double take when he saw the handwriting. He could remember seeing writing like that on a newspaper crossword at his house, following a lazy Sunday morning. What in blazes was Brianna sending him?

He tore open the parcel and sat down on the bed to explore the contents. The laugh he let rip when the toy giraffe tumbled onto his lap was long and heartfelt. It seemed like an eternity since he'd last had anything to laugh about. With a sense of anticipation, he sat back on the bed and began to read the letter.

Dear Mitch,
I missed you Saturday night at the party. I wore a slinky red dress, one I'd bought especially for you. I'd wanted to blow your mind. It had a plunging neckline, daring

low back, and clung to the rest of my body like a silk wetsuit. Is this description turning you on, making you feel uncomfortable? I hope so. It's my way of paying you back for what you said before you left. I was disappointed you had to go, that's all. A girl is entitled to be disappointed if the man she's grown to care for has to leave her for several weeks. You had no right to talk about ending our relationship and then leaving before I had a chance to tell you how I feel.

Anyway, the dress really worked on Frederick. Did I tell you about him? He's the Earl's son Melanie is determined to fix me up with. Frederick couldn't keep his eyes off me. Or his hands, for that matter. Oh, and did I mention he's tall, dark and handsome? Does this bother you at all? If it doesn't, if you're reading this and not feeling a damned thing, then you're right. We should call this relationship – oh, sorry, you hate that word, don't you? The great loner Mitch McBride couldn't possibly get involved in something as serious as a relationship, could he? So let me re-word that part. If you're not upset at the thought of Frederick running his hands over my silk-covered body, then you're right, we should call this 'thing' between us over. On the other hand, if you are feeling the slightest stab of jealousy over Frederick kissing me on the veranda in the moonlight, then you should read on.

You see, you've been honest with me, so it is only fair I'm honest with you in return. I think I'm falling in love with you, Mitch. Yes, I know it wasn't what we agreed, but I'm not going to apologise for my feelings. It's happening and we're both going to have to deal with it.

I hope you're looking after yourself. I hope you're finding some time to sleep, some time to relax. I don't expect a letter back. You've already told me you aren't a hearts and flowers man, so I can't imagine you're a letter writer, either. I wrote this as much for me, as for you. At least, while I'm writing it, I feel close to you.

I'm enclosing Sam, my cuddly giraffe. He will keep an eye on you while I can't. I am going to imagine you putting him into your bed, cuddling him at night, thinking of me. Of course I know in reality you'll shove him straight into your holdall. But I can dream.

Yours, Brianna xxxx

He experienced the whole gamut of emotions as his eyes pored over her stylish letters. Lust and a stab of raging jealousy came first, quickly followed by anger when he read her words of love. He ended on a smile, looking back at the giraffe and wondering what, exactly, *was* he going to do with it?

Overcome with fatigue, and God only knew what other emotion, he put his head in his hands and tried to clear the fog from his over-tired brain. Then he re-read the letter, more slowly this time. It was the statement that she thought she was falling in love with him that wouldn't go away. It kept staring him blindingly in the face. What was she thinking? She couldn't possibly be. Hadn't she understood he wasn't the sort of man that loved, or was loved? God, he'd never been loved, though when he was younger he had tried to love. He'd tried to love his mother. That experience had taught him it was a lot less painful if he didn't let people get close to him, and if he didn't get close to people. If he didn't involve his heart. It had helped in the army, when he'd been laughing with colleagues one minute, and battling to save their lives the next. And it had helped with women, where no emotional attachments enabled him to easily continue doing the job he loved.

So what was he going to do about Brianna? How typical of her to declare her feelings and then tell him he was going to have to deal with it. It was part of what he admired about her. She was pushy, bolshie, but refreshingly straightforward.

He'd never received a love letter before and supposed, in her quirky way, this was one. Unheeded, a wash of emotion came over him as he thought of Brianna, thousands of miles away, bothering to put pen to paper and to parcel up her crazy giraffe. As his eyes filled and the emotion threatened to choke him, he shook himself. He was over tired, that was all. He'd get over it.

It had been two weeks since she'd last seen Mitch. Ten days since she'd spewed out her feelings to him in the letter. Long past the point of caring whether people in the office knew about her feelings for him, she'd asked for his flight details the moment she'd heard he was heading back. The emotional trauma of wondering if he would call wasn't for her. Today she was going to meet him off the plane. If he rejected her ... her heart tightened painfully. Well, if he rejected her, at least she'd know where she stood. That had to be better than mooning around, waiting for a phone call that might never come.

With her heart in her mouth she watched the steady line of weary travellers making their way through the arrivals hall. Some scanned the crowd, searching for the face of the loved one meeting them. Others looked straight ahead, knowing they were making their own way home. Mitch was one of those. As his tall broad figure came into view, Brianna almost shouted out with joy. God, she'd forgotten how gorgeous he was. Wearing tattered jeans and a crumpled leather jacket, his face was tanned but tired. Those deep brown eyes, such a stunning contrast to his fair hair, were fixed at some point in the distance. There was a magnetism about him, something that drew the eyes. She wasn't the only one to feel it. Other women in the crowd, many probably waiting for their husbands or their lovers, turned to watch as Mitch walked past.

For a moment Brianna froze. He looked sexy but distant, remote. Could she really rush up to this man and throw her arms around him? Did she dare? The harshness was there in the set of his jaw, in the lines on his face. She'd forgotten that, just as she'd forgotten what he'd been like when she'd first met him. But that was only one side to him. This was the same man who'd spent a weekend teaching her how to windsurf.

'Mitch!' she cried out, suddenly finding her voice. Her legs started to run towards him, their pace matching the fast beat of her heart. 'Mitch!'

He stopped and turned around, his face blank. She watched as he narrowed his eyes and surveyed the crowd, looking to see where the voice had come from. Pushing past the lady with her buggy and the couple who were enjoying a hot reunion kiss, Brianna forced her way into his line of sight.

Brown eyes found hers and flared with surprise. 'Brianna? What on earth are you doing here?'

He looked shocked, but she didn't think he was cross. Anyway, she was past caring. She flung her arms around his neck, at last feeling the solid, muscular body whose touch she'd craved. He smelt of planes and pure one hundred per cent man.

Mitch dropped his bag and pulled her closer to him, bending his neck to bury his nose in her hair. Her heart sang as he continued to hold her. As if he'd missed her. As if he really didn't want to let her go.

'Well, this is a nice surprise,' he said hoarsely, finally pulling back.

'Is it, really?' she blurted, then kicked herself. She didn't do timid.

Mitch smiled, the effect softening his face, making him instantly more approachable. 'Trust me, a beautiful lady throwing her arms around me when I've just come off a transatlantic flight is definitely a nice surprise.'

Relief gushed through her, making her almost euphoric with happiness. 'Well, in that case, your place or mine?'

This time Mitch laughed, the rich sound warming her heart still further. 'Well yours is closer, but I've run out of fresh clothes.'

Brianna gave him a sly glance, her confidence returned. 'For what I have in mind, you won't need any clothes.' She threaded her arm through his and led him towards the car park. 'But why don't I drive to your house while you have a kip in the car. You're going to need all your energy for later.'

She was willing to wait until he'd showered and sorted himself out, but it seemed Mitch had other plans. While she had no idea where she stood in terms of his emotional feelings, she was left with no doubt about his physical desires. As soon as she'd crossed the threshold into his home he dragged her into his arms and carried her up the stairs. Within minutes she was naked, in his shower, her legs wrapped around his hips, her whole body screaming in delight. He made love like he did most things in life, with an intense passion, a total focus. Even as they dried off, he wasn't ready to let her go. He pulled her down onto his bed and took her once more, his need for her no less fierce.

'Wow. I think I can be reasonably sure no other woman has been in your bed recently,' she remarked lazily as she tried to regain her equilibrium.

Mitch turned to her, propping himself up on one elbow. 'I'm not in the habit of sleeping with more than one woman at any one time, Brianna. I thought that was how you'd see it, too.'

Brianna's heart gave a stupid lurch. Surely that meant they were still together? At least for now. 'Of course it is.' She tenderly brushed back the damp hair from his forehead. 'When you went away, I was angry with you. I wanted to fall into the arms of the next handsome man that came my way.' She felt his body tense alongside her and experienced a flare of triumph. 'But when Frederick kissed me, I felt nothing. You've spoilt me. Even when I was cross with you, I couldn't kiss another man.'

Mitch took the hand that was tracing the lines on his forehead and put it down between his legs. 'Good.'

Brianna knew they needed to talk, but for now it would have to wait. Her man had other ideas and she was more than happy to follow them.

By the time Mitch finally let her out of bed, it was dark and they were both hungry.

'I can make us an omelette while you unpack,' she declared as she wriggled back into her trousers.

Knowing her aptitude for cooking, he raised an eyebrow.

She huffed. 'How difficult can it be? Whisking some eggs together, adding a bit of cheese, maybe some tomatoes.' With her chin up, she sauntered out of the bedroom.

He chuckled and started to sort out his bag. Was this really happening? Had rich, spoilt Brianna really stood in a departure hall waiting to meet him off a plane and then brought him home? He'd been stunned to see her, his mind struggling to sift through the emotions jostling through him. Joy that she was there, terror that he was being dragged into something he wasn't sure he wanted. Wonder that she'd actually bothered to meet him, fear for what that might mean. Of where she was leading them.

'This all feels very familiar,' he remarked when he found her bent over his cooker in the kitchen.

She stopped prodding the contents of the pan. 'What do you mean?'

'Hey, I didn't *mean* anything.' Seeing her wariness, he put his arms around her, drawing her against his chest. 'It was just an observation. The last two times I've come back from abroad, I've had a gorgeous woman in my house, in my kitchen and in my bed. I'm not complaining.'

He felt her relax against him. 'Sorry, it's just I know you don't like being crowded. I don't want to overstep the mark.'

Mitch stood still, his feelings unsteady. What had he done to deserve this woman? Many times he'd tried to push her away, treated her badly, mainly for his own self-preservation. It scared him to think he was starting to let her in. Back at the camp, he'd repeatedly told himself he didn't want a relationship. They were messy and he wasn't cut out for them. Yet here he was, back with Brianna, and feeling a surge of contentment he'd rarely felt before.

'Brianna, I'm not good with words,' he told her quietly, knowing it was about time he gave her something back. 'I've always preferred actions. But you need to know I care for you. I like having you around. It's a new experience for me, having a woman write a letter to me, meet me at the airport.' He nodded towards the now burning omelette. 'Try and cook for me. You'll just have to give me some time to get used to it.'

Brianna ignored the burning eggs and turned to kiss him gently on the lips. 'Take all the time you need, Mitch. I'm not going anywhere.' She went back to turn over the omelette. 'Except perhaps the local takeaway. Bugger, it's only the second time I've cooked for you, and the second time I've burnt it.'

'At least you know I'm not just turned on by your haute cuisine.' He gave her a kiss on the back of her neck. 'I'll get a takeaway.'

Ten minutes later they were once again enjoying a meal in front of the fire. This time, pizza.

'Mitch, have you really never had a woman write to you, or meet you at the airport before now?'

He looked up, surprised. 'Yes. I told you, I don't do relationships.' He laughed at himself. 'At least I haven't, until now.'

Brianna's lips twitched. A second later, a broad grin split her face. 'Does that mean you're my boyfriend now?'

He drew in a deep breath. Facing gunfire in a war zone was less terrifying than this. 'Yes. I guess so.'

For a while she didn't stop grinning. It was so infectious, he found himself shaking his head and grinning back.

'Have you thought any more about what you're going to say on Saturday?' she asked eventually when they'd given up on the pizza. 'You have remembered you promised to talk at the ball?'

Well, that successfully wiped the smile off his face. 'Yes, I've remembered, but no, I haven't thought about what I'm going to say. I've not had a lot of time.' He took their plates and went to pile them up in the kitchen.

'Mitch, can I ask you another favour?' she called out.

He popped his head back round the door, eyeing her suspiciously. 'That depends.'

'During the ball we're going to hold a date auction. I've managed to persuade a few of my friends to put themselves forward as prospective dates, to be taken out by the highest bidder. I'm going to do it as well. Can I put your name down?'

'*What?*'

'It's just a bit of fun,' she replied defensively. 'And all the money goes to Medic SOS.'

Flabbergasted, he leant against the door frame. 'Let me get this right. You want me to volunteer to have a meal I don't want, with somebody who's paid good money for the privilege? You have to be joking.' He shook his head, baffled by the whole concept. 'Firstly, I can't see anyone actually *paying* to have a meal out with me. God knows, I'm not the most scintillating of company. And secondly, why the hell would I want to give up my time to make polite conversation with some rich woman I don't know? Hell, Brianna, I can't believe you seriously thought I'd agree to that.'

'I didn't, but it was worth a try.' She fluttered her eyelids. 'You've got no idea how much those ladies would pay for a night out with a sexy doctor.'

He felt a schoolboy flush creep up his neck. 'I said no,' he repeated tightly.

'Okay.' With a fluid grace she moved off the sofa and draped her arms around his neck. 'And I can't say I'm upset. I don't want to share you with anybody else, anyway. I'll just put an extra cheque into the pot and grab that date all to myself.' She kissed him softly on the lips. 'Come on, Mitch, I'm tired. You must be shattered. Take me to bed.'

'Now that I will do,' he muttered gratefully.

Chapter Twenty-Three

Mitch spent Saturday morning wondering what on earth he was going to say in his speech. God only knew why he'd let Brianna talk him into this, he grumbled to himself as he crossed out the words he'd just written. He was no orator. Yes, he'd spoken to large groups a few times, but with a view to training them, not entertaining them. His audiences had been soldiers, or medical students, there to listen and learn. Tonight his audience was a group of rich men and women who'd paid a ridiculous sum of money to be wined and dined. The last thing they wanted was a lecture on how to deal with injuries sustained by fallen debris. A shame because that was what he was good at delivering.

Frustrated, Mitch put down the paper and went to iron his one and only dress shirt. He'd found it lying crumpled at the back of his wardrobe. The last time he'd worn a tuxedo had been at university, the day he'd graduated. He figured tuxes didn't date much. Having spent what he'd considered at the time to be a small fortune on the thing, he was damned if he was going to buy another one just for tonight. If they didn't like what he was wearing, tough. Maybe they wouldn't let him through the door and he could just slope off home and forget all about the stupid speech and meeting Brianna's crowd of friends.

And there, he thought, in a nutshell, was his real problem. It wasn't so much the speech, though he wasn't looking forward to it. It was the knowledge that he was stepping into Brianna's world now. In the safety of the medical camp, and then back at his place, he'd managed to forget the class gulf that stretched between them. Tonight it was going to flare up in his face again. He was a professional, a doctor. When it came to his work he was confident, some would say brash. But in his personal life he couldn't shake off the blasted feeling of inadequacy. Oh, he was okay with most people, but Brianna's crowd weren't most people. Mitch knew where he'd come from, and was ashamed of it. It didn't matter how hard he tried to put it at the back of his mind, to tell himself it wasn't important, he knew he was kidding himself. It *was* important. It made him defensive, on edge. Not a good combination for socialising.

Gritting his teeth, he shrugged off his thoughts and finished ironing the shirt. It was just one blasted evening. He could get through it. All he needed to do was remind himself of who he was now, not who he'd been. He was proud of what he was doing and it was probably a damn sight more than the idle rich crowd he'd be mixing with. If he could just get through the evening without making a fool of himself, or of Brianna. That was all he asked.

His journey up to London was uneventful and Mitch was soon ringing on the bell to Brianna's apartment. He felt awkward, standing there on the pavement, dressed in his finery. It occurred to him he didn't know the etiquette of picking up a lady to go to a ball, even if she was running it. Should he have brought flowers? Probably. More than likely. Jeez, he was a reasonably good swimmer, but he felt staggeringly out of his depth, in waters with currents he couldn't begin to understand.

He stewed for a few seconds longer, until Brianna opened the door. Then he had no room in his mind for any other thoughts. Transfixed by the sight of her, he simply stared. It might be a clichéd saying, but she took his breath away.

'Mitch, you're looking very handsome. Do you want to come in for a moment? I'm just putting on the finishing touches.' She leaned into him and kissed him slowly, lingeringly on the lips.

'If you keep that up, you'll be starting from scratch again.' Putting his hands onto her hips he regretfully pushed her away. She wore a deep green silk number, which caressed her body and brought out the beauty of her eyes.

Laughing, Brianna caught him by the hand and led him back up the stairs to her apartment. 'Why don't you pour yourself a drink while I find the right necklace to go with this dress.'

It was his cue to reveal a stunning diamond and emerald necklace from his pocket. At least that's what happened in the movies. Of course he'd arrived with nothing. Even if he had thought to have brought something, he couldn't have afforded the jewellery a woman like her desired, or deserved. Damn it, what the hell was he doing here, dressed up in an off the peg, ten-year-old tuxedo? He didn't belong, and if he ever thought he would, he was deluding himself. With a grunt of frustration he stalked into the kitchen and, ignoring the bottle of champagne in the ice bucket, grabbed himself a bottle of beer from the fridge.

That was where Brianna found him a few minutes later. Propped up against the breakfast bar, his face like thunder, drinking beer from the bottle.

'How do I look?' she asked softly.

He glanced up from the floor, his eyes slowly taking in the full appearance. A dramatic single emerald glinted around her neck and matching earrings dangled from her lobes. He didn't dare think who'd given them to her. Ignoring the sharp twinge of jealousy he concentrated instead on drinking in the rest of her. Her hair was now piled on top in a casual fashion, with loose tendrils flowing down her neck. On her feet were dainty silver sandals.

'You look far too good for the likes of me.' Confusion clouded her eyes and he inwardly cursed. *That* was the best compliment he could come up with? Frustrated with himself he swigged again at his beer. 'I should have brought you something,' he told her flatly.

'Why?'

'Isn't that what men usually do when they take a beautiful woman to a ball?' His tone was belligerent and he knew that he was wrong to take his self-directed anger out on her. Damn, he was coming to care for her too much, and it hurt. It hurt to know she could never be his. That he couldn't give her what she needed. A woman like her simply didn't belong with somebody like him.

'I don't want flowers or tokens, Mitch. I've had men bring me both, but nothing has given me as much pleasure as the look in your eyes when I opened the door.'

'What look was that?'

'The look that told me you wanted to devour me, right on the doorstep.' She smiled softly, knowingly at him.

She was a woman who knew exactly the effect she had on a man. And on this man in particular. With a sigh he clasped her by the shoulders and buried his face in her neck, taking in a lungful of her perfume. It was clearly concocted for its ability to bewitch men. 'I did,' he replied at last. 'And I still do. God you smell good.'

She chuckled. 'I should do, it cost me enough.'

Mitch drew back and looked at her. 'I'm still sorry I didn't bring you anything.'

Her eyes seemed to mist over. 'Mitch, if I'd wanted a man who brought me chocolates and flowers, I wouldn't have started seeing you.' Gently she touched his cheek. 'I want you, Mitch, just exactly as you are.'

As Mitch drove to the hotel he was very conscious that his glamorous date should have been arriving in a luxurious limousine, not an old four-wheel drive with windsurfing gear sprawled across the back seat. Brianna though, looked totally unperturbed. He had to hand it to her. It didn't seem to matter whether she was on camp with Medic SOS, dressed up to the nines in her glamorous apartment, or curled up on his sofa. She looked comfortable wherever she was.

Since arriving at the ball, Brianna had barely had time to think. It had been a whirlwind of activity, with so many last minute details to check on. She'd lost sight of Mitch the moment they'd crossed the floor into the vast ballroom. Now she was anxious to find him. However as she set off to hunt him down, she was besieged by Melanie and a crowd of their friends, including Henry and Frederick. Kisses were exchanged, compliments on their respective outfits given and received.

'Brianna, darling, who is the hot-looking man over there, talking to the man from the hotel?'

Brianna followed Clarissa's gaze and smiled to herself. That was where Mitch had disappeared to, obviously checking out the sound levels on the microphone. He did look incredibly gorgeous, even to her biased eyes. The black tuxedo emphasised his tall, athletic build, and the white shirt brought out his tan. For once his chin was freshly shaved, showing the strength of his jaw and the sharpness of his cheekbones.

'Hot-looking? He's wearing an off the shelf tux for crying out loud,' Henry interjected dismissively.

'Umm, but he's filling it out rather well,' added Sophie, another member of the crowd Brianna had gone round with since school.

'That is Mitch McBride, Chief Medical Officer at Medic SOS and my lover,' Brianna announced proudly, laughing delightedly when several pairs of eyes jerked round to look at her.

'So, that's Mitch,' Melanie said quietly, her eyes on the man in question.

'Hang on a minute, Brianna. What did you say?' Sophie almost screeched. 'Crikey, you're a dark horse. How long has this been going on? Why didn't you tell us?'

Brianna held up her hands. 'Hey, calm down, one question at a time. It's been going on since I went out to South America. I didn't tell you because it's early days and I wasn't sure whether it was going to come to anything.'

Sophie swung round to Melanie. 'Did you know about this?' she asked accusingly.

Melanie smiled. 'Guilty, your honour. And before you ask, I didn't say anything because it wasn't my secret to tell. Added to which, I had been hoping to pair Brie up with Frederick, though now I've seen Mitch, I think I can see why she's so hooked. No offence, Frederick,' she added quickly.

'None taken,' Frederick murmured, eyeing up his rival.

'Is it serious?' Henry was looking at her rather oddly and Brianna's heart sank. Bugger, she'd been right. He was jealous.

'As I said, it's early days, but I'm not planning on looking elsewhere.' Disappointment weaved across Henry's face and for a moment Brianna felt a flicker of sympathy for him. Then Mitch glanced over and caught her gaze. He didn't smile, just regarded her steadily with his deep brown eyes.

Abruptly he turned and said something to the soundman before walking purposefully towards her. She watched as he took in her friends, his glance drifting over Henry and Frederick. By the time he reached her, his eyes were glinting possessively. Before she had a chance to make any introductions, Mitch's hand moved to circle her waist and he proceeded to give her the type of kiss that should really be conducted in private.

'Mitch,' she said breathlessly when he slowly drew away. 'I want you to meet some of my friends.' She made the introductions, very much aware of the different reactions from the two sexes. The girls became giggly, as girls often do when faced with an alpha male. Frederick and Henry became wary and aloof.

'Pleased to meet you.' Mitch shook hands with the men, but his expression was as cool as theirs.

Men were so silly, Brianna thought. They became all territorial when faced with other men. It was like watching the gladiators of old, eyeing each other up before a fight.

'You'll have to excuse us folks,' Brianna interrupted the male posturing. 'I need to make sure this man is ready to deliver his pre-dinner speech. We'll catch up with you later.'

Taking Mitch by the hand, Brianna led him over to the entrance of the ballroom. 'What was all that about?' she asked when they were out of earshot.

'All what?' he asked innocently.

'You know. If you were a bird your feathers would be all puffed up by now.'

He shrugged dismissively. 'I know Frederick was the one you kissed at the party I missed, but where does Henry come in? He looked like he wanted me dead.'

Brianna stopped, turned and slid into Mitch's arms. 'He's just a friend. I think he harbours feelings towards me, but I can assure you they aren't returned. I'm only interested in you, Mitch. Only you.' She kissed him softly. 'And now I'm afraid I've got to be the charming hostess. Do you want to come with me to meet and greet, or do you want to escape for a while?'

'Escape.' He gave her a wry grin.

'Okay, but make sure you're back for your speech. You're sitting next to me on the first table. You'll be talking as soon as everyone sits down, before the starter is served.'

'Better hope I don't put them off their meal then.' He

gave her a kiss on the cheek, and disappeared down the hallway.

Mitch's heart was pounding as he walked up to the microphone. The ballroom full of guests, bedecked in their finery, turned expectantly to watch him. His final thought, before he launched into his speech, was stuff them. If they didn't like what he had to say, at least he wouldn't have to do it again.

'You're ten years old. It's dark, almost black. You can only just see your hand in front of you. You're trapped. Can't move your legs. You reach out and feel a lump of concrete. It's lying across you. When you try and breathe, your chest tightens in agony. Your eyes become more accustomed to the light and you make out your mother, on her back, blood pouring from her head. You scream her name, but she doesn't reply. Nobody does. You hear the sound of creaking and notice the place that was once your front room is now destroyed. The ceiling has caved, the walls crumbled, debris is everywhere. A baby cries. Your little sister. You try to move towards her but you can't. Terrified, you claw at the concrete slabs pinning you down, but you're too weak to move them. You scream again, but nobody replies. Your heart clutches in terror. You're going to die here, all alone. You cry.'

Mitch broke off to survey the ballroom, noticing with grim satisfaction that he had their full attention. He'd decided only that morning he wasn't going to stand there and spout facts and figures. He wanted to let them know what it was like for some people in the real world. For those not safely cocooned in their mansion houses.

'This is how I found Ari, following an earthquake in Java. He was one of the lucky ones. We were able to save both him and his sister, though sadly their parents were both dead when we arrived. Ari sends a card to Medic SOS every Christmas, thanking us for saving his life. The more money we have, the more lives like Ari's we can save. Thank you for listening.'

He moved away from the microphone and started to walk back to his chair. The applause began as a ripple and ended as a deafening crescendo. People were out of their chairs, standing to clap him. He halted, stunned by the reaction. He had hoped to make them listen, to make them understand. He hadn't dared to consider they might appreciate his efforts. As shock slowly turned to embarrassment, he raised a hand in thanks and strode back to his place next to Brianna.

He noticed tears in her eyes as she grasped his arm with one hand and laid the other tenderly on his cheek. 'Wow, my hero.'

Mitch sat down with a thud, his ego considerably swollen and his body a lot more relaxed than when he'd arrived. He took a huge gulp of wine and turned to accept the thanks of the woman sitting on his other side. Perhaps, against the odds, he might enjoy the evening.

Chapter Twenty-Four

Mitch watched the dancers glide skilfully across the ballroom floor. He stood alone, having politely turned down Melanie's request for a dance. He didn't know how to waltz. It hadn't been high on the list of essential learning at the inner city school he'd gone to. Over the years he'd managed to adopt a passable shuffle, but he'd decided not to risk standing on Melanie's toes tonight. So he contented himself with watching. His eyes were fixed on Brianna, dancing with a tall, grey-haired man who was making her laugh. He felt a tug of jealousy, even though the man looked old enough to be her father. Perhaps he was her father.

The feeling of possessiveness that gripped him whenever he looked at her wasn't something he'd ever experienced before. He didn't like it, didn't want it but, infuriatingly, he couldn't seem to stop it. Was this what love felt like? He'd never really understood what it meant, but was very much afraid he was teetering on the edge of it. If he wasn't careful, he might fall into it without even realising. The advantages it might bring were all too clear as he gazed at the bewitching sight of Brianna, but the reality was it would end in pain. On both sides. He knew damn well he wasn't cut out for a close, caring relationship. Least of all with a woman who had more class in her little finger than he could hope to achieve in a lifetime. The question was, did he have enough strength to pull away?

At last she made her way towards him, almost gliding across the room, her smile bright, her eyes dancing. He realised she was in her element. Amongst her friends, in opulent surroundings, the centre of attention. So far removed from his own comfort zone it was laughable. She wound an arm around his waist, appearing not to notice his discomfort.

'Are you enjoying yourself?'

He chose not to reply. Instead his eyes focused on a slender, older, striking-looking woman who was coming towards them. Brianna's mother. He'd met her once before, when she'd visited the Medic SOS offices. Not that she'd probably remember him. 'Does your mother know about you and me?' he asked, nodding over in her mother's direction. As he said the words, he felt Brianna's arm slip from his waist. He had his answer.

'Not exactly,' she replied, smiling over at her mother.

'What does that mean, exactly?'

For once, Brianna looked less than confident. 'I mean, she knows we, well, got together in South America. But I haven't really spoken to her about you since.'

'I see.' And he did see, all too clearly.

'No, it's not like that,' Brianna hastily tried to reassure him. 'I'm sure she'd be fine if she knew.' He knew the words were a lie. And that she knew he knew. 'Look it doesn't matter what she thinks ...' she began again, but had to stop as her mother drew up alongside them.

Polite introductions were made. Her mother congratulated Mitch on his speech, which he stiffly accepted. Clearly desperate to put a quick end to the awkward situation, Brianna dragged him away for a dance.

'I hope you're not expecting to waltz,' he began, his voice still tense. 'I don't do dancing.'

They reached the edge of the dance floor and Brianna turned, moving fluidly into his arms. 'And I only want to feel your arms around me for a while,' she whispered, moulding herself to him.

He groaned and felt the warmth zip through his body.

They might be totally wrong for each other, but when he held her close, it felt so damnably right.

As they danced, Mitch allowed his hands to wander slowly, seductively, over her body. Over the curves that glided beneath the silk of her dress. He was out of order. Even he knew that. His technique belonged more to the school disco than a plush ballroom, but he didn't care. Let her mother see. He wanted to touch, to feel. And Brianna wasn't complaining. If anything, she was moving in closer, rubbing against him, encouraging him. He was fast becoming uncomfortably aroused.

'What are you thinking?' she murmured against his ear.

'I'm thinking you can't be wearing much under this dress,' he replied, fighting the urge to grab her hand and take her somewhere private.

She laughed throatily. 'I'm not.' Tugging at his hand, she smiled at him wickedly. 'Follow me.'

Gripping Mitch's hand, Brianna strode through the vast ballroom and moved towards the lift. The doors opened almost instantaneously. As soon as they entered it, Mitch dragged her to him, his mouth eagerly devouring hers. 'Fast and furious in the lift?'

'Tempting,' she replied huskily as his hands slid under her dress and along her thighs. 'But I had in mind something slightly more private, in a bedroom.' As the lift came to a halt, she held out a key card with a saucy grin.

'I can go with that, too,' he replied roughly, taking the card from her trembling fingers and quickly opening the door. 'How long have we got?'

Brianna looked at her watch. 'Half an hour.'

Within seconds of entering the room, Mitch had unzipped her dress, watching as it fell in a cloud of green silk to the floor. 'God, Brianna,' he croaked, staring at her naked breasts, and the wispy silk that barely covered her bottom half.

It was hot, frenzied and over in minutes. The intensity left him reeling.

'It just gets better and better,' Brianna sighed contentedly. 'I'm so glad I had the foresight to book a room. I thought it might be useful if we were too tired, or too drunk, to get a cab home. But I much prefer the use we put it to.'

Mitch, who hadn't even had time to take his shirt off, started slowly undoing his buttons.

'What are you doing?'

'What does it look like?' He threw his shirt over the chair and dived back onto the bed. 'By my reckoning, we've still got fifteen minutes.'

When Brianna walked up to the microphone a short while later, Mitch couldn't help the smug smile that slipped across his face. Her hair wasn't quite as artfully coiled on her head as it had been at the start of the evening. Her skin glowed just that little bit more.

'Ladies and gentlemen,' she began. 'We've come to that stage of the evening when we ask you to dip once more into those deep and generous pockets of yours. It's auction time. Please welcome our auctioneer onto the stage, who will explain how it's all going to work.'

She stepped aside to cheers and whistles. Then the professional auctioneer explained how the auction would run and set the proceedings in motion.

Mitch watched with passing interest as several pretty young women went for £1,000, and a couple of cocky men raised £500 and £1,500.

'And finally, we have the hostess for the evening, Brianna Worthington. Who will start the bidding? Shall we say five hundred pounds?'

He went from couldn't care less to wound up like a coiled spring in the blink of an eye. It might only be a harmless way of raising money, but seeing Brianna on the stage, a prize ready to go to the highest bidder, set his teeth on edge. He didn't want her dating anybody else, even if it was for a good cause. Before he had a chance to think, his hand shot up in the air and he was starting the bidding.

'Thank you, sir,' the auctioneer acknowledged him. 'But surely, for our beautiful hostess, we can get more than five hundred pounds?'

'One thousand pounds,' came the response from a rather rotund man near the front of the stage.

Mitch gritted his teeth. 'One thousand five hundred.' He felt stupid, offering money to go on a date with the woman he was seeing anyway. Especially as the money went to the same charity he worked for.

'Two thousand pounds.' The man at the front wasn't giving in.

Mitch figured he didn't need to eat next month, after all. 'Two thousand five hundred.'

He was relieved to see a shake of the head from the man who'd been bidding against him. Expelling breath he hadn't realised he'd been holding, he risked a glance at Brianna, who was smiling broadly at him.

'Two thousand five hundred pounds with the tall, fair-haired gentleman at the back of the room. Do I hear any further bids?' The auctioneer was ready with his gavel. 'Going once ...'

'One hundred thousand pounds.'

The crowd gasped and turned en masse to stare at the latest bidder.

Mitch didn't need to look. He knew it was Henry. The man's obsession with Brianna was obvious to everyone. Except it seemed to the lady in question. He'd seen the look of jealousy flare in Henry's eyes after he'd deliberately kissed Brianna in front of him. It didn't take a genius to work out that Henry would take any opportunity he could to embarrass Mitch, to belittle him in Brianna's eyes. And he'd succeeded. Other than selling his house, which even Mitch wasn't prepared to do just to save face, he had to accept that Henry had won.

Involuntarily his hands clenched into fists. The smart, grown-up way to admit his defeat would be to acknowledge Henry's bid with a polite smile. But Mitch had never been the polite sort. What he really wanted to do was run a fist into the smug bastard's smooth, handsome face. Glancing at the genteel crowd, watching him expectantly, and then at Brianna's worried face, Mitch knew he couldn't give in to that urge. So he did the only thing he could do. With a single shake of his head, he turned around and strode out of the room, making his escape.

Brianna couldn't get off the stage fast enough. She'd seen the humiliation on Mitch's face, mixed with a hefty dose of anger, and was desperate to get to him before he left. She didn't know what she'd say when she caught him, only that it was vital she did.

'Brianna, darling.' Her mother stood in the aisle, blocking her way. 'Where are you rushing off to?'

'Not now, Mum.' Frantically she scanned the exit, briefly catching sight of Mitch's back view before he disappeared down the corridor.

'You're running after Mitch, aren't you?'

Brianna flinched at the undertone. Her mother certainly had a way of showing her disapproval. 'I'm going to find him, if that's what you mean.'

'I didn't realise you two were still an item until this evening.'

'After the way Henry's just humiliated him, we probably won't be.' None too gently, she manoeuvred her mother out of the way. 'Sorry, Mum, but I don't have time for this now.'

'Just be careful. I warned you about getting involved with a man who's from a very different background to yours ...'

They were words she'd heard before and they rolled off Brianna as she fled through the ballroom as fast as her towering heels would allow her. Then it was down the corridor, across the foyer, and through the revolving door to outside. There, to her intense relief, she found Mitch leaning against the wall, waiting for a taxi. His bow tie was unknotted, shirt open at the collar and his jacket flung over his shoulder. His face was as black as thunder.

'Mitch.' She rushed up to him, laying a hand on his arm.

'Leave it, Brianna,' he growled, yanking his arm away from her touch.

'No, I won't leave it.' He was angry, but so was she. At the moment it was a toss-up who she was more angry with. Henry for being so arrogant, or Mitch for letting Henry get to him. 'Were you going to go without saying goodbye?'

Mitch glared at her, stuffing his hands back into his pockets. 'I'm not a great person to be around right now. Go back to your friends.'

'My rich friends, don't you mean?' She thrust her chin up at him, daring him to disagree.

'Yes, damn it, your rich friends.' His dark eyes glinted dangerously, a sign he was battling to hold onto his temper. He was a proud man and that pride had just taken a big hit.

'Mitch, Henry has just paid a ridiculous sum of money for one evening with me. Something you can do any night you choose for free. What does that make him?' she asked, her tone gentler this time.

'It makes him rich and stupid,' he acknowledged with a grunt.

'And what does it make you?' She risked moving closer to him, putting her arm around his waist.

'Lucky?' There was a twitch of humour to his lips now.

'Exactly right, and don't you forget it.' She tugged his head down and planted a long, slow kiss on his lips. 'Now, are you going to stay out here sulking, or are you going to come back into the ballroom with me, dance in front of Henry's nose and then join me in the hotel room we've already christened?'

He sighed. 'Damn it, Brianna, I hate that people like Henry make me feel inadequate. I know I shouldn't let it get to me, but it does.'

Brianna could only stare at Mitch in astonishment. How could a man as strong, as smart as him, possibly feel inadequate? She couldn't understand it. 'Mitch, you're worth a hundred Henry's. Just because he was born into money, doesn't make him a man.'

Mitch allowed himself to be taken back to the ballroom. Allowed Brianna's words to soothe his rumpled pride. He even had to admit to a spurt of childish euphoria when he saw Henry watching them together on the dance floor. Hell, he knew he was a better man than that pompous twit. He also knew that someone as shallow-minded and mean-spirited as Henry, even with all his money and privilege, wasn't right for Brianna.

But that didn't mean a rough-edged charity medic from the wrong side of the tracks was right for her, either. Lust had got in the way of his instincts. He was becoming tangled up with a woman he had no business being entangled with. Worse, he was now in so deep that whatever he did, they would both get hurt.

Chapter Twenty-Five

Brianna threw the phone down in annoyance. Having paid £100,000 into the Medic SOS bank account, it looked like Henry was after his pound of flesh. He wanted his dinner date and he wasn't going to take no for an answer. Brianna hissed. Perhaps she should be grateful at least one man wanted to have dinner with her tonight, even if it was Henry. Mitch hadn't exactly been inundating her with calls since last weekend, begging to see her. She was starting to get more than a little fed up with the way he blew hot and cold.

Despite Margaret's insistence that Brianna work the proper office hours, she left work early, reasoning that tonight could be classed as work. The man had paid a small fortune for the date, the least she owed him was to look her best. And that meant allowing plenty of time to get ready.

Having showered, she slipped into a short, flirty silk dress and was trying to reach round to do up the zipper when her phone rang.

She gave the zip one last tug, but her arms weren't long enough and the insistent ringing of the phone was driving her crazy. Muttering under her breath she left the unzipped halves dangling and went to answer it. 'Hello?'

'You sound out of breath. What are you up to?'

She expelled a soft curse. Mitch. 'I'm trying to do up the zipper on my dress. Where are you when I need you?'

'I'm better at undoing zips,' he replied dryly. 'Why are you putting on a dress now anyway? Have you got a hot date?'

'As a matter of fact, I have.'

There was a moment of deafening silence. 'Who with?' he asked finally, his voice sounding strangled.

She laughed. 'Come on, Mitch, I'm only teasing. I'm seeing Henry for this flipping date he paid for at the auction.'

'I see.'

Again there was silence. Brianna shook her head, half annoyed, half pleased. Was Mitch really jealous? Of *Henry*? 'Well, if it helps, I'd rather I was seeing you. I would have been, if you'd phoned.'

'I'm phoning now, aren't I?' Then there was a deep sigh. 'Look, I'm sorry I haven't been in touch. I've been a bit busy. Where is he taking you?'

'The Ivy.' Even as she said the words, she cringed, imagining the look on his face at the name of the pretentious restaurant.

'Well, enjoy your evening, Brianna,' he replied quietly, putting down the phone before she had a chance to reply.

With a sigh she gathered up the halves of her dress and went in search of her mother.

'Would you mind doing me up?' she asked when she found her in her study.

'Wow, you look lovely, dear.' Her mother quickly zipped her up before easing her round to face her. 'So.' She coughed delicately. 'Is this all in honour of Mitch?'

Brianna rolled her eyes. 'No. It's for Henry.' Her mother's lips curved into a brief, triumphant smile. 'And before you get any ideas, this is the date he paid for.'

'Oh, I see.' The smile disappeared, but Brianna knew her hope remained. 'Well, have a good evening, darling.'

Brianna mumbled her thanks, disappearing before she received another lecture on how wonderfully suitable Henry was. In contrast to the wildly unsuitable Mitch. There had been a time when she might have looked forward to being taken to dinner by Henry. But that was before she realised he liked her as more than a friend. And before she'd met the rugged doctor who'd stolen her heart.

* * *

Mitch was restless. Ever since he'd spoken to Brianna he couldn't settle. He'd tried to watch the television, but none of the programmes took his interest. He'd thought of taking out his surfboard, but there wasn't much light left and for once the thought of pitting himself against the wind and the waves didn't thrill him. He'd deliberately waited until midweek to phone Brianna, wanting to put some space between them since the saga of the ball. But the moment she'd told him she was going out with Henry, the defensive shield he'd started to erect had shattered. Now he found himself pacing the room, unable to get the image of Brianna laughing with Henry over a glass of champagne out of his head. This scenario should have been perfect. What easier way to put the brakes on their doomed relationship than to push her into the arms of another man?

The thought caused a sharp pain his heart. No. Damn it, she deserved someone far better than bloody Henry. Angrily he punched his hand against the door frame. This was crazy. He couldn't stand it. He couldn't simply sit the evening out in his own home wondering what she was doing. Snatching at his car keys, he slammed out of the house.

Two hours later, he was sitting in his car opposite her place feeling like a stalker, which effectively he was. Thank God common sense had prevailed enough for him to abandon his first idea, which had been to storm into the Ivy and sit down at their table. Yeah, he could just imagine how well that would have gone down. Henry might have been pissed, but Brianna would have been absolutely livid. So instead he'd parked up outside her house and sat and waited, not even daring to think about what he was going to do if she didn't turn up.

Another hour passed. Mitch looked at his watch. It was half past eleven. Where the hell were they? His hands gripped the steering wheel and with a muttered curse he sunk his head onto them. What on earth was he doing here? He was a total fool. He'd spent the best part of three days telling himself he had to cool things with Brianna and now he was sitting outside her place, waiting for her to come home like the jealous boyfriend he'd convinced himself he couldn't be.

Just as he was about to turn the key and drive home, a sleek black Mercedes purred into view. Mitch watched as the car glided to a stop right outside her house. Screwing up his eyes he could see Henry at the wheel and Brianna sitting next to him, her hair pinned elegantly on the top of her head. She looked every inch the lady she was.

Aware he was still clenching the wheel, Mitch made himself relax and sit back in the seat. He'd just wait until she got out, until Henry drove round the corner, and then he'd drive off home. He didn't need to ever admit to this shoddy little venture.

Inside the Mercedes Henry's face bent towards Brianna's.

Without thinking, Mitch yanked his door open and barged over to them, thumping on the passenger window.

A shocked Brianna opened the door. 'Mitch! What on earth are you doing here?'

'I came to check you were okay.' He barely squeezed the words out, his jaw was so tight.

'Why wouldn't she be okay?' Henry leaned across from the driver's seat, his cheeks flushed with anger.

Mitch didn't reply. He just stood and stared at them both, hands in fists at his side, muscles tense.

'You knew I'd be okay with Henry. He's an old friend.' Brianna shook her head, as if she still couldn't believe he was there.

Mitch sucked in a sharp breath, aware of an irrational stab of jealousy at her words and what they implied. The years she and Henry had already shared, even if it was only platonic. 'I wanted to make sure he didn't push for more than he'd paid for.'

Brianna flushed at his coarseness. 'That was uncalled for.'

It was. He was being rude and overbearing. With a jerk of his head Mitch looked away, staring into the distance. He was fast losing his mind. Brianna was making him lose his mind. Why else had he driven all the way here, effectively to spy on her?

Simmering with anger at himself, he left them to it and walked back across the road to his car. He'd done exactly what he hadn't wanted to do at the ball. He'd shown Brianna up in front of one of her friends. At this very moment Henry was no doubt looking down his long, aristocratic nose at him and Mitch couldn't even blame him. He'd not only given him all the ammunition he needed, he'd practically loaded the damn gun and pulled off the safety catch. He'd shown no better manners than the louts he'd grown up with.

As he hunched over the wheel of his car, brooding into the night, Brianna slipped into the passenger seat.

'What on earth are you playing at?' she demanded, her green eyes blazing. 'How dare you embarrass me like this, checking up on me as if I'm some sort of harlot? One you can't trust out of your sight.'

There was nothing he could say in his defence.

'And what if I'd wanted to invite him back?' she continued, her voice softer now, but more deadly. 'What would you have done then?'

He turned to glare at her. 'Don't play games with me, Brianna.'

'Same goes, Mitch.' She moved to slide back out of the car. 'It's been three days since the ball and you haven't bothered to call. I never know where I stand with you from one day to the next. Either you want me in your life or you don't. Which is it?'

This was his opportunity. The chance to do what any sane man would do in his position, once he'd grasped the woman he was falling for was too far out of his reach. He just had to say the word.

'You know damn well which it is,' he ground out, knowing he didn't have the strength to do what he needed to do. If he couldn't bear the thought of her on a platonic date with Henry, how was he expected to finish with her now, leaving the field open for all the other men he'd seen sniffing around, watching her with frankly lustful eyes.

'Do I?' she replied softly. 'Maybe I need to hear you say it.'

'I want you, Brianna. God knows, I want you.' Just like he'd wanted to be part of a normal, happy loving family. He could want all he liked, but some things he just couldn't have.

'Then why are you still sitting in the car?'

She shut the passenger door and crossed the road, her beautiful body rippling under the silk of her dress. As he watched her, his heart was in danger of exploding in his chest. On the outside she was beauty and class personified. On the inside she was funny, warm-hearted and stronger than he'd realised. Once all he'd seen was a spoilt rich girl. Now he knew she was so much more. It was no wonder he couldn't do without her.

With a shake of his head, he climbed out of the car and went to follow her.

As he caught up with her on the doorstep, he put his arm around her shoulders and turned her to face him. 'I'm sorry I embarrassed you,' he told her, running his finger over her soft pink lips. 'I'm not good at jealousy.'

She sighed against his fingers. 'I'm not interested in other men, Mitch. I thought I'd made it clear by now. You are all I want. All I need.'

Her eyes were luminous and Mitch allowed himself to drown in them. Lowering his head to kiss her, he kidded himself that maybe, just maybe, they were meant to be together. If not forever, then at least for a little while longer.

Chapter Twenty-Six

Mitch had never been one for parties of any description. Give him a pint of beer and a cosy pub any day. But here he was at his second party in successive weekends, and mingling with Brianna's friends once more. With a wry shake of his head he had to admit he felt no less like a fish out of water than he had at the ball.

His gaze swept across the partygoers congregated by the vast turquoise swimming pool that glittered invitingly in the early summer sunlight. There, in the middle of the throng, laughing happily and glittering just as invitingly, was the reason why he was prepared to put up with feeling so out of place. Brianna, looking so mouth-watering, that feasting his eyes on her was like a kick to his solar plexus.

At that moment she turned her head and caught his eye. After whispering something to the girl she was talking to, she sauntered up to him, her movements easy, fluid, sensual. 'What are you doing, standing here all alone?' she asked softly, draping her arms around his shoulders.

He expelled a deep breath of contentment as she nestled against him. Was it any wonder he couldn't give her up? 'I'm waiting for a sexy lady to come and chat me up,' he replied, running his hands lazily down her back. She was wearing very little. Just a brightly coloured kaftan and a miniscule pink bikini.

'Will I do?' she smiled up at him.

'Well, you're the best offer I've had so far,' he replied, nipping playfully at her ear. 'But the night is still young.' He received a sharp dig in the ribs. 'Ouch. For that you can get me another drink. I guess it'll have to be the non-alcoholic kind.'

'It was your choice to drive. We could have stayed over. Sophie did offer.'

'I know.' But he hadn't wanted to stay any longer than was necessary. At the first opportunity he was going to drag her away so he could have her all to himself.

Brianna took Mitch by the hand and led him towards the temporary bar. When she'd looked up to see him watching her, her heart had jumped in her chest. Her first thought had been how sexy he looked. Hard, tough, not the sort of man that you messed with. That menacing edge, the one that was there when he brooded like she'd caught him doing just now, gave her goosebumps. Not the cold kind, or the scared kind, but the *shivers up the spine excited* kind. It also set him apart from other men, especially the crowd here tonight. He was, on the whole, older, being in his mid-thirties rather than mid to late twenties. But his age didn't come from the years that he'd lived, but the way that he'd lived them. This crowd had been brought up with a silver spoon in their mouth and a generous trust fund in the bank. Most hadn't done a proper day's work in their lives. Unlike Mitch, who worked his gorgeous butt off to save and improve the lives of others.

As he ordered another round of drinks for them both, Melanie sidled up behind Brianna. 'You know, Brie, if I met your man in a dark alley late at night, I wouldn't know whether to be delighted or terrified.'

Brianna was still chuckling when Mitch came back with the drinks. 'What are you ladies sniggering about?' he asked, looking from one to the other.

'The relative merits of dark alleys,' Melanie replied, batting her eyes at him. 'Now then, Mitch. I hope you've brought your trunks with you.' She cast her eyes over his dark T-shirt and casual linen shorts, clearly assessing what lay beneath.

'If you're hoping for a pair of Speedo's, you're doomed for disappointment.'

Melanie giggled. 'I don't think you're going to be a disappointment.'

Brianna raised her eyebrows. 'Err, excuse me, I am here you know. The only one who'll be getting their hands on my boyfriend's trunks is me.' It felt strange saying the word boyfriend out loud. It implied a certain steadiness to their relationship that, even after his jealous appearance at her place during the week, she knew didn't really exist. She wondered if she'd ever reach that stage when she knew he was hers.

'Fair enough,' Melanie agreed. 'But it doesn't mean to say the rest of us can't look. Come on, Mitch, time to strip off and get into the pool. I want to see if you've got what it takes to be on my team for the water polo.'

Mitch eyed her warily. 'What exactly does it take to be on your team?' he asked as he peeled off his shorts.

'It's all about form,' she replied with a wink. 'Body form.'

'You'll have to excuse Melanie,' Brianna interjected. 'When it comes to an attractive male she turns into some sort of Mata Hari.'

She glanced up to see a crowd walking towards them. Sophie was there. Sadly, so too was Henry and his friend Simon. They were all stripped down to their swimwear, the girls slender in their bikinis, the boys with perfectly sculptured chests and trendy coloured trunks. Brianna hadn't spoken to Henry since their charity date and she wasn't exactly thrilled to see him now. Goodness only knew what Mitch was thinking. She watched the men eye each other up.

'Are you ladies ready to start?' Henry directed his question at Melanie and Brianna, deliberately avoiding Mitch.

'As it happens, I was just asking my star player to strip off,' Melanie replied coolly, clearly sensing the atmosphere between the men and showing whose side she was on.

Though Mitch's expression gave nothing away, Brianna could tell he was uncomfortable. She had a desperate urge to drag him back to the car and far away from the party. He was here only because she'd asked him to come. It wasn't his scene and having Henry prowling round, waiting for him to slip up, wasn't helping. Mitch tugged off his T-shirt and nodded over to Melanie.

'Umm, I wasn't wrong. You do have form.' Melanie ran an appreciative pair of eyes over Mitch's plain black trunks and bare torso. 'Nice tattoo.'

He looked over his shoulder at the black panther. 'Thanks.'

'I've never understood the fascination for grown men, or women for that matter, to adorn their bodies with ink.' Simon spoke the words casually, but Brianna heard the edge behind them. He'd set his feet firmly in Henry's camp.

'I agree,' Mitch replied, his voice equally light. 'I wasn't a grown man when I had it done.'

'I bet you were a man when you received those scars.' Sophie nodded to where her eyes were seemingly transfixed on the long scar that ran jaggedly across his side.

'For some,' Mitch replied tersely.

Brianna clutched at Mitch's hand, noting how tensely he was holding himself. Not surprising, as they were eyeing him up like an animal at the zoo. Tattoos and scars weren't seen very often in the circles these people moved in. They all had perfect bodies. If they weren't born with them, they paid a fortune to have them created through personal trainers and clever plastic surgeons. She felt a roll of shame wash over her. These shallow people had been her friends.

'Come on, Mitch,' Melanie spoke, thankfully breaking

the tension. 'You, me, Camilla and Hugo. We'll be unbeatable.' Reaching out her hand, she tugged a slightly unwilling Mitch towards the pool.

Brianna was left standing and wondering why it felt like she'd just allowed her lover to be fed to the lions.

The action in the pool kept everyone entertained for the rest of the afternoon. Brianna realised she needn't have worried about Mitch. He was more than capable of looking after himself. Though he clearly hadn't played the game before, his swimming prowess and natural athleticism more than made up for his lack of experience at water polo.

'What are you doing with him, Brianna?'

With a start, she turned to find Henry standing next to her, his eyes fixed on Mitch who was still in the pool.

'I'm having a great time,' she replied coolly, 'despite your determination to ruin it with your little stunts.'

'I made a significant contribution to your precious charity,' he countered sulkily. 'You should be pleased.'

'I would have been if your motivation had been altruism, not humiliation.'

Henry snorted contemptuously. 'The man's an easy target. Look at him. What type of man has a panther on his arm and scars on his chest?'

'The sort that's had a tougher life than you,' she spat back. God, had she once been that judgemental too? She shivered.

Henry stared at her for a moment and then obviously decided to change tactics. He draped a friendly arm around her shoulders, pulling her so she was forced to face him. 'Come on, Brie. You and me, we go back a long time. We're friends. In fact I had thought we were going to become more than that, right up until you lost your senses and started dating that loser.'

Something in Brianna snapped. She shoved at Henry, pushing him away from her. 'How dare you call him that? He's more of a man than you'll ever be.'

'Problem?'

She hadn't seen Mitch come up behind her, but was grateful to feel the strength of his arm as it circled her waist.

'Nothing I can't handle,' she replied, looking pointedly at Henry.

Mitch glowered, beads of water trickling over his powerful chest. 'If you've got something to say, Henry, you need to say it directly to me.' The words he uttered were calm enough, but the fire in his eyes betrayed his anger.

Henry smirked. 'I think I will. You see I'm trying to work out what on earth Brianna sees in you and I find myself totally stumped. Of course, when I look at what you see in her, it's blindingly obvious. She's beautiful, but that's not the real attraction for you, is it?'

Henry was clearly enjoying himself, playing to the crowd that had started to gather, sensing trouble. The hairs on the back of Brianna's neck tingled and she clutched the arm that still circled her waist. She didn't know where Henry was going with this, but wherever it was, it wasn't going to end well.

'No,' Henry continued, staring contemptuously at Mitch. 'Looking back at your history, it would seem a woman doesn't have to be beautiful to get your attention. She doesn't even have to be young. She just has to be filthy rich.'

Brianna turned sharply to Mitch. 'What's he talking about?' she pleaded, wanting to understand.

But Mitch's rigid profile wasn't looking at her. 'Spit it out, Henry. You think I'm only with Brianna for her money, is that it?' She felt his arm tighten around her. 'Not a particularly flattering assessment of Brianna's attributes.'

'It's not my assessment,' Henry thundered, on a roll now,

veins pulsing on the side of his neck. 'It's yours. You're quite good at this game now, aren't you? Targeting wealthy, vulnerable ladies. But then you've been practising for a long time. You started off with the older women, didn't you?'

When Mitch remained silent, Henry continued. 'Does the name Catherine ring any bells with you, or have you forgotten all about her?'

Mitch's fingers dug into her waist and Brianna had to stifle a yelp. 'You bastard,' he uttered under his breath.

'Ah, so you do remember your first conquest. I understand she was quite taken with you for a while. Thankfully her family found out, didn't they, Simon?' Henry cast his eyes over to his friend, who looked slightly embarrassed, but nodded. 'You see Catherine is Simon's aunt. She is the sister of Simon's father. Thankfully he was able to explain to his sister who you really were. A chancer, preying on a rich old lady.' Henry stared deliberately over at Brianna. 'It looks like your tastes have improved, though your methods are probably still very similar.'

One minute Mitch was grasping her waist, the next he was grasping Henry's shirt collar and yanking him towards the pool. Henry tried to push away but Mitch was far too strong for him. Stunned by the speed and violence of the action, nobody interfered as Mitch took his right arm back and thrust it into Henry's jaw with brutal force, sending him flying into the pool.

Mitch waited for a few seconds to see Henry bob up to the surface, spluttering. Then he turned back to the now hushed crowd. 'Entertainment over.' His voice was as cold and flat as the expression on his face. Without a backward glance at anyone, including Brianna, he picked up his T-shirt and shorts and strode off towards his car.

Brianna stood frozen to the spot, her mind blank.

'You see, Brianna,' Henry was yelling at her from the

pool, holding his jaw. 'That's the real nature of the man you're sleeping with. He's a bloody thug.'

His words acted like a bucket of cold water on her, clearing her senses. Livid with anger, she walked to the edge of the pool. 'What the hell did you expect, spouting all those lies at him? And what sort of idiot do you take me for? Do you really think I'm stupid enough to be hoodwinked by a man who only wants me for my money?' She looked pityingly at the man now struggling out of the pool, the man who had once been her friend. 'I chased after Mitch, you fool, not him after me.'

She felt her friend's arms pulling her back, but Brianna just shrugged them off. 'I've got to get to Mitch,' she cried, desperate to reach him before he drove off.

Suddenly she was running as if her life depended on it. She ignored the pain in her bare feet as she ran across the gravel to where she could see Mitch's car, the engine running. Panting, she banged on the passenger window. 'Mitch, let me in.'

The door unlocked and she dived inside. Though her instinct was to wrap her arms around him and apologise, she stopped as soon as she saw the bleak look on his face. Anger, pain, humiliation all vied with each other. There was no warmth when he looked at her, nothing to indicate that any show of sorrow or compassion on her side would be gratefully received. 'Are you okay?' she settled on, not daring to touch him.

'I've just been accused of conning rich women out of their money by one of your friends. Why wouldn't I be all right?' His voice was so tight she wondered how it had squeezed past his vocal cords.

'He's no friend of mine, not any more. Look, I'm sorry he said the things he did. I know none of it is true—'

'Do you?' Mitch interjected harshly.

She frowned. 'Of course I do.'

'How do you know?' He snapped the words out as he put the car into gear and crunched down the driveway.

'I know you, Mitch. You're honest and you're proud. There is no way you would prey on rich women.'

He laughed, a bitter sound that had her shivering despite the warmth of the evening. 'You don't know me, Brianna. You don't know me at all.'

Brianna gazed at the harsh, rugged face she had come to love. She wanted to beg him to let her get to know him. To tell her about his past, open up to her. Sadly anger shimmered round him like a shield, one she didn't dare try and penetrate. This was his dangerous side back in action. She had a feeling Henry had been lucky to escape with a single punch. The best thing she could do was keep quiet and hope the drive home would calm him down.

Chapter Twenty-Seven

As Mitch drove, the white-hot anger continued to fester inside him. It was only a lifetime of learning how to handle his temper and hide his emotions that gave him the necessary calm to drive Brianna home. Catherine. It had been a long time since he'd heard her name, over fifteen years. And it still hurt.

As he neared Brianna's house, he glanced in her direction. Her face was pale, her eyes fixed unblinkingly on the road ahead. His heart squeezed. He had become terrifyingly attached to her, as he feared he would. Over the years, since Catherine, he'd sometimes wondered if he was actually capable of caring for anybody. At least now, looking at Brianna, he knew he was. It was small comfort. Deep in his heart he'd been living an illusion, a fantasy that, despite everything he'd told himself to the contrary, there was a chance for them both. A chance for a future together. That had just blown up in his face.

He pulled up outside her house and turned off the engine.

'Are you coming in?' she asked quietly.

He shook his head, fearing if he allowed himself to speak he would give in to the temptation to say yes.

'I see,' she replied coolly, her beautiful eyes brimming with tears she was clearly determined not to allow to fall. 'Is that not tonight, thanks, or not ever again, because it sounds a lot like the latter?'

Mitch let out a deep sigh. He hated this part, the part when he had to say goodbye. God knows, he'd gone through the routine enough times, though with Brianna he'd come closer than ever to thinking of a future with both of them in it. This time it was going to hurt like hell. 'Brianna, you and

I both know it's time for us to go our separate ways. We had fun, like we said we would. But now it's over.'

'Why? Are you really going to let the words of a spoilt, immature twit come between us?'

Mitch almost smiled. He couldn't have described Henry better himself. 'His methods are crass, but you can't deny the truth behind them. We don't belong together, Brianna. We don't fit. It's not just our backgrounds, though that alone would be enough. It's also what we want out of life. I warned you right at the start, I'm not cut out for relationships. You want marriage, a family. I'm not capable of giving you that. It's time for us to call it a day before we get in too deep and one of us gets hurt.'

Brianna let out a bitter laugh. 'It's too late for that. I love you.' Her voice grew softer and was on the verge of breaking. 'I've damn well fallen head over heels in love with you.'

He felt as if a hand had opened up his chest and clutched at his heart. How could she love him? She didn't even know him. If she knew the truth about him, where he'd come from, she wouldn't love him. 'Then you're a fool,' he replied, his tone deliberately harsh.

Brianna recoiled, but not for long. Soon her eyes flashed back at him. 'No, Mitch. If you're turning down what we have between us, then you're the fool.'

He couldn't disagree with her quietly spoken words. He was a fool, because he'd never find someone quite like Brianna ever again. But wasn't it better for her to think of him as a fool, than to know the truth about him? He'd grown up in an environment where the only relationship between a man and a woman had been about sex and money. What did he know about love? And he sure as hell couldn't accept her love, when he wasn't sure how much he could love back. He cared for her. He knew that. Cared so much it hurt. But was it love? Jesus, he didn't know what that meant.

He watched as Brianna climbed out of the car, her head held high. She was one classy lady, which only served to remind him of their differences. Still barefoot, her sandals hanging from her fingers, she walked away from him with her spine straight and her demeanour dignified. She never once looked back.

He waited for her to step inside before speeding off, screeching the tyres in his determination to get away. He ignored the pain he felt in his chest. After all, he'd known all along this would happen. And it was fine. He was fine. He was meant to be alone. Relationships weren't for him. Brianna might think she loved him, but she didn't. Couldn't in fact. Because there was so much about him she didn't know.

As soon as she shut the door, Brianna ran to her bedroom and flung herself onto her bed. There she did the only thing she was capable of. She cried her heart out. Great wailing sobs she couldn't control. At some point she must have crawled inside the bed, but she wasn't aware of it. The tears just wouldn't stop flowing. Now she understood why they called it a broken heart. It really felt as if her heart had smashed into lots of tiny pieces.

The next morning, though the tears had finally dried up, a dark cloud of despondency hung over her, sticking to her wherever she went. It was there during her shower, still there when she got dressed, and weighed heavily on her now as she answered the door.

'Oh, my darling, you look awful.' Her mother stood back and gave her the sort of once-over that only mothers can do.

'You sure know how to cheer a girl up,' Brianna replied

dryly, letting her in. 'I take it the gossip grapevine is working well and you've already heard about what happened at the party.'

'Well, Abigail did phone me this morning to say Henry had been grabbed by the throat and then punched,' her mother told her as she took a seat opposite Brianna in the living room. 'Apparently he was lucky his jaw wasn't broken, but there's an awful bruise coming up. What on earth did Mitch think he was playing at?'

'I don't think he was doing much thinking,' Brianna acknowledged sadly, hugging at a cushion. 'He'd been called a con artist, Mum. One who tricks women out of their fortunes.'

Her mother bristled. 'Whatever Henry might have said, there is never any excuse for violence. From what I hear, Mitch could have killed him.'

Brianna thought back to the look on Mitch's face as he'd lunged at Henry. Cold, menacing, dangerous. 'If he'd wanted to kill him, Mum, he would have.'

'And you admire that?'

'I admire people who stick up for themselves. What I don't admire are people who go around deliberately trying to humiliate others. You weren't there, Mum. You didn't see how Henry provoked him. Trust me, Henry got off lightly. Mitch made sure he had a soft landing in the pool.' She sighed. 'And if you're going to say in your next breath that it isn't how gentlemen behave, then don't bother. True gentlemen don't behave like Henry, either.'

Her mother had the grace to agree. 'It wasn't nice of Henry, you're right. But he was looking out for you. You are worth a lot of money. That would be quite an incentive, in many men's eyes.'

'Well, you don't have to worry any more, either of you. Do you know why? Because the man who is clearly only after me for my money, has dumped me.' The stupid tears began to fall again, tears she thought she'd run out of.

'Oh, darling, I am sorry.' Her mother moved to sit next to her and gave her hand a sympathetic squeeze.

'Don't be a hypocrite, Mum. You're not sorry at all. Mitch was good enough to work for your charity, but never good enough to date your daughter, was he?'

'It doesn't have anything to do with being good enough,' her mother replied sharply. 'But it's not easy being in a relationship where the two parties feel unequal. Especially when it's the man who feels inadequate next to the woman.' She gazed at her daughter. 'I know you're hurting darling, but you're young. Mitch has done the right thing by you. In time you'll see that.'

'No I won't. All I'll see is a man too damned scared to allow himself to fall in love.' She looked down at where her mum was holding her hand. 'It doesn't all add up. He's a strong, confident man. Why would he let someone like Henry undermine him?'

'Probably because Mitch can't handle your wealth, darling. It's a lot to ask a man to take on. Those that don't see it as an opportunity for sudden richness can find it a massive dent to their pride. We might live in a modern era, but it's still more socially acceptable for a woman to marry a rich man, than the other way round.'

Brianna sighed. 'You're probably right. It was always a bone of contention between us.' Then she threw her arms around her mother's neck. 'God, I wish I'd been born poor.'

While Brianna was being comforted by her mother, Mitch was on his own, praying for the phone to ring. He didn't want to wish a disaster on anybody, but right now he needed something to take him away from his solitude. Why was it he couldn't look at his kitchen without imagining Brianna there, burning the bacon? Couldn't even sit on his own sofa without picturing her curled up on it. And his bed. Christ, his bed even smelt of her. It was driving him crazy. More than ever before in his life, he needed to work. That focused him like nothing else, allowed no time to think. Then, when he returned home, he would be fine. There wouldn't be anybody waiting at the airport for him, but he'd quickly get used to that again. Used to the way things had always been.

With a gesture of sheer frustration, Mitch grabbed the wetsuit from the living room floor and began to pull it on. The sea had always been a great solace. A place he could lose himself, for a while. He would spend his day windsurfing, and trying to forget the time he went with Brianna.

Chapter Twenty-Eight

In the office a few days later, Brianna hesitantly picked up the phone. She had never had to do this. Never had to contact an ex-lover. In previous relationships she had said goodbye and never looked back. This was different, on two levels. Firstly, Mitch had been the one saying goodbye. Secondly, they worked for the same organisation. Not seeing each other again wasn't an option, unless one of them left. She couldn't see Mitch leaving. Neither was she prepared to take that route. Not when work was the only thing keeping her sane. Taking in a deep breath, she dialled his number.

'McBride.' At the sound of his deep, clipped voice, her heart lurched.

'Mitch, it's Brianna.' She hesitated. What did you say to an ex-lover? 'How are you?' she asked formally.

'Well, thank you,' came the clearly amused reply. 'And you?'

'Damn you, Mitch,' she replied crossly. 'You can stop your mockery. I'm feeling my way here. I don't know the etiquette for greeting an ex-lover.'

'What did you do with your other ex's then?'

'I never spoke to them again.'

He let out a soft laugh. 'Ouch, so cruel. I suppose I should be flattered then.'

Annoyed by his apparent ease with the situation, Brianna turned frosty. 'No. This is a work call. I'm making it because I have to, not because I want to.'

There was a pause. 'Consider me put in my place. Fire away then. What do you want?'

'I've been talking to the chief medic in the army about the possibility of a mutually agreeable liaison.'

'You've been talking to Gerald?' His voice rose dangerously with each word he uttered.

'Yes,' she replied coolly. 'He speaks very highly of you.'

'Where is this going, Brianna?' Annoyance crackled over the line.

'I discussed the possibility of you doing a few training sessions with the medical staff there. Nothing major, just a couple of times a year. Sharing your experiences might provide them with valuable insight on handling field-based trauma situations. In return it would give Medic SOS a high profile within the army. Hopefully, in the longer term, some of them may choose to join us in the future.'

The silence stretched across the phone wires. 'And did you consider, for one minute, that it might have been polite to contact me first, before you started offering my services around?'

The words were slow, measured and deadly and uttered in exactly the right tone to put her back up. Anger was a good antidote to a broken heart. 'I didn't realise I had to go running to you every time I wanted to speak to somebody.'

'You're being deliberately obtuse. I want to know why you didn't bother to talk to me first before contacting my old boss, and discussing my time.'

All at once the heat of her argument fell away, leaving her empty. She loved him. She missed him. Talking to him now was agony. 'The truth is, I didn't want to talk to you,' she admitted, her voice wobbling slightly. 'This is hard for me, Mitch. I figured if I contacted him first and he wasn't interested, then I would be saved a conversation with you.'

There was a long, deep sigh on the other end of the phone. 'Just your bad luck he liked the idea then.' She could almost picture his wry smile. 'Look, it's a good initiative, Brianna. If I haven't told you already, then I'll do it now.

You're one smart cookie.' A pause. 'And if it helps any, this isn't easy for me, either.'

Tears, unbidden, crept down her cheeks. *Why did you end it then?* she wanted to scream down the phone at him but she was in an office, surrounded by interested females. And anyway, it was old ground and she had to move on. He was a stubborn man. Once his mind was made up, there would be no changing it. 'Good,' was all she said, before asking Mitch to follow up with Gerald, and quickly ending the call.

The conversation with Mitch had churned up her feelings again. She knew she had to stop brooding about him, but she couldn't. And when she pictured him, it was often right at the moment that Henry had shouted off about Catherine. Mitch had looked devastated. It kept preying on her mind. It hadn't been the look of a man shamed by his actions. No, it had been the look of a man tortured. A man who had obviously cared about Catherine very deeply. Which meant nothing Henry had said made sense.

'I can't let this drop,' she told Melanie later that evening as they shared a bottle of wine in her apartment. Part of Melanie's *cheer up Brianna* strategy.

'And meddling in Mitch's past is going to get you back into his good books how, exactly?'

Trust a friend to be blunt. 'I'm not meddling. Think of it this way, if he is a gold-digger ...' Melanie's mouth gaped open. 'No, of course I know he's not, but *if* he was, if he had embezzled money out of a rich old lady. Well then, I'd have a right to know, wouldn't I? He was my boyfriend.'

'That's some pretty warped logic, if you ask me.'

'No, it's not. It makes perfect sense. Us rich girls have to be very careful, you know.'

'Hey, who am I to stop you? I'm just the sidekick. If you

really believe this is the right thing to do, I'm right behind you. Wincing and rolling my eyes, maybe, but I'm here. I'll even get you Simon's number.' She fished around in her handbag and pulled out her phone. 'Here, go for it.'

Brianna took the phone, gulped, gulped again, then punched in the numbers. 'Simon, it's Brianna.'

'Well, this is a nice surprise. What can I do for you?'

Melanie leaned in to listen, nodding reassuringly at Brianna.

'I'm a bit embarrassed really,' she began, acting the part of the dumb rich girl. 'All that business last week with Mitch. I'm ashamed I was so easily conned by him. I wondered if you wouldn't mind telling me what happened with your aunt. How Mitch managed to play her.'

'Well, it was a long time ago,' Simon replied slowly. 'I remember Dad telling us his sister, who's quite a bit older than him, had instructed the family solicitor to change her will and leave her house to a boy who'd been living with her. That was Mitch. Dad wasn't happy. We were the original beneficiaries of the will, as Aunt Catherine had no children.'

'What did your Dad do when he found out?'

'He knew Catherine must have been conned. After all, why else would an elderly woman leave money to an eighteen-year-old the rest of the family had never heard of? So he told the solicitor to stall on the changes and to send a letter to Mitch saying he wasn't to contact Catherine again or they would call the police. It seems he'd already tricked her out of some money. They didn't want her duped into giving anything more. Especially her home. That's something that should go to family, not some chancer who came in off the streets.'

Brianna bit back all the ripe responses that immediately came to her mind. 'It sounds like your aunt had a lucky escape,' she murmured instead.

'And so did you from the sound of things.'

'Yes, it would appear so. What did Catherine think about all this?'

'I don't know. I've never spoken to her about any of it.'

'Simon, do you think Catherine would mind if I contacted her? I don't want to upset her, but it might help both of us to talk about how we were taken in by this man.'

Beside her, Melanie stifled a gasp and gaped at her.

'I'm sure my aunt wouldn't mind,' Simon replied, oblivious to Melanie's muffled sounds of horror. 'She's a bit old now, but you'd never know to talk to her. She's bright as a button. She'd probably enjoy the company.'

A minute later, Brianna was clutching Catherine's phone number in her hand. The key to Mitch's past.

'Well, that was ridiculously easy.' Melanie glanced down at the scribbled number. 'But now you've got it, what the flipping heck are you going to do with it?'

'I don't know,' Brianna admitted shakily. 'God I need a drink.' As she poured herself a glass of wine her hands trembled.

'If you phone Catherine now, you really are meddling in stuff that's not yours to meddle in,' Melanie warned.

'I know.'

'And if Mitch ever finds out, he won't just be angry, he'll be apoplectic. From what I've seen, and what you've told me, the man guards his privacy as if it were the crown jewels. Invading it like this would be, well, tantamount to betrayal I guess.'

'I know that, too.' She took another large gulp of wine. 'But what if there's been some sort of misunderstanding? What if my interfering can help Mitch in some way? He did once mention a kind lady who'd taken him in and helped him go to university. If this is that lady, he might want to speak to her again.'

'So why hasn't he? He's hardly the shy retiring type.'

'Maybe they lost contact.' She stood and snatched up the phone. 'Bugger it. I've got this far, I might as well follow through with it now.' Ignoring Melanie's grimace, Brianna took another swig of wine, for Dutch courage, and dialled Catherine's number.

'Hello?'

'Good evening, is that Catherine?' Before the lady had a chance to reply, Brianna continued in a rush. 'You don't know me. I'm Brianna Worthington, and I'm a friend of Mitch McBride.'

There was silence on the end of the phone. It went on for so long Melanie mouthed at her to check Catherine was still there.

'Yes, dear, I'm still here,' the old lady confirmed. 'Hearing Mitch's name, it's such a shock. I haven't heard it for so many years.'

Brianna's heart was pounding so much she could hear it. She hoped to God Catherine couldn't hear it, too. 'I wondered if you could spare me a few minutes to talk about him?'

'Well, of course. Is he all right? He's not in any trouble?' The concern in her voice was clear, and Brianna felt a rush of relief. Whatever had happened, Catherine clearly didn't still hate Mitch for it.

'He's fine, really. It's quite a long story though. Would you mind if I came over, perhaps tomorrow evening, to talk to you in person?'

Next to her Melanie let out a strangled noise and mimed slitting her throat. Brianna ignored her and concentrated on Catherine's reply and the warmth of her voice.

'I wouldn't mind at all, dear. In fact, I'd love to talk to you about Mitch. I always wondered what happened to him. He used to write so regularly, and then, out of the blue, his letters stopped coming, and I never heard from him again.'

Brianna's still pounding heart skipped a beat. 'Catherine, are you sure you didn't ask your family to write to Mitch, instructing him you didn't want him to contact you anymore?'

'Why ever would I have done that? He was like a son to me. No, dear, I may be in my dotage, but I know for a fact I would never have wanted Mitch to stop seeing me. I assumed he got bored of writing to an old woman. That he'd found himself a new life and didn't need a constant reminder of his old one.'

'Catherine, I think there's a lot we need to talk about,' Brianna replied softly. 'I'll see you tomorrow.'

Melanie waited for Brianna to take down Catherine's address and put the phone down before clearing her throat. 'So, you're not meddling, but you've now arranged to visit a very important lady in Mitch's past without his knowledge.'

Slowly Brianna leant forward and put her face in her hands. 'It would appear that way, yes.'

'God Brie, I hope you know what you're doing.'

Hysterical laughter bubbled out of her. 'Of course I don't.'

Chapter Twenty-Nine

All through the following day Brianna could think of nothing but her pending visit to Catherine that evening. She guessed it made a welcome change from daydreaming about Mitch. Following the directions Catherine had given her, she pulled up outside an imposing town house in a very upmarket area of the city. No wonder Simon's father had been keen to make sure the property didn't go to a stranger. It was clearly worth several million.

The lady who greeted Brianna was far from the doddering old woman she'd been expecting. Yes, she was probably in her eighties, but she wore it really well. She was elegantly dressed, her white hair fashionably layered, and her face, though wrinkled, still had the fine bone structure of a beautiful woman.

'You must be Brianna. Please, come in. Would you like a drink?'

Brianna accepted a coffee, and was shown into a grand living room. The furniture was antique, but homely. 'This is my posh room, where I bring all my visitors. When it's just me, I sit in a cosy little snug round the corner,' Catherine confessed as she sat herself down on a high-backed chair by the fireplace. She smiled at Brianna. 'My dear, since you called last night I've not stopped thinking about what you said. I'm anxious to hear everything you know.'

Brianna settled back against the sofa and wondered where she should start. 'Last week I was at a party with Mitch and your nephew, Simon. At the party Mitch was accused of being a gold-digger, of preying on a rich woman. Your name was mentioned.'

Shock spread across the old lady's face. 'Mitch? A gold-digger? What a load of old nonsense. He never took a single thing off me I didn't freely give.'

'Catherine, I spoke to Simon last night and it appears that his father, your brother I believe, was concerned when he heard you'd wanted to amend your will. Leaving your house to a stranger, rather than your family, was a big step.'

'That was nobody's business but mine,' Catherine retorted sharply. 'Mitch wasn't a stranger. He was like a son to me. And that so-called family of mine would have known that if they'd ever bothered to visit. Why wouldn't I want to leave him my house? He'd lived with me here for four happy years. I wanted to give him a family home, something he'd never had before.'

Brianna's shoulders slumped in relief. It was only then that she realised she'd been harbouring a fear that maybe, just maybe, her instincts about Mitch had been wrong. But now she knew she was right, was what *had* happened really any of her business? Her desire to hear more about Mitch clashed fiercely with the knowledge she was prying into private matters.

She shifted in her seat. 'Catherine, I feel a little awkward talking about your family like this. It has nothing to do with me. I probably shouldn't have interfered at all, but when Mitch was accused of conning you out of money, I knew it couldn't be true.'

'It certainly wasn't. What was it you said on the phone about a letter?'

'Simon said his father instructed the solicitor to write to Mitch telling him never to contact you again, or they would call the police.'

Catherine rattled her cup down into the saucer. 'Oh, my,' she whispered, totally taken aback. 'Poor Mitch, whatever must he have thought of me? No wonder he suddenly stopped writing.' The old lady had gone as white as a sheet and slumped back against the chair. 'I should have guessed there was more to it than him simply not being bothered. He was always so good to me, so caring. And now I think of it, around the same time Mitch's letters stopped arriving, my brother started asking about him. He told me Mitch was all manner of horrid things I knew were lies so I simply ignored them. What I should have done was realise the connection. How stupid.' Her voice began to break and tears slipped down her cheeks.

'Oh, Catherine, I'm so sorry. I didn't want to upset you.' Brianna was mortified. 'I shouldn't have come. I shouldn't be meddling in things that don't concern me.' Wondering how she could comfort somebody she barely knew, Brianna walked over to the older lady and offered her a tissue. She was surprised when Catherine put a hand around her fingers, and clasped them tight.

'Don't you dare go apologising, my dear. You've just given me back the son I thought I'd lost. When I've got over the shock, I'll feel so much better, so much happier.' She paused to blow her nose. 'I just wish I'd believed in him more. I wrote a few more times, asking him why his letters had stopped, but when I didn't get a reply, I didn't push it.'

Brianna put her arm around Catherine's bony shoulders. 'You loved him, Catherine. You chose to let him go, thinking that was what he wanted. You can't blame yourself for that.'

Catherine wiped her eyes and gave Brianna a shaky smile. 'Sorry, dear, I just needed to get that out of my system. Now tell me, how is he? Did he become a doctor in the end, like he'd always wanted to?'

Reassured that Catherine was over her tears, Brianna went to sit back down again. 'You would be so proud of him. Yes, he's a doctor. He spent some time in the army and now works for a charity that helps victims of natural disasters anywhere in the world that might need their expertise. He's smart and very brave.'

'And is he happy? Has he found love?'

Brianna looked down at her coffee cup for a moment, unable to hold the steady gaze of the other lady. 'I think these are questions you'll need to ask him.'

'Brianna, you said you were his friend. Are you his girlfriend?'

'No, not anymore.' A ball of emotion lodged in her throat and she coughed to loosen it. 'I was for a short while. But now, well, we work together at the same charity.'

'But you love him, don't you?'

This time Brianna couldn't avoid the old lady's astute look. 'Yes, I do. Is it that obvious?'

'Well, I don't think anybody would stick their neck out like you have, or come to visit a stranger from his past, if they didn't care.'

Sighing, Brianna put down her cup. 'Mitch is strong, compassionate and clever, with a sharp wit that makes me laugh. But he's also a man who doesn't want anyone to get too close to him. I did, and I think it terrified him. He said our backgrounds were too different, but when it comes down to it, I think he just prefers to be alone.' Tears began to prickle under her eyelids. 'Sorry, I didn't mean to pour out my feelings quite like that.'

'Don't be silly, dear. It's lovely to hear how much he means to you. He must have turned out well if he's inspired such passion in you.' As if choosing her words, Catherine paused and took another sip of coffee. 'Did Mitch ever tell you about his upbringing? About his mother? About how we met?'

Brianna shook her head. 'No. I know bits and pieces. How he didn't have a father, so when his mother died, you took him under your wing.'

'Well, his childhood is Mitch's tale to tell, not mine. But I can tell you about when I became involved. I had just come back from a month long holiday. I let myself into this house, and there he was, large as life, sitting on my sofa, watching television. He'd been squatting in my home for nearly two weeks.'

'Squatting?' Brianna repeated, shocked.

'Yes, my dear, and I have no doubt I looked as horrified as you when I first saw him. He was fourteen. Confident, cocky, tough as you like, but underneath the bravado I could see he was a lonely, sad, young boy.' Brianna watched as Catherine's face softened at the memory. 'I remember doing a quick check of the house, but nothing was taken. Everything was perfectly tidy. I threatened to call the police but he simply gathered his things together and told me I could if I wanted. He gave me some money for the food he'd eaten and proudly walked towards the door.'

Brianna saw tears hovering in Catherine's eyes and knew her own tears were spilling down her cheeks and onto her hands. 'I take it you didn't call them.'

'Of course not. I told him he could stay for a while, but then he needed to go home. Gradually it became clear he had no home to go to. No parents, nobody. He'd been squatting in houses because he didn't want to go into care.'

Her tears were now flowing so freely Brianna had to drag out a tissue for herself. 'What happened then?'

'Well, of course I wanted to adopt him properly, as my son, but there was no chance an old lady like me would be allowed. The authorities kept threatening to put him in foster care, or a home, but he refused to budge and I refused to let them take him in. Eventually, after a lot of legal to-ing and fro-ing and a large donation to the council funds, I became his legal guardian. I'd never been lucky enough to be blessed with children. Looking after Mitch for the next four years was as close as I came.' She dabbed at her eyes and let out a watery smile. 'Not that I did much looking after. He was fiercely independent. Too much so. Having not had the luxury of a proper childhood he'd had to grow up too early and far too fast.'

'Do you mind me asking, was it you who helped him go to university? I only mention it because he once told me a kind lady had paid for him to go.'

'Why yes, of course it was me. It was his dream. Why should a boy who'd had such a horrid start in life not be allowed to follow his dream? The day he turned eighteen I put a lump sum in a bank account for him and told him he had to use it to become a doctor. He was acutely embarrassed, kept telling me he didn't want it, but I told him there was a time for pride, and a time for gratitude.' She smiled at the memory. 'He said he'd shut up and choose gratitude.'

As Catherine finished recounting her tale, the grandfather clock chimed ten o'clock. Brianna looked at it aghast. She was torn between wanting to hear more about Mitch and consideration towards the older lady who was surely feeling tired. Consideration won. 'Catherine, you've been really kind, but I've taken up far too much of your evening.'

'No, dear, you've been the kind one. Will you tell Mitch you've seen me? That I didn't have anything to do with that letter?'

'Of course I will. I'm sure he'll be in contact as soon as he can. You both have so many years to catch up on.' She saw Catherine move to get up. 'No, stay where you are, I'll see myself out.' She bent to kiss her on the cheek.

She was walking out of the room, when Catherine's voice stopped her. 'Brianna. Mitch hasn't seen much love in his life. If you care for him as much as I think you do, you might need to be very patient.'

Brianna nodded slowly, and let herself out of the house. She could be patient, she thought. It wasn't her natural forte, but she could do it. However there was being patient and there was pining away after a lost cause. She had a feeling this would turn out to be the latter.

While Brianna was talking to Catherine about his past, Mitch was focused very much on the present. For him that meant being knee deep in rubble in a remote part of Indonesia.

He'd been almost ridiculously relieved when the phone call had finally come. An earthquake on one of the islands, Medic SOS were needed straight away. At last he'd been able to focus his mind on doing good, rather than allowing it to brood on a chestnut-haired beauty. For the most part, it had worked. Since he'd been out here, he'd barely had a chance to take breath, never mind think about Brianna. Of course he'd have to face up to his feelings sooner or later, but for now he had work to do. He surveyed the grim scene in front of him. They weren't going to be leaving Indonesia for a while.

'Mitch, they've found a survivor in one of the buildings.' It was Tessa, her voice urgent. 'He's trapped his legs. The rescue workers want you to come and take a look.'

Grabbing his bag of medical supplies he followed Tessa towards the crumbling ruin that had once been a shop. The rescue team were huddled outside, eyeing up what was left of the structure. He started to walk towards the entrance, but was held back by one of the group.

'I don't think you should go in there. It's not safe.' The man wiped a weary hand across his brow. 'We went in a few minutes ago when we heard his voice, but the whole place began to creak. It's got to be made secure before we can go back.'

'What about the patient? What are his injuries?'

The man shook his head. 'He's trapped by a steel girder. It fell right across his feet. No way can he be moved quickly.'

Mitch looked at the ruins in front of him. 'You and I both know this building can't be made more secure. We've got to get him out now, fast, or he'll die when the rest of it collapses.'

'We can't get him out. I've already said ...'

Looking down at the bag in his hands, Mitch made an instant decision. 'I'll amputate his feet, that way we can move him. When I give the signal, come in and help me drag him out.'

He strode purposefully into the ruins, ignoring the plea from Tessa not to go in. This is what they were here for. To rescue the injured.

Inside it was eerily dark but using his torch he found a path through the broken masonry and towards a faint voice. 'Don't worry, we'll have you out in no time,' he reassured as he moved closer, though the words were said with a lot more confidence than he actually felt. Amputating one foot was bad enough. Doing two, with the groans of the crumbling walls echoing around him, was going to require nerves of steel and a great dollop of good fortune. He knew from past experience he could muster up the former. As for the luck. Well, he wasn't so sure.

Resolutely he opened up his medical bag.

Suddenly his world went black.

Chapter Thirty

Following her visit to Catherine, Brianna had a troubled night's sleep. She kept picturing a fourteen-year-old Mitch, lost and alone. A child who'd had to resort to squatting in strangers' houses and fending for himself. Her heart ached at the thought. At least it helped explain his fierce independence, his reluctance to share his life with anybody else.

The next morning, when she'd finally given up on getting any more sleep, she tried to phone Mitch. Frustratingly his mobile was turned off, and his home phone just rang and rang with no reply. Where was the man when she needed to talk to him? It was so early in the morning she had to conclude he was either a very heavy sleeper, which she knew he wasn't, or he wasn't at home. Jealousy ripped through her, sharp and painful. Of course there could be any number of explanations for him not being at home. Being with another woman was only one of them, but it was the one that kept her mind occupied throughout her journey to work.

'Sally, do you know where Mitch might be?' Brianna asked the office manager as soon as she arrived in the office. She wondered if the other woman knew about their relationship, or lack of it, and felt slightly foolish. 'I've tried his mobile and his home phone but not had a response from either.'

'Didn't we tell you yesterday? The team were called out again. There's been an earthquake in Indonesia. I expect he's knee deep in casualties at the moment.'

'Damn.' The words were out before she could stop them.

'Is there a problem?'

Brianna smiled, recovering her poise. 'No, no problem.

I just wanted to follow up with him on this proposal with the army.'

With apparent casualness, Brianna walked slowly back to her desk. So Mitch was away again. Her first selfish thought was at least he wasn't with another woman. Then she remembered Catherine, who would at this moment be waiting for a call from her surrogate son. Sadly she'd have to let her know it would be a while before that happened.

Turning her mind to work, she mused that she'd never realised how therapeutic it could be. She'd always considered work a chore, something she didn't have to do but thought she should. Since joining Medic SOS, all that had changed. She still didn't have to work, but now she wanted to. It was a huge difference.

The next few hours flew by as she immersed herself in proposals for the next fund-raising ball. So great was her concentration she almost jumped out of her skin when her phone sprang into life.

'Hi, Brie. It's Melanie. I wondered if you fancied meeting me for lunch? I know what you working girls are like. I promise I won't take up more than an hour, and you can stick to sparkling water.'

Wondering where the time had gone, Brianna rubbed at the back of her neck, tight from staring at a computer screen. 'That sounds like exactly what I need. I'll meet you at the Italian place in half an hour.'

Three quarters of an hour later, for she knew Melanie always ran late, Brianna sauntered into their usual haunt and found herself a table by the window.

'Brie, darling. Sorry I got held up.' Melanie finally arrived, a further five minutes later, gushing with all the usual apologies.

'You always do,' Brianna replied dryly, but gave her friend a warm hug.

'How have you been? Did you go and see Catherine?'

'Yes.'

Her friend's eyes widened in delight. 'So, what did you find out? Is Mitch a nasty scheming gold-digger after all?'

Melanie was smiling so wickedly, Brianna had to chuckle. 'You know he's not.'

'Well?'

'Let's order first, then I'll tell you everything.'

For the next half an hour, they talked and ate. And talked some more.

'Well, how dramatic. Fancy being left orphaned, running away from the authorities and then being looked after by the person in whose house you'd been squatting. No wonder there's such an air of mystery about the man. He's had one heck of a life.'

'And that's just what we know from the age of fourteen. I dread to think what happened before that. Catherine wouldn't say. I'm not sure if she knows the full story.'

Melanie finished off her salad and placed her knife and fork carefully back on her plate. 'No wonder he found it so hard to mix in our world. It must be hard for him, coming from nothing. When I think of how Henry treated him, it makes me sick.'

Brianna sighed and pushed away the rest of her sandwich. 'Well, I just hope he won't be too cross with me when he finds out I went to see her.'

'I had my reservations, as you know, but hearing what you've just said, you've done him a huge favour. He clearly cared for Catherine. When he knows she didn't send the letter, they can find each other again. It's a gooey, soppy, happy ending.'

Brianna wondered if the dour, intensely private Mitch would see it that way.

* * *

The afternoon sailed past. Brianna followed up on the leads she had with potential sponsors, and felt a real sense of achievement when one of them promised to donate regular amounts of money in return for a mention on their website. Work-wise, her life was going well. Donations were already up and the team were in the happy position of deciding how to manage the new level of investment. Even Margaret was smiling at her. If only her love life was going down a similar smooth road, life would be perfect.

'Oh my God.' Looking up sharply, she saw Sally's tortured expression. 'How badly is he injured?'

Brianna's heart flew into her mouth. It had to be one of the team. *He* narrowed it down to a male. There were only three males she was aware of out there. A one in three chance it was Mitch. The odds were in the right direction.

'Keep us posted, won't you? Yes, I'll tell the office. Look after him, Tessa. I don't need to tell you, he's rather special.'

When Sally came off the phone, they all surrounded her. 'Mitch was trying to rescue a man when the building collapsed on him. They managed to get him out, but he's been badly injured.'

Brianna felt the blood rushing from her head. The room started to spin and she staggered back towards her chair, just managing to grab hold of it before everything went black.

'Brianna, wake up.' Coming to, her eyes focused on Margaret's face. 'Are you back with us?'

Brianna nodded her head, trying to get up from the floor where she was currently lying.

'Hey, careful, we don't want you blacking out on us again.' Margaret helped to ease Brianna to her feet and onto her chair.

'Sorry,' Brianna mumbled, trying to clear the muzzy feeling from her brain. 'I don't know what happened. One minute I was fine. The next—'

'You were rather gracefully collapsing onto the floor,' Sally interjected.

The fog cleared. 'Oh God, it was Mitch. You were telling us he'd been injured.'

Margaret took Brianna's hand and rubbed it, clearly trying to get some warmth into her clammy circulation. 'Yes, it sounds like he has. Why don't you come into my office for a bit and get yourself together?'

With a sensitivity Brianna didn't realise Margaret was capable of, she was helped into the office, sat down with a coat to warm her up and given a hot tea. 'How bad is he, Margaret?'

Margaret moved to the chair opposite her. 'From what I can gather, he's got the usual broken bones and bruises, but it's his head they're worried about. He's unconscious and has fractured his skull. They think he'll need an operation to remove bits of the skull from his brain.'

Brianna threw a hand to her mouth. 'Oh God.'

'Sorry, that sounded more gruesome than I'd intended.' Margaret glanced at her sharply. 'You're not going to black out on me again, are you?'

Brianna tried to shake her head, but she felt so dizzy she had to stop. 'What can I do? How can I increase his chances? Can he be airlifted home?' The words tumbled out of her.

'Honestly? If he can be moved, then yes, he'd have a much better chance of pulling through if he's treated in a specialist centre.'

'Then that's what we'll do.' Brianna leapt to her feet, grabbing at the back of the chair when the floor seemed to move slightly. 'I'll arrange for him to be flown back here to a centre specialising in brain injuries.'

Margaret held up her hand. 'Hold on a minute. There are a couple of issues here. Firstly, we need to check with the team whether he's okay to fly. And secondly, arranging for the flight, if you want it done quickly, would have to be done privately, which means enormous cost. We are insured, but that could take time—'

'Time he doesn't have. The money is no problem. I'll sort it.' Brianna's hands tightened on the chair. 'He can't die, Margaret,' she said quietly. 'He's too important.'

Margaret gave her an understanding smile. 'And I think you don't just mean in terms of his work here.'

Brianna flushed. 'No, I don't. He's important to me.'

'I can see that. I'll give the guys a call; see if he can be moved. You sort out the transport and receiving hospital.' Brianna was almost out of the door when Margaret spoke again. 'He's tough, Brianna. I can't see Mitch letting a brain injury stop him, can you?'

It was wobbly, but Brianna managed a smile. 'I hope not.'

Brianna didn't know how she got home. When she opened her front door, she glanced back over her shoulder to see her car parked outside. She must have driven, but she had no recollection of the journey. She was functioning on automatic pilot, going through the motions of everyday life, but her mind was with her heart. In Indonesia.

Mitch had been given the okay to be moved. Now the ball was in her court.

'Mum, Dad,' she shouted, knowing they were in the house somewhere, as they'd promised to meet her here.

'Brianna, darling, what is it? Your message on the phone sounded so urgent.' They were waiting for her in their sitting room.

She rushed over to them and for a few seconds allowed herself to take comfort from their tight, loving embrace. Then she pulled away. 'It's Mitch. He's been hurt and it's serious. He's got a brain injury. We need to get him back to England quickly, so he can be treated by specialists.'

Her father took one look at her face and simply drew his arms around her tighter. 'Do whatever it takes Brianna. I'll find the money.'

The floodgates opened and tears streamed down her face. 'Oh, Dad, thank you, thank you.' She took a moment to absorb the strength and love from her parents. How good it felt to know she was loved, to know they would do anything for her, without hesitation, without question. She thought of Mitch, alone in a makeshift hospital bed somewhere. Had he ever experienced that sort of love? She didn't think so.

'I've got to go and sort it all out ...' She broke away, desperate to get things moving, to get Mitch back where he belonged.

'Darling, calm down,' her father took her hand. 'I'll call my personal assistant and get him to make the arrangements. You need to rest a while. You'll be no use to anyone in this frazzled state. I take it you want to fly out with the plane, to fetch him?' Brianna nodded. 'Right then, wait here with your mother while I make a call.'

With amazing speed, a few hours later Brianna was climbing up the steps into a private medical plane.

'Are you sure you don't want me to come with you?' her father asked for the hundredth time. Bless his heart, he'd not only made sure of the arrangements, he'd also insisted on seeing her off.

'You've got a business to run and besides, I'm a big girl now.'

'I know, but to me you'll always be my darling child.'

She brushed at her eyes. 'Crikey, Dad, don't go getting mushy on me. My emotions are all over the place as it is.'

Gently he kissed her forehead. 'You love him, don't you?'

She felt so choked she could barely speak. 'Yes.'

'Then he's going to be fine. With you looking out for him, how could he be anything else?'

Biting her lip, she tried to smile. 'You mean I'm a stubborn cow who won't let him die.'

'Well, I would have put it more delicately. You have a determined streak in you. If something is important enough to you, you've always found a way to achieve it.'

'Let's hope Mitch's survival isn't going to be any different.'

He lifted her chin and made her look at him. 'You'll phone as soon as you get the chance, won't you? Don't worry about the time differences. Just let us know how things are going.'

'I promise.'

A few moments later the pilot signalled they were ready. Her dad climbed back down the stairs and the door closed.

She waved at him from the tiny window. How her life had changed. Until a few months ago the only plane trips she'd ever taken were for holidays. Now she was off to her second disaster zone in as many months.

And this time she was dreading what she'd find even more than the last time.

Chapter Thirty-One

For as long as she lived, Brianna would never forget her first sight of Mitch as he lay unconscious in the back of the makeshift ambulance at the airport. To see such a strong man so helpless, cut her in two. His usually tanned, rugged face was pale and lifeless. Though his body was covered with a sheet, she could see nasty bruising on his shoulder. Tessa was kneeling next to him, holding the drip, checking his vital signs. She looked as ragged as Brianna felt.

'Apart from the head injury, he's broken some ribs and fractured his lower right leg, right arm, collarbone and pelvis.' Stuart was taking her through his injuries but all Brianna could think was how battered he looked, how beaten. For the first time since she'd set out on her rescue mission, she really started to believe she might lose him.

'But it's just the head injury you're worried about, yes? Everything else is easily fixed?'

Stuart gave her a tired smile. 'That's probably an accurate summary. We can't be sure, without proper X-rays, how bad the injury is to his pelvis. We don't think it's affected any other organs, but they'll be able to sort that out back in England.'

'Okay then. Let's get him there as fast as we can.'

The unconscious Mitch was lifted carefully onto the plane. When he was secured, Tessa turned to her. 'Take care of him, please.'

Though they'd clashed in South America, both competing for the same man, now that man was a common bond between them. Brianna knew Tessa loved Mitch, just as she did. It was etched across the nurse's tired face and evident in her worried eyes. 'I will, Tessa, I will.' Briefly they hugged each other, each acknowledging the other's pain.

'He shouldn't even have been in the building,' Tessa whispered as they moved apart. 'But he's so damn stubborn. A man was crying out in pain and the rescue team couldn't move him because his feet were trapped. They told Mitch the building was too dangerous to operate in, that it could collapse any moment. But Mitch went in anyway. Bloody stubborn fool.'

Brianna looked over at Mitch. 'Let's hope he doesn't pay for that stubbornness with his life.'

'When he pulls through this, I'm going to give him such a bollocking,' Tessa muttered.

For the first time in twenty-four hours, Brianna smiled. 'You'll have to stand in line.'

They exchanged a look of complete understanding. 'You'll keep me updated, won't you?' Tessa asked. 'I know the phone signal is sketchy here, but we've got the satellite phones and the office have the numbers.'

Brianna squeezed her hand. 'You have my promise. I'll let you know the moment anything changes.'

Tessa reached into her pocket. 'Oh and I found this next to his bed.' She handed over a small toy giraffe. 'It seemed an unlikely find. Was it your doing?'

Brianna's heart flip-flopped in her chest. Big gruff Mitch had kept the giraffe? 'Err, yes. I gave it to him.'

'Then it should go with him now. It's obviously important to him.' Brianna stared down at the toy, chosen because its big brown eyes had reminded her of Mitch's. She was too overcome to speak. 'I didn't think I'd ever say this,' Tessa continued, 'but I'm glad he's got you, Brianna. Mitch and I are obviously not meant to be but I'm glad he's got somebody looking after him, fighting for him.' With tears in her eyes, she gave a final wave and walked back to the truck.

Brianna climbed into the plane beside Mitch and tucked

the giraffe next to his face. When the doors closed, she took hold of his hand and held it close to her heart. 'We'll soon have you back in England, my darling. They'll put you back together again, I promise.'

As the plane thundered down the runway, Brianna kissed his stubble-roughened cheek and prayed.

Once Mitch was in the hands of the hospital, Brianna found herself sitting alone and feeling helpless. They were doing tests and would operate as soon as they had the results. She was reassured several times, in the placatory voice healthcare professionals use with people they really want to throttle, that Mitch was in good hands and that she needed to go and rest. But how could she possibly go home, when he was still here, fighting for his life?

'My darling daughter.' Brianna turned to find her parents and Melanie striding up the hospital corridor. 'You look absolutely shattered.' They all huddled around her, hugging and kissing her. 'How is he?'

Brianna focused on trying not to cry. 'He's still unconscious. They've taken him off for tests and then they'll operate.'

Her mother took her by the shoulders. 'Right then, there's nothing more you can do for him for the moment. It's time you started looking after yourself for a while. Your father's going to take you home, where you're going to have a shower and rest. Melanie and I will stay here. We'll let you know as soon as there is anything to report.'

'But I can't leave him ...'

Her protestations were drowned out. 'Nonsense. When he regains consciousness, the last thing he'll want to see is you looking like something the cat's dragged in.'

Melanie tried, and failed, to hide a smile. 'You do look a bit of a state, Miss Worthington.' She stared, pointedly, at

Brianna's scruffy khaki trousers and creased T-shirt. 'Not exactly an ambassador for the Worthington name.'

Brianna held her hands up in surrender. 'I give in. I'll go. But if there is any news ...'

'We'll let you know,' Melanie and her mother chorused.

Reassured, Brianna allowed her father to take her home. Once there, before she did anything else, she made the phone call she'd been dreading.

'Catherine? I'm afraid I've got some bad news about Mitch.'

She heard the sharp intake of breath at the other end. 'Oh no, don't tell me he's—'

'No, he's alive,' she reassured quickly. 'In a serious condition, but still alive. He's back in England and they're operating on him shortly. He's in good hands, Catherine.'

When she'd given Catherine all the details, Brianna went to get a much needed shower. As she let the hot spray pummel her exhausted body, she hoped Mitch was somehow aware that there were at least three ladies who were praying desperately for him to pull through.

She arrived back at the hospital several hours later, feeling slightly better for a short nap and a change of clothes.

She met Melanie at the hospital entrance where she'd obviously been trying to have a sneaky cigarette. 'I know,' her friend acknowledged shamefaced, 'a really bad place to light up, but crikey these places give me the heebie-jeebies.'

'Me too.' Brianna glanced longingly at the cigarette Melanie was now stubbing out. 'Is Mitch still in surgery?'

'Yes, but we're expecting to hear from the surgeon any time now.' She studied Brianna's pale face. 'How are you holding up?'

'I've felt better. But if the surgeon comes out with a smile on his face, I'll perk up no end.'

They walked arm in arm to the private lounge they had been given, one reserved for families of patients in intensive care. It was rather soulless, but the sofas were a lot more comfortable than the usual plastic chairs and at least they had some privacy.

'Miss Worthington?' Brianna looked round with a start and nodded at the man in the green surgical gown.

'I've just finished operating on Mr McBride. Are you the next of kin?' The surgeon wore a neutral expression on his face, giving nothing away.

'I, well, not really. He doesn't have any family. I'm the one who brought him here.'

Seemingly satisfied with that, the surgeon sat himself down next to her. 'Then I guess you'll be the one who wants to hear that the operation went well. I don't think there will be any long-term damage but the next few hours will be the key, as we see how he comes round from the anaesthetic. So far, so good.'

Brianna slumped against the back of the chair. 'Thank God.' She turned to look at the surgeon. 'And thank you.'

He smiled. 'He managed to get himself pretty beaten up. We've put casts on his leg and arm, and we've had to put a metal plate in his pelvis. It'll be a while before he's up and about. I hear he was out in Indonesia, as part of a medical rescue team?'

'He's a doctor with Medic SOS, a charity that gives immediate medical support in crisis struck areas.' She felt almost drunk with relief. 'I could give you the whole blurb, when you've got time. We're always looking for funding.'

The surgeon laughed. 'I suspect I'll see you around this hospital for a while to come, so I'll look forward to having my arm twisted.'

'Can I see him?'

'He's in the recovery room at the moment. When we're

sure he's out of immediate danger, we'll let you know and you can sit with him.' He eyed Brianna with undisguised appreciation. 'I'm sure having a beautiful woman like you by his bedside will speed his recovery no end.'

'That is so typical of you,' Melanie muttered as soon as the surgeon had left the room. 'Even in a flipping hospital you manage to attract the male talent.'

'Talent?'

Melanie shook her head in amazement. 'Yes, Brie. The surgeon was quite a dish.' She took in her friend's strained face and put a sympathetic arm around her. 'But I guess you've only got eyes for one man, haven't you?'

A short while later the medical team came in to tell Brianna she could go and sit with Mitch. Her parents and Melanie offered to stay but she sent them all away. She had Mitch. That was all she needed.

The monitors by his bedside gave out reassuringly steady bleeps. His face still looked awfully pale against the stark white hospital sheets and his hair had been shaved and a bandage wrapped around his head. She kissed his lips, reassured when they felt warm. 'Oh, Mitch, you've got to pull through. There are people rooting for you. Don't let us down.'

Brianna was dozing off in her chair when she heard her name being whispered. She jolted awake to find Catherine at the foot of Mitch's bed.

'Catherine, what a surprise.' She leapt out of the chair and went to kiss the older lady's cheek. 'Come and sit down here.' She wagged her finger at her. 'I told you not to come. He's asleep. I would have called and let you know if there was any change.'

'I know, dear, I know.' Catherine looked down at Mitch. Brianna could see the love shine from her eyes and the fear sweep across her face. 'But I had to see him for myself. What if he doesn't pull through? I would have lost my chance to see him as a grown man.'

Brianna nodded, completely understanding. 'He usually looks a lot better than this.'

Catherine's eyes travelled over his bruised body and his bandaged head. 'He's a fine young man, isn't he? I can tell, despite the bruises. He looks handsome and strong. He always was a good-looking boy. Had all the young girls after him.'

'He still does,' Brianna acknowledged with a wry smile.

'You must love him an awful lot, Brianna, to go to all this trouble for him.'

'I do,' she replied simply.

'He doesn't find it easy to let people into his life, as you've already discovered. He's never had anybody who really took care of him, made him feel loved.' She looked down at the man in the bed. 'I tried, but the damage had already been done.' She transferred her gaze to Brianna. 'I hope you can find a way to get through to him. He needs somebody like you, although he probably doesn't realise it and certainly won't thank you for it.'

The lump in her throat was so large Brianna had trouble swallowing. She certainly couldn't talk, so she settled for trying to smile instead.

'Well, dear, I'll go now. I know he's in good hands.'

With that Catherine vanished, leaving Brianna alone once more with Mitch. She held his hand and, curling up on the chair next to his bed, she dozed.

Mitch was struggling to come out of a huge black hole. He felt the pull of light and heard the soft sound of a female voice. He tried to open his eyes, to see who it was, but as much as he struggled to wake, the blackness kept descending. There it was again, a voice he recognised, a voice that spread warmth throughout his body. Forcing his eyes open this time he could just make out the outline of a woman's face. Long, brown hair, high cheekbones, beautiful green eyes. They were gazing into his.

'Brianna?' He attempted to move, to get up, but the pain shot through him and he fell back with a groan.

The woman he thought must be Brianna was smoothing his brow, pushing his body back against the pillow. 'Don't try and move, Mitch,' she murmured softly. 'You've taken a bit of a beating. Do you remember? You were playing the hero when a building fell on top of you. You've broken a few bones, so you need to lie still.'

Mitch relaxed back against the mattress. He had a vague memory of trying to amputate a man's foot. And then blackness. But he couldn't work out what Brianna was doing here. 'Where am I?' he croaked, his voice unsteady.

'You're back in England, in hospital. They've operated on your brain, so you'll be feeling a bit groggy for a while. Now just relax.'

Soothed by her words and her presence, he closed his eyes and allowed the blackness to take over once more.

When he awoke again, it was easier. He moved his head to the side and saw Brianna, asleep on the chair next to him. Memories of earlier came flooding back. He was in hospital, she'd said. He looked down at his body. Saw the plaster casts, the drips and the monitoring equipment. He must have taken quite a hammering. He could remember what had happened more clearly now, right up until the moment the building had started to collapse in on him, but he couldn't recall anything of how he'd managed to get from there back to England. He glanced at Brianna again and smiled to himself. She looked so peaceful when she was asleep. Peaceful and achingly beautiful. He felt his heart lurch, but he quickly looked away. Wasn't their relationship over? Hadn't he ended it? He blinked, trying to clear his head. Then why was she by his bedside? From the way she was sleeping, she must have been there for hours. What was the point of sleeping in a chair in a hospital, when she had a perfectly good bed at home?

As if aware that he was staring at her, Brianna stirred and opened her eyes. 'Mitch, you're awake again.' She unfurled her body gracefully from the chair. 'How are you feeling?'

He grimaced. 'Like I've been run over by a herd of rhinos.'

Laughing softly, she ran a hand gently across his forehead. 'You have no idea how good it is to have you back.'

He tried to move, but found he didn't have the strength so he fell back against the pillow. 'How the hell did I get here?'

'You needed an urgent operation. We got a plane to bring you back.'

He noted her discomfort; the slight flush, the way she twisted her hands. He wasn't so groggy he didn't know exactly what that meant. 'You paid for an air ambulance, you mean.'

She flinched. 'Yes. What was I supposed to do? Leave you to die out there?'

He was too tired to argue. 'I guess I should thank you then. I owe you my life.'

Tears glistened in her eyes. 'I don't want your damned thanks,' she muttered. 'I just want you to get better.'

He cast his eyes sideways and caught sight of the giraffe, staring accusingly at him from the side of his bed. *Why are you being so graceless?* it seemed to be saying to him. 'What's that thing doing here?' he demanded.

'Tessa said she found it by your bed at the camp. She thought it might be important to you.'

Busted. What sane man has a stuffed animal by his bed? Only one who's hopelessly attached to the woman who sent it to him. Something he wasn't going to tell her. So he needled her instead. 'Why are you sleeping here, on that chair, when you should be at home, in bed?'

'I wanted you to have somebody waiting for you when you woke up.' Her face dared him to mock her.

Mitch remembered the last time he'd been in hospital. It was during his stint in the army, after his medical team had been ambushed. There had been nobody waiting for him then when he'd come round. He tried to reach out his good arm to touch her, to convey his gratitude, but the strain was too much. He let it fall back onto the bed. 'Thank you,' he whispered, before falling back to sleep.

Chapter Thirty-Two

The more Mitch improved, the grumpier he became. He was still prone to headaches, but was now thinking clearly, which only made him increasingly frustrated at the relative slowness of the rest of his body to mend. Brianna, his one constant visitor, took the brunt of most of his temper.

'Why the hell can't I get up and go to the toilet?' he snapped at her. 'It's a man's basic privilege, to go to the damn toilet. Peeing in a bloody bottle is degrading.'

Brianna tried to hide her grin. Now she knew he was going to make a full recovery, the sight of this strong man temporarily weakened was surprisingly cute. Even when he was being surly and bad-tempered. 'I'm sure they'll let you get up soon. I'll go and see if I can find a nurse.'

'Thanks,' he grunted. 'And while you're there, you can tell her I'm thirty-four-years old. I'm capable of going to the toilet by myself.'

Laughter bubbled out of her as she went in search of the nurse, who promised she'd come round as soon as she could. Brianna was still smiling as she ambled back to Mitch's ward. Right up until she rounded the corner and saw him trying to lever his body out of bed. His good arm was clenched tightly to the neighbouring chair, his face contorted with pain. Even as she shouted his name the chair moved and Mitch let out a deep grunt of agony as he ended up with his upper body hanging precariously out of the bed.

Brianna dashed over. 'What the hell do you think you're doing?' she fumed, angry with his stupidity. He was a doctor, for goodness sake. He should know better than to try and push his body beyond what it was capable of at the moment.

Carefully she reached her arms under his shoulders and hauled him back against the pillows. As he sank back, his face deathly pale and wreathed with pain, he shut his eyes.

Smoothing his brow, she reassessed her earlier opinion. It was no longer cute to see him like this. It was heartbreaking. Sighing, she sat down on the chair, giving him a moment to recover. Knowing his pride, she had a feeling it wasn't just the pain that had knocked him sideways. The embarrassment of being so helpless must have added a sharp twist.

When he opened his eyes again, it was to lash out at her. 'Haven't you got anything better to do than sit here?'

Though she knew he was suffering, his words were like a slap around the face. 'Apparently I haven't.' Stiffly she stood and picked up her bag. 'But as my presence here clearly upsets you, I'll leave you alone.'

Tears stung her cheeks as she hurried out of the ward. She was a stupid woman, at least when it came to Mitch. Why had she been visiting him every day, anyway? He'd told her in no uncertain terms he didn't want her in his life and yet, since the accident, she'd continued to act as if they were together. She was his work colleague. That was all. It was about time she started acting like one.

Mitch had plenty of time to mull over his choice of words during the following, lonely week. Even by his own low standards, he knew he'd acted deplorably. He was an expert at pushing away people who got too close, and Brianna was still too close. But that didn't give him the right to treat her so damn shabbily. How had he thanked her for effectively saving his life? He'd as good as told her to leave him alone. Not surprisingly, she'd taken him at his word and hadn't visited since. That had been seven long, dreary days ago.

In truth it wasn't just his desire to thank her and

apologise that had him cursing yet another visiting time when she didn't show up. He missed her, period. He hadn't realised how much he'd looked forward to her visits until they'd dried up. They had been the highlight of otherwise really crappy days. Visiting time in his now full ward buzzed with the chatter of family and friends calling on his fellow patients, but no one came to see him. All he had for company was a stuffed giraffe and even that was glaring at him from his bedside, reminding him what a bastard he'd been.

He'd had one visit from Margaret and Sally from the office but they hadn't stayed long. No doubt put off by his foul temper. It wasn't much to show for thirty-four years.

He had to get fit again and get home.

With that goal in mind, he really put his back into his sessions with the physiotherapist, his desire to get out of hospital far greater than his pain threshold. The hard work seemed to be paying off and he finally managed to haul himself across the ward on a crutch. Not easy when you had a cast on your right arm as well as your right leg.

'When can I get out of here, Mandy?' he asked for the hundredth time as he levered himself carefully onto the bed. Though he was shattered from the effort of trying to walk, he was also desperate not to show it.

The physio sighed. 'Mitch, it doesn't matter how many times you ask, the answer will still be the same. You can go home when I believe you're capable of being able to manage by yourself. Unless of course you're going to reconsider and agree to a carer staying with you?'

'Somebody I don't know sleeping in my home? Not bloody likely,' Mitch answered angrily. 'I don't need a nursemaid. I can manage. I've got a crutch. I'll sleep downstairs. Damn it, Mandy, I'm going to discharge myself soon if you won't let me go.'

'That would be your privilege but you won't get my approval until I can see you're capable of looking after yourself. At the moment you aren't,' she stated bluntly.

Mitch cursed under his breath and sat back further on the bed. Damn Mandy, damn them all. He wasn't going to put up with this much longer. He'd give it until the end of the week. He'd already been in hospital three weeks. It was too much of anybody's life.

Shifting himself back onto the bed, he caught sight of a slim female figure hovering at the entrance to the ward. The immediate spurt of joy he felt was impossible to ignore or dismiss. He was pathetically grateful to see her.

'Brianna.' A broad smile stretched right across his face. 'I thought I'd scared you off.'

Brianna had debated long and hard about whether she should come to see Mitch again. In the end her desire to see him and check up on his progress had overtaken her pride. The genuine warmth of his smile was a welcome reward. God, she was a sucker where he was concerned.

'It would appear I don't scare off that easily,' she replied, walking towards the bed and taking a moment to appraise him. He looked a lot better. The bruises were fading and his face less pale. His new short hairstyle suited him, emphasising his lean cheekbones. 'How are you?'

'Feeling ready to go home, but apparently I can't because I'm not mobile enough yet.' He looked up at her, his face a picture of determination. 'But bugger it, I can't stay here much longer. It's doing my head in. I know the best place for me to recuperate is at home.'

'Would Edna keep an eye on you? Make sure you were okay?'

He snorted. 'I don't need an old lady looking after me. Edna has enough trouble looking after herself. No, I'll be fine.'

'How about if you come and stay with me until you're on your feet?' The words flew from her mouth before she'd had a chance to consider what she was offering. Have him live with her, in her apartment? Was she some sort of masochist?

'What?'

His strangled response, together with the look of horror on his face, made Brianna wish to God she'd kept her mouth firmly shut. It had been her heart talking, certainly not her head. Mortified, she stared at the floor. When it failed to do as she prayed and swallow her up, she drew in a shaky breath. 'You know what, forget I said anything.' She threw the windsurfing magazine she was clutching onto the bed. 'Here, I brought this for you, to help relieve the boredom. I hope you manage to escape soon.' Legs rigid with humiliation, she stalked away from his bed.

'Brianna, I'm sorry. Please, don't go.'

She wanted to ignore him, wanted to get away so she could lick her wounds in private, but the plea in his voice stopped her. When she slowly turned round, his eyes were full of apology.

'It seems upsetting you has become a habit of mine,' he said quietly. 'One I need to break. God knows, you don't deserve it.' He paused and ran a hand across his shaven head. 'I was surprised by your offer, that's all.'

'You were horrified.'

Mitch flushed slightly. 'Okay, yes, I was horrified, but not for the reason you think,' he added hastily. 'It's not the thought of staying with you. God knows, anything would be an improvement on this place.'

'Wow, thank you. You really know how to make a woman feel needed.'

Mitch threw up his good hand in despair. 'Hell, I'm making a real hash of this, aren't I?'

Brianna could only agree. Still, it made a change to see him on the back foot. She watched as he sagged back against his pillow, sighing deeply. When he raised his head to look at her, it was the first time she'd seen his brown eyes look quite so unguarded.

'I've never had anyone look after me, Brianna,' he admitted slowly. 'I'm used to taking care of myself. For me to have to admit I need help is incredibly hard.' He gave her a rueful smile. 'But here I am, in plaster casts from head to foot and as helpless as a bloody baby. I don't have the luxury of being proud. You made a very kind offer and I'm really grateful. Hell, I might not show it, but I'm grateful for everything you've done for me.' His voice was as serious as the look in his deep brown eyes. 'You saved my life, Brianna. Your visits also saved my sanity. I didn't realise quite how much until you stopped coming.'

Brianna shifted awkwardly. She wasn't sure she liked seeing him so humble. 'Yes, well ...' she trailed off, unsure how to respond. To say it was nothing would be totally untrue. To tell him he meant everything to her, that she'd done what she had because she loved him, would be received with equal mixtures of horror and pity. 'I did what I could, for a friend,' she settled on, hoping it was the right response.

It seemed to be, because he smiled. 'Well, as your friend, would it be okay for me to come and stay with you for a short while, until I can get rid of these damn casts? It should only be for a week or so.'

Brianna nodded, wondering what on earth she was letting herself in for. It was going to be so hard to have him stay with her but not touch him, not kiss him. But she'd gone from losing him as a lover, to almost losing him full stop. Having him as a friend was better than not having him at all.

Chapter Thirty-Three

Only hours after Brianna collected him from the hospital, they were having their first argument – over his determination to make them a cup of tea.

'If you tell me once more to stop mothering you, I'm going to scream. I'm supposed to be helping you. Stop fighting me all the time and let me.'

'I've got it,' he replied through gritted teeth, not prepared to admit the simple task was causing him agony. Jeez, he couldn't even fill a bloody kettle. He was useless. As the thing filled it became heavier and he found it increasingly hard to hold onto it, while also balancing on a crutch. There was no way he'd be able to carry it over to the plug socket. With a clatter he let it fall into the sink. 'I didn't want a cup of tea anyway,' he declared with bad grace, before swinging out of the kitchen as fast as his one good leg and crutch would allow him.

'You know I don't have much experience with children,' Brianna fumed after him. 'But I'm beginning to realise what it might be like to have a stroppy toddler.'

He tried to block out her words as he lowered himself onto the sofa. He wasn't stroppy. A little stubborn, maybe.

A few moments later she handed him a steaming mug. 'Here you go. I thought about putting some sugar in to sweeten you up, but I don't think I've got enough.'

Sheepishly he accepted the cup. 'Thanks.' He took a sip, and looked back over at her. 'Regretting your offer already?'

Laughing, she sat down on the comfy chair opposite him. 'Let's see what the rest of the day brings. You know, you've got to relax and let me help you out for a while, Mitch. It won't make you less of a man, just because I have to make your meals, help you up, drive you around.' He grunted. 'Right then, I've got to log on and check my emails. Is there anything else you need before I go?'

It was on the tip of his tongue to ask for a new leg and arm, but he stopped himself. Bitterness was going to get him nowhere. 'Could you bring me the list of exercises the physio set out for me? I think it's on top of my holdall.'

Within seconds she returned and held out the list for him with a flourish. 'Here you go, sir.'

Her green eyes shone with mischievous amusement, her mouth twitched with barely controlled laughter. He allowed himself the sheer pleasure of looking at her. 'You know, maybe I could get used to being waited on hand and foot after all.'

With a chuckle that pulled at his insides, she turned to leave the room. 'Make the most of it, buster. You'll soon be back home and fending for yourself once more.'

As Mitch watched her saunter out, the warmth he'd felt at her laughter suddenly turned into a chill. He couldn't understand why. He wanted to get back home, didn't he?

Later on in the day, having done his exercises, which hurt like hell, Mitch decided to take a shower. He'd had a couple at the hospital and knew he could just about manage by himself, as long as he put the protective covers over his casts. Making sure Brianna was still locked away in her study, he lay on his bed and shrugged off his clothes. The hardest part done, he hauled himself up and crossed the hallway to the bathroom. As soon as he closed the door, he realised his mistake. There was nothing to sit on. It was literally a huge, walk in shower room. There wasn't even a toilet. He eyed up the shower gel. How the hell was he going to put the stuff on his body, and wash it off, when his only good arm was holding the crutch supporting him? He grabbed the bottle and tried to squirt it onto his skin, whilst at the same time supporting his body with the crutch. It was impossible. With a gesture of total frustration, he let out a loud oath.

Brianna was typing away when she heard Mitch's loud curse. Without a second thought she dashed into the shower room, stopping abruptly at the sight that greeted her. Stark naked, he was leaning against the wall and looking despairingly up towards the ceiling. He turned his head towards her as she entered.

'Sorry,' she whispered, quickly averting her eyes, but not before she'd managed to get a tantalising glimpse of him. He might be broken and bruised, but he still cut one magnificent male figure. It was the one that filled her dreams and even now made her heart race. 'I heard you curse,' she explained, looking him squarely in the face. 'Is there anything the matter?'

Clearly embarrassed, he dropped his gaze to the floor. 'I'm fine. I just haven't got enough arms to support myself and wash at the same time.'

Her heart went out to him; he looked so fed up, so utterly frustrated. Unthinkingly she picked up the shower gel. 'Here, let me rub some of this over you. Then you can just stand under the shower and wash it off.'

The moment her hands smoothed across his naked flesh, she knew it was a mistake. The sexual chemistry that had always been strong between them instantly flared. She heard his sharp intake of breath, and her own gasp.

'Leave it, Brianna,' he growled. They'd both felt the flash of desire at the feel of her hands on his skin, but his reaction was more obvious. He twisted away from her. 'Leave me alone.'

* * *

She gave him some space, figuring the shower episode had probably been the last straw for him today. So after asking the cook to bring up two plates of whatever her parents were having, she went to watch television. Mitch would come and find her when he was ready. His empty stomach would lure him out of his room, if nothing else.

Right on cue, as the cook knocked on the door to deliver the delicious smelling dinner, Mitch appeared, his damp hair a reminder of his thwarted attempt at a shower.

'I'm sorry about earlier. I umm …' she sighed, taking the plates through to the kitchen. 'I was just trying to help.'

Mitch nodded and sat himself down at the table. 'I know. And it's not as if you haven't seen me naked before.' He gave her a crooked grin. 'Heck, at least I know everything is still in good working order.'

Brianna chuckled, relieved at his change of mood. 'How did you manage to wash in hospital?'

A slight flush crept across his cheeks. 'A lot of bed baths, at least in the beginning.' She raised her eyebrows. 'Was it humiliating, I can see you wondering. Yes, it damn well was. Did I enjoy it? No.' He took a mouthful of the beef stew. 'Mind you, when the pretty blonde nurse was on, there were moments …' he let the sentence hang.

'You are a walking cliché, Mitch McBride,' Brianna replied coolly, pouring a bit more wine into both their glasses.

'Hey, I can't help it if what they say about a nurse's uniform is true. At least on the right nurse.' Obviously enjoying his memory, he smiled and shovelled more food onto his fork. 'Seriously, when I had a shower, they had one of those plastic seats, so I could sit down and wash with my good arm.' He shrugged. 'I guess I could do with one of those.'

'Then that's what we'll get.'

'Not much of an alternative to a sexy lady washing me down, but I guess it's the most sensible solution.'

Brianna glanced up to see him gazing at her with an amused twinkle in is eye. This time it was her turn to blush. She concentrated on her food, trying to ignore the image that burned in her mind. One of his stirring arousal as she lathered his muscular body with shower gel.

The next few days passed by quickly. They settled into a routine where each accepted the other's need for space, but enjoyed their time together, mainly over meals and in the evening. Working from home instead of the office, Brianna found it useful to have Mitch alongside her and often picked his brain over the initiatives she had ongoing. Although she was very much aware of the sexual spark that still lay between them, it was obvious that nothing could happen, even if either one had wanted it to. So with sex no longer on the agenda, it was an opportunity to talk, to get on together as friends. It surprised her how easy Mitch was to live with. He ate everything she put in front of him, kept his room tidy and even put the toilet seat down. All in all, he was the perfect house guest.

The one thing that stopped Brianna from really enjoying her time with him, that nagged at her almost constantly, was the thought of Catherine. She'd put off telling Mitch about Catherine while he was in hospital, convincing herself he was too weak. But as the days went by, Brianna found it harder and harder to justify her silence. It wasn't right that she knew something about a major part of his life and he didn't. So, though she knew it would upset their current status quo, she finally broached the subject one evening as they were eating.

'There's something I need to talk to you about,' she began, pushing her plate away. She knew she wouldn't be able to eat anything further.

'Fire away.' When she hesitated, he frowned. 'Should I be worried? You look kind of serious.'

She tried to smile. 'No, there's nothing to worry about. Hopefully it will be a good thing.' As she grasped for the words she'd rehearsed off by heart the night before her mind went alarmingly blank.

'Brianna, you're scaring me.' She felt Mitch's hand cover her own. 'What is it? You've gone pale.'

She withdrew her hand and stood up. 'It's about Catherine.'

At the mention of her name, he froze. Slowly he put down his fork and sat back in his chair. 'What about her?'

'You mentioned once there was a lady who took you under her wing. I presume that was Catherine?'

He nodded, his jawline tense.

'From the sound of your voice when you told me about her, I guessed she was somebody you cared about, a lot.' She looked at him for some sort of agreement, but was met with a stony wall of silence. Pausing, giving herself some time to think of the right words, Brianna walked to the table and picked up her glass, taking a quick sip of the crisp white wine. 'After Henry threw those accusations at you at the party, I couldn't seem to get you and Catherine out of my head. You weren't just angry when he said what he did. You were upset. Then I remembered you'd said it was her that broke off the contact. I couldn't understand why someone who cared for you enough to take you in, would suddenly do that. So I followed up with Simon. I wanted to find out what had happened.'

'Who gave you the right to interfere in my life, Brianna?' he asked coldly, his eyes flat, his face rigid.

She'd been expecting a flash of temper. The controlled, icy anger, was far more unnerving. 'I know it was wrong. For what it's worth, I did it with the best of intentions. I thought there must be a simple misunderstanding.' She raised her head again to look at him. 'And there was.'

Mitch hauled himself to his feet. He didn't want to hear

any of this. It was part of his past that he'd locked away and he didn't want ever dragged out again. Feeling equal parts fury and fear he grappled around for his crutch, swearing as it clattered to the floor.

'Wait, you have to hear me out.'

'I don't have to do anything,' he replied curtly, lunging for the crutch and then propelling himself awkwardly towards the door. There he leant weakly against the frame, dreading the answer to his next question, but knowing he had to ask it. 'Did you speak to her?'

She flushed, but still looked him directly in the eye. 'Yes.'

His heart clattered against his ribs. 'What did she tell you about me?'

Briefly she closed her eyes. 'She told me how she found you squatting in her house, then became your legal guardian,' she admitted quietly.

'Anything else?'

When she shook her head, he sagged against the door frame in relief. 'Good.' When he'd mustered his strength, he grasped the crutch and set off down the hallway.

'Don't you want to know the rest? How Catherine didn't have a clue about the letter that was sent? That she loved you, still loves you? That she visited you in hospital when she thought you might die, because she so desperately wanted to see the man you had become?'

The words rung in his ears but Mitch wasn't listening. He ploughed all his efforts into escaping down the corridor and reaching his room as quickly as possible. Once there he hurled himself onto the bed, allowing tears he was ashamed of to fall down his cheeks. He didn't want to think about Catherine. He didn't want to be reminded about his past.

And there was no way in hell he wanted Brianna to know about any of it.

* * *

Mitch barely spoke to Brianna the next day. His anger towards her still simmered, though in truth he was now more angry with himself than her. Angry for not realising Catherine hadn't been behind the letter he'd received. At the time he'd been so concerned with his own feelings of hurt and rejection, he hadn't thought about it from her side. He should have known Catherine wouldn't have done such a thing. It hadn't been in her nature. Through his selfishness he'd managed to hurt the one person from his past who'd cared for him.

His bad temper wasn't helped by the phone call he took from Frederick. Pompous ass. 'Yes, she's here,' he barked down the phone. 'I'll get her.'

He found Brianna in her study. 'Phone call for you.' They were the most words he'd spoken to her all day.

'Thank you,' she replied, accepting the phone.

He didn't intend on listening, really he didn't, but he wasn't very quick on his crutch, so he couldn't help but hear her politely decline what was obviously an offer of dinner. 'I don't feel I can leave Mitch alone just yet,' he overheard her saying.

He cursed under his breath. What did she think he was? Some sort of charity case? A kid who needed constant supervision? He barged back into the study just as she was putting the phone down.

'You don't have to babysit me,' he told her cuttingly. 'I'm not a child.'

'No, I know you're not,' she agreed calmly. 'Though at times you act like one. However, I would feel better staying in while you're under my care.'

'For God's sake Brianna,' he snarled. 'You need to find yourself a life. Maybe it would stop you interfering so much in mine. Go out with the man.'

She appeared startled at the harshness of his words, but

maintained her composure. He admired her for it, even as it irked him. Instead of crumbling, she jutted her chin forward.

'Right then, I will. Please close the door behind you.'

He did more than that, he slammed it before stalking back to his bedroom in a foul mood. For years he had been almost viciously in control of his emotions. Now they were all over the place. His broken body frustrated him, thoughts of Catherine and how she must have felt when he stopped writing to her, haunted him. At the bottom of it all though was Brianna. He could snap and snarl at her all he wanted, but there was no denying that once again he was letting her get under his skin. If he wasn't careful she'd go even deeper into his body. Into his closed off heart.

The following evening he watched Brianna greet Frederick with a kiss on the cheek, and wondered what on earth he'd started. This time he hadn't just pushed her away, he'd shoved her straight into the arms of another man. Sure, he'd been angry with her, but what sort of excuse was that? Especially as it now seemed clear Catherine really hadn't told Brianna anything about his early life. If she had, Brianna would have found it impossible to hide her disgust from him.

With that worry out of the way, he'd grudgingly started to realise Brianna had done him a great favour. Now he had the opportunity to see Catherine again. To put things right and make up for the wasted years. The tragedy of it was, instead of going down on his knees and thanking Brianna, he'd bellowed at her. Then ordered her to go out with Frederick. Rich, titled, handsome Frederick.

The thought of them together was like a knife to his gut. And the more he pictured them, so similar, so flaming made for each other, the more that knife twisted.

Chapter Thirty-Four

How was it possible to miss a man so much? Especially when that man was grumpy, uncommunicative and angry with her. It had been three days since she'd taken Mitch to have the sling and cast removed from his arm. Three days since she'd dropped him back at his own house.

During their last few days together they'd settled on a reasonably amicable truce. He had been courteous, civil and distant. She had tried to be the same. He had enquired with polite interest how her date with Frederick had gone. In the same manner, she had replied she had enjoyed it. And she had. So what if she felt nothing when Frederick kissed her goodnight? Surely that zing, that passion, would come. She just needed to allow her body time to adjust to a different man holding her, that was all. And anyway a few dates with a handsome, charming man, no matter how platonic, would at least help soothe her wounded ego, if not her damaged heart. Mitch was gone, back to his own life. It was time to pick up the pieces of her own.

She dialled number two on her phone, making a note to herself to relegate Mitch from his number one status after the call.

'Melanie, it's Brianna.'

'Well, knock me down with a feather. You've finally decided to come out of the woodwork again, have you?' her friend replied with her usual bluntness.

'Sorry, I've been a bit tied up looking after Mitch. But hey, he's gone now, so I'm free again.'

There was a pause down the line, then an exhaling of breath. 'Let me guess. Despite saving his life and nurturing him back to health, the guy has buggered off home without declaring undying love for you?'

'Something like that.' To her annoyance Brianna could hear her voice breaking. 'I feel such a fool. Of all the men in the world, why did I have to fall for one who doesn't love me back?'

'I don't know, honey, but you always did like a challenge. I'll get the girls together. What you need is a night of wild dancing and unlimited champagne.'

'I'll be there.' Brianna put the phone down with a deep sigh. What she really needed was a complex, compassionate, sexy man, but it seemed he wasn't up for grabs.

Mitch worked on his fitness like a man possessed. Where the physio had stated thirty repetitions, he did sixty. He doubled the weights and walked along the seafront, with his cane, twice a day. His leg was still in a walking plaster, but that was coming off next week. His shoulder and arm were mended and though they might be weak, he had full movement. The ribs and pelvis were doing fine, giving him only the occasional twinge of pain. Even the scar on his head was fading, covered by a new growth of hair. Getting his leg back would be the last major milestone in his recovery. After that he could pick up his swimming, get back in his car and start to claw his life back together. They told him he wouldn't be fit for work for another few weeks, but he was damned if he was going to let them keep him to that. He needed the focus of work more than ever.

Throwing the newspaper down in disgust, Mitch went to get his coat. Time for another walk. Staying in the house was driving him crazy. He couldn't understand why he was so restless. He was used to enjoying his own company, the peace and quiet of his home. Now, it felt like a tomb. The silence seemed to scream at him *you're alone, you're alone*. It was how he'd always wanted it, so why did he crave someone to talk to? To drink a cup of tea with. To laugh over the articles in the papers with.

Slamming the front door, Mitch set a fast pace along the coast. It wasn't just anyone he wanted to do those ordinary, everyday things with. It was Brianna. God, he missed her more than he'd ever thought possible. He hadn't heard from her since she'd quietly dropped him off nearly two weeks ago. Not that he'd expected to. After the business over Catherine, they hadn't exactly left on best friend terms. More polite work colleagues. Mitch thrust his free hand into his pocket and stared out to sea. That had been his fault and he knew it. With his self-righteous anger he'd finally succeeded in driving her away. He deserved to be alone.

As he let the sound and smell of the sea wash over him, Mitch forced his shoulders to relax. There was one thing Brianna had left him with, and that was Catherine's contact details. He still had them, pinned to the fridge. He hadn't phoned her yet because he knew when he did, he'd want to see her. He didn't want to do that looking banged up. Next week though, he was going into town to get his cast removed. It would provide a perfect opportunity to drop in on her.

The thought finally lifted his heart. He might have lost the second woman he had ever cared for, but he had a chance to make everything good again with the first.

A week later, his leg free of the cast and his heart hammering like a trip engine, Mitch rang the bell of the house he remembered so vividly as a child. Feeling like a gawky teenager again he took a moment to study the grandeur of it all, noting that outwardly at least, the place hadn't changed. Then the door opened and he could do nothing but stare at the elegant lady who stood before him. She was something else that hadn't changed. Without a word, he reached out his arms and she moved into them. They hugged for what seemed like hours, neither willing to let the other go. She even smelt the same, Mitch marvelled, remembering her distinctive perfume. As a child it had represented sophistication and security. So different from the memories of his mother.

Finally he eased away, though his arms were still around her. 'You haven't changed,' he whispered, amazed at how hard it was to find his voice.

She chuckled and gave him a gentle dig in the ribs. 'And you've turned into quite the charmer. I've got a lot more wrinkles, my fingers are arthritic and my hair is white.'

He smiled. 'To me, you are still beautiful.'

Her eyes filled with tears. 'Oh, my darling boy, I've missed you so much.' She gave him a final, tight embrace before ushering him in. 'Come on in, you know where to go. I'll sort us out a drink.' Smiling, she raised a hand to his face. 'Look at you, a real man now, and so handsome. I don't suppose you'll want a hot chocolate.'

Laughing, he followed her through to the sitting room. 'I think I need a beer, or a whisky if you've got one.'

'Mitch McBride, you know there is always whisky in this house.'

While Catherine walked off to get the drinks, Mitch took in the familiar surroundings. She'd decorated, moved things round a bit, but in essence it was still the house he'd lived in for four years. The only one in his childhood he had ever called home. It was in this very room he'd acquired the taste for whisky. Catherine would treat herself to a tot while they played chess. Every time her back was turned, he had a crafty sip, something he knew she was probably aware of, but never mentioned.

When she came back into the room, she stood for a

while, gazing at him. 'I can't believe you're really here.' She handed him his whisky and sat down on the sofa, patting the seat next to her. 'Come on, you've got fifteen years to fill me in on.'

Chuckling, he sat down beside her. 'I'm going to need a few more of these then, before the evening is over.' As he took a sip, his face turned serious. 'Catherine, first I have to apologise. When I got that letter, I should have realised you hadn't had anything to do with it. I don't know why I didn't. All I could think was how gutted and hurt I felt—'

Laying a hand on his, she interrupted gently. 'It's my brother who should be apologising, not you. You were used to being let down. It's not surprising you thought I had let you down, too. Besides, I should have tried harder from my end. When you didn't return my last few letters, I just assumed you were busy with your new life and didn't want a reminder of the old one.' She looked at him questioningly. 'Did you not receive them?'

He groaned and clasped her hand. 'I moved digs right after the letter from the solicitor arrived. The threat of police scared the life out of me. I figured they'd dredge up my past and kick me off the course, so I scarpered and didn't give anyone my forwarding address.'

'Oh, Mitch, you poor soul. What you must have gone through.'

Her voice caught and he squeezed her hand. 'Hey, forget it. It's all over now. And just so you know, I never thought of you as a reminder of my old life. I thought of you as the closest thing to a mother I'd ever had. I still do.'

Tears ran freely down her cheeks and she half sobbed, half laughed. 'Oh my, you've really turned my waterworks on now.' She patted at her face with a tissue. 'But what a lovely thing to say, thank you.'

'I don't say anything I don't mean, but please can we

change the subject now. You know how rubbish I am with this emotional stuff.'

She smiled. 'Okay then. Let's start with your answers to these. How did you feel when you graduated, why did you choose to join the army and why aren't you married yet?'

Roaring with laughter, and feeling as if some of the weight had lifted from his heart, Mitch settled back into the sofa and started to talk to Catherine. Just as he'd done so often, many years ago.

Two hours and several whiskies later, he'd brought Catherine up to date with his life story.

'I'm so proud of you, Mitch. Look at you, at what you've achieved. You save lives.' She took another tissue and dried her eyes. 'I always knew you would turn into something special.'

He looked at her sceptically. 'What, even when you first found me squatting in your house?'

She chuckled. 'Yes, even then. That's why I didn't throw you out.' Putting the tissue back into her pocket, she assessed him carefully. 'Now, tell me why you aren't married to that gorgeous lady who's responsible for getting us back together.'

Mitch, who'd been taking another sip of whisky, swallowed it back too quickly, making him cough. 'Brianna?' he croaked.

'Of course, Brianna. She's smart, beautiful and with a heart of gold. Why haven't you snapped her up yet?'

'I'm not sure what Brianna has told you, but we're just friends,' he replied carefully, feeling as if he was walking through a verbal minefield. 'Work colleagues, actually. Of course she's been fantastic since the accident. It was her who arranged for a private air ambulance to get me back to England. She saved my life.'

'I know all about that, dear. Brianna and I have become firm friends since she first came to see me. We've talked about many things, including how much she loves you.'

Once more Mitch had cause to nearly choke on his whisky. 'She might have thought she did, a while ago.' He shook his head, his chest tightening painfully as he thought of how he'd left things. 'But not anymore. As I said, we're just friends. She's seeing some other guy now. Rich bloke, son of an Earl, apparently.' He stopped, aware bitterness had crept into his voice.

'Jealous?'

He winced. Shouldn't the last fifteen years have dulled her senses, made her less astute? 'It doesn't really matter whether I'm jealous or not. The fact is she's moved on. She's better off with Frederick. He's more her type.'

'And what exactly is her type then?'

Mitch scowled into the bottom of his glass. 'Charming, well-bred, rich, perfect manners. You know the sort of man.' It hurt to think of her with someone like that. It really hurt.

Catherine shook her head at him. 'You silly boy, that's not her type at all. That's just what you think she likes. I have to say, much as I love you, none of the attributes you've just mentioned come to mind when I think of you. But Brianna loves you anyway. What I'm interested in is do you love her?'

Mitch wanted to palm Catherine off with a trite reply about caring for Brianna, as a friend, but he knew she'd see straight through it. 'The truth is, I don't really know. I've never been in love. I don't know what it should feel like. All I know is I miss her. Every time I think of her, I feel a deep ache inside me. When I eat, I want to have her sitting opposite me, her eyes filled with laughter. When I walk by the coast, I remember how good it felt to walk with her, to hold her hand. When I go to sleep, and when I wake up, I feel lost because she's not there.'

'Then you are in love.'

He exhaled slowly. 'Yes, I guess I am. For all the good it will do me.' He turned to Catherine, trying to get her to understand. 'Whatever I feel, nothing will ever come of it.'

She frowned. 'Why ever not? You love her and she loves you. I know she does.'

Mitch snorted. 'Did Brianna forget to tell you that she's Brianna Worthington? Sole heir of a multimillion pound business?'

'And why should that make any difference?'

'Do you honestly think someone like me belongs with someone like her? You and I both know exactly where I come from. Brianna doesn't. I'd rather we kept it that way.' Angry at the way the conversation had headed, Mitch leapt to his feet and began to pace.

'She wouldn't care, Mitch. You know that.'

'Maybe, maybe not. But we'll never know because nobody is going to tell her.' He glanced back over at Catherine. When he'd arrived her eyes had shone with happiness. Now she looked sad and hurt. God, what was wrong with him that he continued to upset the people he cared for the most?

He sighed. 'I'm sorry I shouted. I didn't mean to take it out on you. Brianna and I stopped being lovers a while ago, before my accident. I knew it was better that way, for both of us. It hurts now, but in time she'll marry someone who deserves her.' He shook his head at her when she tried to talk. 'No, please, respect my views on this. I couldn't live with myself if I saddled her to me. Don't get me wrong, I'm proud of who I am now, of what I do, of what I've achieved. But it doesn't take away what I was. Brianna and I, we're from two different worlds. I've tried to mix in her world.' He thought back to the auction at the ball and to him punching Henry into the swimming pool. 'It didn't work.'

'But could she live in yours?' Catherine replied softly.

Mitch just shook his head. 'I've kept you up too late. Time for me to go.' God knows, his head couldn't cope with much more tonight.

When they reached the front door, Catherine took his hand. 'I understand your feelings, my boy, but this is one time you're wrong.' She kissed him gently on the cheek. 'It was lovely to see you. Make sure it isn't another fifteen years before I see you again.'

He smiled finally, enveloping her tiny frame in his arms. 'You can count on it.'

Chapter Thirty-Five

Brianna was delighted to receive an invitation to dinner from Catherine. It had been a while since they'd last caught up, though they'd spoken on the phone only last week. Catherine had done the phoning this time, obviously dying to tell her all about the visit she'd had from Mitch. Brianna had listened avidly, her heart desperate for news about him. She'd learnt he'd been given the all-clear regarding his rehabilitation and he would be allowed back to work in another week.

She knocked on Catherine's door, really looking forward to the evening. Despite their difference in age, the older lady was a good companion, very easy to talk to. She was also someone she could open her heart to about Mitch, someone who loved him as she did.

The moment Catherine opened the door Brianna could see she wasn't her usual self. She seemed flustered and wouldn't even look her in the eye. 'Catherine, how nice to see you.' Brianna kissed the other woman's cheeks. 'Is everything all right? You look like you're hiding something.'

'I think perhaps she is.'

Brianna's face snapped round at the sound of that deep voice. 'Mitch,' she almost squawked in shock. 'What a surprise to see you here.'

'And vice versa,' Mitch replied dryly, looking over at Catherine with suspicious eyes. 'What are you playing at, Catherine?'

'Oh, silly me,' Catherine replied, ushering her two guests into the sitting room. 'As you get older, your memory goes.' She nudged Mitch. 'You should know that, being a doctor. I must have forgotten to tell you I thought it would be a nice idea to have you both round for dinner. My way of thanking Brianna for getting us back together.'

Catherine breezed off to organise the drinks, leaving Mitch and Brianna alone, standing awkwardly together. 'Sorry, I didn't realise—' she began to say.

'How are you—' Mitch started to speak at the same time. He stopped and gestured for Brianna to continue.

She smoothed down the non-existent creases on her suede skirt. 'I was just going to say I didn't know Catherine had invited you too. If I'd known—'

'You wouldn't have come?' he supplied.

She blushed and looked away. Why did she have to feel so uncomfortable in his presence? So acutely aware of him and how fit and healthy he looked. With his face tanned once more and his body relieved of all outward signs of his injuries, he looked, frankly, gorgeous. 'Of course I would still have come, if you'd wanted me to,' she replied stiffly. 'I just don't want to interrupt anything. I'm an outsider, after all.'

Mitch shook his head. 'You stopped being an outsider the moment you entered our lives.'

'Interfered in them, don't you mean?'

He gave her a small, slightly awkward smile. 'Yes.'

'Here you go, my dears. A glass of sherry.' Catherine walked back into the room, seemingly oblivious to the discomfort of her guests. 'I know it's probably an old lady's drink, but you have to humour me.' She raised her glass and looked at them both. 'A toast. To Brianna, to whom I will always be grateful. And to Mitch, my surrogate son, who has finally made it home.'

They ate together in the large dining room and Brianna's discomfort began to ease as Catherine and Mitch traded humorous anecdotes from their time together. When Catherine divulged how stubborn Mitch had been as a teenager, Brianna laughingly joined in, adding her own tales of how Mitch tried to cope on his own despite his broken limbs.

'Oh, he's stubborn all right,' Catherine agreed, speaking to Brianna. 'Take now. He's managed to convince himself he's not good enough for you. It doesn't matter what I say to him, he won't change his mind.'

Confused, Brianna stared at Catherine. 'What do you mean, not good enough for me?'

'Exactly what I say. The man's crazy about you, but for some reason he's got it into his head that because he came from a poor background, he doesn't deserve somebody like yourself. Of course, I told him you won't care where he came from, but he won't listen. Tell me, Brianna, does it matter to you where a man was brought up? How much money he has?'

Brianna's shocked brain was having trouble dissecting the conversation. Had Catherine really just said Mitch was crazy about her? She stole a glance at him, but his shuttered, angry face didn't help. 'I'm sorry, Catherine. I'm not sure what's going on here. But for the record, of course I don't care about a man's wealth, or his background. Mitch knows that. It's what he is now that matters, not what he was.'

Catherine nodded triumphantly. 'There you go, Mitch. Just what I told you.' She stood and walked towards the door. 'Now, if you'll excuse me, I need to go and lie down for a while. One of the privileges of being old. I'm sure you both have a lot to talk about.'

With that Catherine swept out of the room, leaving Mitch and Brianna alone. Silence echoed and her thumping heart sounded like gunfire in her ears. Mitch made no move to speak. Of course he didn't. He simply crossed his arms, his face like thunder. The only thing Brianna could think to say, the only thing she was interested in, was whether what

Catherine had said was true. Glancing at the rigid set of Mitch's face, she found herself unable to ask. He looked as blindsided as she was. Stiffly, she rose from the table.

'I think its best I go now. It's been,' she shook her head and sighed, 'an interesting meal.'

Still he didn't speak. Not until she'd reached the door.

'Brianna.'

She stopped in her tracks. 'Yes?'

'I think we need to talk.' He spoke the words quietly and without looking at her.

'You don't have to, if you don't want to. I know Catherine's rather pushed you into this situation.'

'That's putting it mildly. I feel as though I've been flattened by a bulldozer.' He gave her a wry smile. 'But now the words are out there, we can't just ignore them, much as I might like to.' He stood up from his chair. 'Let's go and sit somewhere more comfortable.'

Nodding her agreement, she walked back with him to the sitting room. Brianna perched on the sofa, but Mitch chose not to sit. He prowled the room like a cornered tiger.

'What Catherine told you, about my feelings for you. It's true.'

Brianna let the words slowly sink into her bemused brain. 'You're crazy about me? Crazy good or crazy bad?'

He stopped his movement and gave her a brief smile. 'At times you do drive me crazy, but that's not what I mean.' Sighing deeply, he carried on. 'Brianna, I told you once I don't know what love means. Well, I think I've started to find out.'

The words sparked off explosions of delight in her head. It was as if all her Christmases had come at once. But as she moved to throw her arms round him, she caught sight of the expression on his face. It wasn't that of a man happily in love. Instead he looked almost defeated.

'What is it? What's wrong?' He'd finally said the words she'd been longing to hear, but he was holding something else back. 'If you're worried I might not still feel the same, you shouldn't be.' She could no longer stand to see his tortured expression. Flinging herself at him she buried her head against the hard wall of his chest. 'I love you, Mitch. I love you so much.'

'No.' The words tore out of Mitch as he flung his arms at Brianna's shoulders, holding her off. But then he looked into her eyes. They blazed with such love. Love for him. The realisation was so incredible for a selfish moment he wanted to pretend it was all that mattered.

With a groan he pulled her against him and gave in to the desire to kiss her. A desire that had pulsed through him since he'd first caught sight of her standing on the doorstep. As always, she gave herself to him completely, opening her mouth wider, pushing her body up against his. He was drowning in her, in the taste, the smell, the feel of her. But he couldn't accept what she was offering. He had things he needed to say. Truths she needed to hear.

Breathing hard, he gently eased her away. 'Brianna, I need to talk to you. I need to tell you about my childhood.'

'Okay,' she replied huskily, withdrawing slowly but still with her arms wrapped around his waist. 'But I don't think Catherine would mind too much if she came back and found us canoodling on the floor.'

'Canoodling?'

'Necking, snogging.' Her voice softened. 'Making love.'

'Don't tempt me.' Needing to distance himself, he took a deliberate step back and tried to gather his thoughts.

Wordlessly, Brianna sat back on the sofa.

This was it. As tension gripped him, weighing down his shoulders, he cleared his throat. 'Brianna, you know I never knew my father and that my mother died when I was fourteen. What you don't know is that my mother was a prostitute. My father was one of her clients, though she never knew which one.'

'Oh my God.' Brianna sank back against the sofa.

'My real name is spelt Mich,' he carried on, grimly determined, not daring to look at her. 'It's short for the tyre company, Michelin. A little joke from my mother, as I was a constant reminder to her of the importance of using rubbers. I changed the damn thing as soon as I was old enough.' Finally he looked at her, and what he saw made his voice falter. 'So ... well, now you can see why I never really spoke about my childhood.' God, she looked shell-shocked. Maybe he could live with that, but then there was the expression in her eyes. They were filled with a disgust that left him reeling. He'd expected it – what woman wants to know she's slept with the son of a whore? – but still it hurt. So damn much.

'Was she a good mother?'

Her question caught him by surprise. At least she was still willing to talk to him. 'It depends what you mean by good. My friends thought she was great. I could go out as late as I wanted. I didn't need to let her know where I was, or who I was with. She didn't shout when I had poor marks at school, or when I was caught by the police for stealing or joyriding.' Oh boy, the bitterness wouldn't stop flowing out of him. 'Frankly, she didn't care. All she was bothered about was when her next client was due and when she could get her next fix.' He forced himself to look Brianna in the eye. 'She was an addict, too. Started off small time, but ended up on the hard stuff.'

'Is that what killed her?'

'Yes,' he replied shortly. 'I came back from school one day and found her lying on the bed next to a syringe. I could tell straight away she was dead. I called 999 and was waiting with her when I suddenly realised if I hung around,

I'd be taken into care. I'd heard rumours of what that was like, and there was no way it was happening to me. So I took what money I could find and scarpered.'

'And that's how you came to be squatting in Catherine's house,' Brianna murmured.

He shrugged, trying to give the appearance it didn't bother him much now. He didn't think he was deceiving either of them. 'I tried living on the streets at first, but it was cold and uncomfortable. That's when I started wandering round the roads further afield. The ones with the fancy houses. A lot of them looked like they weren't lived in. I watched Catherine's house for a week, didn't see anybody enter or leave, so I decided to make it my temporary home.'

'You broke in?'

'Yes. It wasn't the first time I'd done that, either.' He spoke harshly, full of self-loathing. 'You've seen my tattoo?' Brianna simply nodded. 'I was a member of the Panthers. We were a group of teenage kids who liked to think we were hard. We stole cars, broke into houses.' He turned away, too ashamed to look at her, too disgusted at the boy he'd been. He could tell himself he'd managed to straighten himself out. He could hope he'd done enough good since that it had counterbalanced some of the bad. What he couldn't do anymore was hide away from what he had once been. 'I think you've heard the rest, from Catherine. So, there you have it, my full life history.'

Brianna felt the tears on her cheeks and knew she'd been crying for a while. As he stood, shoulders rigid, staring out of the window, she realised she finally understood him. No wonder he fought so hard not to let others get too close. He'd practically been abandoned as a child; had never experienced a parent's unconditional love. Something she had always taken for granted. So he'd coped by telling himself he didn't need anybody.

She walked over and put her arms around his shoulders, pressing her face into his back. 'Mitch, I'm so glad you've told me all of this. It helps me to understand you. But you have to know, none of it matters.'

'Well it should,' he returned bluntly, still with his back to her.

'How can it when it's helped make you the man you are today? I don't just love your compassion and sexy body, you know. I also love your strength and complexity.' She moved round to face him, forcing him to look at her. 'When I think what you had to live through—'

'It disgusts you.'

'It horrifies me,' she corrected him. 'It makes me want to cry. But don't you see, it's made you into the very special man you are now.'

'No,' he snarled, pushing her away. 'Haven't you been listening? My mother was a hooker, and a drug addict. I grew up amongst pimps and crooks. I've stolen cars and burgled houses. Good God woman, I'm far from special.'

'Well, you are to me.'

He shook his head. 'Don't say that. Look at me, Brianna. What can I offer somebody like you?'

'Yourself,' she replied quietly. 'It's all I want.' When he didn't respond, she cursed. She'd tried sympathy and got nowhere. Perhaps it was time to play hardball. 'Is that what it's going to be like then, Mitch? Feeling sorry for yourself for the rest of your life? Forever pushing away the people who love you, because you can't deal with who you are, and where you came from?' She bent to pick up her handbag. 'Maybe I got you wrong. Maybe you're not the man I had you down for, after all. That man had this unbelievable inner strength. A real sense of his own worth.' She was aware of him quietly following her as she walked to the door. 'When you go to sleep tonight, alone, remember this.

You could have been with me. I love you. I don't care about any of the other stuff. You shouldn't, either. Rich or poor, upper class or working class, childhood angel or teenage rebel, it's all totally irrelevant when you love somebody.'

Her legs trembling, she dashed out of the house and into her car.

When Catherine came back down the stairs, she found Mitch sitting alone, nursing a whisky. 'Where's Brianna?'

'Gone home.'

'Then why haven't you gone with her?'

'I don't know.' He shook his head. 'It all happened so fast. One minute I was telling her about my childhood, which she said didn't matter. The next she was shouting at me, telling me I wasn't the sort of man she thought I was.'

Catherine smiled. 'Well, if you're still here, moping around an old lady's house when you could be in bed with a beautiful woman, perhaps you're not the man I thought you were, either.' She took hold of his glass, removing it from his clenched fingers. 'If you love her, you need to claim her, before somebody else does.'

Mitch looked into Catherine's pale blue eyes and realised she was right. If Brianna was foolish enough to love him, and not care about his background, then who was he to argue? The alternative was letting her go. Watching someone like Frederick, or, God forbid, Henry, snap her up. He rose to his feet and hugged his substitute mother. 'You are a very meddlesome, but very wise, lady. And I love you, too.'

He saw the pleasure creep over her face, and wondered how he had managed to earn the love of two such very special women.

Half an hour later he was ringing on Brianna's doorbell. She opened it dressed in a slinky silk dressing gown, her hair cascading loosely around her shoulders. For a moment he was lost for words.

'I don't want to sleep alone,' he said at last, his voice hoarse from the lump that had wedged in his throat.

She smiled serenely and held out her hand. 'Good. Neither do I.'

Chapter Thirty-Six

As he followed Brianna to her bedroom, Mitch was determined, for the first time in his life, to put his fierce passion on hold. At least for a while. Tonight, he wanted to show Brianna tenderness. Show her with his actions what he was so poor at saying with his words. After undressing quickly, he joined her on her bed. Where before he would have plundered and taken, now he took the time to caress, holding back his more primitive urges until he was sure she understood how much she meant to him. He kissed her everywhere, enjoying her sighs of pleasure. He held her close and murmured his love for her over and over again. Only when she begged for release did he enter her, and even then he did it slowly, carefully. They rocked together and Mitch understood how beautiful making love could be when it involved your heart, as well as your body.

When he woke the next morning it was to find her snuggled against his side.

'Tell me I'm not dreaming,' he asked in a voice thick with sleep and desire.

In answer, she rose and nibbled his bottom lip. 'Well, if it is a dream, I hope I never wake up.'

He drew her tight against him, but though his heart was full and content, there was something he knew he had to do. 'Brianna, are your parents at home today?'

'Umm, I think so. Why?'

'I want to talk to them about us.'

She lurched up, unaware her breasts were gloriously uncovered. 'Why?'

'Princess, you need to cover up a moment or I won't be able to concentrate.' She pouted at the nickname she hated, but lifted up the sheet. 'I want to tell them my history. I want it out in the open. I'd rather they heard it from me, than from somebody else.' He gave her a wry smile. 'Your friends seem to have a habit of finding out about my past.'

Sighing, Brianna lay back on the pillow. 'That's fine. I understand your feelings. But you have to understand mine. It doesn't matter to me what they say. I love you, and there is no way I'm going to let you push me away again.'

He gazed at her face. Who would have thought somebody so beautiful, so soft and genteel, could have such a stubborn streak. 'I'll count on it,' he replied huskily.

He wasn't feeling quite so convinced about his idea when he was summoned into the sitting room by the Worthington housekeeper later that morning.

'Mitch, this is a pleasant surprise,' her mother greeted him. 'Come on in, and we'll get you a drink. Coffee?'

He tried to remind himself he was a man, not a shy teenager. 'Yes, thank you.'

'Mitch.' Brianna's father shook his hand. It was a strong, firm handshake, one Mitch did his best to return. Mr Worthington gestured for him to sit down.

'How are you?' Brianna's mother gave him a long, appraising assessment. 'You look fully recovered.'

He tried not to squirm under her scrutiny. Tried not to think about the fact that she was expensively dressed, in flowing trousers and a silk blouse. He had on black jeans. 'I'm good, thank you. Still a bit weak where the bones are knitting together, but getting there. I should be back at work soon.'

'Good. You were very brave.'

He shook his head. 'No. Just doing my job.' He hesitated a moment. 'Brianna did a marvellous thing, arranging for the air ambulance. I expect you both had a lot to do with it, too.' He hoped his sincerity was clear in the tone of his voice. 'Words are inadequate, but they are all I have. Thank you.'

Her father shrugged off the thanks. 'Any friend of Brianna's, is a friend of ours. Now, I take it you've not just come round to tell us that.'

'No.' He fidgeted, very conscious the elegant chair he was sitting in was probably worth more than the entire contents of his own home. He didn't know how to start and was relieved when the housekeeper brought in the coffee, serving as a momentary distraction. As he thanked her for the cup, he wished he wasn't in yesterday's clothes. He wished he'd taken the trouble to shave. He wished a lot of things.

He decided to dive straight in. 'I'm here to talk about Brianna.'

'Ah.' Her mother smiled slightly, and sat back against her chair.

'I love her,' he said simply. 'I want to spend the rest of my life with her.' He watched the reaction on their faces. It wasn't horror, thankfully, but it wasn't joy either. He sighed, and wished again. That he was anywhere else but here.

'As I hope to become part of her life,' he continued, desperate to get this over and done with, 'I want to tell you something about me, about where I came from. I don't want any surprises coming out of the woodwork later on.' He went to stand. He felt more in control that way. 'I grew up in the inner city. My mother was a hooker, my father one of her customers ...' The words came out in a rush as he gave them a short and to the point version of his sleazy childhood.

Only when he'd finished the full story did he dare to look back at them. He wished he hadn't. Telling them all this now had been stupid. He should have let them get to know him a bit more before throwing all the gory details at them. But hell, this was who he was. He wasn't proud of it, but he'd spent too much of his life hiding from it, being ashamed of it. Brianna had heard it all, and still loved him. That was the most important part.

'You've spoken a lot about your background, Mitch, but not about yourself.' Her father spoke, his expression not giving anything away.

Hell, what could he say? 'I've been called bad-tempered, surly and rude.' He forced a smile. 'Mostly by Brianna. I also like to think I'm determined and fiercely passionate about the things I care about. That includes your daughter.' He swallowed and took a deep breath. Here it was, his heart on his sleeve. 'I can't offer your daughter much in the way of material things, but I can tell you I love her with a strength I hadn't thought possible.'

'Isn't that the most important thing, love?' Had her mother's eyes softened, or was that wishful thinking?

'In my opinion, yes. But then I would say that. I have little else to give,' he replied honestly.

'Are you asking for our permission to marry her?' Mr Worthington's eyes were green, like those of his daughter. They were also just as sharp and hard to avoid.

Mitch shook his head. 'No. I can't risk you not giving it. I just wanted to let you know the full picture, before you heard it from anybody else. I will ask Brianna to marry me, though. I want her in my life, permanently. I know how much you love her, and she loves you. I never want to get in the way of that love, never want her to have to take sides. If she'll have me, I wanted to reassure you that I'll sign any document you want me to. If she ever wants out, I will only walk away with what I came in with.'

Finding the tension unbearable, Mitch ran a hand through his hair and tried to slow his words. 'I realise I have everything to gain from this and she has nothing, but I've tried to do the right thing, tried to walk away and I can't.

Life without her is only half a life.' Aware his voice was breaking, Mitch stopped his monologue there. He'd said what he set out to say. He couldn't do any more than that.

Her mother cleared her throat. 'Mitch,' she said softly, glancing at her husband for support. 'All we've ever wanted for our daughter is for her to find a purpose in life and find happiness. Since she met you, she has found both.'

Her husband reached out and held his wife's hand. 'My wife is right. If Brianna is happy, then we're happy. As to the rest, it doesn't matter where a man comes from. It's what he does with his life that counts. You're a fine example of that. All we ask is that you promise to take care of her and to love her.'

Mitch smiled at last, relief washing over him. They weren't going to make life difficult for him. 'That, I can promise.'

Her father stood and held out his hand. 'You might not want our permission, Mitch, but you've got our blessing.'

Choked, Mitch shook his hand and then found himself hugged by her mother.

He walked away with his head held high. He'd told them the worst parts about himself and yet they'd accepted him. That was one giant hurdle over. Only one more to go.

Chapter Thirty-Six

As Brianna packed her case, ready to spend the weekend with Mitch, she wondered if she should broach the subject of them living together. Surely, now they'd both confirmed their love for each other, it was the next logical step? Of course it might be for most men, but she wasn't dealing with most men. She was dealing with Mitch McBride. Passionate yes, but also stubbornly independent. Though he'd opened up to her finally, she knew she couldn't rush him. Mustn't rush him in fact, or he might back off, as he had done before. No, he would do what he wanted, when he wanted to. For now, she had to be content with the fact that he loved her, and had been as keen to see her this weekend as she had been to see him.

Zipping up her bag, she went to find her parents to let them know she wouldn't be around. She hadn't really spoken to them since they'd met with Mitch. Both evenings she'd come home from work ready to grill them, only to find they were out. Frustrated, she'd let the matter drop, hoping it had just been a coincidence and they weren't deliberately avoiding her. She'd meant what she'd said to Mitch. She loved him, and would continue to love him, no matter what her parents thought. Deep inside, though, she knew it would be so much better to be seeing him with her parents' approval, instead of against their wishes.

'Mum! There you are.' Finally, she found her mother home. 'I've been looking for you for the last few evenings. Where have you been? I thought it was the daughter who should be out on the town, not the parents.'

'Your father and I aren't old yet, you know. We still have a social life, and friends who want to see us.' She gave her daughter a quick squeeze. 'But if we'd known you wanted to see us, we'd have stayed in. What did you need us for?'

Brianna laughed. 'As if you didn't know. I thought you might be avoiding me, because you were too worried about what to say to me about Mitch.'

Her mother looked genuinely shocked. 'Good heavens, where did you get that from? I hope you don't really think we're such ogres.'

Brianna sighed and considered her words. 'No, but I also know you weren't all that keen on me seeing him in the first place. And that was before you knew about his childhood.'

Her mother sat on the bar stool in the kitchen and motioned for Brianna to do the same. 'Darling, your father and I only want you to be happy. Yes, I was worried that Mitch wasn't right for you, but only because I know from personal experience how much easier it is to be with someone who comes from a similar place. There wasn't only your father, you know, but when I met him, I knew straight away he was the one.'

Brianna smiled. 'When I first met Mitch he was rude, but the sexiest man I'd ever seen. He got under my skin and filled my mind so I couldn't think about anything else but him. He's the one, Mum.'

Her mother patted her gently on the arm. 'I know. I'm not blind, Brianna. I can see how much you love him, and what you see in him.' She chuckled. 'But aside from his looks, to have lived through what he has and come through the other side shows a strength of character we can only respect and admire. He's a good man, my darling, and we're delighted you've found him.'

Brianna threw her arms around her mother's neck. 'You don't know how happy that makes me. He's the man I want to marry, have children with.' She sighed. 'I just hope he feels the same. I guess I'm going to have to be patient while he figures out he wants to spend the rest of his life with me.'

'I guess you are.' With a smile and a twinkle in her eyes, she ran a loving hand down her daughter's cheek before getting up off the stool.

Brianna sat, puzzled. 'Why are you grinning?'

'My daughter's in love. Why wouldn't I grin?'

Far from satisfied with her mother's answer, Brianna raised herself off the chair and went to pick up her overnight bag. 'Okay. I won't be home this weekend. I'll be with Mitch.'

'Well, have fun.'

When she waved her goodbye, her mother still had a smile on her face.

As she pushed open the door to Mitch's house, she was struck by how different it looked. It was positively gleaming, as if he'd spent the whole day tidying up for her. And were they really fresh flowers in the vase? She shook her head. No, she must be dreaming.

'Mitch?' she called out, following the scent of garlic to the kitchen. There he was, standing over the stove, turning something over in a pan. It was like the scene out of an old domestic handbook. Only Mitch was playing the role of the anxious to please wife, and she was the husband coming home after a hard day.

He turned and there was no doubting his pleasure at seeing her. It was clear in the deep brown of his eyes, in the easy smile that spread across his rugged features. He turned down the gas, and gently put his hands on her shoulders, drawing her tight against him. 'Umm, you feel good,' he murmured against her hair. 'And you smell good too.'

Delighted, she wriggled closer. 'You know what they say. Absence makes the heart grow fonder.'

'I don't know about that, but it certainly makes a man frisky.' He cupped her face and gave a deep, searing kiss. 'I hope you're not hungry because it's going to have to wait.'

He lifted her into his arms and carried her up the stairs.

Later, after Brianna had changed into some casual silky little number that made Mitch's eyes water, they headed back downstairs. Mitch hunted out the champagne he'd put in the fridge and wrestled it open, handing her a glass.

'Are we celebrating?'

He gave what he hoped was a casual shrug of his shoulders. 'Not really. I thought you might like some.'

'Oh, I do. It's just, what with the champagne, the tidy house and the flowers, I wondered if something was up?'

Heck, what was he supposed to do now? The ring he'd bought yesterday burned a hole in his pocket. But he'd planned to wine and dine her first. He wanted to do this properly. 'Can't a man tidy his house without arousing suspicion?' he replied a touch irritably.

She was used to him by now. Instead of taking offence, she smiled. 'Of course. The flowers, they're lovely. Did you buy them?'

Now she had him feeling like a twit. What man in his right mind goes out and buys flowers for his home, just for fun? 'Yes,' he snapped, before reigning in his temper. This fancy setting was meant to soften her up for the proposal. Not piss her off. 'I thought, as you were staying the weekend, you might like them,' he ventured carefully.

Brianna stood and gave them a long, deep sniff. 'You're right. I do. You can't go wrong with flowers and champagne.'

'Yes, well, I'll go and see if our first course is ready.'

Mitch turned sharply and went back into the kitchen, aware he'd left Brianna staring after him in confusion. Not half as confused as he was. Was he really about to throw together king prawns sautéed in garlic butter?

Why hadn't he stuck to his original plan of fish and chips?

'Umm, these prawns are delicious,' Brianna told him a while later as she tucked into the starter. 'I didn't realise you were such a good cook. You haven't cooked for me before.'

'No. I thought it was time I did.' Inwardly he groaned. What on earth was wrong with him? He couldn't string two sentences together without feeling stiff and nervous. Heck, he'd faced far more terrifying circumstances than this. He'd had to stare down men with machine guns, for goodness sake. Why was he making such a big deal out of saying four simple words? *Will you marry me?* They weren't even hard to say. But then it wasn't actually saying the words that was the problem. It was hearing her reply he was scared to death of. He'd finally found a woman who had broken down his defences and pushed her way into his heart. He'd never find another like her. He knew she loved him, but how much? Enough to marry him?

'Brianna ...' The ringing phone cut across his words. With a muttered oath he went to answer it. Whoever it was, they were in for a brusque conversation.

He was soon back and clearing the plates away. After popping the steaks under the grill he went to sit back down opposite her. She looked achingly beautiful, her hair tousled from their love-making, her soft pink top draped over her curves. He cleared his throat. 'Did you have a good day?' he asked, immediately biting down on his lip, exasperated beyond measure at his inane question. He should be telling her how gorgeous she was. God, he was so crap at this.

Clearly surprised by his question, Brianna smiled. 'Yes, thank you, I did. Did you?'

He saw the playful smile, the teasing light in her eyes. 'Oh, hell. Look Brianna—'

The smoke alarm went off in the kitchen. Swearing loudly, Mitch leapt out of his chair and yanked open the grill, only to find his steaks looking decidedly charred.

Bloody great. He couldn't even get that bit right. Annoyed, he snapped off the grill and plonked himself down on the kitchen stool before briefly putting his head in his hands in despair.

It wasn't long before a comforting arm crossed his shoulders. 'Don't worry about it. I've burnt enough food in front of you. It's only fair you retaliate.'

He raised his head and managed a weak smile. 'It's not the food, at least not only that. It's everything. Who'd have thought proposing to a woman would be so damned difficult.'

Brianna stood for a moment, motionless. Then her heart leapt into life, pounding against her ribcage. 'Is that what you're doing?' she asked, her voice a breathless whisper.

'I've been trying to. But between the phone call, the burnt food and my nerves, it's not quite as I'd planned.'

He looked so pained, her heart swelled still further. Easing herself gently onto his lap, she circled his neck with her arms and gave him a long, deep kiss. 'Then let me take away some of your nerves. My answer will be yes.'

Surprise, relief, joy. His eyes lit up with all three. 'Are you sure? Really sure? It's a big step. I won't put up with anything less than the rest of our lives.'

She rained kisses over his face. 'I'm sure. Why, are you trying to put me off?'

'God no.' He returned the kisses then pulled his head away, holding her face in his hands. 'I'm sorry I made such a hash of this. I wanted to do it properly, because you deserve nothing but the best. Somehow I mucked it all up. I can't seem to find the right words to tell you how much I love you, how much I need you in my life. I've tried living without you and I can.' The deep brown eyes that stared into hers were as dark as she'd ever seen them. 'But with you in it, my life is different. I'm different. You bring me happiness, laughter, joy. Jesus, you complete me, Brianna. I can't offer you much in return, but everything I have, everything I am, is yours.'

Tears streamed down her face. 'You've just found the right words.'

'Thank God.' He stared at her tears. 'Those are happy tears, right?'

She smiled and rubbed her thumb across the planes of his face, lovingly tracing the high cheekbones, the grooves at the side of his mouth. 'Of course they are. Oh Mitch, you always have been and always will be all I've ever wanted.'

She leant back in for a cuddle, but he was rummaging around in his back pocket. 'Before I forget.' He pulled out a box and awkwardly thrust it at her. 'I didn't know whether you'd want to choose your own, or whether you wanted the romantic gesture. I won't be offended if you don't like it, but I figured as I'd never bought jewellery for a woman before, now would be a good time to start. I made the lady in the shop promise we could take it back and change it for something else.'

Brianna knew that whatever was inside the box, she would love it. The gesture, knowing he'd gone into a shop to choose something for her, was so much more important than the actual ring itself. But she was genuinely delighted by the simple, emerald cut diamond set in platinum. 'You can throw away the receipt. It's beautiful.'

'It bloody should be. It cost me most of my savings.' Before she had a chance to interject, he was talking again. 'Speaking of which, we need to talk about where we're going to live and about your money. I've spoken to your parents, told them I'll sign anything to make sure your inheritance is protected.'

Brianna held out her hand. 'Come with me.' She led him up the stairs and into the bedroom. There she slid into his arms. 'I want to live here, in this house, with you. We'll manage off your salary. The rest of the money can stay in the bank. It can be a trust fund for our children, a large donation to charity or something for us to splurge with in our old age. I don't care. All I want is right here.' Gently she pushed him onto the bed. 'Now, it's time to make love to your future wife.'

Epilogue

Brianna looked at her reflection in the mirror and knew she looked like a bride should look. It wasn't the artfully dressed hair, or the stunning slim-fitting white bridal gown that made the perfect picture. No, it was the sheer happiness radiating from her eyes that really said it all.

Her father came up behind her, circling his arm around her waist. 'I know I should be feeling sad at this moment, giving up my daughter to another man, but to be honest, that isn't how I feel.' He took a step back and studied his daughter. 'You look so radiant, so full of life. Just like your mother did on her wedding day. I know you've found that special someone. The love of your life. So I don't mind handing you over to Mitch, because I know that's what you want. Besides, it actually feels as though I'm gaining a son, not saying goodbye to my beloved daughter.'

Brianna leaned in close, as she had done so many times over the years. 'Good, because you will never get rid of me.' She gave her reflection one last look. 'I hate to sound conceited, but I think I look pretty damned good.'

Her father chuckled. 'So do I.' He gave her a gentle kiss on the cheek. 'Come on then, let's not make Mitch wait any longer. I imagine he's having a hard enough time in that church.'

When it had come down to choosing guests for the wedding, it had become only too painfully obvious how few people Mitch had in his life. His family had consisted only of Catherine, though her utter delight at the news had surely been worth more than an army full of distant relatives. His list of friends had also been a short one. The Medic SOS team – those who weren't abroad – and two mates from his army days, one of whom he had chosen as his best man. It had been a stark reminder to Brianna of how much Mitch had once isolated himself and how much he'd moved on since. He'd even agreed to a large wedding, which meant right now he was sitting in a chilly church, surrounded by a congregation most of whom he'd never met in his life. Suddenly she was anxious to see him.

She had imagined gliding serenely down the aisle, bestowing an elegant smile on the guests as she did so. Instead she almost ran down.

Her father tugged her back. 'Slow down,' he whispered. 'It's not the hundred metres sprint.'

But she couldn't. All she wanted to do was get to Mitch. To make sure he was there, that he hadn't got cold feet and fled at the sight of the crowded church.

When he came into view, she finally slowed. He looked amazing. Though he'd baulked at the suggestion of wearing a morning suit, he had agreed to a tuxedo and white bow tie. With his face glowing with health and his hair cut short, just as she liked it now, he was to die for.

But even better than his rugged good looks was the love that radiated out of his deep brown eyes when he turned and saw her. She took his outstretched hand and beamed as he squeezed it gently.

All too soon the service was over, the photographs taken, the meal served and the speeches made. Her father had been charming, the best man witty. Mitch had been achingly sincere. He had begun by thanking her parents for accepting him into their family. He had ended with his deep gratitude to her for giving his life meaning and for teaching him how to love. When he promised to love and cherish her for the rest of his life, she had wept for the first time that day.

Having now repaired her make-up, Brianna was ready to catch up with her family. She spied her mother talking with

Abigail, Henry's mother, and strode over to them. Thank goodness her parents had agreed Henry wouldn't be invited.

'Darling, I don't want to worry you,' she overheard Abigail saying, feeling a weird sense of déjà vu. 'But Henry tells me Mitch comes from a rather unsavoury background, if you know what I mean. I hear his mother was a working girl ...'

Brianna froze. Damn Henry and his ridiculous desire to ruin what she and Mitch had. She was about to wade in and say her piece, when her mother interrupted Abigail with a curt wave of her hand.

'Abigail, I know all about that poor boy's childhood and what he had to endure. How he found the strength to get through it and become the man he has, I will never know. I'm proud to have him as part of my family, as my son. If you value my friendship, you'll remember that.'

To Brianna's surprise, her mother rose from the table and headed off towards the bar, leaving Abigail alone and red-faced. Trying to hide her grin, Brianna shot off after her. 'Did you and Abigail just fall out?'

'When that woman bad-mouths my family, she is no friend of mine.'

Brianna grinned, hugging her. 'Oh, Mum, you're priceless.'

The day blended into the evening, when more guests arrived and the party really started to liven up.

'Here, bride, have another glass of champagne.' Melanie thrust yet another glass into her hands. 'If you can't get drunk on your wedding day, when can you?' Brianna accepted the glass gratefully and took a sip. 'So where is that heart-throb husband of yours?'

For a moment Brianna was puzzled. Then she broke into a huge goofy smile. 'Oh, Melanie, it feels so strange, thinking of Mitch as my husband.' She scanned the dance floor. 'Look, there he is. Dancing with my great aunt, would you believe. He even looks like he's enjoying himself.'

'Umm, and I do believe she's flirting with him a little. Look at her, gazing up at him in adoration. You're going to have to go and claim him soon.'

Brianna laughed and settled back to rest against the table. She was delighted at how well Mitch had settled into her family during the six months since he'd proposed. Especially how he'd got on with her parents. Because they all loved her, they'd been determined to make their relationship work. Somewhere along the line though, their mutual like and respect for each other had meant they'd stopped having to try.

'Well, as you've bagged the hottest male here tonight, I've had to look for the next best, as usual.' Melanie's eyes weren't on her. They were fixed on the dashing man walking towards them, elegant in his handmade evening suit. 'And, do you know what? I think I've found him.'

'You and Frederick?' Brianna exclaimed.

'Umm, yes, it would appear so.'

'That's fantastic.' She gave her friend a tight hug. 'Will I be attending another wedding soon?'

Melanie snorted. 'Slow down, we're not quite at that stage yet. But you never know.'

'Never know what?' Frederick asked, kissing Brianna's hand. 'May I say, you are quite the most beautiful bride I have ever seen.'

Happily accepting the compliment Brianna risked a sly glance towards her friend. 'Let's see if you're still thinking that in another year.'

Melanie whisked him off to the dance floor before he could ask any more questions. Brianna smiled as she watched them. They made a striking couple. She had a good feeling about them.

Mitch tried to extricate himself from the arms of Brianna's great aunt. How many flipping relatives did she have?

When he'd agreed to a big wedding, he'd had no idea what that meant. There were hundreds of these people. All very pleasant, but he'd had enough of polite conversation to last him a lifetime. 'Sorry,' he told the feisty-looking old bird, who hadn't been backwards in coming forward. 'I need to find Brianna.'

Hastily he slipped away, scanning the room in an almost unseemly desperation.

'If you're looking for your wife, she's over by the bar.' He turned to find Catherine smiling at him.

'I was, but I can hold off dancing with her when the second most beautiful woman in the room is smiling at me.'

Catherine chuckled. 'My goodness, who is this smoothly handsome stranger, and what has he done with my Mitch?'

'Hey, don't knock a man when he's trying.' He reached for her hand and kissed it dramatically. 'How about that? And please tell me you don't want to dance, because I bloody hate all that shuffling.'

'Now that's more like it. And no, I don't need a dance. Just your attention. I wanted to let you know that I finally managed to change my will. Something I thought I'd done years ago, but it seems my brother managed to put a stop to it. I don't know if it will help ease that chip you probably still have precariously balanced on your shoulder, but when I finally pop my clogs, my estate will go to you.' Her eyes twinkled. 'And I might not be Worthington rich, but I am pretty loaded.'

Flabbergasted, Mitch gaped at her. 'Hell, Catherine. I don't know what to say.'

'You don't need to say anything. I'm doing what any mother would do. Leaving my inheritance to my son.' She reached up to kiss his cheek and had disappeared before he had a chance to close his mouth.

Now he really needed to find Brianna.

Once more his eyes swept the room. Thank you God, there she was. His wife. His heart lurched and he let out a smug smile. Bloody unbelievable.

'At last, I find my beautiful wife alone.' He moved up behind her, placing a kiss on the back of her neck.

She turned and smiled at him. 'Hey there, husband. I've just been talking to Melanie. It seems she and Frederick are an item.' She nodded over to where Melanie and Frederick were getting as close as two people could get on the dance floor.

Mitch stilled. Suddenly all his insecurities came flooding back. 'That could have been you,' he said quietly, then kicked himself. He was on his wedding day, for crying out loud. How could he still doubt her love for him, when she'd just declared it in front of legions of her friends and family?

Brianna blinked, then shook her head at him. 'You silly man, it could never have been me. Don't you realise that by now? From the first day I met you, I was yours and yours alone. As I've told you many times already, you always were, and always will be, all I've ever wanted.' His body relaxed against her. 'Of course, if I'd wanted a man with money, a title, charm and sophistication, then Frederick would have been perfect.'

Growling, Mitch took hold of her hand and dragged her across the room and out into the hallway. 'I'll show you my version of charm and sophistication.'

Finding a quiet doorway, he pulled Brianna against the door and proceeded to devour her mouth with a hunger that left them both breathless. 'Does that work for you?' he asked when he finally pulled away.

'Oh yes,' she sighed, sagging against him. 'You work for me, Mitch. Every single part of you.'

'Good, because you work for me, too. Now, we need to say our goodbyes to everyone and get the hell out of here. I want to start our honeymoon.'

About the Author

Kathryn was born in Wallingford, England but has spent most of her life living in a village near Windsor. After studying pharmacy in Brighton she began her working life as a retail pharmacist. She quickly realised that trying to decipher doctors' handwriting wasn't for her and left to join the pharmaceutical industry where she spent twenty happy years working in medical communications. In 2011, backed by her family, she left the world of pharmaceutical science to begin life as a self-employed writer, juggling the two disciplines of medical writing and romance. Some days a racing heart is a medical condition, others it's the reaction to a hunky hero …

With two teenage boys and a husband who asks every Valentine's Day whether he has to bother buying a card again this year (yes, he does) the romance in her life is all in her head. Then again, her husband's unstinting support of her career change goes to prove that love isn't always about hearts and flowers – and heroes can come in many disguises.

Do Opposites Attract? is Kathryn's second novel with Choc Lit, but her first book to appear in paperback. Her debut novel is *Too Charming*, which was published by Choc Lit Lite and is available online.

For more information on Kathryn visit:
http://kathrynfreeman.co.uk
www.twitter.com/KathrynFreeman1
www.facebook.com/kathrynfreeman

More Choc Lit

From Kathryn Freeman

Too Charming

Does a girl ever really learn from her mistakes?

Detective Sergeant Megan Taylor thinks so. She once lost her heart to a man who was too charming and she isn't about to make the same mistake again – especially not with sexy defence lawyer, Scott Armstrong. Aside from being far too sure of himself for his own good, Scott's major flaw is that he defends the very people that she works so hard to imprison.

But when Scott wants something he goes for it. And he wants Megan. One day she'll see him not as a lawyer, but as a man … and that's when she'll fall for him.

Yet just as Scott seems to be making inroads, a case presents itself that's far too close to home, throwing his life into chaos.

As Megan helps him pick up the pieces, can he persuade her that he isn't the careless charmer she thinks he is? Isn't a man innocent until proven guilty?

More from Choc Lit

If you enjoyed Kathryn's story, you'll enjoy the rest of our selection. Here's a sample:

Is this Love?

Sue Moorcroft

How many ways can one woman love?

When Tamara Rix's sister Lyddie is involved in a hit-and-run accident that leaves her in need of constant care, Tamara resolves to remain in the village she grew up in. Tamara would do anything for her sister, even sacrifice a long-term relationship.

But when Lyddie's teenage sweetheart Jed Cassius returns to Middledip, he brings news that shakes the Rix family to their core. Jed's life is shrouded in mystery, particularly his job, but despite his strange background, Tamara can't help being intrigued by him.

Can Tamara find a balance between her love for Lyddie and growing feelings for Jed, or will she discover that some kinds of love just don't mix?

Visit www.choc-lit.com for more details including the first two chapters and reviews, or simply scan barcode using your mobile phone QR reader.

Sugar and Spice

Angela Britnell

The Way to a Hero's Heart ...

Fiery, workaholic Lily Redman is sure of two things: that she knows good food and that she always gets what she wants. And what she wants more than anything is to make a success of her new American TV show, Celebrity Chef Swap – without the help of her cheating ex-fiancé and producer, Patrick O'Brien. So when she arrives in Cornwall, she's determined to do just that.

Kenan Rowse is definitely not looking for love. Back from a military stint in Afghanistan and recovering from a messy divorce and an even messier past, the last thing he needs is another complication. So when he lands a temporary job as Luscious Lily's driver, he's none too pleased to find that they can't keep their hands off each other!

But trudging around Cornish farms, knee deep in mud, and meetings with egotistical chefs was never going to be the perfect recipe for love – was it? And Lily could never fall for a man so disinterested in food – could she?

The Wedding Diary

Margaret James

Where's a Fairy Godmother when you need one?

If you won a fairy-tale wedding in a luxury hotel, you'd be delighted – right? But what if you didn't have anyone to marry? Cat Aston did have a fiancé, but now it looks like her Prince Charming has done a runner.

Adam Lawley was left devastated when his girlfriend turned down his heartfelt proposal. He's made a vow never to fall in love again.

So – when Cat and Adam meet, they shouldn't even consider falling in love. After all, they're both broken hearted. But for some reason they can't stop thinking about each other. Is this their second chance for happiness, or are some things just too good to be true?

Visit www.choc-lit.com for more details including the first two chapters and reviews, or simply scan barcode using your mobile phone QR reader.

Introducing Choc Lit

We're an independent publisher creating
a delicious selection of fiction.
Where heroes are like chocolate – irresistible!
Quality stories with a romance at the heart.

Choc Lit novels are selected by genuine readers like yourself.
We only publish stories our Choc Lit Tasting Panel want to
see in print. Our reviews and awards speak for themselves.

We'd love to hear how you enjoyed *Do Opposites Attract?*.
Just visit www.choc-lit.com and give your feedback.
Describe Mitch in terms of chocolate
and you could win a Choc Lit novel in our
Flavour of the Month competition.

Available in paperback and as ebooks from most stores.

Visit: www.choc-lit.com for more details.

Keep in touch:
Sign up for our monthly newsletter Choc Lit Spread for
all the latest news and offers: www.spread.choc-lit.com.
Follow us on Twitter: @ChocLituk and Facebook: Choc Lit.

Or simply scan barcode using your mobile phone QR reader:

Choc Lit Spread

Twitter

Facebook